Off Kilter

Off Kilter

DONNA KAUFFMAN

BRAVA

KENSINGTON PUBLISHING CORP.

www.kensingtonbooks.com

BRAVA BOOKS are published by

Kensington Publishing Corp.
119 West 40th Street
New York, NY 10018

ISBN-13: 978-0-7582-5089-6
ISBN-10: 0-7582-5089-4

First Kensington Trade Paperback Printing: January 2011

10 9 8 7 6 5 4 3 2 1

For Joanne . . .

Your Grasshopper appreciates everything you've taught her.

I would also like to acknowledge, once again, the talent, generosity, and support of all the wonderful weavers I have met while researching this series. Joanne and Linda, you have introduced me to such an amazing world! I can't thank you enough. Please excuse the artistic liberties I've taken, and know that any mistakes made were surely my own.

Chapter 1

Roan McAuley had never been opposed to getting naked. He wasn't even averse to the idea of cameras being involved. Or being outside all the while. He drew the line, however, at having an audience and being the only one going full monty.

Shee sighed deeply.

He'd only known her a few hours, yet he was already intimately familiar with the deep sigh.

"Drop the kilt, hot stuff, and let's get on with this, okay?"

Because he wasn't having enough fun getting naked in front of his fellow clansmen—and women—he also had the distinct pleasure of going full commando in front of never-so-pleasant Tessa Vandergriff. What had he done to deserve that? And, more to the point, her?

"Aye, drop the plaid, mon! What are ye afraid of?"

That hearty exhortation brought cheers from the assembled crowd.

Roan scowled in the general direction of his soon to be ex-best friend, Graham MacLeod. "Careful, there, mate, or I'll run off with your lovely fiancée and leave *you* eligible for this particular disgrace."

"Disgrace? I dinnae think so, lad. 'Tis an honor."

"*Donning* the plaid is an honor." Aiming to maintain some semblance of being in charge of the insanity, he sent a cheeky wink in the general direction of the ladies assembled in the crowd. Some of them were old enough to be his grandmother. What had the world come to, he wanted to know? "Doffing the plaid," he went on, "while often a prelude to fun is something I prefer to do in a more intimate gathering."

Graham chuckled, but Tessa merely rolled her eyes, so Roan played straight to his strength, and called out to the crowd directly. "The lot of you surely have better things to do with yerselves, now," he admonished with a twinkle in his eye and the flash of a dimple, "than stand about, hopin' as ye are, to ogle the naughty bits of the mon who's made it his duty and honor to do right by ye no matter the circumstance—including putting his integrity and pride aside to save our puir, wee island home. So, go on now with yer husbands and loved ones and ogle each other's bits and pieces. I'm guaranteeing we'll all hae a more enjoyable end to our day."

There was a pause, which continued on long enough for hope to build in his heart that perhaps his good humor, not to mention being a good sport about taking part in that cocka-mamie scheme, had shamed them into leaving him be. Then auld Eliza MacLeod—his very own secretary, no less—who'd celebrated her seventy-third year of tyranny on this good, green earth a mere week ago Tuesday, stepped forward . . . and began clapping her hands. Along with that, she let loose a whistle that likely set half the dogs on Kinloch to howling.

"Och, young Roan McAuley, charmin' scamp that ye are, dinnae ye be tellin' us how to spend our Saturday eve. I daresay we know how to amuse ourselves. If that includes ogling yer Godly gifted bits, then we'll do what pleases us." She looked to the other women gathered around her and winked. "What say you, ladies? Is watching this bonny lad make a spectacle of himself what pleases us?"

The grins grew wider, and others picked up the clapping, which turned quickly to cheering. The men that peppered the crowd, initially abashed by the openly assertive stance of their women, quickly picked up the chant, perhaps sensing the benefits to be had later that evening if they supported their partners. Hoots and hollers followed, along with repeated taunts of "Drop the plaid!" and "Are yer bits truly so Godly gifted? Proof! Proof!"

Roan turned a scowl toward Graham. "You know, there is surely some law about this on the books somewhere. If Shay were here—"

"He'd be standing right here, betting me money on this," his friend cut in with a chuckle. "In fact, I have a few pounds riding on this myself."

"We're burning daylight, gentleman." Tessa straightened, her long red curls catching in the warm breeze and lifting out from around her head.

Rather like Medusa's snakes.

As if she could read Roan's less-than-charitable thoughts, she shielded her fierce, crystalline blue eyes from the Western slant of the sun and scalded him with a single, silent look. "Man up, for God's sake, and drop the damn thing."

"We're not sending in nude shots," Roan replied with an even smile, as the chants and taunts escalated. "So I don't understand the need to take things to such an extreme—"

"The contest rules state, very clearly, that they're looking for provocative," Tessa responded, sounding every bit like a person who'd also been forced into a task she'd rather not have taken on—which she had been.

Sadly, that fact had not brought them closer.

She shifted to another camera she'd mounted on another tripod, he supposed so the angle of the sun was more to her liking. "Okay, lean back against the stone wall, prop one leg, rest that . . . sword thing of yours—"

" 'Tis a claymore. Belonged to the McAuleys for four centuries. Victorious in battle, 'tis an icon of our clan." And heavy as all hell to hoist about.

"Lovely. Prop your icon in front of you, then. I'm fairly certain it will hide what needs hiding."

His eyebrows lifted at that, but rather than take offense, he merely grinned. "I wouldnae be so certain of it, lassie. We're a clan known for the size of our . . . swords."

"Yippee," she shot back, clearly unimpressed. "So, drop the plaid, position your . . . sword, and let's get on with it. It's the illusion of baring it all we're going for here. I'll make sure to preserve your fragile modesty."

She was no fun. No fun 'tall.

"The other guys did it," she added, resting folded hands on top of the camera. "In fact," she went on, without even the merest hint of a smile or dry amusement, "they seemed quite happy to accommodate me."

He couldn't imagine any man wanting to bare his privates for Miss Vandergriff's pleasure. Not if he wanted to keep them intact, at any rate.

He was a bit thrown off by his complete inability to charm her. He charmed everyone. It was what he did. He admittedly enjoyed, quite unabashedly, being one of the clan favorites because of his affable, jovial nature. As far as he was concerned, the world would be a much better place if folks could get in touch with their happy parts, and stay there.

He didn't know much about her, but from what little time they'd spent together that afternoon, he didn't think Tessa Vandergriff had any happy parts. However, the reason behind her being rather happiness-challenged wasn't his mystery to solve. She'd been on the island for less than a week. Her stay on Kinloch was as a guest, and therefore temporary. Thank the Lord.

The island faced its fair share of ongoing trials and tribulations, and had the constant challenge of sustaining a fragile economic resource. Despite that, he'd always considered both the McAuley and MacLeod clans as being cheerful, welcoming hosts. But they had enough to deal with without adopting a surly recalcitrant into their midst.

"Well," he said, smiling broadly the more her scowl deepened. " 'Tis true, the single men of this island have little enough to choose from." The crowd took a collective breath at that, but his attention was fully on her. Gripping the claymore in one fist, he leaned against the stacked stone wall, well aware of the tableau created by the twin peaks that framed the MacLeod fortress, each of them towering behind him. He braced his legs, folded his arms across his bare chest, sword blade aloft . . . and looked her straight in the eye as he let a slow, knowing grin slide across his face. "Me, I'm no' so desperate as all that."

He got a collective gasp from the crowd. But rather than elicit so much as a snarl from Miss Vandergriff, or perhaps goading her so far as to pack up and walk away—which he'd have admittedly deserved—his words had a rather shocking effect. She smiled. Fully. He hadn't thought her face capable of arranging itself in such a manner. And so broadly, with such stunning gleam. He was further damned to discover it did things to his own happy parts that she had no business affecting.

"No worries," she stated, further captivating him with the transformative brilliance of her knowing smile. She gave him a sizzling once over before easily meeting his eyes again. "You're not my type."

That was not how those things usually went for him. He felt . . . frisked. "Then I'm certain you can be objective enough to find an angle that shows off all my best parts without requiring a blatant, uninspired pose. I understand from Kira that you're considered to be quite good with that equipment."

The chanting of the crowd shifted to a few whistles as the tension between photographer and subject grew to encompass even them.

"Given your reluctance to play show and tell, I'd hazard to guess I'm better with mine than you are with yours," she replied easily, but the spark remained in her eyes.

Goading him.

"Why don't you be the judge?" Holding her gaze in exclusive focus, the crowd long since forgotten, he pushed away from the wall and, with sword in one hand, slowly unwrapped his kilt with the other.

He took far more pleasure than was absolutely necessary

from watching her throat work as he unashamedly revealed thighs and ass. He wasn't particularly vain or egotistical, but he was well aware that a lifetime spent climbing all over the island had done its duty where his physical shape was concerned, as it had for most of the islanders. They were a hardy lot.

The crowd gasped as he held the fistful of unwrapped plaid in front of him, dangling precariously from one hand, just on the verge of—

"That's it!" Tessa all but leapt behind the camera and an instant later, the shutter started whirring. Less than thirty seconds later, she straightened and pushed her wayward curls out of her face, her no-nonsense business face back. "Got it. Good! We're all done here." She started dismantling her equipment. "You can go ahead and get dressed," she said dismissively, not even looking at him.

He held on to the plaid—and his pride—and tried not to look as annoyed as he felt. The shoot was blessedly over. That was all that mattered. No point in being irritated that he'd just been played by a pro.

She glanced up, the smile gone as she dismantled her second tripod with the casual grace of someone so used to the routine and rhythm of it, she didn't have to think about it. "I'll let you know when I get the shots developed."

He supposed he should be thankful she hadn't publicly gloated over her smooth manipulation of him. Except he wasn't feeling particularly gracious at the moment.

He couldn't believe she was Kira's best mate. Kira MacLeod was kind, gentle, and sweet of nature . . . whereas Tessa was a temperamental virago. It was hard to comprehend what could have drawn the two together.

"Wasnae so painful after all, was it then?" Graham pushed away from the tree he'd been leaning against as the crowd disbursed. "Ye didn't even have to show off yer manly bits."

He walked over, handing Roan his shirt, and, big as he was, momentarily provided a natural screen that Roan took full advantage of, making quick work of wrapping the plaid around himself again.

"Much," Graham added, with a dry note and an all-too-pleased look on his face.

Roan waited until he was decently covered before shooting his friend a quelling look. "You're taking far too much pleasure in all of this, ye ken. I realize ye think yer gettin' some sweet bit of revenge for me sendin' ye all the way across the pond to retrieve yer beloved—"

"From her own wedding," Graham interjected. "A wee tidbit of information you'd neglected to share."

"Only because ye'd never have gone if I hadn't!" He waved his hand, dismissing the topic. They'd hashed it out already upon Graham's return a month ago. The trip had landed him a bride, and simultaneously given every inhabitant of their tiny Hebridean island a reason to celebrate. With Graham's marriage to a McAuley bride, they had peace of mind, knowing their clan lairdship would continue uninterrupted, in his very capable hands. "I did it for your own good, and if ye dinnae stop going on about it, I'll simply whisk your lovely bride-to-be off to my own lair and book Iain passage back here so he can take the job away from your miserable, thankless—"

Graham frowned. "Has there been any indication of Iain returning?"

Roan knew Graham didn't share his personal concerns in that matter, so he didn't mind ribbing him from time to time. Iain McAuley had been a long lost heir to the island lairdship after the previous chief's death. He had shown up, out of the blue, intending to take what was rightfully his. And would have, if Graham hadn't beaten him to the punch and gotten engaged to Katie. Iain had taken off as quickly as he'd come, and Roan wasn't entirely certain they'd seen the last of him, "No, of course not. I was merely pointing out that you should be thanking me. Several times over. Because of my brilliant discovery and strategy, we've no' only managed to thwart the still unexplained attempt by your late grandmother's heir to usurp your title . . . but you might want to be thinkin' on how if it weren't for me, your bed would still be a cold, heartless, wasteland." His smile returned as he swiftly regained his equilibrium, post-virago. "Of course, my own bed still qualifies as such, so I believe the sacrifice on my part could rightly be called sainted."

Graham chuckled. "Aye, yer nobility is second only to your humble servitude."

Roan grinned. "As long as we're in agreement, then."

Graham shook his head at that, then turned in time to watch Tessa stow her gear in the boot of Kira's little Fiat. "She's an interesting one, that one is."

Roan looked past Graham's shoulder. "I can think of other adjectives that come more quickly to mind, but she does make an impression."

Graham glanced back at Roan, squinting against the sun that was dipping lower behind his back. "So, how is Kira these days?"

Roan suddenly found himself fiddling with the buttons on his shirt as he continued to dress. "Fine, I suppose, I dinnae much keep track. Far too much going on, what with your wedding less than a fortnight off, now combined with this ridiculous calendar scheme." He looked up at Graham and quite deliberately changed the subject. "Do ye think we're daft for trying to get into this thing? I mean, when Eliza brought the contest to my attention, I thought she'd truly gone mad, but once I looked into it and realized just how widely distributed the damn things are, it was almost too foolish not to try for it. The attention our inclusion in the calendar would bring to Kinloch would be marketing gold. Only, now—"

"Now you're just pouting because you ended up having to stand in front of the camera and be part of the ridiculous scheme, instead of remaining mercifully anonymous by running the show from behind it."

Roan opened his mouth intending to refute that statement. He'd devoted his entire adult life to doing everything he could to promote their island and its sole supporting industry, keeping them afloat economically, even hoping to push further, to a place where they could thrive. For that he'd do a hell of a lot more than be photographed with nothing more than his ancestors' claymore. Roan smiled. "Says the man who'd rather be out in his fields, taking test samples of flax seeds. You're just relieved that only the single blokes can participate."

"Damn right," Graham said on a laugh.

"And I dinnae pout." Roan straightened and settled the rest of his garb into place. "It's more a scowl. Surly and manly."

"Here." Graham handed over the sword he'd held while Roan got dressed, then turned and started off toward the Land Rover he'd left parked on the side of the road. "Don't think I missed you changing the subject just now," he called back over his shoulder.

Anything Roan might have said to that was lost when several of the villagers went up to Graham and started to excitedly discuss the wedding plans—in minute, excruciating, but ever-so-enthusiastic detail. Roan folded his arms and leaned against the wall again, taking pleasure in watching Graham's knowing smile freeze into something passably congenial as he did his best to nod and agree and look like he was truly interested . . . all the while making the escape to his vehicle as fast as humanly possible.

Roan had no doubt that his childhood friend was reel to sinker hooked by his bride-to-be. The two were like besotted love birds when they got within so much as viewing distance of one another. It was enough to make a single lad choke. With envy. No one was more anxious to get to his wedding day than Graham. But Roan also knew from listening to his friend vent over ales and darts, that as happy as he was to see everyone else fall as swiftly in love with Katie as he had, he could live quite happily for the rest of his days without another soul mentioning tea roses and tatted lace to him ever again.

Smiling to himself, Roan followed behind at a decent pace. Most everyone had gone. More of them than not would likely head down to Angus's for an ale and some gossip, second only to a game of darts as the most popular pastime on the island. He thought that sounded like a good end to a bad day, until he realized that he'd likely be the focus of a large portion of that gossip. Perhaps he'd head into the office instead, get a little work done without Eliza or anyone else sticking their noses in and about.

The sound of a slamming boot brought his head up. He'd been so lost in thought, he hadn't been paying attention to the fact that Kira's Fiat was still on the side of the road—which meant Tessa hadn't left yet.

Brilliant.

His lorry was beyond her car, on the opposite side of the single track lane, so he could hardly ignore her. He found himself thinking that a nice conversation about tatted lace sounded pretty good at the moment and wished he'd kept up with Graham. He nodded, forcing a smile and hoping to ease on by without further incident.

"Tessa! Roan!"

They turned to see Katie ducking around another departing car, waving and smiling at them.

Out of the corner of his eye, he saw Tessa's shoulders slump a little. The fact that he felt the exact same way didn't endear her to him. He adored Katie, but wished she'd caught up with him after Tessa had departed.

"Katie," Roan responded with a ready grin. "Ye've missed the show entirely—for which I'm eternally grateful—unless of course, witnessing my manly display would have furthered my suit with you. In which case, we can probably set up something a bit more intimate later on." He glanced at Tessa. "Have no fear, I won't be requiring your services."

"For which *I'm* eternally grateful," she said, eyeing the two of them.

Katie punched Roan in the shoulder, which was the expected and now traditional response to all of his teasing and flirting. Rubbing his shoulder, he accepted her follow-up hug and adopted

European mode of kissing him on both cheeks, which always amused and charmed him. That was the effect Katie had on everyone.

She turned to Tessa and grinned. "Feel free to ignore him when he's like that, or just punch him."

"Does it help? The punching? I've tried ignoring."

"If you mean will it make him stop, no. But it does make you feel better."

Roan watched the exchange, not entirely sure whether Tessa was being droll, or completely lacking in humor. If it wasn't for her dazzling display toward the end of their photo shoot, he'd have insisted to anyone who asked that it was the latter.

Katie stuck her hand out. "We haven't officially met. I'm Katie McAuley, Graham MacLeod's fiancée and therefore the source of a great deal of what I'm sure is very annoying wedding minutiae you could well live without. For that I apologize. I'm also a very distant cousin to this guy." She elbowed Roan in the ribs and he tugged at one of her blond curls. "I apologize for that, too. Frequently."

Roan watched Tessa take in their byplay, and though there might have been a flicker in her eyes, her expression remained smooth. "Completely understandable." She took Katie's hand in a short, but not impolite handshake. "Tessa Vandergriff."

"I understand you're Kira's friend," Katie went on, with her infectious smile still wide and natural, despite Tessa's less than effusive reaction. "I can't tell you how much it's meant to us all that you were willing to step up and help us out. You came here for a vacation, to catch up with an old friend; the last thing you needed was to get pressed into service. Not to mention I realize getting you to take photographs for a hunk of the month calendar is on par with asking a surgeon if he can help with a paper cut. Overkill!"

She laughed, which made Roan grin, because it was impossible not to when you were around her.

Unless, apparently, you were Tessa Vandergriff. "That's okay. I don't mind helping out Kira, and by extension, all of you." A polite smile made a brief appearance. "If you don't mind, I'm going to get back to her croft and look into setting up something to get these developed." She patted the single camera bag she had slung over her shoulder.

"It's no' digital?" Roan asked, then immediately wanted to kick himself. Why on earth would he want to prolong the conversation?

"Oh, I have plenty of those as well, but occasionally I like working with film. I like having my hands in the process—it makes me feel more connected to the work. You think differently when what you get is what you get. Digital is wonderful, but in some ways it's too easily transformed. Film is true."

It was the most animated he'd seen her since their introduction at his office earlier that morning. If he didn't know better already, he'd think she was actually human. Rather than, say . . . Borg.

She also seemed to realize the aberration in demeanor, and cut herself off with a quick, tight smile. "I'm sure you don't really care about all of that. I'll leave you two, to . . . whatever your business is."

"Please extend my thanks to Kira as well," Katie said, stepping back so that Tessa could open the door to the little red two-seater that had seen better days. Years, actually.

"I will," Tessa said, making one last effort at curving her lips upward, then closed the door.

Roan lifted a hand in a silent salute good-bye. He wasn't sure what to make of her, all commanding and bossy on one hand, but kind of socially awkward on the other. Quickly he reminded himself that figuring it out wasn't any of his concern.

As Tessa turned the key and started the engine, she looked through the windshield at him. Straight at him.

He got all caught up in her turquoise eyes. They were so intense, and he heard again the echo of quiet passion with which she'd spoken about her work. It was clear that while she might not love taking pictures of half-naked Scotsmen, she did have a love for photography itself. He hadn't had any chance to look into her credentials after Eliza had introduced her and announced she'd be taking the photos for the contest. He'd figured it didn't really matter. The amount of gear she traveled with alone was testament to the fact that she was no amateur.

He found himself wondering . . .

She abruptly broke their gaze and looked over her shoulder so she could back onto the road. Turning the car in a tight U she headed off down the road without a backward glance.

Roan and Katie turned and watched, Katie framing her eyes with a hand on her forehead.

"And so delightful, too," he said calmly.

She glanced at Roan, and smiled. "What did you do to piss her off?"

He gaped and plastered his free hand over his heart. "Me? I'm fairly certain she was dropped from the womb that way."

"Roan," Katie chided, though there was still a decided twinkle in her eye. "Maybe she was just having a bad day."

That was what he loved about Katie McAuley. Aside from the fact that she made his best friend a happier, more well-rounded human being, she'd also proven the perfect partner in crime for Roan. Unlike the scientific-minded Graham and the natural-born mediator, Shay, she was of sunny disposition, like himself, and also had a rather droll view of life. She didn't share that side with everyone, but seemed to have found a kindred spirit in him.

He'd initially been quite taken with her. Even though he'd never have acted on the attraction, they had quickly moved on to form a kind of familial bond that he'd come to cherish. He'd grown up with Graham and Shay as his ready and steady mates, so he'd never felt a lack of friendship or kinship, but it was a new and different thing, having what amounted to a sister in his life.

"You don't get that kind of attitude from having a single bad day," he said.

Katie watched the Fiat disappear into the distance. "Well, given what she does for a living, I'd guess she's seen a whole lot of bad days, so maybe we shouldn't be so judgmental. I know I couldn't do what she does. It was nice of her to help us out." Before he could follow up on that comment, she turned and checked out his garbed form, wiggling her eyebrows. "My, what a big . . . sword you have."

He wiggled his right back. "That's what they all say, luv." They laughed and he quite willingly let his curiosity about Tessa die an unexplored death as he turned his attention to more pleasant matters. He slung a casual arm over Katie's much narrower shoulders as they walked across the track to his lorry. "Did you see Graham just now as you arrived?"

"I saved him from death by wedding details, yes. He'll owe me for that, later," she added wryly. "But I came by because I wanted to tell you that I have the mock-up of the new home page done for the site, with the details about the calendar, and I wanted to know if you'd like to give it a look."

Katie's background had been in management for her family's ship-and-yacht-building empire, but her heart was in marketing and graphic design. She had quickly found a niche on Kinloch as his much needed creative consultant. She had already contributed several fresh ideas to the promotion he did for the island economy, which centered on the artisan baskets that were woven exclusively on Kinloch and sold worldwide.

"Pretty confident. We haven't even developed the photos as yet," he said with a laugh, while also trying not to cringe at the thought that he was the featured attraction of at least some of them. Surely the other blokes on the island who had already posed for Tessa would provide plenty of shots for her to work with. "We're a long way from advertising the thing. We need to win a spot in it first."

She just smiled up at him. "I'm a believer. I've looked back at everything you've done here. In the past five years your accomplishments in getting the baskets to a more global market have been nothing short of incredible, given the limited set of tools you have to work with. When you set your mind to something, you get results. I know folks are grateful, but I don't think everyone realizes just how much you do, because you don't toot your own horn."

"Well, I'd love nothing more than toot my horn, but word is you're already taken."

She just rolled her eyes.

"But that's okay. I've accepted my singular future. I'm thinking of getting a few cats, actually," he went on, adopting a rather pious expression, "and looking onward to a life dedicated to the service of others."

"Give me a break. If Kira would so much as blink in your direction, you'd be happily servicing your own needs with her a heartbeat later."

He was used to her ribald comebacks by now, but he'd rarely been the source of one, so he choked a little. First Graham, now her. "I dinnae ken where ye got that idea," he said, even though he knew she was too keenly observant not to see right through his protestations. "I'll die a monk, writing sonnets to your ethereal beauty, and pine for the perfect love that I can only observe, but am destined never to have for my own."

"I dinnae know how 'tis that the lovely villagers of Kinloch put up with yer multitudinous mountains of crap." She laughed, her accent dead on despite her brief tenure on the island. "But I certainly won't. So ask her out already. Sheesh. It's pathetic watching a grown man pine for no good reason."

"I pine only for you."

She had the most feminine snort. "Who did you use as your front woman before I came along? Seriously, Roan, I don't know what you're waiting for. She's not attached and—"

"And presently letting Morgan le Fay live under the same roof with her." He gave a shudder that wasn't entirely feigned. "No thanks. I'll wait until Tessa's taken her leave."

"Aha! So you admit it then. Well, that's a start." She patted him on the arm. "But I know you, you'll only find some other excuse entirely. You don't strike me as a chicken, Roan, so seriously, man up."

"I'm no' a chicken, as you put it. And my manhood isn't in question." He waggled his brows. "You've seen my sword?" He lifted it, then stowed it in the back of the lorry when she merely shook her head and gave him a sad, pitying look.

"Don't think you're going to charm me into forgetting this conversation," she warned, unwittingly echoing the same dire warning as issued by her fiancé earlier. "I'm on to you, Roan McAuley. You run around this island, being roguishly adorable and making everyone else feel good about themselves. It's about time you got some of that love back."

He shot her an affronted look. "I'll have you know I'm beloved by all here. Treated like a veritable prince. What more could a man ask than the admiration and love of his people?"

"A warm bed and an open heart," she said, quite a bit more sincerely than he'd have anticipated. "One that's accepting of yours."

He didn't have a quick rejoinder for that.

"You have so much to give the right person," she went on as they trundled toward town. "And she's right here, all but on your doorstep. What is it that's holding you back?"

His smile faded a bit. "It's a complex tale, Katie."

"It couldn't be. You're a man. And therefore too one dimensional for complexity."

He barked a laugh, though a quick glance at her proved that while she was willing to keep things light, she was far from letting it go.

"Speaking of our one-dimensional capacity," he said, changing the subject back to work, "what integrity-challenging marketing campaign has that wickedly brilliant brain of yours devised? Despite what you think, we men like to think we're more than just the sum of our manly parts. We're sensitive blokes, you know, with fragile egos. We need them stroked." He glanced at her and grinned. "And stroked often."

"Oh, brother."

"Roguishly adorable, I believe you said."

"And already regretting it."

They laughed together as he drove the rest of the way into town, but his thoughts remained partly on his conflicted feelings for Kira . . . and far more annoying, his apparent inability to stop thinking about her temperamental houseguest.

Chapter 2

"Well, doesn't that just bite." With a disgusted snort, Tessa clipped up the final series of shots on the cotton cord she'd strung inside Kira's narrow pantry, which temporarily doubled as her dark room. It was cramped and the jury-rigged lighting sucked, but she'd operated in far, far worse conditions. "Figures."

She wasn't surprised. Not really. She'd known exactly what she was getting when she'd started running the shutter. She'd just hoped that maybe, for the first time, her illustrious eye for things might have failed her.

So much for that.

With the last of the film processed, she needed to clean up so Kira could have her pantry back before breakfast. But she couldn't seem to stop staring at the last half dozen shots she'd taken.

She could tell herself she was interested in the integrity of the shot, the point of view she'd chosen, and how the angle allowed the sun to perfectly filter the light across the tops of the mountains and spill down over the fortress tucked between the peaks. She had an affinity for capturing the natural beauty of any landscape in her scope of vision, and had done it for so long it was second nature to her.

Of course, what had always drawn her was the juxtaposition of the staggering splendor of nature's bounty . . . contrary to the horrifying atrocities committed by man.

She closed her eyes briefly against any threat of invading visuals, then opened them once more to look at the subject of the photos in front of her. There was nothing remotely horrifying or atrocious about their human subject. In fact, she could argue that his natural beauty almost eclipsed that of the stunning backdrop.

He wasn't ruggedly hewn like their island leader, Graham, whom she thought of as Paul Bunyan in plaid. Roan was tall, as well, but where Graham was linebacker big with a square jaw, Roan was rangy and lean, broad of shoulder, lean of hip, his muscles perfectly and tightly defined, and his skin surprisingly golden, which only leant a gleaming, gladiator feel to the whole image. Unruly, sun-bleached brown hair shagged around his head in wayward curls, looking as if he did nothing more than rake a hand through it now and again. There was a shadow of stubble on his cheek, but she sensed it was more a result of the afternoon hour than through any deliberate design. In fact, she doubted he gave his appearance much thought. Mostly because he didn't have to.

He was roguish and charming, with a devilish glint of mischief in his green eyes and a deeply grooved dimple that winked often given his penchant for grinning. She was quite certain he was well used to incorporating all of that to further his own agenda whenever it suited him. Probably because it had netted him an alarmingly high, ego-inflating ratio of success.

She had no patience with people like that.

She knew her own unusual looks and her taller-than-average height set her apart from the crowd, but she'd spent a lifetime playing them down to get what she wanted, and where she wanted to go. She took a lot of pride in the fact that her work spoke for her. And only her work. No one could argue that she'd earned her way to her current pinnacle of success by employing any asset other than her pure, unmitigated talent behind a camera.

And yet . . . she looked at all that rugged, charming beauty, and it tugged at something inside her. Something intensely . . . female. She responded to it, to him, almost viscerally, and no amount of intellectual arguing with herself could divert her from that singular truth.

She closed her eyes with the sole intent of ridding herself once and for all of his unwanted hold on her attention, but all that did was drive her thoughts in steamier, more primal directions. She thought about how he'd smiled and dangled that kilt. How he held that sword. His palms were wide, even the muscles in his forearms were rigidly defined, as he'd gripped the hilt. Her lips parted as she imagined him letting go of that tartan, and striding to her, planting that sword deep in the earth, then taking her by the arms and yanking her up against him, plunging his tongue into her mouth and making her—

A tap on the door jerked her from her reverie.

"How goes it in there?"

"Almost done," she choked out, cheeks flaming as she realized how almost "done" she'd actually been.

"Can I see?" Kira asked through the closed door.

"Not yet with these," she said, rallying herself back to the moment at hand. And away from where she'd like to have another pair of hands at the moment. "But I have a ton of digital stuff to sort through, so you can give me your expert advice about them."

There was a snort. "I have an eye for weaving patterns, but you don't want me tellin' ye anything about photography."

"They're pictures of half-naked men." Tessa opened the door a bare crack and slipped through, shutting it quickly behind her. "The appeal is universal, requiring only gut instinct."

"So shallow," Kira said, then smiled. "I like it."

"Then you are officially my assistant."

Kira's smile broadened, and the light it brought to her eyes made Tessa feel slightly less than the schmuck of a friend she'd been of late.

"I've got the tiffin almost done," Kira said, as she turned into the small, but tidy kitchen. She smiled over her shoulder. " 'Tis only appropriate we enjoy the rush of chocolate endorphins while drooling over naked men—even if I did grow up with most of them." She paused then and made a face. "Come to think of it, I'm not sure I can be the least bit objective after all. I still remember what each of them looked like with freckled cheeks and the complete absence of body hair."

Tessa wrinkled her nose. "Ew."

"I know. But there is chocolate—which can only help."

"I can be shallow enough for the two of us. Let's proceed, shall we?"

Kira slid the pan of tiffin—chocolate and crushed cookies baked in warm, buttery goodness—and set it to cool on a rack on the butcher block counter, while Tessa propped open her laptop on the small kitchen table. She plugged in one of the three digital SLR cameras she'd used that day. It had been simpler than changing lenses back and forth.

Kira slid two heavy stoneware mugs onto the table and filled them with hot water, before dropping tea bags in each to let them steep. "I would ask why you need so many of those, but any explanation you'd give would go right over my head. I'm fortunate if I can get both the head and the feet of my subjects in the same shot. But let me tell you, I never cease to be amazed that you look through that little window and capture what you do. I look through that same tiny porthole and can't even hope to decide where to frame the scene so that it looks like anything more than a disorganized jumble."

Kira continued chattering away and Tessa kept one ear marginally tuned in, but the lion's share of her focus was on the file download and creating separate folders for each subject.

It was only when the chatter died down that Tessa looked up and blinked. "What?"

"I know today was a pain in the arse." Kira reached across the table and laid her hand over Tessa's arm. Kira was a toucher by nature, a nurturer of the first order.

Tessa had discovered she was neither—which worked out well in her line of work. It was usually intrinsic to her job to operate apart from whatever was going on around her, so it was rare that anyone touched her deliberately, and certainly not so casually. Or kindly. When someone put hands on her, it was usually in an attempt to separate her from her equipment, or remove her bodily from wherever she happened to be standing at the moment.

That she could handle. That she expected. It went with the job.

This . . . this threatened her. She didn't know how to handle it. Especially now. So she carefully slid her arm free under the guise of needing to type on the keyboard.

"I know taking pictures of any kind wasn't what you came here to do. For that, I'm sorry."

Tessa purposefully didn't meet Kira's direct gaze. She had made plenty of acquaintances in her years traveling the globe as a photo-journalist. But there was only one person who knew her. Truly knew her. Tessa was well aware that her story about wanting to take a little holiday and catch up with her old friend had only been accepted on the surface. She'd told Kira she was experiencing a little burnout, hoping that would explain her fatigue and general crankiness. She'd be fine if Kira would just allow them to operate under that pleasant façade.

"Maybe shooting half-naked Scots was exactly what I needed," Tessa said, though not with any real conviction. "Who wouldn't like a break from the ravages of war and mother nature for a little time spent staring at some beefcake instead? Who knows, could be the launch of an entire new career direction." *And God help me, I need one.*

Her attempt at levity was met with a sincere smile that had everything to do with extending compassion and little to do with amusement.

"Do they give Pulitzers for beefcake shots?" Tessa asked, pretending to ponder the question quite seriously as she went back to her computer screen. And hid.

Kira picked up her tea mug and scooted her chair around so she could look over Tessa's shoulder. "Lord, give me mercy," she said on a choked whisper and put her mug down.

"Looking a little different to you now, are they?" Tessa's smile came more naturally, and she was thankful to shift the focus to her work. Even if the series of shots weren't exactly her proudest accomplishment.

"All I can say is, I'm thinkin' the Pulitzer panel might create a new category just for you if they got a load of these."

"Who knows, the world might be a better place if they did." Tessa clicked open another file and forced her shoulders to relax. She was safe now. And, for the first time since she and her gear had been thrust back into service, she was thankful for the distraction of it all. It provided a topic of conversation, which was an easy way to keep the focus off her personally. The way she always preferred it to be. "Where is that chocolate, anyway? This is just the beginning. We'll need stamina."

Kira fanned her face as she pushed her chair back. "Well, it's grueling work, but somebody must do it if we're to help boost the local economy's infrastructure." She got up and went over to the counter. "We're such altruistic, caring women, that's what we are."

"Hearts of gold," Tessa said with a dry laugh. For the first time, she felt like she'd made the right choice, truly, in coming to Kinloch. She'd known Kira since they'd gone to boarding school together in London. She'd been bad at keeping in touch with everyone else who'd crossed her path, mostly because she hadn't felt compelled to stay connected. But despite their lives taking completely disparate paths, Kira had doggedly refused to be dropped from Tessa's orbit. Over the years, Tessa had done her level best to keep from exasperating her only true friend too badly, but even with her best intentions, long periods would elapse between their communications.

When she'd finally capitulated to the overwhelming evidence that she needed to exit the field for a bit . . . there was only one place she could go. Only one person she could trust herself to turn to. Being holed up alone somewhere was the last thing she needed. She'd at least admitted that much to herself. So she'd tracked Kira down, stunned and shamed to learn her happily settled, London-based friend was recently divorced and had retreated to her own childhood home with the same need to exit her personal battlefield.

Tessa was thankful Kira had found the solace and healing she'd needed in coming back to Kinloch, but that didn't ease her shame in not being there for her best and only friend in her dire time of need. She was objective enough about herself to know that while Kira might love her despite her faults, she had probably also known that Tessa hadn't been the one to turn to for help or comfort.

It made her deeply question what kind of person she'd become—because Kira would have been right. Keeping herself from feeling . . . well, anything, was the only way Tessa had managed to do her job.

Fortunately, Kira had had a real home to return to. The only home Tessa had wasn't a place she could go. Frankly, and possibly quite pathetically, the only home she had was wherever Kira was.

She'd been blessed by the open-armed welcome she'd received when she'd shown up on her oldest and only friend's doorstep—duffel bag and camera gear in tow—and a haunted, ravaged look on her face.

Kira busied herself cutting up pieces of tiffin and digging out plates, while Tessa slid mercifully into the autopilot zone of work. They weren't challenging images. And that was fine with her at the moment.

Kira slid the plate of freshly baked heaven onto the table, and topped off Tessa's mug with hot water. "Stop worrying."

Tessa looked up and frowned, truly nonplussed. "About what? The calendar guys? I'm not worried. We've got some decent shots. It was good light out there yesterday. And the subjects were willing enough." *Most of them, anyway.* Her thoughts veered to Roan and his affable grin and his big . . . sword, and she veered them right back. "You'll have as good a chance of winning this thing as anybody else."

Kira smiled. "I've always admired your ability to own your talent."

Tessa shrugged. "It's not ego, it's—"

"Honesty. I know. That's why I like it. Your confidence will go a long way to making everyone here feel better about our chances."

"I'm not giving any guarantees," she warned, even as her thoughts drifted to the shots presently drying in the pantry. "But if they don't pick at least one of your island heathens for their pretty boy collection, then they're either blind, or lack a pulse."

Kira laughed. "They're not all heathens, ye ken." Then she pretended to think about that. "Wait, yes they are." She sat down again and nibbled some chocolate crunch while she watched Tessa click open her editing software and begin working on a se-lect few shots. "What I meant, earlier," she went on, her voice a soft comfort as the silence stretched companionably, "was you don't have to worry that I'm going to pry."

Tessa sent her a sharp sideways glance, feeling a little caught off guard. She'd let her defenses down and had no immediate response that wouldn't either be a flat-out lie or simply confirm what Kira was already suspecting. "What do you think of this one?" she asked instead, and shifted her laptop monitor to cut the glare.

She held Kira's gaze as steadily as she could, and felt like a jerk for not finding a better way to acknowledge her friend's support. But she simply couldn't go there. Not yet.

Kira held Tessa's gaze only a beat longer, long enough to confirm that she knew something wasn't right with her friend, then mercifully turned her attention to the monitor. "Ranald?" She glanced at Tessa, then back to the screen. "Really?"

Tessa frowned and switched instinctively back into professional mode. Lately that had been a special hell all its own, but, at the moment, it felt like the haven it had always been for her in the past. She narrowed her gaze and critically studied the photograph. "What's wrong with it?"

"It? I'm not talking about the composition. I'm talking about Ranald. He's . . ." She scrunched up her nose and shook her head.

"What's wrong with him?"

" 'Tis simply no' right, Tessa, for a man to have that much hair." She shuddered. "Everywhere."

Nonplussed, Tessa looked at the picture once again. "This is the sexiest Highlanders calendar. Highlanders aren't the waxed and shiny types. Leastwise not the ones I've met so far. I was going for rugged mountain man." Again, her thoughts went, unbidden, to Roan. He was neither waxed nor shiny. In fact, he had hair in the exact right amount, in the exact right places. Damn the man and his perfect perfection.

"Aye, Ranald is rugged, if by rugged you mean 'has been covered by a rug.' "

Tessa spurted a little laugh at that, even as her eyes widened. "Listen to you."

Kira's cheeks grew pink and she glanced down, suddenly looking self-conscious. "I know it, I'm being evil. It's no' right of me."

"Actually, I was about to clap my hands together and say 'finally!' Welcome to the land of us normal mortals. I don't think I've ever heard you say anything that could be construed as less than kind and sweet. It's downright annoying, that kind of karmic perfection."

"And a fat lo' of good it did me, eh?" Kira quipped. To her credit, there was barely a flicker of pain behind the self-deprecating smile. But Tessa hadn't missed it.

She turned around in her chair and jutted out her chin toward Kira. "Go ahead," she offered. "Pop me one. Right in the kisser. I deserve it, you know."

"What on earth are ye goin' on about now?"

"Punch me. Hit me. Whatever. Just inflict some pain and we'll both feel loads better."

Kira looked properly horrified, and Tessa laughed. It was the closest she'd felt to normal in a very long time.

"What's funny about that?" Kira asked, looking more worried and concerned than since Tessa had shown up on her doorstep a week ago.

"You haven't changed so much after all. Don't worry. But you can still hit me if the mood strikes."

Kira frowned and took up another piece of crunch. "I dinnae know what's gotten into you, my closest, dearest friend," she said as she munched, "but if you want me to pretend that I'm no' aware there's something deep and dark lurkin' about in there—which I'm willin' to do if it'll help ye heal—then at least try not to act like a loon."

Tessa's laughter subsided. Normal time was over. She opened her mouth, shut it again, then sighed. Heavily. "I'm not in the best place at the moment, you're right about that. But I don't want to—can't—talk about it. I . . . I just needed to be away from some things for a bit." And connected to other things . . . like her only family. "I'm certain I'll work through things on my own." That was an out and out lie. She was certain of no such thing. No such thing at all. But she didn't want Kira to worry. More than she already was, anyway.

Tessa stood up and walked over to her friend, tugging her arm free from where she'd wrapped it around her middle. "I wasn't here for you, when things ended with Thomas," she said, never more sober and serious. "And I hate that, more than you might ever believe. I've been such a lousy friend. But that doesn't mean I don't hurt for you, and wish I was a better person, a better friend. I don't know how you're really feeling. You seem good, you sound better than good. But I don't truly know. So, I just want to say, I'm here now, and if you need anything, I'm willing. Whatever it is. Whatever helps."

"Weaving."

"What?"

"Weaving. It helps. I think it healed me. Mostly, anyway." Kira looked up and Tessa saw, for the first time, the toll of what the last eighteen months had taken on her sweet, gentle-natured friend.

"I'm so sorry," she whispered.

"I am, too." Kira took a breath, regrouped, and squared her slender shoulders. "I came back here to hide, lick my wounds, feel sorry for myself. But instead, I found the thing I should never have left behind."

"The baskets?"

Kira nodded. "I thought it was so sentimental and backward, marking me as some kind of uneducated Highlander. Outlander. You remember, when I came to London, how I was so enthralled with everything it had to offer? Big city, big moments, everything that was a world away from"—she stepped back and gestured to the tiny croft that had once been her grandmother's home, and home to her mother before her, albeit in an even more antiquated form—"this."

"It's not a bad thing to dream, to explore," Tessa said. "To want something different than what you have."

"I know. Truly, I do. I know I was fortunate to have the life I led in London. Perhaps I had to do that, to better respect where I came from. When I came back here . . . I didnae intend to stay. I just wanted time away, to reset myself. The weaving . . ." She looked over to the studio that had been added onto the croft sometime close to a century before. "I couldn't sleep. At first. It's so quiet here. I'd forgotten how quiet. It almost drove me mad. But . . . I couldn't go back. I wasn't sure I ever wanted to. So many memories." She hugged herself again. "Many of them so good. So beautifully, wonderfully good. It was torture, in its purest form. Seeing where we'd lived, where we'd laughed. Where we'd loved. So fully and completely. Me, an idiot, apparently, believing in the fairy tale, because it was all I ever wanted."

"Kira—"

She held up her hand. "But in the quiet of the night, with too many memories and no' enough sleep, I started with a basket. Mostly to give my mind a focus, and get it mercifully off the rest."

"And it helped." Developing film was much the same for Tessa. For all the photos she took of death and destruction, she'd taken equally as many of beauty, of life. Most of those didn't make it into the newspapers or the magazines, but on many a long, very long night, bringing them to life had kept her sane. "I understand that, Kira. Maybe more than you know."

She nodded. "I believe it saved me. No' at first, perhaps. But when I gave myself fully to it, going back to the roots of where I began—I-I don't know, Tessa—something came over me. Or into me. Visions of the patterns, the colors, the shapes, and textures. I don't know where it all comes from, but it fills me up. And letting it out, indulging in it, exploring it, and seeing the result of it . . . fulfills me. So I've stayed, thinking I'll leave when it feels right."

"Do you think you will? Leave? Go back to London? Or start over in a new city?"

She shrugged. "I dinnae know. I'm no' sure it matters so much now, what comes next. Right at the moment, being here is good, enriching, life giving. I'm good. Better than I've been, and better than I thought I'd ever be again. So, I'm here. Right now."

Tessa listened to the words, and heard the soul of the truth in her best friend's voice. She supposed there would always be a place inside Kira that mourned what was, what might have been—should have been, if you asked Tessa . . . but Kira very specifically hadn't. Tessa would still like to look Thomas up. And kick his sorry ass. For starters. But Kira hadn't expressed that desire either.

In fact, she'd said little to nothing about what had taken place, other than she'd been blissfully happy, planning a bigger home, thinking about starting a family . . . when Thomas announced their seven-year marriage and almost decade-long relationship was over for him. He'd already leased another flat before making his announcement and had moved out immediately, leaving her nothing to fight for.

Broken-hearted, broken-spirited, and, from what Tessa could tell, even a full year and a half later, still not certain of the why of it, Kira had had no choice but to move on with her life.

And she had. Brilliantly so, if there was truth in what Tessa had overheard the locals saying about Kira's unique and untraditional new artisan basketry.

She looked into Kira's eyes and saw the hint of lingering shadows . . . but mostly she saw hope and light. Maybe that was the best a person could wish for, coming out on the other side of a tragic set of events . . . hope, and a little light.

Tessa had no doubt that light would grow stronger for Kira. Her friend wasn't destined for a life lived in shadows. In contrast, it made her wish there was a glimmer of light in her own life, or that she could trust it would be there, at some point. The darkness she was in felt pretty complete at the moment. And she didn't know if that would ever change.

Chapter 3

"Only me?" Roan grabbed up the thick envelope of rejected photos and pushed his chair back from his desk. "Well, that's a load of rubbish, that is. Let me take a look through these. Surely there are others that are better."

Eliza merely folded her arms over her short, stout figure, and sighed the sigh of the long put upon. "You're quite well aware of yer appearance, lad. Dinnae pretend to be all aghast. We've got a shot at it, or so Miss Vandergriff believes. I trust her opinion."

"She's not a fashion or a model photographer." About as far from the pretty and the shiny as she could get, actually. Despite efforts to the contrary, Roan hadn't been successful in eliminating Kira's houseguest from his thoughts. At all. So he'd finally given in and done his research, telling himself it was merely the wise thing to do, given the level of responsibility they'd placed in her hands—which was a lie he hadn't been able to sustain for the time it took to Google her name.

When the long list of responses to his search had scrolled onto the screen he'd stopped telling himself anything. He'd been too busy reading. And reading some more. To say he'd been impressed—and, aye, intimidated—by everything she'd achieved at barely a few years past the age of thirty, would be as vast an understatement as saying that he was only a wee bit stunned at what she'd witnessed by that same young age.

"I'm fairly certain her list of awards qualifies her to be a judge of just about any subject that can be caught on film," Eliza rejoined. "So if she thinks yer pleasant-enough features are the ones we should be pinning our hopes on, then that's what we'll do."

"Pleasant-enough is it now? Wasn't it just last week when you referred to my assets, as it were, as God-given?"

"Well, they all are from his hand," she said, then glanced over Roan with studied disregard. "No matter the abundance. Or lack thereof."

Roan had to laugh at that, and caught Eliza's satisfied smile as well. Theirs was a well-honed routine and though neither would have admitted it, they enjoyed the challenge and the comfort to be found in their spirited exchanges.

"Well, then might I just say I'm surprised that my lack of abundance, as you put it, will be put on display for the judges' panel. Surely there are other candidates—"

"Well, there would have been Shay, had he returned from Edinburgh in time. I'm certain he'd have taken your place. Easily."

Roan didn't rise to the bait. "And I'd have gladly let him. But what about—" He flipped through the discard stack, but the mere sight of his clansmen, ridiculous and goofy grins on each and every face, simply didn't bear perusing. He definitely wasn't ready to see the same expression on his own face.

He put the discard stack down, and didn't touch the envelope with the finalists' photos—all of which featured him. He glanced up to find Eliza still standing there, staring him down.

"I'll . . . handle it," he told her. "Thank you for bringing them in." He should be thankful he only had Eliza to deal with. When he'd gotten word she'd be dropping them off earlier that day, he'd expected a showdown with Tessa—which did nothing to explain his disappointment when he'd learned she'd merely left the photos with his secretary.

"The deadline is—"

"Friday. I know." He blew out a short huff of annoyance,

then made himself smile. It was his only hope of getting his privacy back. "I willnae be missing it, rest assured."

"I'm sure. We're all countin' on ye, lad." Eliza pointed to the discard pile. "Dinnae be thinkin' of making any substitutions, is all I'm sayin'. We're trusting Tessa's experience. We're fortunate she was here and willing."

"Aye, I know it."

Her gaze narrowed, but when she couldn't shake his ready smile, she finally nodded. "Good. I'll post the package when you have it ready. Ferry schedule is changing tomorrow. Coming at half past now, instead of on the hour."

"Got it," Roan said, his smile tightening. "Were you able to get hold of the Malaysian distributor? Set up a call?"

Eliza bristled, as he'd known she would. "Of course I did. Set it up for tomorrow at seven."

"In the morning?"

"I should hope so. You wouldn't want to be trying to set up a distributorship at three in the morning Kuala Lumpur time, would ye?"

"Right. Seven. In the morning. Brilliant." He swiveled his chair so he faced his laptop screen. "I'd better go over my notes, make sure they're coherent enough for me to interpret at the crack of dawn."

"If ye didnae stay up so late working, it wouldnae seem so early to ye. The rest of the world rises every day as the sun comes up."

"Which is why I thank the world every day I have a job that leaves rising at such an ungodly hour to those who appreciate it." When she continued to give him the chiding eye, he turned and smiled more sincerely at her. "Thank you for setting it all up, Eliza. I appreciate all that ye do, and well ye must know it."

She harrumphed . . . but finally retreated from the field of battle. "Wouldn't be able to keep this place afloat for ten minutes if I weren't around to—" Her grumbling was mercifully cut off as she closed the door behind her, though he could have recited the rest from memory.

Lips curving as they typically did after a hearty round, he brought up the notes he'd taken for the new distributor. After a few minutes of staring at them and retaining nothing, he swore under his breath and gave up pretending he was going to get anything else done until he'd dealt with the more pressing matter at hand—looking at those damn photos.

Just as his hand was hovering over the packet, there was a tap on the door, which opened before he could respond.

Katie stuck her blond head in first, a smile on her face. "I heard a rumor that the finalists have been chosen! Or, should I say, finalist?"

"Go away."

She just laughed. "Ha! So you are the chosen one. I knew it! Lemme see!"

She came dancing into the office and he barely had time to snatch the packet off his desk and out of her reach before she lunged for it. "What do you mean, you knew it?" He frowned. "Don't tell me Tessa went and announced it at Angus's or something."

"Since when does anyone have to make an announcement around here for word to get out? Actually, Tessa didn't say anything. If you want to blame someone, you can aim that at Blaine. And he only told me. So far," she added with a twinkle in her eyes.

"Blaine?" He turned his chair to face her directly. "How the hell—"

"From Kira."

"Kira?" He leaned back in his chair. "What did she say?"

Katie shook her head, a look of pity on her face. "You were all ready to throw Blaine under the bus before I even explained, but I bring up Kira and suddenly you're all thoughtful and open to listening."

"Because Blaine loves gossip second only to . . . well, nothing, as far as I can tell. And Kira wouldn't hurt a soul, much less blurt out something like that, to someone like him."

"Careful," she warned, her smile still warm, but a bit of steel entering those dark blue eyes of hers.

Though Roan definitely enjoyed having a new friend and sisterly playmate with whom he could enjoy viewing the world around him, he was also well aware that he was second—third in line, actually—for her affections. Right after her soon-to-be-spouse, Graham . . . and her lifelong friend and former fiancé, Blaine Sheffield.

He held up his hand. "I'm sorry. Even though you know I'm not saying anything that's not true."

The storm clouds cleared and she nodded as she grinned. "I know. He really is hopeless. He's just insatiably curious about . . . well, everything. And, you know, go with your strength, right?" She held her hand up to stall his rejoinder. "Anyway, the story is that Kira was on her way here with the goods—"

"Kira dropped them off?"

The pitying look returned. "Seriously, you should see yourself right now. It's as if you've been told someone took your present from under the tree before you'd had a chance to shake it. How is it a man as confident as you won't just walk up and ask the woman out, for God's sake?"

"Like I said before, it's complicated. And I'm not going to talk about it," he added, with enough warning in his voice to make sure she understood he wasn't simply baiting her. Kira had been back since the spring before last, but she'd not been the delightful girl he'd remembered growing up with, at least not upon her immediate return. In fact, she'd looked downright . . . ravaged. She hadn't talked much to anyone, taking refuge, instead, in her grandmother's old croft, spending all her time making it livable again. Then she'd surprised everyone by re-birthing the unique weaving her direct lineage of MacLeods had been well-known for. Even the best of the island gossips had only been able to learn that her life in London, including her marriage to a university professor, had come to a bad end, and that she'd returned home to get on her feet once again.

The last thing she'd needed then was a childhood friend hitting on her, not that he'd have intruded on her solitude during those early days. But he'd always had a soft spot for her growing up, and that soft spot, it seemed, was still there. Though she'd kept mostly to herself, he'd become sort of a self-appointed protector. She didn't know it, but he'd kept watch over her, in a general, non-stalkerish way, and . . . more or less made sure she was okay. She'd begun weaving a month or so after her return, and her work was the means by which he had made contact with her; it was strictly professional. She'd never encouraged his attention, or that of anyone else, as far as he knew. And he'd know. He'd made it his business to know.

He'd watched as she'd come back into her own, observed the color returning to her fair skin, the vibrancy in her voice as she interacted with the other villagers, and the light sparkling in her lovely, hazel eyes. But even as she'd healed, there was no indication she was viewing their personal interactions as anything but professional inquiries as to her work output and when it would be ready for sale. Roan well knew all the signs when a woman was interested in him. She exhibited none of them.

So . . . he didn't go there. Not with her. Not for fear of being shot down, per se. But because he didn't want to put any awkwardness between them, or harm what rapport they did have. Losing that would matter to him. So . . . he simply didn't ask for more—not without some indication it would be welcomed. He consoled himself that she wasn't encouraging interaction of that kind with anyone on the island.

He was biding his time. It wasn't as if there was anyone else sparking an interest.

Tessa's scowling face and wild red curls flashed through his mind, but he promptly dismissed that subconscious blip. She'd sparked his notice, all right, but not in a good way.

"So, what happened with Kira and Blaine?" he asked Katie as much because he wanted to know, as to banish thoughts of Tessa. Again.

"She was on her way here, but stopped in at Mildred Anne's to pick up some dye for a new weaving design she's hatching. Blaine was there, and they struck up a conversation."

"And?"

"And, what? If Blaine wants to know things, he has a way of getting people to talk. If Sheffield-McAuley had ever bothered to figure out his strengths and exploit them, who knows the things he might have accomplished—which, you know, you could do, too. He's very useful. Instead of disparaging him or underestimating him, you should consider how he could help you, industry-wise. He's a very smart guy."

"I'm sure he is. Speaking of Sheffield-McAuley, when is Blaine going back to your family's firm?"

She just rolled her eyes. "I don't know. Possibly about the same time I do. Never. By following me here, he's managed to break free, just like I did. That freedom is amazing and not a little terrifying. But while I have a path laid out for me now, he doesn't. He has dreams, goals, ones he's craved for a very long time, and I have no doubt, at some point, he's going to follow them, and be ridiculously successful. But you have to understand we just escaped a life of familial tyranny, so until we've figured out exactly where we stand with our respective mummies and daddies," she went on, adopting a credible Scot accent, " 'tis no' likely he'll be headin' anywhere." She propped her hands on his desk. "In the meantime, be smart and use his mad information-gathering skills to help grow your market."

"I've got my hands full with your mad skills—"

"Hey," she said, pretending to be affronted, "my new site concepts are going to revolutionize how you do your custom ordering and you know it. Blaine, on the other hand, could probably dig up markets you haven't even considered. In fact, just before the wedding apocalypse, he'd surprised me with his ideas on expanding Sheffield's hold on the custom sloop and catamaran market."

Roan didn't point out that marketing yachts to rich people was slightly different from finding toeholds in the global traditional artisan craft market, mostly because she was likely right where Blaine was concerned. "I thought you had him working on the whole Iain story. Has he found out anything yet?"

"He's working with Shay, actually."

Roan's brows lifted. "Shay? *Our* Shay?"

"Um, yeah," she said, looking at him quizzically. "What other Shay do we have?"

"None, I just"—he shook his head—"I can't quite picture those two teaming up, is all. Shay is so . . . dry. And Blaine is—"

"Anything but," Katie laughed. "I know. But he owns that and you know it. That's what I've always loved best about him. I've so thoroughly enjoyed getting to see him be fully himself all the time, since coming here."

"It stretches the imagination to consider that he'd be capable of being anything other than the . . . vibrant personality he is."

Katie laughed. "I know you won't believe this, but he was *the* most straight-laced executive at Sheffield-McAuley."

"I'm not even touching that one," Roan said, finally relenting and laughing. It wasn't that he didn't like Blaine, it was that he didn't really understand him, or his motivations for being there. He trusted Katie that the guy was harmless, and from what he'd seen, Blaine was definitely not there to get in the way of his childhood friend's future happiness . . . but it was still odd, no matter how you looked at it. So Roan tried not to. "What you're telling me is that, if this little conversation they had happened a good, what, hour ago, then probably the whole damn island knows by now?"

Katie nodded and grinned, then leaned forward before he knew what she was about and snatched the finalists' envelope away from him. "Ha!"

He didn't even bother telling her to give them back, or not to look. He merely sighed, swore under his breath, and swung his attention back to his laptop screen and the Malaysian business meeting notes. "No mocking. No taunting."

"In your dreams, pretty boy."

He did smile at that, a little.

"Why is it you're so annoyed by this anyway? I dinnae ken, mon," she added with a bit of sass. "You know you're a hot commodity on the island, that all the women want you, even the ones old enough to be your grandmother—"

"Don't."

"I'm just saying, you're a flirt and a charmer of the first degree. I'd think you'd be making T-shirts and posters of the damn photos and seeing what side business you could strike up. In fact, I'm surprised you're not soaking up every bit of this added attention."

"Well, that's where the brief tenure of our friendship might be showing," he said, keeping his gaze on the screen, even though he saw nothing but a blur of text. "My behavior with the people on this island is just me being me. I enjoy them, they enjoy me, we enjoy each other. It's . . . natural, for want of a better word. But there's nothing natural about me posing in the all together to be flaunted about for the world to see in some damn calendar."

Katie sauntered closer, wiggling the stack of photos in her hands.

"I'm tellin' ye," he warned, "I dinnae want to see them. I'll be haunted for life. I'm no' jokin with ye on this, darlin' Kate."

She lowered her hand with the photos, and her expression, or what he could see of it from the corner of his eye, sobered a little. "You're really serious, aren't you?"

"I really am, aye. My thought has been that we've grown close as friends so quickly because we have an understanding of each other. 'Tis true we both embrace laughter and fun, and think most folks would be far better if they just lightened up a wee bit and didnae view all things with such dour seriousness. But because you are betrothed to my closest friend and our island leader, and clearly besotted with the lucky sod, your open and fun nature is seen as friendly and puir of heart, which I know it to be. Just because I am an unattached male, it doesnae mean I should be viewed any differently. I am a happy, hearty soul who enjoys the excitement life brings and embraces it fully, but I dinnae conduct my life in a way that would be considered immodest or amoral."

She stared at him for a beat, then another, making him feel more than a wee bit ridiculous for his outburst. But he'd been taking the ribbing of everyone on the island for the past week and he was tired of it. Most especially when it came from those he expected to support him.

"Well," she said at length, "these aren't amoral or immodest." Then she fanned the photos out a bit. "Okay, maybe a wee bit on the immodest side," she added with an inviting grin. Upon seeing his scowl, she grew a little impatient. "Oh, for heaven's sake, Roan, you could use some lightening up yourself right about now. It's not like it's pornography. They're good natured and sexy, which, to my mind, is natural and perfectly healthy. They're a bit of fun and if they bring business to Kinloch, then what's the harm?"

He didn't respond right away, and hoped the subject would naturally come to a close. He should have known better.

"Wait." She walked around the desk until he finally looked up at her. She held his gaze for a long moment. "I think I see what this is really about. It bothers you a lot that Kira saw these, doesn't it? Is that it? You don't care what the world thinks of you or your behavior, but you do care what she thinks."

He refused to answer—on the grounds that she was one hundred percent correct. He knew he was being a sheep's arse about it, but the fact was, he didn't need whatever respect he might have fostered in Kira over the past year and a half to be blown to middling hell because she saw him as some halfwit more interested in exposing his manly bits than he was serious about growing the island economy.

He reached over on the desk and picked up the reject packet. "Here," he said, in lieu of a direct response. Katie knew she was right. He didn't need to confirm it. "Look through these, and find something else we can submit. I know Tessa is a hotshot in her field, and I'll be the first to applaud the successes she's had, but that doesn't necessarily qualify her to judge this."

"But you'll trust my judgment?"

Roan looked at her. "Let's just say I think you have a better understanding of the attraction between women and men than she does."

"Well, I'd like to argue that, strictly on feminist grounds."

"But you've met her."

"I have."

"So, do me a favor, okay?"

Katie held his gaze, and he was thankful for the sincere affection he saw there.

"When is the deadline?"

"Has to be on the ferry tomorrow."

"Okay, I'll look them over tonight. But you get to call Graham and explain why I'm ogling half-naked photos of his childhood buddies."

"He's no' to be part of this selection process," Roan warned.

"Oh, not to worry," she replied. "I don't know that this would be his preferred way to spend an evening together."

Roan grinned. "Point taken."

Katie juggled the packets and slid the finalist photos back in their envelope. "You'll be here in the morning?"

"I have a seven o'clock phone conference, then computer lab at the school at eleven."

"Hey, I heard the soccer team did well with their game against Castlebay. Good job, Coach."

"Football, ye Yank," he said, even as his face split in a wide grin. He was proud of his kids. "Kicked Castlebay's arse, they did."

"Graham told me those kids have played together since being old enough to go to school and hadn't won a single game in two seasons. I think what you've done to help out is great."

"All they needed was some steady direction. It gives me a chance to kick the ball about again, prolong that whole growing up thing a wee bit longer."

"I hear you, Peter Pan. But they're lucky to have you." Katie walked to the door, and glanced back. "Roan, if Kira knows you," she said, making a circle in the air with her hand to indicate the whole of him, "the real you, then your posing for this picture will make her laugh, and be proud that you're willing to step outside your comfort zone for the sake of the island. If she doesn't, then maybe you need to set your sights on someone else."

Caught off guard yet again, he took a moment too long to come up with his ready response. "I would, luv, but Graham has already won your heart."

"Maybe you were right then. You should think about getting a few cats after all. Being as you're so pathetic and all." She winked at him and ducked out before he could lobby a response.

He was smiling as he went back to work, but with her comments about Kira echoing through his mind, he wasn't nearly as settled as he'd like to be.

Chapter 4

Tessa finished lacing up her hiking boots and tugged the legs of her jeans down over them, before quietly letting herself out the back door of the croft.

The sun hadn't quite made its way over the horizon yet, and the rock-strewn meadows that bordered Kira's property were still drifted over with a thick, morning fog. She could barely make out the fuzzy bodies of sheep clustered just beyond the closest stone wall, much less those farther out. The occasional grumbling bleat was the only sound in the otherwise quiet dawn.

The weight of her favorite, standard issue, classic Nikon F-301, circa 1985, was a familiar comfort hanging around her neck, one she wasn't taking for granted on the peaceful September morning. Pulling her fleece jacket a bit closer, she zipped it up against the morning chill and set out through the side gate, across the rear field, heading toward the stacked stone wall in the distance. She planned to take the herding trail she knew led well beyond it, circling the base of the sole mountain peak to be found at that end of the small island. Beyond it lay the single-track north road that eventually looped around the entire island, but her destination was the rocky shoreline on the far side of the north track.

She couldn't make out the mountain at all; the fog was too thick. Actually, Ben Cruinish was more a very large hill than a real mountain. Nothing like the towering twin peaks that formed the stunning skyscape at the western end of the island. The flaxseed crops that were the basis of the baskets woven on the island were grown in the protected valley between them. The easternmost tip, where Kira's croft was situated, was more meadow and stream, populated by sheep-rearing crofters and the fishermen who plied their trade off the northern coast, out past the Sound of Ailles in the waters of the Atlantic.

The rhythms of island life might seem slow, even rustic, but the islanders were methodical in accomplishing the daily tasks required to subsist off the land and sea. Their work ethic was positive and hopeful, something she'd witnessed in places with far, far less to be positive or hopeful about. The people didn't seem to take for granted the natural bounty they had available to them. They took deep pride in the traditional artistry of their intricately woven baskets, their single export and source of income.

She'd traveled enough, seen enough, to have an honest respect for cultural traditions, and marveled at how they persevered the world over, through centuries of strife and constant challenge. The people on Kinloch had every right to be proud of their heritage, and how it had not only kept them a viable, thriving community within their homeland, but had grown into a commodity being traded in a global marketplace, where people around the world enjoyed the fruits of their very creative labors.

But it wasn't Kira's wildly imaginative waxed linen baskets or the quiet calm of island life that were the focus of Tessa's thoughts. She'd woken again, with adrenaline pumping through her so hard she'd been shaking, nauseous with it, her skin hot and flushed, the bed linens damp from sweat. For the fifth night in a row, her unconscious mind had dragged her through the harrowing journey it kept insisting she take when she finally, exhausted, had closed her eyes and prayed for uninterrupted sleep.

Since arriving on Kinloch, she'd been safely tucked away in Kira's croft, quite consciously secure in the knowledge that no bombs would be dropped, burning the roof over her head, or leveling the buildings around her; that no vicious, virus-carrying insects would be feasting on her flesh; no night-marauding animals—two legged or four—would be hunting for her. Nor was there even a remote threat that anyone would storm the cottage, looking to roust her from her sleep and drag her off to a cell somewhere, to question her endlessly about her reasons for being in the village in the first place.

No. None of those things would ever happen to her there.

But tell that to her subconscious. All of those things had happened to her in other places. Often enough that it felt perfectly normal for her to sleep with a knife under her pillow, a net over her bed, and a fire extinguisher within easy reach—which could also double as a Louisville Slugger when necessary.

She'd spent the past nine months trying to figure out how to come to terms with the tricks her mind had started playing on her, while still maintaining a full assignment load. She understood it was a form of post-traumatic stress, and was smart enough to know she couldn't just ignore it, outrun it, or out think it. Extensive counseling had helped her understand it and why it was happening, and even change the way she thought about it and dealt with it. But counseling hadn't stopped it from happening.

Mostly because it *was* still happening . . . for real.

Several months into counseling, she'd heeded the counselor's advice and taken a brief, five-week sabbatical. She'd made huge, confidence-building strides. But back in the field, one bomb had gone off, and everything had come screaming right back with it. No amount of employing all the techniques she'd learned would stave the terror off. Not as long as the bombs kept exploding. And people kept dying. The counselors and therapists who'd helped her had all said the same thing: find a new career. You can't handle this one any longer if you want to stay healthy.

She'd rejected that diagnosis. Out of hand. She'd tried alternative methods, including hypnosis and acupuncture, among other more off-the-wall therapies. Those who knew her would have been boggled at the things she'd experimented with. Even she was surprised by the lengths she'd gone to. But she'd have tried anything if she could find a way to manage her disorder effectively so she could stay in the field and continue her work. Photojournalism was what she did. It was who she was. She couldn't contemplate an alternative.

But it had finally gotten so bad that she wasn't functioning, wasn't sleeping . . . and she sure as hell wasn't doing her job effectively. In fact, for the six weeks prior to coming to Kinloch, she'd missed deadlines and struggled to complete her assignments, with no hope left that things were going to improve— unless she made some additional changes. Deep down, she knew there was only one additional change left to make.

Feeling more lost than she'd ever been, not knowing where else to turn, she'd finally decided to take the "vacation" everyone who worked with her had been gently, and not-so-gently, suggesting. She'd come to Kinloch, to Kira. She'd come, initially telling herself a break from the road would give her time to find a realistic solution that would allow her to heal, while continuing in the only profession she'd ever known, or ever wanted. As she'd debarked from the island ferry and been engulfed in Kira's tight hug, she'd already known that for the lie it was. There was no realistic solution—other than walking away.

She knew that. So what she was really doing there, was hiding—taking a vacation from the inevitability of the truth. Only, in the wee, shaky hours of another restless, terror-filled night, she'd decided that wasn't exactly working, either.

Sometime around three-thirty that morning, she'd found herself going back over some of the calendar prints she'd taken. Her eye focused on the scenery . . . and not the kind that had to do with bulging muscles and artfully placed swaths of plaid. There was beauty on Kinloch—natural, staggering amounts of it, no matter the direction in which she'd pointed her camera.

But there was also a history there. While the fields were no longer strewn with the carnage of this battle or that blight, what grew was a direct result of what had come from the survival of those brutal challenges.

That had gotten her to thinking . . . about the travesties she'd spent her professional career recording, exposing to the world the atrocities suffered by so many, often in places of equally staggering beauty and bounty. It had always struck her as so needless, so . . . reckless. All of her work, her determination . . . had done absolutely nothing to stop it from happening again. And again. With an infinity of agains yet to occur.

Similar madness and mayhem had happened right on these shores, on the very ground where she was walking at the moment. She juxtaposed the savagery of the past . . . with the bucolic scenery of Kinloch as it was today. There were ruins of an ancient abbey just off shore, and the towering fortress of a castle, slowly crumbling, yet still standing boldly as a symbol to the clansmen and women who made their home there—direct descendants of the men and women who'd laid those very stones, whose very blood had been shed beneath her feet in order to preserve it and all it stood for, and what it would continue to stand for.

A thread of an idea was born of that.

She couldn't stop the madness or the mayhem, either in the world or inside her head. Maybe it was that very helplessness that had eventually taken such a heavy toll on her psyche. So . . . if she couldn't continue to subject herself to the ravages of war . . . perhaps she could turn her attentions to what happened after. What had those wars eventually wrought for the people who'd fought in them?

Maybe it was time to train her lens on the other side of the equation.

Smokescreen? Cop out? She wasn't really sure. It was only a shadow of an idea . . . and she was aware she might simply be fooling herself into thinking there was merit to it, or substance in it worth pursuing. She was trudging over rocky soil at dawn, dodging sheep, and heading to the shore to take pictures of the abbey . . . and the tower . . . and later, the castle. From there, she wasn't certain. She had research to do. And, if the wisp of an idea took on substance, there would be interviews to schedule.

It shouldn't excite her, that burgeoning idea of hers. It should terrify her. But her fingers were itching to get to work. And she hadn't felt like that in a very, very long time. Longer than she would have ever admitted—even to herself.

She scrambled over the second stone wall, navigated through another herd of mingling, black-faced sheep, then headed west around the base of Cruinish, toward the north track. The shoreline was still a mile off, but the distance melted away as the hike gave her time to think, to plot, to plan.

Kinloch wouldn't be the most interesting place to document a history of then and now, but it was where she was, away from everything, and everyone who worked with her. No one would ever have to know if it turned out to be a ridiculous folly.

Deep in thought, feeling physically weary, but mentally energized by the new plan, she jumped a shallow gully that ran alongside the north track. She'd barely scrambled to the side of the road, slipping a little as she tried to gain purchase on the stretch of loose dirt and rocks between her and the pavement, when a single headlight pierced the fog, followed by the blare of a horn. The motorbike was right on her, leaving her no time to leap out of the way. Then came the sound of skidding tires, as it left the road on the far side and slid sideways in the soft dirt before depositing its rider into the bordering gully just beyond.

"Oh my God." Tessa managed to right herself without falling back into the gully behind her, then ran across the narrow track. "Are you okay?" She had to shout over the sound of the motor that was still humming on the bike, but was more interested to find out if the driver was injured. "Are you hurt? Should I go for help?"

She gingerly skidded down the steep side of the gully, then hopped across the mud-and-water-filled trench at the bottom, slogging through the muck on the other side as she made her way to where the rider was presently rolling to his back, groaning. Well, swearing, actually, she realized, as she got closer.

"Just wait a second, I'll help you."

It wasn't until she was almost on top of him that the heavy mists, still thickly banked down in the gully, parted enough so she could see him more clearly. "You," she said, stopping short, the hand she'd been extending freezing in mid-reach.

"Christ, I should have known." Roan sat up, ignoring her half-hearted gesture to help pull him up, then made a face as the muck oozed in around the waistband of his trousers when he shifted backward to reposition his booted feet. "Brilliant. Bloody brilliant."

"Here," she said, resolutely sticking her hand out. "Let me help."

He eyed the hand as if she was shoving a snake at him.

"Look, I get that we're not best buddies, but I'm not an ogre who takes pleasure from the misery of others."

"Could have fooled me," he muttered, as he pushed himself up. He climbed from muck to bank, then up to the side of the road where his bike still lay, the motor spinning.

"No, please," she said flatly, "I can climb back up on my own." She hopped the gully again, and found a rocky section that made climbing back to the roadside a bit easier.

He wasn't paying any attention to her, but was crouching over his motorbike, which was now silent.

"Will it run?" she asked, walking toward him, despite the urge to simply turn around and keep on walking toward her original destination.

"Run, yes. Roll, I'm no' so certain."

She skimmed her gaze over the frame, and noted that one of the wheels did look a bit . . . warped. "That's not so good."

"No, it's not. And I have an appointment at"—he glanced at his watch from habit, no doubt, only to swear under his breath again as his shirt cuff slid back to reveal the timepiece was covered in thick gunk, with a few choice pieces of gully debris sticking to it as well—"doesnae matter much now, anyway." He straightened and moved the bike so it was well off the road.

"What are you going to do?" she asked, though she wasn't certain why she was still engaging him in any form of conversation. He was clearly unhurt, and just as clearly not remotely caring whether she stayed or left. It was just . . . she didn't feel right walking away from the scene of an accident. Especially one she was at least partly responsible for.

"Walk into town. Borrow Graham's truck, pick up my bike, take it to Magnus's shop." He finally glanced at her. "What on earth were you about, wandering out here in the wee hours of dawn? The sun's no' even fully up yet."

"Heading to the shore," she answered, not that it was any business of his. But he didn't look so smug with his ridiculously perfect dimple filled with gully mud. And that made him slightly less annoying to her. "I'd give you a lift, but as you can see"— she gestured to her feet—"I'm sorry though, for making you crash. I didn't see the headlight until it was too late."

There was a beat, then he said, "Not to worry. Worse things could have resulted." He scraped the mud from his face and combed his gunked-up hair back from his face.

It was all kinds of wrong that looking like something from the La Brea Tar Pits made him seem much more rugged. She could imagine how smug he must have been when he realized she'd chosen him, and only him, as their best chance at getting into the Highlander calendar. It probably annoyed the hell out of the village charmer to look anything other than his GQ best.

"You might want to consider a shower first, before borrowing a truck," she said. "Just a thought."

He glanced down at himself, then surprised her with a smile and a short laugh. "I'd like to think Graham is a good enough friend no' to mind a bit of mud." He plucked a twig and a clump of muck from the pocket of his khakis. "But perhaps ye have a point."

She refused to become one of the charmed. It would be a lot easier if he'd stop smiling. A gunk-filled dimple only diluted his charm so much.

He turned and looked back up the track from the direction he'd come, then the other way, which led into the village proper.

She had no idea where he lived, but she assumed they were closer to town than to his home. She couldn't have said what prodded her to offer an alternative. Surely it was her guilty conscience talking. "Kira's place is probably closest," she said. "I'm sure she wouldn't mind if you cleaned up there. She'll be up and in her studio by now."

To her further surprise, she could have sworn he blanched. Just a little. Right before all the good humor left his face. "Uh, thanks. But, ah, no. I'm—I'll be fine. Good."

She folded her arms. "Really." He was stuttering—which made the otherwise cocksure man she'd had the displeasure of being saddled with earlier in the week seem almost . . . endearing.

"Yes," he said, gathering himself rather quickly. "Quite. You—carry on with what you were doing, then. And I'll—"

"Walk into town. Looking like a creature from the black lagoon. Perhaps I'll join you on the hike in. Maybe snap a few pictures as we go along. Could be amusing. Who knows, maybe you'll actually like those."

"What do ye mean?"

"Well, from what I hear, you couldn't be bothered to even glance at the ones I took of you last week. Pretty sure of your appeal"—she shrugged and gave him a frank onceover—"with reason, I suppose. I guess we should all own our assets."

He took a step closer, real irritation on his face. "You're so smug, thinking you have me pegged. But you have no idea, in the least, who I am, or what motivates me to do anything I choose to do."

"Me, smug?"

"Aye. But then, I've read your resume and I guess, likewise, you have reason to be. Owning your assets and all that. I'll just say that while your career impresses me—mightily, in fact—I dinnae know how it is you've done all ye've done."

"Because I'm a woman, you mean?"

He looked honestly confused. "What does gender have to do with pointing a camera at something? No, I was speaking of yer attitude about the rest of us poor blokes."

It was her turn to be confused. "What on earth are you talking about?"

"Your people skills leave a lot to be desired, lass. Although, I suppose, anyone who has seen all of the things that you have, wouldn't be expected to have much softness left."

He hadn't said the last part unkindly, which was why it undid her. Or that's what she told herself, anyway. It was easier to think of him as an opinionated, uninformed, too-good-looking-for-his-own-good jackass. "Why on earth would you take the time to look at my career highlights?"

"I just insult you and you're only concerned that I peeked at yer curriculum vitae?"

"You didn't insult me. You just spoke the truth. You're probably right—too right—about my people skills. But given your lack of enthusiasm regarding my involvement with this project in general, and you in particular, it just struck me as odd that you'd spend any amount of time digging up information on me."

"No' so difficult. You're quite Google-able. I looked you up because we're trustin' yer judgment on something that might seem trivial to you, but could bring us a great deal of help."

"Kira explained," she said. "And I get that the ... ah ... added exposure could potentially be a boon for your basket sales. And probably boost tourism. I just hope you're not banking all your marketing on a Hunks of the Highlands calendar."

Rather than be insulted, he laughed. "No, it sounded ridiculous to me, too, at first. But when it comes to the welfare of this island and every last person on it, I'm willing to do whatever it takes. It's the only reason I agreed to gettin' Kira to ask you to man the camera, or stand in front of it myself. I needed to know who I was trustin' to make what might turn out to be an important decision. But did I need to see the photos of my smiling, idiotic face? No. I didn't look at any of them, no offense meant to you. I looked at your history, and I trusted you with the choice."

Strangely enough, she believed him even though it didn't jibe with who she thought he was. "Me and Katie McAuley, you mean.

"What?" she asked, when he looked surprised. "I know you asked her to double check my choices. Do you honestly think anything stays secret around here? I haven't met a single soul other than you since setting out on this hike, but I'm fairly certain someone could probably tell you the color underwear I have on right now."

Bad example, she thought immediately, when his gaze drifted over her. There'd been nothing remotely lascivious about it. More a casual cataloging. Like he'd done with her career highlights—which annoyed her, but for all the wrong reasons. Surely she didn't care what he thought of her? As a photographer, or as a woman.

"We're a tightly knit group. We rely on each other," he said as his gaze returned to hers. "It's like that on a wee island. Has to be."

"I understand that, but correct me if I'm wrong—in the grand scheme of things, you've only known Katie McAuley slightly longer than you've known me."

"Aye, 'tis true. But . . . it's different with Katie. Spend any time with her, and it's like ye've known her yer whole life. Everyone here feels it."

"Good people skills, then," she said dryly, and earned a smile.

"Something like that. We're all close, but we're not close-minded. We have our differences here, but we're accepting of new people, new ideas. We'd never have survived otherwise. We respect and hold each other in high esteem, or we certainly try to."

"Yes, I believe I witnessed a whole raft of that esteem the other day, while you were undressing for me."

She'd meant the comment to be amusing, but perhaps her delivery was even rustier than she'd thought. He folded his arms and rocked back a little on his heels. How it was that all the mud and muck made him look sexy, she had no idea. She had a lot of personal experience with mud and muck and there was usually nothing remotely attractive about it.

"What was it that put you off me?" he asked, sounding surprisingly sincere, like it really mattered.

"Is it so hard for you to take, having one less woman giggling and blushing when she's around you?"

He grinned. "I'm a likable guy. What can I say? Except to you."

She smiled briefly. "You'll get over the loss, I'm sure. Since you seem to have pretty much the same impression of me, I can't imagine why my thoughts on you matter one way or the other."

He lifted a shoulder, continued to regard her with that dimple-flashing, half smile of his. "I don't know that they do. Although I admit I'd be interested to know if you've got a giggle in you." He just laughed when she rolled her eyes. "Mostly, I'm . . . curious. It's no' an ego thing. You're right, it's healthy enough, with or without your admiration of my manly bits."

She couldn't help it, she laughed. More like a snort. But still. *Dammit.* "Yes, well, given I chose your manly bits exclusively as potential daydream fodder for women everywhere from ages sixteen to sixty, I'm fairly certain your ego is fully intact, if not additionally inflated. If you do make the calendar, your throngs of admirers will merely grow to an international level. World domination is surely only a centerfold away after that."

She paused because he was frowning. "What?" she asked. "Don't try to tell me you're not going to eat that up. You're a red-blooded man who is quite well aware of his charms."

"Aye. Believe it or not, I'd rather my charms, as you call them, weren't put on display for the masses. The idea of hanging on walls in places ye dinnae even know of, being ogled by God only knows who . . . that's a wee bit odd to contemplate, now isn't it?"

"Are you honestly telling me this was some kind of sacrifice for you?"

"Did I, at any point, look like I was having a good time? Was I encouraging you in any way, other than to mercifully get it over with as soon as possible?"

"You loved playing the crowd and—"

"I was trying to get them to leave!"

She thought about that for a moment, and realized he had a point.

He walked closer to her, until she could see his green eyes quite clearly through all the muck still splattering his face and neck. It must have been the contrast with all that mud that made them seem so . . . mesmerizing.

"You don't know what to think about me, do you? Because you already had your mind made up on what kind of man I was before we even got started. I'd have expected you, of all people, with your background, to be more open-minded, to get the facts first. At the very least, consider that simply because I'm male and might enjoy charming a smile or two from folks I've spent my entire life around, doesn't necessarily mean my ego and identity are linked directly and only to what's under my kilt."

"I was just—"

"Being condescending, patronizing, and a wee bit narrow-minded. After seeing your work—I did look at a fair share of it—that mentality doesn't seem to fit. But what do I know? Maybe you're great behind the camera, but face to face with people . . ." He shrugged, then turned around and started toward his bent-up motorbike, apparently done with the conversation. And with her.

"You're right."

He stopped, and turned back to look at her.

Why . . . why was she prolonging the conversation? She held

his gaze with equanimity, then finally sighed, and felt the starch go out of her just a little. What the hell was wrong with her, anyway? Well, besides the obvious. "I have seen a lot. More, maybe, than anyone should. And . . . I've developed some very strong ideas and opinions. About a lot of things. And . . . people, as well. I'm not shy about expressing them."

He held her gaze with seeming ease, but rather than looking disgusted with her—which would have been understandable, because she was a little disgusted with herself at the moment—he appeared . . . amused. "So," he said, a flicker of that devilish twinkle sparking into his eyes. "How is that working out for ye?"

He was relentless with the charm. And it was working. A smile hovered at the corners of her mouth. "Well, at the moment, I'm here shooting photos for a Highlander hotties calendar. Not to be patronizing or condescending, but that's not my usual caliber of assignment."

He nodded. "I thought you were here on vacation."

"I did the shoot as a favor for a friend, true," she said, purposely not responding directly to his comment. "But . . . I didn't need to be pompous about it. Or take my frustration out on you."

"You were frustrated because you deemed shooting those photos to be that far beneath you? Even as a simple favor? Were you afraid to have word leak out? Your name attached to them? Now who has the unhealthy ego?"

"No, of course not. I stand by all my work. Though it's not something I'd have ever imagined myself doing, I was happy to help Kira. I'm frustrated because I can't—" She managed to cut herself off just in time. She waved a hand, striving for the insouciance she used to have, but had lost over the past year. Actually, longer ago than that, if she were honest. She felt the sting of Roan's casual observations once again. The sting of truth.

"Because you can't relax and enjoy time off?"

"Something like that."

"I imagine there are always stories that need telling some-where. That kind of urgency must be hard to turn away from."

His insight caught her off guard. She wouldn't have pegged him as a man who bothered to notice much beyond his own charming influence on others. Clearly her powers of observation had completely failed her where he was concerned. She was seeing what she wanted to see—which was the worst possible thing. But then . . . that was what she did. She just hadn't realized it was who she'd become.

Instead of blowing him off with some smartass answer, she decided his sincerity at least warranted an honest response. It bothered her, more than a little, that she had to work at it. And not because it was him. She hadn't been able to talk to Kira, either.

"Let's just say that I haven't taken a vacation in a while. Perhaps I should have been better about scheduling them into my assignments." That was about as much as she was willing to share. His savoir faire with the opposite sex might make him seem somewhat superficial on the surface, but she was quite aware there were greater depths to him than she'd anticipated. She didn't want to encourage any more of his curiosity. To that end, she lifted the camera from where it hung around her neck, and continued before he could say anything else. "So, if you're sure you don't need or want my help with the bike, or"—she made a general gesture in the direction of his mud-coated self—"I guess I'll get back to what I was doing."

"Which was?"

"Taking vacation photos," she said dryly. "For fun."

He flashed a grin and the dimple winked out through the drying muck. "You know anything about that? Fun, I mean."

She opened her mouth, fully prepared to shoot back an equally smart-ass answer, but instead just let the whole damn thing go and laughed instead. That's what he made her feel like doing, and it felt surprisingly good. "I used to have a passing acquaintance with the idea, but possibly it's been a while."

"With the kind of work you do, that's not surprising," he said, sincere, but not somber about it.

She appreciated that, and felt shamed again for her rather shabby treatment of him. "Perhaps my journey today will reintroduce me to the concept." Not true, but at least the intent was to be friendly. The last thing she would have told him was that she was technically on assignment . . . and while she was energized at the idea that she might have discovered the first step toward mental redemption, she would hardly call the day she had planned fun. Terrifying, portentous, intimidating, maybe. The day's agenda was nobody's business but her own.

"Maybe," he replied, but sounded dubious. "Where are you headed?"

"To the shore."

"Ah, the abbey and the tower?"

"In part."

"I'm sure you'll do them better justice than most."

The compliment—sincere by the sound of it—caught her off guard. "I—thank you."

He shrugged. "Just because we started off on the wrong foot, doesnae mean we have to stay wrong-footed. Does it?"

There was no charming smile or mischievous twinkle, just a plain, sincerely asked question. So she lifted a shoulder—casually—which belied the sudden pounding of her heart, and said, "No, I suppose it doesn't."

He laughed.

"What?"

"You're a tough one, Tessa Vandergriff."

That stung a little, deserved or not. She was all done being under Roan McAuley's microscope for the day. "Having seen my work, you'd understand that a softie would never make it out there, doing what I do."

He walked closer again, almost too close. He studied her for an unnervingly long moment, but she let him, determined not to allow him to get to her. Damn her racing heart. He'd rattled her good, but as soon as she moved on with her day, that moment in time would be forgotten—by her mind if not her body.

"But you're no' as much a hard-arse as ye think."

Rather than bristle, she found herself swallowing a bit stronger than was absolutely necessary. "What makes you say that?"

He lifted his hand toward her. She instinctively flinched away—and hated giving him even that much of a glimpse at just how messed up her instincts were. He wasn't going to hurt her. Far from it, if his expression was any indication. His eyes widened momentarily, but he let his hand drop rather than push it. "Because you needed this vacation. Or break, or whatever this time here really represents to you. A real hard-arse . . . the time off wouldn't have mattered, so why bother?"

"Maybe that's why I'm frustrated, because it's precisely a bother."

"And maybe you just wish you were more a hard-arse than you actually are."

That was far too dangerously close to the truth she'd been forced to confront the past year. She definitely didn't appreciate hearing it, ever-so-dismissively, from him. "As you said to me, you have no idea who I am, or what motivates me to do the things I do. Now, if you don't mind, I'll be continuing on with my hike. I hope things work out for you getting into town and getting the bike fixed. I'll be happy to contribute to the latter, since I was partly responsible. You can leave a message with Kira."

She walked around him, with no intention of looking back, no matter the provocation.

"I'm glad you did, you know."

Dammit. She kept on walking, then swore under her breath and stopped. Without turning around, she said, "Did what?"

"Took a break. You picked a good place for it. We're happy to take ye in, Tessa. You'll always be welcomed on Kinloch. No matter what." Amusement entered his voice as he added, "We've a thing for misfits." Then, a beat later, with humor still clear in his tone, he added, "I should know."

She wanted badly to turn around. How could he think he knew anything about being a misfit? He'd been born and raised in the bosom of a loving, tightly woven community. As far as she could tell, he'd flourished under that umbrella of adoration and support, and seemed quite happy with himself and content in his life, whatever it was he actually did around there. Misfit? She didn't think so. And she did know. She was an expert on the subject.

She managed to hold her tongue and continued walking. "Good," she called back, without looking over her shoulder. "Then, one misfit to another, you won't be insulted if I just walk away now."

She heard him chuckle. And damn if she wasn't smiling as she continued on her way.

Chapter 5

He couldn't stop thinking about her.

For the first time since she'd moved back to the islands, the woman on Roan's mind wasn't the hazel-eyed, sweet-hearted Kira. The eyes in his thoughts of late flashed aquamarine, and were paired with wild red curls and a lanky body that did things to his pulse that made no sense to him. Especially given that the entire package came coupled with a cranky attitude and a smart mouth.

A smart mouth that made him laugh. Made him think. And made him want things he had no business wanting. Not with her, anyway.

But he did. Want. All the time, it seemed. He woke up hard and spent half his days trying not to get hard again, which was an issue every time he thought about Tessa. He thought about making those aquamarine eyes flash for entirely different reasons, thought about what those lanky legs would feel like wrapped around his waist, and wondered just how smart her mouth would be if it were wrapped around his—

He swallowed a groan and closed his eyes briefly as Father Madaig droned on, but rather than block her from his mind, the action only served to further clarify his mental image of her. He pictured her smiling the way she did, the kind of half curve of her lips that told him she knew far more than she had a right to know. He could all but hear her voice . . . all throaty and authoritative, telling him what was what. She didn't like to be pushed around, but she sure didn't mind doing the pushing. His body leapt again at the idea of what a fun challenge that could be.

"Earth to Roan."

He blinked his eyes open and glanced sideways at Shay. "Right here, mate."

Shay angled his chin to Roan's right as he subtly nudged the back of Roan's arm. Roan turned to find both Father Madaig and Graham staring at him with varying degrees of patience.

"Ring?" Graham said, clearly amused.

Roan glanced between him and auld Father Maddy, who was decidedly less entertained by his lack of attention. But then, he'd been rather stern where Roan was concerned since the time, as an eight-year-old altar boy, he'd almost burned out their centuries-old church by tipping over the votive prayer candles during a rather impromptu race against Graham to the double doors leading outside. A race he'd won, by the way.

Graham hadn't seemed to earn the same level of consternation. Of course, Graham had been the future laird and a model little altar boy. Or so Father Maddy thought. Roan had discovered his gift of charming himself out of sticky situations at a right early age . . . but Father Maddy had always been particularly immune. Roan had eventually concluded that the dour old man simply couldn't comprehend those with a natural, sunny nature. Likely he was confused by why Roan didn't spend more time being terrified of the fire and brimstone that seemed to dog Father Maddy's every waking thought.

Poor bloke.

Because he'd probably never completely outgrow his more impish impulses, Roan smiled beatifically at the good Father, as he automatically groped in his pocket, then just as abruptly stopped. "We're rehearsin'. I dinnae have it on me. It's in safe-keeping." He'd given it into the watchful eye of Eliza—which was almost the same as having it guarded by the queen herself.

He glanced past Graham and winked at Katie, who was also smiling. *See*, he wanted to tell Father Maddy, *even the bride isn't put off by my brief bit of daydreaming.*

He could hardly be blamed for his wandering thoughts. It was a spectacular September afternoon, and they weren't in the church proper, but standing in a field on the northeast side of the island, near enough to the water for the ruins of the original abbey, situated just offshore, to be in easy view. Where they stood was the very spot where Graham had proposed to Katie, a surprisingly lush little bower of green meadow, tucked in the midst of an otherwise rocky bit of grazing pasture.

He grinned and gripped Graham's outstretched hand in a hearty handshake. "Go for it, lad. I have a feelin' she'll say yes, ring or no'." Katie laughed, Father Maddy scowled at their unscheduled levity—he was a stickler for ritual—then all of them, except Roan, glanced over to a point just behind Shay as another voice intruded into the moment. A throaty, authoritative voice.

"Father, I'm sorry to interrupt, but would it be possible to restage this so you're all angled just a bit"—Tessa walked up to the small, gathered group and gestured with her hands—"that way? It would make for a stunning backdrop to the photos."

Photos. What, she was a wedding photographer, now?

Roan realized he was bracing himself before turning to look fully at her. He consoled himself that his hesitation was merely due to the mental images he'd been entertaining only moments ago. The bracing didn't help in the least. He shifted his weight, fighting the natural response of his body as his gaze took in all of her. He hadn't seen her since their unfortunate run-in a few days before, and he'd rather hoped that seeing her again would put his odd preoccupation into some rational perspective. The one where she annoyed him, he annoyed her, and he could go for more than five minutes without thinking about her with anything other than stifled irritation.

Katie and Graham had both turned around and were following Tessa's hand motions while she explained how the shot would be best framed as they said their vows. "So, from the back, you get a nice view of the mountains in the distance, and if I'm shooting to get your faces"—she nimbly climbed up and tiptoed across a jut of rocks to position herself on a taller outcropping just behind Father Madaig—"from here," she said, not even a little bit out of breath, "then you'll be framed by the shore line and the abbey as well, but this way the tower won't be in the shot."

She smiled quick and natural, and it was such a normal thing, as if she did it often . . . except, in his experience, she didn't. That smile wasn't any less impressive than the only other time he'd seen it. Truly transforming. The witty rejoinder that sprang to mind died unspoken as he simply got caught up in the glory of it.

"I know you said the abbey was important," she continued, "but I'm thinking having what amounts to an ancient jail in your wedding photos isn't something you're really interested in."

It was, more or less, what he'd have said—if he wasn't so awestruck by how greatly a warm smile transformed her otherwise sober and serious face, and by how the rest of her seemed to be affecting him.

"Also, once we've concluded here, I think it would be great if we went back to Flaithbheartach, so we can frame a few shots of you there. I know you're holding the reception in the village, but I think the historical and ancestral significance might be a really wonderful addition to your album, and one that you'll appreciate having later."

Tessa pronounced the Gaelic-named clan stronghold where Graham and Katie lived, as if she'd been born to the language. Katie had been there a month and still called it Flyvertuck—

which made him smile. Of course, she'd named the village Port
Joy, opting for a loose translation of the Gaelic meaning rather
than take a shot at its given name, Aoibhneas. It was only surprising she hadn't nicknamed the fortress the Castle of Lordly
Deeds or something equally amusing.

But when the often amusing Katie turned to more serious
and sober Graham, Roan thought there was no way any man
presently drawing breath could say no to the sparkle and enthusiasm that so naturally lit up her face.

"It would add time between the ceremony and reception,"
she said to him, "but I think Tessa is right."

Graham, the studious scientist, was a completely different
man when he was around his bride-to-be. He smiled broadly
and often, and there was something quite vulnerable in his expression when he looked at her. Roan felt his heart tighten up
as he unashamedly witnessed their obvious love for one another. It was as if they didn't have to speak words to truly com-
municate with each other. He wasn't jealous—he couldn't be
more sincerely happy for the two of them—but there was no
denying he'd grown deeply envious of what his best friend had
found.

Despite Roan's own untraditional childhood, he'd always
known he wanted to spend his life growing old and doddering
as half of a united pair. He'd never known his own parents, but
being raised by an entire village had its advantages. He'd witnessed, close up, more strong unions than he could count. The
entire history of the McAuley and MacLeod clans on Kinloch
was specifically and legally bound by the sanctity of the marriage bond. Vows were taken quite seriously on that tiny spit of
land, and Roan was right on board with those deeply held, traditional beliefs.

In fact, he'd been the one to push Graham into fulfilling his
own obligation as the new reigning laird by completing his role
in the centuries old Marriage Pact that guided the leadership of
the island. In order to keep the strength and unity on Kinloch

intact, for the past four hundred years, each McAuley or Mac-Leod island chief was legally bound to marry a member of the opposing clan in order to retain clan leadership. Graham's fulfillment of that ancient pact had directly resulted in Katie being welcomed into their island fold. What he'd told Tessa the day of their close collision was true. Katie might not have been on Kinloch for many weeks, but everyone on the island would agree it was as if she'd been part of their clan for a very, very long time.

Tessa might not be enjoying the same hearty welcome, but she wasn't exactly embracing her good fortune in being there, as Katie had. Watching her, Roan wondered if there had been a change of heart . . . and what had provoked it. He had a hard time believing, after talking to her about her burnout—at least as he'd interpreted it—that she'd have willingly or happily taken on another such assignment. It was important to the islanders, as had been the calendar shoot . . . but certainly not something she'd have otherwise done. He could imagine, much like a physician being asked to perform surgery on vacation, she was put out by another request for her services.

And yet, she seemed quite in her element, scampering over the rocks, figuring out shots, lining up angles, and ordering everyone about. He hid a smile. That she truly embraced the last part wasn't such a stretch.

Katie, Graham, and Shay were all smiling and happily accommodating her suggestions. Even Father Madaig didn't seem too awfully put out by the disruption of the established order of events. In fact, he seemed almost . . . flattered, when Tessa asked if he wouldn't mind turning just a bit, so his profile would be handsomely displayed. Perhaps he'd Googled her, too, Roan thought, then immediately dismissed that, finding it impossible to imagine the curmudgeonly and pious minister embracing technology any more advanced than that requiring a wick and a match.

Perhaps Tessa had taken to heart Roan's comment about

Kinloch's open arms when it came to welcoming misfits, embracing the lost, or simply offering solace and shelter to those who needed it. Kira had been a little bit of all three of those things. She'd grown up on Kinloch, but had gone off, as so many did, to find her fortunes elsewhere. But she was welcomed back as warmly as if she'd never left.

Roan turned and skimmed his gaze over the field behind them, glancing toward the road; though Kira's car was parked on the verge, there was no sign she'd accompanied her friend. In fact, he was somewhat surprised the entire village hadn't turned out to watch the rehearsal, given everyone's gleeful obsession with the whole event. Perhaps out of deference to Katie and Graham they'd decided to leave them to at least conduct some of the preparations in peace. The field where they stood would be filled with every man, woman, and child come Friday, as they witnessed Katie and Graham's vows firsthand. Roan wouldn't be surprised if even the livestock was somehow appropriately festooned for the occasion.

All and sundry would head into Aoibhneas to celebrate the most important union to take place on Kinloch's bonny shores since the last chief, Ulraig MacLeod, had married well over a half century before.

Shay had barely made it back from Edinburgh in time for the nuptials, and Roan was reminded he'd yet to ask him if he'd found out anything further about his distant cousin, Iain McAuley. A cousin they'd all met when he'd come out of the woodwork to stake his own claim to Kinloch as the heir next in line if Graham hadn't found a bride. Once Graham's engagement to Katie had been set, Iain had disappeared on the next ferry, gone as swiftly as he'd come.

Graham seemed willing to shrug off any lingering concerns about whatever it was that had prodded Iain to show up in the first place. Roan wasn't so certain. And neither was Katie. To that end, she'd put Blaine on the case.

Roan's gaze moved past Katie to where Blaine stood to her

right. Tall, blue-eyed, and blond like Katie, he had that aristocratic look about him, though at least he didn't sneer through it, as so often seemed the case with those born into privilege. He seemed a decent enough sort, all in all, but Roan had long since given up pretending he had any real understanding of Blaine and Katie's lifelong relationship. In the end, the only thing that mattered to Roan was that Blaine was no threat to Graham's future happiness. Other than being an annoying distraction, he seemed relatively harmless.

Roan looked away from Blaine and got tangled up momentarily again in watching Tessa as she continued staging discussions with a smiling Father Maddy and the happy couple. He'd never been able to get more than a reluctant nod from the auld man and she'd charmed a smile from him. Roan hadn't known the Father's dour expression had any upward mobility. And charming? Tessa?

He looked at her and had to admit there was an infectious vibrancy to her that hadn't been there the day of the calendar shoot. He'd seen a flash of it the day he'd wrecked his bike, but thought his imagination was in overdrive. However, there was no denying she'd reclaimed at least a little of the energy she said she'd come there looking for. Unlike their first project, she was clearly committed to this new one. Whether it was for the sake of the happy couple, he couldn't say, but she seemed sincerely interested in what she was doing. She was confident and clear-minded about how she envisioned things, but rather than coming off dictatorial or overbearing, there was a level of confident enthusiasm radiating from her that was palpable even from where he stood. She hadn't so much as glanced his way. He wanted to be relieved by that, but instead was feeling a bit put out at the moment.

Katie and Graham appeared openly thrilled to have her on board for their special day, and though Roan might not have been willing to admit it even as recently as a week ago, he thought they really couldn't be luckier.

"Now, if we could get the best man and . . . what were you calling him again?" Tessa looked from Katie to Blaine.

"Man of honor," Katie said, with a truly affectionate smile aimed at Blaine. She squeezed his arm and he took her hand and leaned in to kiss her on the cheek. Their affection was sweetly sincere but most definitely of a familial nature. Since Blaine was obviously gay it was not surprising. Roan couldn't fathom the two of them ever agreeing to marry in the first place, no matter the family pressure on them. But it had all worked out in the end. Well, except for Blaine. But then, he'd used the breakup to get out of the clutches of the family's evil empire, so Roan supposed he wasn't complaining. He didn't have to live a big whopping lie for the rest of his life.

"Right," Tessa said. "Man of honor." For some reason, her gaze sought out Roan's. Up to that point, he'd have sworn she didn't even know he was part of the proceedings. But if he wasn't mistaken, they were sharing a moment, the kind of moment reserved for private jokes and nods of understanding between two people who got each other. There was a dry curve to her lips and a quick flash of acknowledgment at the absurdity of the whole Blaine-Katie confluence—at least that's how he interpreted it—and because he did get it, he found himself returning the same quick flash of a dry grin.

"I'll need you to move here," Tessa went on, barely skipping a beat as she motioned Blaine to move to his right.

Funny, Roan thought, his mind still on that mini-moment. He'd just been marveling over Katie and Graham's instinctive communication. Who'd have thought he'd achieve even a blip of that with Tessa Vandergriff, of all people. Maybe, in their case, contempt had bred familiarity. Only . . . he was finding it really hard to recall what it was he'd found so contemptible in her.

"Roan," Shay muttered, causing him to look up again.

Tessa was the one with the patient expression. "You'd be here, then," she said to him, apparently repeating herself.

"We'd like to get out of here sometime today, old chap," Shay said under his breath. "If you could find your way clear to paying attention for more than a full five minutes at a time, we'd all be ever so grateful."

"Oh, don't go gettin' yer wobbly bits in a twist," Roan muttered in his general direction, before moving to where Tessa was motioning. "Here?" he asked her.

She hopped down from the rocks and went about sorting them each into place with a quick, impersonal clasp of the shoulders. She even commandeered Graham, which, given his height and breadth, most wouldn't have done with such casual intrusion, but she didn't even pause.

Roan was coming to see that perhaps her people skills weren't nearly as lacking as he'd first assumed. She simply employed hers very differently from most people. Her approach wasn't traditional or particularly warm and homey like Katie's. He doubted she suffered fools gladly, but her very air of confidence bred a certain sense of loyalty in those around her, making them feel equally confident about following her directives.

That confident leadership faltered, ever so slightly, when she moved in front of him, hands raised to grip his shoulders, too. At the very last second she paused, then dropped her hands to her sides rather than touch him. "Just angle yourself so you are at Graham's immediate left, your right shoulder a half foot or so behind his left one, facing the exact same way. If you were to look backward over your own left shoulder, you'd see the abbey ruins set out in an almost straight line behind you."

For preservation of both sanity and the fit of his trousers, Roan forced his gaze away from the vivid awareness he spied in her blue-green eyes. They were almost turquoise. No way was she thinking anything close to what he'd been thinking about, so he chalked the expression up to what was probably her normal tenacity and focus when truly into the job at hand. Whatever the case, he broke eye contact and turned to look behind him, shifting until he was in the exact position between Graham and the abbey in the distance behind him. "One question," he asked, still staring at the space behind the assembled group.

"Which is?"

"If we're standin' *here,* how will we shift the assemblage behind us?" He motioned to the rocky field that was directly behind them. The remainder of the grassy spot where they stood was off to their left. "Won't it be awkward if the guests are standin' over there, and we're facing over here? And Katie's path to the altar might require a bit of rethinking in terms of footwear."

Shay chuckled, which turned into a cough when Tessa shot him the kind of glare that Roan was more accustomed to seeing from her.

He found it more amusing than annoying. *Now you see what I meant?* he silently messaged to Shay as he shot him a quick grin. He'd tried to explain to Shay why Tessa had gotten so quickly on his bad side. His friend had only crossed paths with her one time, and they'd been in the company of Blaine and Kira, so the introductions had been easy and friendly.

Tessa turned to the bride and groom. "Which would you rather have," Tessa asked, not at all unkindly, "the view of the water and abbey behind you? Or the crowd of friends and family?"

"Is there no way to achieve both?" Graham asked. Up until then he had deferred all wedding decisions to Katie. Roan knew the slight tension in his jaw indicated he'd much rather be out in the fields, testing new hybrid samples from the flax crop.

"I'd rather see the people," Katie said, "if we have to choose. We can take an after ceremony shot with the abbey view."

Tessa strolled a few feet away, her attention tightly on the layout of the property in their immediate vicinity, and Roan could see her blocking it all out inside her head as she quietly muttered to herself.

He wondered if all the preparation and involved planning was foreign to her. From the stills he'd seen of her work when he'd looked her up, it didn't appear she ever had an opportunity to stage things. Even so, she somehow had a unique vision that zeroed in on the event at hand, while also scaling back to take in the whole of the area, coming up with the exact shot to combine or juxtapose the two in a way that was thought-provoking. It made the viewer think about things in a whole new, often profound, and even disturbing way—which was exactly what she intended.

It was difficult to imagine how she ever slept at night after witnessing such things. Maybe her strength came from knowing she was doing something to expose the plight of whomever was the target of her lens. Still, Roan couldn't imagine that would be enough to stave off the kind of haunting a profession like hers would put on a person. He certainly couldn't imagine enduring it himself. In that regard, she was one of the toughest people, in spirit and in mind, that he'd ever met.

Watching her tackle something as comparatively lightweight as a wedding, and seeing the kind of attention and focus she was giving it, was more than a little surprising to him. Especially when she had barely seemed to tolerate guiding them all through the calendar shoot.

"Okay," she announced, turning back to face them. "We can make this work and get the best of both. How about if we shift things like this?" She lithely tiptoed across the tops of the rocks dotting the field between the meadow and where the wedding party was facing, and began reblocking the entire tableau.

Roan and Shay moved as they were told, and he had to admit he was impressed with her solution. Who knew her eye for framing warfare would make her the go-to person on a wedding shoot? He supposed, there might be some parallels, though it was one big, happy family event. As he was watching her place Blaine, he leaned closer to Shay. "So, I hear Blaine contacted you about information on Iain. Anything we should know?"

Shay shook his head. "I think Graham's right about this. I don't think there's anything else to it. I can't find anything out of line." He shrugged. "Iain's doing quite well for himself, is well liked at his company, has a good reputation professionally and personally. No skeletons that I can find. None with his immediate family, either. He's well on his way to making his own fortune, but his family on his mum's side has provided him with a trust fund that could have bought Kinloch outright. So, I don't see any reason he'd come back again."

"Except all of those things were true when he came out here the first time."

"Maybe it was just a lark. He gets an out-of-the-blue inheritance from a relative he knew nothing about, and decides to check it out. What the hell. Sow some wild oats."

"Is he the sowing-wild-oats sort?"

Shay shook his head. "From what I uncovered, he's worked hard to get himself in the position he's in, hasn't traded too much on the family name. The fact that he works at all, given his net worth . . ." He let that trail off and finished with another shrug. "I think it's a closed story. He's not coming back. Nothing will spoil this wedding."

Roan glanced again at Blaine, who was talking quite animatedly with Tessa about God only knew what, and he wondered what the wunderkind's take on the Iain story was.

He made a mental note to ask Blaine directly what his thoughts were on the matter. If Blaine concurred with Graham and Shay, he'd let it drop for good.

"Okay, I think we're done here," Tessa announced.

Father Maddy looked relieved. Apparently the rehearsal was also over, because he accepted help from Graham in maneuvering around some of the tumbled rocks and such until he had a clear path to the road where his vehicle was parked.

"Will you be joining us for dinner, Father?" Katie asked, following in their wake.

"I'm afraid I won't be able to make it, but I hope you enjoy your evening," he said, nodding and shaking hands with the small wedding party before making his final escape. Roan barely made the edge of the road before the man was in his car and pulling away.

"I dinnae think he's been outside the church in far too long," Shay murmured as Roan came to stand beside him and they watched the priest drive off.

"Aye. And I've no' had a problem with that," Roan said, making Shay smile.

They walked over to Graham. "You're both joining us," Graham said, not making it much of a question.

"Aye," Shay responded, and Roan nodded.

Katie and Tessa joined them as Katie was saying, "If you'd like to round Kira up, she's welcome, too."

Roan turned to find Tessa shaking her head. "It's very nice of you to invite us, but I won't intrude on your special—"

"No, really, come with us," Katie implored. "I promise I won't talk photography." She smiled with obvious guilt but little actual regret. "Much."

Roan watched as Tessa clearly struggled with her response. He wasn't sure if her unwillingness to join them was because she wasn't much for socializing, or she truly didn't want to intrude as the outsider of the bunch . . . or because he was going to be there.

"I'll contact Kira," she said, relenting in the face of Katie's imploring expression, "but I know she was deep in studio mode today, so—"

"Roan could swing by to pick her up," Katie offered brightly. Possibly a bit too brightly. "He'll talk her into coming out, won't you, Roan?" She turned to him with a perfect smile on her sweet, calculating face.

He realized he'd been set up. Tessa's gaze turned to his, the questioning look in her eyes making it clear she'd picked up on Katie's not-so-subtle matchmaking attempt, too. It made no sense whatsoever, but he almost felt compelled to explain—although he had no actual idea what to say. His thoughts hadn't been on Kira all day. Or for the past several, for that matter. They'd been on the woman currently staring at him, expressionless. When Katie had been talking of them both joining the party at the intimate rehearsal dinner, it hadn't been the mention of Kira's possible attendance that had snagged his attention.

Roan wanted to tell Tessa she had it all wrong, that Katie was wrong, and that . . . that what? He brought himself up short before he uttered a single word. He hadn't done or said anything, so why in bloody hell was he feeling guilty?

He turned to Katie, fully prepared to make it clear that while Kira was welcome at dinner, he wasn't going to be the persuader she'd hoped for, but Tessa spoke first.

"We can both ride over. I'd like to put my equipment back in the croft, and we'll see if we can talk her into coming back into town with us." Her gaze shifted to Roan's, and there was amusement in her eyes.

Oh, so she thought it was funny, did she? He wondered how fast her expression would change if she knew who'd been the real source of the wayward thoughts he'd indulged in that afternoon.

He turned to Katie. "Well, if she'll be going by, then you'll hardly need my assista—"

"Go with her," Katie said, her gaze darting between Roan and Tessa, finally settling on him.

He gave her a steely gaze back, but rather than look chastened in any way, she merely grinned at him.

"Hurry back!" she added, with a little wave.

"Aye," Shay said, looking between the three of them, then only at Roan, the droll note clear in his steady tone. "Please. Hurry back."

Roan glanced from Shay to Graham, and realized in that

moment that he hadn't been fooling anybody about his interest in Kira. Any other time, he'd have been embarrassed or even a bit annoyed—at himself for thinking he could hide anything from those closest to him—but, at the moment, he was actually relieved. As long as they were thinking to shove him in Kira's path, no one would be paying the slightest bit of attention to the fact that he couldn't seem to string two intelligent sentences together around her redheaded best friend.

Except Katie—whose expression had taken on a far too considering look.

"I'll follow you over," he told Tessa, thinking it better to end the little cluster before things went any further. "We can all go to dinner in my lorry, then." And Graham and Katie could be responsible for getting the two women back home again. It was the least they could do as far as he was concerned. That would teach the bride-to-be to play at matchmaking.

Tessa glanced around the group one last time, and he thought she might add something—heaven only knew what that might be—or reject his offer outright, but in the end, she merely nodded and shoved a long, black canvas tote at him. "Good. Then you can help carry the gear."

Everyone alternately chuckled, grinned, or gave them a little send off wave. He shot Shay and Graham a meaningful look that promised later retribution, then leaned in and bussed Katie's cheek. "Dinnae get yer hopes up, lass," he murmured in her ear. "Things aren't always what ye think they are."

She merely smiled at him as he straightened. "We'll see," she said, then, for the rest of the group, added, "you both at dinner! Don't take too long!"

Deciding retreat was definitely the better part of valor, he hiked the tripod bag over his shoulder, and turned toward Kira's car, which was stationed a few meters up from where Father Maddy's car had been. Tessa caught up with him and he could swear he heard an amused little chuckle behind him.

If she only knew. He doubted she'd be laughing then. He

sure as bloody hell wasn't. How he had gotten himself into that, he had no idea. But he was going to excuse himself right the hell back out of it again. No Kira, no Tessa. No women of any stripe.

At least until after the wedding was over and everyone got the nuptial stars out of their eyes. Himself included.

Chapter 6

With Roan's truck trundling along somewhere in the distance behind her, Tessa pulled into the small courtyard on the north side of the croft. She left enough room for him to pull in next to her, and cut the engine, wishing she had a better handle on how she was feeling at the moment. Partly amused, yes, but also . . . disconcerted.

It had been clear to her that Katie was doing her level best to shove Roan and Kira together. A shoving that Roan had just as clearly been trying to avoid. That part was amusing. And it explained a lot. The day she'd been an unwitting player in his motorbike fiasco, he'd balked when she'd suggested he shower and clean up at the croft. She hadn't known what to make of his sudden stuttering self then, but she suspected she understood now.

Either Roan had the hots for Kira and wasn't acting on it, or Katie was trying to play matchmaker and Roan wanted no part of it. The latter possibility would have rung more true—had it not been for the motorbike incident.

Katie hadn't played any role then. Surely Roan could have accompanied Tessa back to the croft, cleaned up, and even if word had gotten out that he'd done so, she hardly thought anyone would have assigned any meaning to the visit other than the obvious. Kinloch might be a relatively isolated spit of an island, but from what she'd observed, the villagers who made their home there weren't backward or particularly prudish, not if their behavior during the calendar shoot had been any indication.

It left her with the other alternative. Roan was interested, but wasn't openly pursuing Kira because . . . well, she had no idea. Though she might have pigeonholed him a bit too quickly as a guy who got by on his charm and good looks, he certainly had no lack of ego and self-awareness. Surely he wasn't shy about women, or the pursuit of them. It was clear the women on the island all adored him. Some more vocally than others, she thought, recalling the moment he'd started peeling off his kilt.

Her mind stayed on that image perhaps a bit longer than was wise, but it also reminded her about his comments regarding his unease with the whole photo shoot, and having not looked at any of the pictures she'd taken. She smiled, then she grinned, then she shook her head as she laughed to herself. *Could it be? Roan McAuley, shy?* She hardly thought so. He was confident, outspoken, the island darling. But . . . maybe that's because on Kinloch, where his role was assured, he could be brazenly charming and wallow in the love and affection directed his way. He trusted those people.

Would he be so brazen in other situations? Was it his nature to flirt and flatter, or was it just expected of him? Maybe he was only giving the crowd what they wanted, so to speak, as he had at the photo shoot—using other people's preconceived notions of him to get what he wanted. She thought about that for another second and dismissed it. *No. He loved his role here.* He reveled in it. He might not be personally all that invested in his own appearance or what it could get him, because, frankly, he didn't have to be. That he would turn heads no matter where he was probably didn't even occur to him. Maybe having to think about that was what had made him uncomfortable during the photo shoot. But that still didn't explain his odd behavior with Kira.

Why wouldn't he openly pursue her if he was interested?

They'd both grown up there, and though Kira had been gone from her teen years until just recently, it wasn't as if he couldn't trust her to accept him for who he was, as he did the rest of the islanders.

She let her thoughts spin out a bit. Maybe he'd tried and Kira had shot him down. Her friend hadn't talked at all about how she felt regarding dating again, much less becoming emotionally entangled . . . but Tessa wouldn't be surprised if Kira simply wasn't ready for any part of it. Wouldn't Roan know that? Everyone knew every last damn thing about each other. It was disconcerting. And maybe a little endearing. Their hearts were good. So . . . either Kira had shot Roan down, or he'd known better than to try. Yet.

Oh, for God's sake, Tessa. Why on earth do you care?

She could say that it was concern for her best friend. That certainly played a role, but she knew Kira could hold her own. She'd certainly held up through far worse. Though guilt pinged Tessa again, she knew from personal experience there was absolute truth to the saying that what didn't kill you, did make you stronger. Turning down Roan's advances likely wouldn't have tested Kira's mettle. Though initially Tessa had less than generous thoughts about the man, she had no sense that he would do anything to jeopardize Kira's peace of mind.

No, she knew why she really cared.

She looked up as Roan pulled in next to her. And her pulse tripped all over itself when their gazes briefly collided.

Yep. She knew exactly why.

She shoved open the door of the car and climbed out just as Roan was coming around the back of his lorry. She took one look at him, all rangy body and messy curls, his trousers hanging just a bit low on his hips, the fit of his plaid work shirt just a bit too snug across his wide shoulders, and her libido joined her pulse in the little salsa number they liked to do every time she caught a glimpse of the guy. So she was attracted. So what, she reminded herself. She was female, after all. Didn't mean squat.

He smiled. She scowled. "I'll unload. Why don't you go see if you can drag Kira out of her studio." She shot him a glance. "That is if you can man up and ask the woman to dinner."

Roan stopped short, the smile that had been on his face fading. "What?"

"You heard me," she said, and popped the boot open so she could unload her gear.

"Aye, I did. I'm no' deaf. But what in the hell was that supposed to mean?"

"Don't play dumb, McAuley. Despite my initial impression of you, it doesn't suit you." She lifted the trunk top, blocking her view of him, only to have him push it gently, but firmly, right back down again.

"It's no' a lack of intellect when you haven't an earthly idea of what the other person is spoutin' on about."

Tessa knew she should stop talking. She was keenly aware that she'd likely already made a huge tactical error. Until such time as she could be around the man without wanting to throw him up against the nearest wall or down on the nearest flat surface and do every last thing she fantasized about doing with him, it might behoove her to keep her damn mouth shut. And while she was keeping her damn mouth shut, it might also be a good idea to figure out what was really going on with her where he was concerned.

"Nothing," she said. When he merely stared at her, his hand still pinning the trunk lid down, she let out a sigh and repeated the word, but more calmly this time. "Nothing. Ignore me and my attitude. Let's go see if we can roust Kira out of her nest. She could use some time outside these four walls."

Roan's expression immediately changed to one of sincere concern, but when she thought he was about to say something, he remained silent.

It took her aback, to see how much he cared about her friend. It had been an instinctive gut reaction she'd just witnessed. She wasn't sure why it bothered her, that he obviously had feelings for Kira, but she wished—fervently—that it didn't.

"What?" she prodded him, deciding the only way to diffuse . . . whatever the hell it was she felt and thought when he got within spitting distance of her, was to poke and prod it out into the open—so she could deal with it, and squarely tuck it away where it belonged.

"I—" He broke off, clearly unsure about talking to her at all on the subject of Kira, then relented. "You're her friend. Do ye think she's doin' okay?" Gone was the cocky guy, gone was the guy who had no problem getting right in her face the instant she got in his. Instead, there was a man who was obviously worried about someone he cared about. She had no way of knowing if it was simply because they had grown up together, or if his concerns ran deeper, and were more personal. That he cared and the feeling was sincere, wasn't in question.

"I don't know," she answered truthfully. When his expression grew even more vulnerable, she felt a twinge of something far too close to envy for comfort. "Kira doesn't talk about . . . things. And, to be honest, I haven't been the kind of friend I should have been in recent years, so I don't know what I'd otherwise know. She seems to be doing well. I know she's here because it's a good place for her to be."

Tessa held his gaze directly. She wasn't sure how much Kira had shared, or how much anyone knew about why she'd come back. Tessa wasn't about to be the one to spill anything Kira didn't want spilled. "If you're worried, though, you should talk to her yourself. You have a common past here. Maybe she'll open up to you."

He held her gaze for a beat longer, and his expression shifted from one of concern to one that was more focused on her. It made her feel like stuttering.

"You said she should get out more. Do you think she's hiding? I mean, she does stay pretty holed up. I haven't been certain if that's just her way now . . . if she's merely someone who enjoys her privacy, or if . . ."

Tessa swore silently. He was looking at her in the way women everywhere would pay to have their man look at them.

With concern, intent, and focus. Only his thoughts weren't really on her, but on what she could do to help him figure out the woman he was really interested in.

"If what you want to know is if she's ready to go out socially—with you—then ask her and find out," Tessa said, a bit more flatly than she'd intended. It wasn't Roan's fault, after all, that his interests lay elsewhere. He'd certainly never led her to think otherwise, and, again, why in the hell should it even matter? She couldn't be interested in him anyway.

Even if her life wasn't already upside down and turned inside out, whatever her future held, it was most definitely not on Kinloch.

Roan lifted his hand off the trunk lid and stepped around the back of the car until he was standing right next to her—right inside her personal space. "I worry about her because I care. Just like I care about everyone on this island."

"Don't kid yourself," she said, trying like hell not to respond to his nearness in any visible way, even if her throat was suddenly dry, and her knees weren't quite as steady as they'd been moments ago. It was stupid and foolish to let him get to her like he did. She'd be damned if she'd let him get even an inkling of it. "The whole island seems to get that it's more than just neighborly concern on your part. Does Kira know?"

She'd expected his expression to cloud over, or for him to look at least a little self-conscious, or even get a tiny bit defensive. He clearly wasn't at ease with his feelings where Kira was concerned and not remotely like his normal confident, charming self when she was the subject of the conversation. Other than Katie's playful nudge, no one else seemed willing to push him on the matter. Tessa was willing. Especially if it got him out of her face and beyond touching distance.

But he didn't retreat. No. He grinned. Suddenly he was all charm and dimples and self-assured swagger. "There isn't anything for Kira to know."

She snorted, which only served to widen his grin. And add a mischievous light to his devilish green eyes.

"What I wonder," he said, "is why you're so bothered by my concern for Kira."

"Don't flatter yourself. She's my friend, she's had a few big life changes, and she's come here for some peace and quiet. I'd get in anyone's face if I thought they were planning to disrupt that."

"But you just told me to ask her out. Grudgingly, I might add."

"Maybe I don't consider you a threat. And I might worry—that's what friends do—but, trust me, she can hold her own. She'll be the first one to shoot you down if she's not interested. But rather than dance around and stutter and fall all over yourself—so unattractive, by the way—why not just go ahead and ask? Find out one way or the other and put yourself out of your obvious, pining away, misery."

"I've asked myself that many times."

"You've—what?"

"You heard me," he said, and his grin was tempered just a bit. Mostly because that damned vulnerability had crept back in again.

Her heart sank, which was her heart's own damn fault. It knew better than to get all fluttery. "So, what's holding you back?"

"We grew up together, and I guess"—his smile turned wistful and affectionate—"I guess I'd always had a bit of a soft spot for her." He grinned broadly then, making his dimple wink. "She didn't have the time of day for me, of course."

"Some women become discerning at a very early age."

He laughed at that, and she couldn't seem to help herself or the wry smile she gave him in return.

"But that didn't stop me from showing off, of course," he said.

"Of course. Unimpressed, was she?"

"Deathly so, aye. Then we grew up and she left for school in London, and"—he lifted a shoulder—"it was a nice childhood memory."

"Except then she came back, and . . . the memory, or the feelings that went with it, weren't completely buried in the past after all?"

"To be honest, I don't know what they were. But she returned, and . . . I noticed."

"And . . . you did nothing. Fat lot of good that'll do you."

"I hadn't seen her since we were kids. Word was she'd come back home again after . . . that life change you were talking about. I was being polite, didn't think she'd appreciate the full-court press right off."

"She's been back for a year and a half. How polite do you think you need to be?"

He didn't take offense at her directness. Actually, that was one of the things she admired about him. He gave as good as he got, and didn't seem intimidated by her take-no-prisoners attitude.

"Initially," he replied seriously, "I was deferring to her state of mind. She didn't talk about her time away, so everyone here left her to her own path. I figured when she finally stepped out and became more social, I'd pay her more than a business call."

It was Tessa's turn to frown. "Are you saying she doesn't? Socialize, I mean? At all?" Her eyebrows lifted and she smiled. "Or did you wait too long and someone beat you to it?" She knew that wasn't true. She and Kira might not have kept in close contact, but no matter what life changes occurred while they were apart, they always picked up right where they left off.

She'd noticed their dialogue had been a bit more stilted. Tessa had written it off to her own unwillingness to reveal all her reasons for coming to Kinloch, but perhaps there was more to it than that. She'd thought Kira was a bit too closed up for her own good, but she hadn't realized her friend never went out.

"She might be communicating with someone, somewhere else, but she's no' seeing anyone on Kinloch," Roan said. "And to answer your other question, she comes in to town to do her shopping, and is friendly enough with everyone. She keeps up with island business, and she's definitely dedicated to contributing to our catalog inventory. In fact, she's very engaged in trying to push the art forward, trying new designs and materials. But she's no' one to hang about and chat or down a pint. It's work with her, no' play."

Tessa looked at him again, really looked at him. "Well, I can't tell you what Kira's thinking, but you clearly care about her. Maybe if you let your intentions be known, you'd be happily surprised." He started to speak, but she lifted her hand to pause him. "If she shoots you down, then you'll know where you stand. No one should just sit in purgatory. Where does that get you?"

He didn't say anything right off, but held her gaze. He studied her face, looked into her eyes . . . and, quite suddenly, she didn't think his thoughts were on Kira any longer.

"What about you?" he asked. "Do you heed your own advice?"

"About what?" She tried to focus, but the tension between them was hard to ignore. And it had nothing to do with annoyance and irritation. At least not as she—or her body—interpreted it. "About socializing? I socialize."

"Right," he said, the corners of his mouth curving. "A regular party animal."

"I—"

He placed his finger across her lips, and she was so stunned by the contact, that she stopped speaking.

"If your life was in balance, you wouldn't be here trying to find that very thing." He said it kindly, gently even, without accusation. "I've seen your work. I don't know that I'd be able to find a way to play, either, if that was my life, if that's what was in my line of vision every single day."

"You find ways," she said, when he took his finger away. Their gazes were still locked, and it was as if she'd entered a private confessional, where the world didn't exist beyond the circle where they stood. "You have to."

"Right," he said, "but do you? Have you? Or did it, some-where along the line, become all work and no idea how to play anymore?"

He was probing way, way too close to her most vulnerable place. Even though she'd begun to make strides on Kinloch—amazing, surprising strides—toward something that could be her redemption, those had been tiny, baby steps. She was still far too fragile to handle that examination, especially by some-one who had no idea what he was poking at.

She wanted to be all wounded bear and strike out at him, but he was looking at her with the same sincere concern on his face that had been there during their conversation about Kira. While the honest affection was absent—which wasn't surpris-ing since they were otherwise strangers to each other—the fact that he truly seemed to care about her situation was as alluring as his probing was terrifying. She couldn't deny a part of her hungered for that affection, too.

Roan McAuley was making her feel—a whole host of things. All of them dangerous to her health.

It didn't explain why she didn't back away, or push him off. Much less why she answered him. Honestly. And far more thoroughly than she'd intended.

"Yes, it did. I used to play. At some point I forgot how. Or maybe I simply didn't feel like playing anymore. I had a job to do. The stress accumulates inside of you, until it affects your every waking thought. And socializing? Yeah, that doesn't seem as important as just getting through to the next day and figuring out how you're going to find a way to detach enough to do your job. Socializing is a form of attaching. After a while, I couldn't, no matter how inconsequential or trivial. Not if I wanted to keep my focus. So, to answer your question, yes, I know how to. But no, I stopped playing around a long time ago."

She thought her unplanned outburst might have come tum-bling forth because a part of her wanted to punish him for poking at things he didn't understand. But the instant sorrow that flooded his expression did nothing whatsoever to make her feel victorious. Instead, it made her feel like the pathetic victim she was striving very, very hard not to become.

When she tried to step back, wanting—needing—to put some distance between them, he blocked her so she was trapped between him and the back of the car. She put her hands on his chest, intending to shove, but he covered her hands. Not tightly. Not even firmly. He just laid his palms over the backs of her hands, and kept that steady gaze of his on hers. There was no pity in his eyes, only concern. And maybe even a little worry.

It undid her. Tessa's issue wasn't his business, it sure as hell wasn't his problem, and she had made it clear she was perfectly willing to walk away.

"Go inside," she said tightly. "Talk to Kira. You want to talk to Kira. You do not want to be talking to me. Take all that care and concern that's written all over your face, and go shower her with it. She might not believe she needs it, or wants it, but I think you may prove her wrong."

"What about you?"

"This isn't about me. It's about you growing a pair and getting in there and finding out if the woman you've been making googly eyes over for the past year and a half has any interest in making googly eyes back."

"Do you know what occurs to me?" he said as conversationally as if she wasn't so worked up.

She wanted to roll her eyes, but his hands still covered hers and her heart was pounding too hard. "I haven't a clue how your mind works."

His lips twitched, just a little. "You might be surprised then." His hands curled more tightly on hers. "What occurs to me is that I've had a year and a half, and I haven't made a bloody move."

"That's what I've been saying."

"Right. I've known you, what? A few weeks now?"

Her gaze narrowed. And her pulse tripled. "Something like that."

"It occurs to me, that if I was really interested in making a move where Kira is concerned, it's likely I would have. You might have noticed, but I'm no' particularly shy."

"So noted. What is your point?"

"I told myself it was because of her recent divorce." His eyes widened, mirroring hers. "Aye, I know. We all know. We just dinnae speak of it, until or unless she does. But we know. Not the details, but then, I dinnae suppose that's necessary. It's beside the point."

"It is."

"Aye. Because, difficult times or no', I'm beginnin' to think I'd have made my move anyway—if I was truly invested in the outcome."

"You've come to this conclusion because?"

"Because I've known you less than two weeks and we've spent most of that time sparrin' with each other. Yet, you've been on my mind like a plague."

"Please. Stop. I could get a swelled head."

"Shhh, let me finish."

He shushed her? Worse, he was amused.

She merely arched a brow.

And his smile grew to a wicked sexy grin. "There is absolutely no reason I should attempt a pursuit of you. We're all wrong for each other. You're temporary. I'm no' leaving here. And it's quite likely we'd kill each other long before we'd get to any kind of payoff for the work it's going to entail."

"What on earth are you talking about?" Her heart was thumping so hard it made the pulse in her ears thrum. She surely hadn't just heard him say something to the effect of him wanting . . . her?

He lifted one hand from hers, and caught at a red curl that was dancing in the wind swirling about. He wrapped it around his forefinger, and gently, so very gently, tugged her face closer to his.

"I'm talking about the kind of want where a man doesn't wait. No matter what. Because I have every reason to go in that croft and do exactly as you say. And no reason—no sane reason—to do what I'm about to do. And yet, that's all I can truly think about."

"D-do what?"

He was far too close, and his mouth was far too perfect, and those eyes of his were fair to dancing as he looked quite happily into hers. And she wasn't even going think about that damn dimple and how impossibly adorable it was.

"This," he said simply, then did the least simple thing any man had ever done to her.

He kissed her.

Chapter 7

He hadn't planned to do it. In fact, he'd spent the drive to Kira's place listing all the various reasons why he should do exactly as Katie was prompting him to do—ask Kira out. Then put Tessa out of his mind completely. He thought he'd had himself convinced.

Yet, the longer Tessa had stood there, trying to convince him to do the very same thing, the more he knew something was missing. Yes, he cared about Kira, he worried about Kira . . . but if he'd honestly thought she was the one—he'd have done something about it.

Sort of like he was doing, only with the very last person he would have ever considered doing such a thing with.

Her lips weren't soft or pliant. At first.

Her fingers had curled under his hand, and he'd heard her breath catch in her throat. But he had no interest in kissing anyone who didn't want the attention. He lifted his mouth, just a breath from hers. "Have I been mistaken that we've just spent the past few weeks in some kind of perverse foreplay?"

Her eyebrows rose, but her gaze dipped to his mouth. "What?"

He smiled, and brushed his lips across hers. She moaned. Softly. But he heard it. "We dinnae want to want each other," he said, crowding her a wee bit closer to the car, so she had to tip her head back, just a little more.

"No—"

"But we do," he said, then very, very lightly brushed a soft kiss on her lips. "Want each other." He caressed her cheek with his curl-wrapped finger. "Don't we, Tessa?"

"Roan—"

He brushed her curl across her lips, and felt her tremble.

"We shouldn't," she said, her voice a husky rasp that did surprising things to his control.

He trembled a bit. "But we will."

Her gaze lifted to his. It wasn't the annoyance he saw that almost made him step back. It was the vulnerability. He hadn't expected that.

"Nothing good can come of this," she said, her gaze dipping once again to his mouth.

His body leapt in response.

"You don't want to start anything with me."

"You don't scare me," he said, and it was true. Mostly. She didn't scare him, but the feelings she stirred in him were downright terrifying. Especially because she wasn't even trying.

"I should," she said quite seriously.

"I'm certain you're right about that," he said, then wanted to laugh when she looked the tiniest bit outraged. "But in this case, the fire looks so much more enticing than the frying pan." He toyed with more of her red curls, then slid his hand under them and cupped the back of her neck. "And I do think this is going to be like fire."

"Is that what turns you on?" she said, pliant in his hands, yet still keeping her gaze on his. "Playing with fire?"

"No' usually, no." He pulled her up against him. And she held on. Tightly. He moved so his mouth was next to her ear. "But, you know what they say, Tessa, darlin'."

"What do they say?" Her voice was barely a whisper of sound.

He grinned, and pressed a hot kiss to the side of her neck, then gently bit the lobe of her ear. "There's a first time for everything."

"Roan," she said, half warning, half . . . want.

"I know," he said, "me, too." Then he turned her head to his and took her mouth like it was the last kiss he might have on this green earth.

There was perhaps a split second while she didn't respond. Then she tugged him against her, until she was leaning half back across the open trunk, and took charge of the kiss.

And he let her.

Fire, indeed.

Her kiss was aggressive, claiming. It was hot, and intense, and equally intoxicating.

He got caught up in it immediately, his body responding so swiftly he wanted more. A lot more. Right there on the car, if necessary. It was a primal reaction that shot him straight to the edge, like an untried youth who lacked any control, without a drop of finesse.

She was sliding her tongue into his mouth, slipping her hands up the back of his neck, then raking her nails across his scalp, and all he could think about was getting her naked, getting her under him . . . getting her.

Instinct took over, and he pulled her up against him, moving them until the side of his truck was at his back and she was pressed up against him, between his thighs. She was tall, with lean hips, and legs that went on forever, but he was taller. She fit perfectly.

His hands were in her hair, and he tilted her face, intent on staking his own claim in that visceral mating dance. He felt a gut-clenching, voracious thirst for her, as if he'd been near death and she was the oasis within which he could quite literally drown himself. He took over the kiss, the duel of tongues, intent on assuaging his every need. And hers.

She tasted sweet and he craved more. Their tongues dueled and tangled as he pulled her legs over his hips, then slid his palms up to cup her breasts. She moaned into his mouth and arched hard against him, her thighs clenching tight around him as he pushed harder between her legs. She grabbed his shoulders so she could move against him, and he moaned. He rubbed his thumbs over hard nipples pressing through her shirt and nipped her lower lip even as she broke off and nipped his chin.

He cupped her cheek, wanting to bring her mouth back to his, to plunge into it because he wanted to plunge into her, but as he shifted her mouth, he caught her expression. Her eyes were open, her body was tense . . . but she was a million miles away, going on instinct. Nothing more was there.

That should have been enough. He'd known she wasn't personally invested when the kiss began, that it was purely an animalistic response to the sexual tension screaming between them.

They were breathing heavily. She tried to grab his face, move his mouth back to hers. Still mindless, just wanting the escape. He understood that. It was tempting.

"Tessa," he said against her mouth.

"Roan, please, just—"

"I could," he said. "It would be easy."

"Easy is good," she said, her breath coming in gasps. "Easy is perfect."

"Easy is cheap," he responded, and she pulled back as if he'd slapped her.

He took her face in his hands. "I wasnae saying you were. The opposite, Tessa. You're worth so much more than just this."

"You have no idea what I'm worth," she said quite heatedly. "Maybe this is all I'm capable of. If you can't handle that, then we should stop this right now."

Roan stroked his fingers gently over her cheeks. She didn't smack them away. He considered that a small victory. "I think you're capable of anything. Everything. Maybe you only want that much. Because it's safe."

"Or because it's all I can handle," she said, and there was a thread of something other then defensiveness in her tone. One that he picked up only because he saw the flicker of fear in her eyes.

"Have you reached for more?" he asked, keeping his hands on her. She was still entwined between his thighs.

"Have you?" she challenged.

"Fair question. I want to. I want it all. It's only been for lack of having someone to reach for."

"Kira's not worth reaching for?"

"The lack of having the *right* someone to reach for," he amended. "I don't know what stopped me from reaching for Kira. I didn't stop with you. I couldn't. That's the difference."

"What makes you think it's been any different for me? I'm not stuck on an island, but I'm stuck in a life cycle that's not exactly conducive to long-term anything."

"Was there someone—anyone—you would have reached for, if things had been different?"

"Things weren't different. Whatever might have been for me was so long ago I've forgotten it. That was another life. A life before the one I'm leading now. I'm not mourning the loss, trust me."

He set her back just enough so he could see her entire face. "And now this life is changing, too. Isn't it?"

"I don't know what my life is anymore."

He could see as well as hear the stark, almost bald honesty in that statement.

"Whatever this is," she said, jerking his hips against hers, "one thing it isn't, one thing it can't be, is anything more than this."

"And that's enough for you?"

She laughed, but there was no humor in it. "It's more than I've had in a while. A long while."

He was fairly sure she'd meant to toss that off as a little verbal swat, intending to put him squarely in his place. Provider of cheap thrills. What she might not have realized was that her sharp mouth was saying one thing, but the yearning in her eyes was saying something else entirely.

"Do you truly believe that?" he asked.

"That this is more than I've had in a while? Oh, that is pretty much fact. For the past nine months, sex has been the last thing on my mind. Probably for some time before that, too. It shouldn't be on my mind now. But you make that kind of difficult to remember." She was trying to tease him, taunt him out of his probing questions.

His body surged to a more painfully erect state with her all but grinding against his hips. A large—and getting larger—part of him was more than willing to say bugger it and take what she was so willingly offering. It had been a long while for him, too, and he had a pretty good idea that Tessa could quite easily eclipse anything in recent or long-term memory. Hell, she already had. Just the taste of her was downright intoxicating.

But some other part of him refused to give up the fight. He couldn't have said what the bloody hell he thought he was fighting for. The situation had zero chance for improvement beyond the moment. He should take the fun and be thankful for the dalliance.

"That's no' what I meant," he said instead, stilling her questing fingers, then twisting so he had her pinned against the lorry, stilling her hips along with the rest of her.

"Let me go."

"Not yet."

"Roan—"

"Tessa," he shot back, feeling a tweak of anger himself. "I don't know what I want from you. But what I want—from anyone—is more than being a convenient piece, and more than a quick toss."

"Aww, you're more than a pretty face, is that it?"

"Stop it," he demanded.

"Stop what? Telling you the truth as I see it? I don't know what fairy-tale world you live in, but my world is as far removed from make-believe as it comes. So you'll have to forgive me. I can't spin some lovely story for myself to make this all okay. I know exactly what I'm getting into here. Your pants. And you into mine. That's it. It can't be anything more. What is so hard to understand? And what man on the planet doesn't was a vow he would keep. "I have you.

I can," she said, her voice a rough, shaky
I know how, Roan. Even if I wanted to. I

ct you to stop. But you don't have to do it

usiness doing it for me."

r, Roan. We—"
at's what you have to wrap your head around."
r head. "I don't know that I can do that, ei-
ed him square in the eye. "I don't know that I

ldin' on to me. And we're talking. And the world
spinning. Bad things aren't happening."
t know anything yet."
l."
n what? What if you can't handle it? I don't want
on't want help, I don't want anyone standing up for
count on that, no matter what you say, I can't. Don't
stand?"
than you could possibly know. I've stood on my own
life. But it was only when I became an adult that I re-
could only stand on my own because I had a founda-
love and support under me. And behind me. We don't
thing alone, Tessa."
o."
ot anymore."
ig words."
Big desire."
You could have had me. The easy part of me. Why not just
pt that and leave the rest of me be?"
I already told you. You're more than that. And that's what
mpels me. No' just the sex. You're so much more. And I'd
ke to think I am, too."

say, 'thank God' and take what I'm offering? It sure as hell is
the best deal you'll ever get."

"This man," he said, every bit as intensely fired up as she
was. "This man doesn't take a side dish when the main course
could be everything he's ever wanted."

He felt her entire body tense under his. Her eyes flared. Her
mouth parted. There was yearning in all of it. Just a flash of it.
But so deep, so clear. Then she got a grip. A shield dropped
over her expression, as impenetrable as if she'd put up a wall
between them. "You don't know what you want. Not if you're
considering tangling yourself up with me. I'm a disaster, Roan.
There would never have been a good time for us to cross paths,
but this is the absolute worst."

"I don't think so."

"You don't know anything."

He took her face in his palms and had to stifle the urge to
shake her. He was angry and confused, and never more serious
in his life. He had no earthly idea why. But it felt monumental
to him, in that moment, to make her understand. "I know I
want to know you. The good, the bad, the ugly. I want you in
bed, I want you right here, I want you every last place I can
have you. Then I'll very likely want to start all over again and
see if we can improve on the first round."

Instead of making her shore up her defenses further, his
heated declaration caused the wall to crack. Her pupils had
gone wide, and the irises were vibrant, captivating pools of
teal. Like liquid flame. He'd never wanted to leap into a fire
more.

"But that's not all I want, Tessa. That's not all I'd accept.
There's something here. And it isn't just about sex. If that was
all it was, we'd have been on each other within five minutes of
saying hello. Instead, we've been trying our damnedest to avoid
each other. There's a reason for that."

"It's called sanity. But I'm pretty sure my grip on that is ten-
uous at best, so you'll have to forgive me if I've made some less
than sensible decisions in the past twenty minutes."

"Stop it, Tessa. I told you, you don't scare me."

"Then you're too dumb for me. Certainly too dumb for your own good. I'm trying to warn you here, don't you get it?"

"Why? Why are you so damned invested in making sure I know what I'm gettin' into? Why not just tell me what I want to hear, take what I'm offering, and the hell with what I'm feeling? If I dinnae matter to ye, if I canno' matter, if this is just about getting our respective rocks off, then who the hell cares if I know the first or last thing about you?" He pinned her more tightly with his body when she began to squirm. "It's uncomfortable, having to face that it matters. That I could matter. That anyone could matter. Maybe it's you who should be afraid of me. I think you *are* afraid of me."

"In your dreams."

"This is no dream."

She laughed. Harshly. "No, it's a nightmare."

"No," he said, and pushed his face right up into hers. "It's reality. It's your reality. Your new reality. So you'd better get used to it."

"To what?" she shot back, but he could see the cracks in her control starting to fissure.

"To me," he said gently, his fury spent, leaving only the core of the new, raw, and very disconcerting feelings he felt for her. "I'm not letting you run and I'm not letting you hide."

"I don't want you."

"You're not exactly pushing me away. Or haven't you noticed?"

Her legs were wrapped tightly around his and her arms were twined so tightly around his neck, he thought it might cramp. He touched his forehead to hers. "What's in your head is pushing me off, but the rest of you is hanging on. Tightly. So . . . hang on to me, Tessa. Just . . . hang on." Then he leaned in and kissed her, softly, gently, on the lips.

Her moan was one of almost pain. It made something inside his heart break, but he kept kissing her, the sides of her mouth, her cheeks, her jaw, softly, sweetly, as gently as he knew how.

"Doesn't mean we can be more to each other."

"Doesn't mean we can't."

"God, you're stubborn."

He smiled. "I'll take that as a personal endorsement from someone who would know."

"Why is it you're charming with everyone else, and such a hard-ass with me?"

"I have no earthly idea. Maybe that's what you need."

"And what do you need? Surely not someone like me. Kira would have been the perfect—"

"Safe bet. And I told you, if I'd really wanted that, I'd have done something about it. Maybe I was waiting for you, for something like this. Something I couldn't ignore. Something that makes it impossible to wait. I just didn't know it."

"What gave it away?" she said dryly. "My sparkling personality, or my easygoing, approachable demeanor?"

She probably didn't even realize it, but he was acutely aware of it. Her hold on him had relaxed, her fingers were toying with the hair on the back of his neck. She was nestled around him, against him, as if it were the most natural, comfortable place to be. Held by him, all but sheltered by him. He thought it felt about as right as anything he'd ever experienced.

"I know. Everything you're saying makes perfect sense," he said.

"And yet, you're going to stand by me anyway?" Her smile was wry. "Gee, thanks."

"We're . . . this," he said, and pulled her more snugly up against him, making her realize how trusting she'd already become. She had to hold on more tightly to him as he swung them around. "We spar, we challenge, we strike sparks. We get at the truth of each other in ways no one else bothers to do. Maybe because we're so different. I don't know. I think, at the core, maybe it's because we're very much the same. All I know," he said, as he slowly disengaged her legs from around his waist and let her slide to stand inside the circle of his arms, "is that this is the most challenging, and the most natural spot I've ever found myself standing in. And I'm betting you'd say the same, if you let yourself be honest. We're comfortable in each other's space, the way we couldn't be, unless—"

"One of us was hallucinating?"

He smiled at that. She wasn't going to make it easy. But, again, she hadn't stepped outside the circle they'd formed. A circle that had begun the moment they'd finally put their hands on one another, and one, he noted, that had remained unbroken since.

He intended to keep it that way. If not literally, certainly in spirit.

"Unless one of us was simply smarter than the other." He leaned down and kissed her.

It only lasted a second, until she regrouped, but that moment had been telling. "Ye want to get inside now and ask Kira to dinner. Allow me a moment or two to . . . regroup. As it were. No' embarrass myself with too-tight trousers.'"

"We could have been taking care of that instead of all this crazy talk, you know."

He pushed her hair from her face, enjoying the knowledge that he could reach out and casually touch her, connect with her. Ground her. And himself. If only with a touch. It was odd how centered he felt, in that moment. As if things had suddenly become crystalline clear. Where before there were just huge gaps in knowledge, now he had a sense of purpose.

"We'll take care of that soon enough."

Her eyes widened a bit at his bold statement, and her lips parted slightly. His body renewed its battle to be more directly involved in the exchange, and when she smiled, he thought perhaps that moment was going to happen right then and there anyway.

"Dinner," he managed, past a suddenly dry throat. "People waiting."

"Right," she said, but her smile grew, and she moved in closer, taking the upper hand once again. She kissed him deeply, with a smoldering sensuality that had surely left singe marks in all kinds of places.

So, that was to be the battle then. She'd try to make this physical. And he would push for more.

At least he understood where the lines had been drawn.

He yanked her up against him, pulled her hips tightly to his, and kissed her back until they were both breathless.

"Right," he said, then set her back. She merely cocked an eyebrow. He smiled. They both laughed.

Shaking his head, he abruptly turned around and took a short walk to get his body back under control. A few minutes later he finally heard the croft door open, then shut.

He smiled out at the pasture full of sheep. "What in the hell did I just do?"

The bleating of the sheep didn't provide much enlightenment. It occurred to him then that he was about to head back into the village to have dinner with the three people who could read him best. *Holy hell.*

"Maybe she was right," he told the sheep. "I am hallucinating. Or I'm going to wish I were."

Chapter 8

Tessa still felt entirely out of sorts as she entered Kira's weaving studio. What in the hell had just happened out there? "You have to go," she announced abruptly. "I—I can't. I'm staying here."

Kira continued weaving without looking up, studying each spoke as she slid a variety of beads over the blunt tips. "I'm sorry," she said distractedly. "Who are you and what have you done with my friend, Tessa?"

"Sorry," Tessa said, trying hard to corral her thoughts. What did Roan mean by holding on to her? What nonsense had he been spouting out there? Surely she wasn't going to buy into that load of crap. He hadn't the first clue what she was about and he was being all knight in shining armor. What was up with that?" "But it's the best thing. You go. I stay."

Kira set the delicately woven waxed linen basket down on her work table and shifted her gaze to Tessa. Upon looking at her, she lifted a brow. "What happened to ye? You look like ye've run a marathon. Was it rough as all that out there gettin' the photos set up?"

Tessa frowned. "Photos? No. That went fine. Once we got the angles right."

"Then what are ye spoutin' on about? And what's got you lookin' so spooked?"

"Nothing. I'm fine. I just—I don't want to go. It would be better if you went."

"Where is it I'm going now?"

"Oh. Sorry. Rehearsal dinner. In town. Graham, Katie, Shay. And, uh, Roan."

Kira's other eyebrow raised, and a far too knowing smile curved her lips. "Ah. Now we're gettin' somewhere."

"No, you're getting somewhere, which is out of this house. You need to socialize. Why don't you socialize?"

Kira's expression changed to one of confusion. "Who said I don't socialize? I'm a social person."

Tessa worked harder to gather her very scattered wits. But it was next to impossible, knowing Roan was just outside, and could decide, at any moment, to come inside. She couldn't deal with him again right now. Maybe ever. That was it. She'd just never lay eyes on him again. Then she wouldn't have to worry about the crazy things he might say. And how they would make her feel.

She paced the length of the narrow studio, glancing once out the small, mullioned windows on the far end of the built-on room. No sign of him. She wasn't sure if that was good, or merely a warning. All she knew was that she needed to get Kira out there with him. And stay inside herself, away from him. Simple solution, really.

She turned back to Kira. "Name the last time you went out for anything that wasn't chore or work related? When did you last go to the pub? For fun?"

"What? I-I'm not an ale drinker," Kira said, half defensively. "And I'm a complete loss at darts. Besides, I see everyone there is to see when I go in to pick up mail and my supplies from the ferry. No need, really, to spend other time with them in a place where I'm no' comfortable."

"Do you spend other time with anyone?"

"Why does it matt—wait, you're changing the subject, aren't ye? Wha' happened? You came in here like you'd been run over. If it wasn't the photo rehearsal, what on earth was it?" She narrowed her gaze thoughtfully, and Tessa found herself wishing her friend didn't know her quite so well. "Or should I say, who on earth? I was on to it, wasn't I? This *is* about Roan. What did he do?"

"What makes you think this has anything to do with him? I just don't feel comfortable barging in on the rehearsal dinner, that's all. I thought you might like an evening out with friends. They specifically sent me back to get you to come along."

"So why am I going along without you, then? What happened between the rehearsal and here?" She pushed back her cane-woven stool and got up to go have a look out the window herself.

"Okay," Tessa said abruptly. "So, Roan is outside. He's waiting. For you."

That had Kira looking at her with a bit of surprise, then a narrow gaze that was full of suspicion. "What did you do, Tessa? Please tell me you didnae try your hand at settin' me up on a blind date."

"No, that would be everyone else on Kinloch."

"What?"

"I know you've spent this past year and a half focused inwardly, and on your weaving. But . . . have you not been paying any attention at all?" Tessa debated all of three seconds before blurting out the rest. It was a truth, of sorts, and she told herself she was doing this for his own good. And Kira's, too. She thought Roan had had it right all along. Kira was truly perfect for him. With his upbeat personality and positive outlook, not to mention his well-grounded life on the island, he would be just the thing to bring her friend the rest of the way back to the land of the living. Tessa was doing them both a favor. She ignored the hard twinge of conscience, not to mention the pang of . . . something else, and went on. When they both thanked her later, she'd get over it.

"Roan's had a thing for you since you were kids. He's been biding his time, waiting for you to leave the cave, before saying anything. But he cares about you, Kira. Everyone sees it. Or, at the very least, Katie, Graham, and Shay do. They're all happy about the prospect. So, why don't you put the guy out of his misery, agree to go in for a casual dinner with the gang, and . . . see where things lead?"

Kira's expression had gone from confusion to utter shock to guarded consideration. But she said nothing. Not immediately.

"He's right outside," Tessa said. "Waiting."

Kira left the studio and walked across the great room area between the kitchen and the two bedrooms to look out the front window. "That's his lorry."

"Yep."

Kira spun back around, eyes narrowed, but with a surprising edge of hurt in her voice when she said, "I can't believe you took it upon yourself to sign me up for this. How dare you?"

"How—what? I was trying to help."

"How? By promising a man a date with me—to nothing less than an intimate wedding rehearsal dinner. There is nothing casual about that, by the way. What were you thinking?" Then Kira stopped in her tracks, and looked at her friend again, with a far more calculating expression. "Wait a minute. You came in here looking like—" She walked right up to Tessa and ran her gaze assessingly over her.

Tessa instinctively raised a hand to cover her throat. "What do you think you're doing?"

"Looking for signs." She lifted her gaze to Tessa's. "You're shoving me off on Roan because you need a defensive screen. That's even more insulting."

"It's not—" But Tessa broke off, then hung her head, and swore under her breath. When she looked up, it was with the humbling knowledge that she really had sunk to the bottom. "He really does have a thing for you," she said. "I didn't make that up."

"But he didn't come here after me. Did he? Not really." She looked Tessa right in the eye. "I know we haven't been close lately—and I'm to blame for that, too, by the way. We've both been through some pretty tough stuff. But if we are wanting to make the most of this friendship, of getting it back to what it used to be, then we have to be honest with one another. If you're not ready to talk about why you really came here, fine. But we will talk about it at some point. I don't particularly want to dredge up everything I went through two years ago. But I will. At some point. Because, as my closest and dearest friend, you should know. Just as I should with you. But right this second, you are going to tell me what in the bloody hell is really going on with you and Roan and why I'm being shoved into the middle of it. We might have past stuff that needs discussing, but there's no excuse to not keep current on what's going on right this very second."

Tessa felt like she'd had the wind knocked out of her. But once she'd regrouped, and let Kira's announcement sink in she knew it for truth. It wasn't easy taking that step. Even with Kira. "I—it was you," Tessa began. "Why we came out here. Truly. And he has been thinking about you, interested in you, since you came back."

"Roan's not particularly shy, if you haven't noticed, and we've developed a good working relationship in regards to our respective roles in the weaving industry here. I find it very hard to believe, if he were truly interested, he wouldn't have already said something about it. He's had ample opportunity."

"And . . . if he had, would you have been interested?" Tessa knew she had to tell Kira the rest of the truth, but this part was important. Just because Roan had passed up the chance to find out what was what with Kira, and just because Tessa was trying pretty much anything to get out of having to deal with her very confusing feelings for him, that did not mean it wasn't still a potentially viable avenue for Kira and Roan. Because of that, she needed to know—before she could do anything else or decide how she felt.

"I honestly don't know," Kira said. "He's easy on the eyes and the heart. I know he's a man of integrity."

"Have you looked at him and thought, hmmm, maybe?"

Kira looked away then, and Tessa saw a flash of something else on her face. "What?" Tessa asked. "What was that? Because you can't go lecturing me on being honest, and then clam up when things start getting—"

Kira looked at her. "I don't think I'd have pursued things with Roan, though that would likely have been my loss."

"Why not try then?" Realization hit. "Oh. Oh! There is someone else, isn't there? You wouldn't pursue him because your interest is already elsewhere."

"My attention has been diverted, aye. But I've done nothing about it and dinnae intend to anytime soon. Don't badger me about it. Ye dinnae even know the man and talking about it will make it far too real. I'm only up to a good daydream and an occasional hot flash over him as yet." She smiled then, and it was playful and happy, and made Tessa feel the best she'd felt about her friend since coming to Kinloch. "But I'm working on it."

Tessa smiled, honestly and sincerely happy for her friend. "Then that's enough. For now. But you will spill all later. I have my ways."

Kira laughed lightly, and there was something delightfully sweet in the sound that warmed Tessa's heart immensely. A new love would be such a good thing for her friend, but it was also a hopeful thing. Just in general. To know, to see and hear, for that matter, that bad things can happen, but that rebirth happens, too. "I'm happy for you," she said quietly, with a quick smile. "Just having those urges again must feel pretty good."

"Thank you," Kira said, just as sincerely. "And aye, it does feel good. When it's not scary or terrifying. So . . . with me out of the way, that gives you clear shot then, doesn't it?"

Tessa frowned. "You didn't just make up that whole—"

Kira shook her head. "No, it's quite real, I assure you. I wish it wasn't, most days, trust me. It's . . . distracting." Her eyes twinkled. "But no' entirely in a bad way." She walked over and sat back in her work chair. "Okay, your turn."

There came a tap on the door, and Tessa jumped as if she'd

been shot at—which she had been in the past, but it didn't stop her from feeling particularly ridiculous at that moment. Nor did it stop Kira from laughing. "Oh, we've really got to talk then, haven't we?"

"If you'll just go tell him we're not going into town, I'll tell you whatever you want to know." Thankfully, there wasn't much to tell. At least, that's the story Tessa was going to stick to. Personally and publically. What had happened was simply an aberration. She and Roan acted on their crazy hormonal pull, and it was done. She'd make it clear to him that she appreciated his whole Rob Roy act, but that she didn't need or want a protector, or, after much thought, a lover. But she wished him the best of luck in the future and all that lovely rot. Just not with Kira. She'd have to tell him that part, too. Didn't seem right for the guy to strike out twice. It was for the best he knew right off so he could regroup and start a new campaign elsewhere.

What she needed to do was dive back into the work she'd begun on the fateful day of his motorbike accident. Focus on the beginnings of her own potential new path. Focus on the future. No matter where it took her, it would be away from Roan McAuley. Better to start putting him out of her mind right away.

"All right," Kira said as she came back into the studio a few minutes later. "All taken care of. Now tell me what happened with the two of you. I thought you were oil and water. I should have realized that the amount of time you spent complaining about the man meant something was going on there."

"That makes no sense. I was complaining about him because he was a thorn in my side then, and he's a thorn now. He makes things a challenge when they don't need to be. And, frankly, I don't need more challenges."

"I know you did the photo shoots as favors to me, for the people here, but I'm so sorry if—"

Tessa waved Kira silent. "I don't mind helping with the calendar, or even the wedding, but sometimes he makes me wish I wasn't involved with either project." Truth be told, framing out the shots for the wedding, and watching Katie and Graham and the almost inexplicable bond they shared, had moved her quite unexpectedly. Maybe it was all of that, the wedding, the vows, that had made her vulnerable to Roan's unexpected advances. She found herself glancing out the window again as she heard the sound of his truck engine rumbling to life. "What did you tell him?"

"That we'd decided to leave tonight's dinner to the wedding party members."

"Did you say anything else?"

"If you mean did I tell him that you squealed about his childhood crush on me, or that you're hiding in here, too afraid to deal with him directly, then no."

Tessa's jaw dropped, and she had every intention of calling Kira out on those statements. Except, they were mostly true. Okay, completely true. She sighed and her shoulders slumped a little. So much for her good deed of the day scenario. "I'm sorry. About both of those things."

Kira waved a hand and her smile was sincerely good-natured. "Consider it partial payback for me rooking you into the photo shoots."

"I shouldn't have tattled on him, that was wrong. I don't want that to affect your friendship. You were right about one other thing, too. He did say that if it was really meant to be, he'd have made his move. So, you don't have anything to worry about." She wanted to poke a little, find out who this mystery man of Kira's was, but she'd done enough poking at people for one day.

"Why did he tell you that?" Kira asked.

"Tell me what, about his crush on you? Because they're all shoving him at you, trying to get him to stake a claim."

"Not that part. Why did he tell you that he'd have made his move if it was really meant to be? What made him realize that?"

"I'm sorry," Tessa repeated. "Now your feelings are hurt and—"

Kira laughed. "No, that's not why I'm asking. I'm trying to figure out why the two of you were talking about me."

"I was pushing him at you, too. Okay? There, my conniving, bad friend example is complete. But, to be honest, I did think he'd be good for you."

"This after ye just got done tellin' me he's a pain in your arse?"

"*My* arse," Tessa clarified, then smiled herself. "Which is a totally different arse than yours. Mine's far more stubborn and ridiculous."

"I don't know about that. I have been holed up for too long. It's just been . . . comfortable, I suppose."

"Well, maybe this is the impetus you need to make a move yourself."

Kira waved her finger. "You'll no' distract me from my stated mission here, ye know. I'll have it from ye. You promised me that much."

Tessa swore silently, but she knew she was well and cooked. "I know. It's just that I don't know what to tell you, much less how to explain it all. We just—"

"We meaning you and Roan."

She nodded. "We are kind of . . . combustible, I guess is the right word. We strike sparks off one another, and I guess it was inevitable that some of them would turn out to be a bit sexual in nature."

Kira's brows both lifted. "Sexual now, is it?"

"No, no, nothing like that. I mean, we kissed, but it was more like a battle of wills. It was hot, but it wasn't remotely romantic." No, her traitorous mind reminded her, that part came afterward.

"You kissed each other," Kira repeated. "Where?" Then her eyes widened to match her raised brows. "That's why you came in here looking as if you'd been in a windstorm!" She grinned, then clapped a hand over her mouth to stifle the hoot of laughter.

Probably because Tessa's scowl was a tiny bit on the fierce side at the moment.

"Right out in me courtyard, don't ye know. Well . . ." She managed to keep the laughter inside, but that didn't stop her from grinning like a Cheshire cat. "So," she asked, her eyes a lively twinkle, "how was he?"

Tessa swore and stalked over to the window. "Okay, I am so not having this conversation. I didn't promise kiss and tell details."

"Oh, come on. I'm a puir single lass, starvin' for attention here. Let me live vicariously through yer steamy and salacious social life."

Tessa snorted. "I don't have a social life. What happened out there in the courtyard isn't going to change that, no matter what he thinks."

"What does he think?" Kira stood and came over to stand by Tessa, who was watching Roan's truck trundle off down the single track lane.

"Ridiculous things that can never happen," Tessa muttered, suddenly too tired to put up much of a fight. She turned to Kira, but it was too hard to look into those knowing, wise eyes of hers and bring herself to reveal how terrified she'd been. So she looked back out the window.

"Like?" Kira prodded gently.

"Like he doesn't just want hot sex. And it would be the best damn hot sex we've both ever had. I'd stake a bet on that. Stupid man."

"He doesn't want sex? What does he want then?"

"Oh, don't get me wrong. He wants the hot sex. But he has this insane moral code or something. At least, what else could it be? He refuses to just romp in the hay. Apparently he needs to at least fool himself into believing it could be more."

"He wants more? With you?" Kira hadn't asked the question unkindly. It was more in sincere surprise.

Tessa understood it and wasn't insulted. In fact, she hoped

Kira could explain Roan's stance to her. Because she sure as hell wasn't seeing it. She looked at Kira. With a dry smile to match the wry note in her tone, she said, "Now you can see why I was pushing him off on you. You two? Match possibly made in heaven. On paper, anyway," she added, palms up. "Me and Roan? Match made in hell. No matter how you add it up or where you write it down."

Kira didn't agree or disagree. She just kept that considering look on her face. "So . . . what did you tell him?"

"That. More or less. I mean, there's the obvious part. He's a lifelong islander, I'm a world vagabond. Mismatch, right there. I explained that I'm not ready for a relationship, even if I was sticking around. I came here to work some things out." She looked starkly at Kira then. "And I know I owe you an apology for not talking with you about it—"

"We covered that. More than once. It's okay, truly. When the time is right, I'm here. We both know that. So . . . you told him? About that?"

"Not in detail. I haven't talked with anyone. Anyone who's not a paid professional, anyway."

Kira's expression changed to one of real concern.

"It's okay," Tessa reassured her, even though there was plenty of reason to be concerned. Hell, she was concerned. That's why she was there. "I'm handling it. The right way."

Kira nodded, but didn't press. Tessa wondered then if Kira had likewise sought help beyond that of friends or coworkers or neighbors to get her through. And she knew that their talk would happen sooner rather than later.

"But I didn't have to tell him," Tessa said. "I mean, he figured out I wasn't here for a fun holiday, that I was working something out. I alluded to burnout, which is part of it. I don't know, though, he seemed a lot more . . . intuitive than I'd have expected. It was disconcerting."

"And downright scary, I'd bet," Kira added. "I'd have run off right then, I can assure you. Being made to feel vulnerable when you're in a fragile state is no' the best thing. I know it. So, when you laid that all out there for him, what did he say? Did he get it? Is that why you came inside?"

"I came in to get you, but it was escape, pure and simple. Because no, he doesn't get it. Or just doesn't want to. It's like he's got this complex or something, because he kept telling me it didn't matter what was going on with me, or what our current paths were. He was just spouting on about not having to do things alone, about sticking and not running, about giving people a chance to be there for me, and being open-minded enough to see what could be."

"And first chance you had—"

"I ran. Well, I exited. But, he'll realize soon enough if he doesn't already . . . I don't plan to make a re-entry."

"He'll honor your choice. He's no' a disrespectful man."

"I'd agree. If it was anyone else—but . . . it's different with us. It's like we're always inside some giant karmic test, or karmic joke. I can't tell which most times"—she looked back out the window, even though he was long gone from view— "but I don't think he's going to give up on me just yet." She wasn't sure how she felt about that—which bugged the hell out of her.

"What about you?" Kira asked, maybe seeing something in her expression. "Certainly there is something going on here if you're this thrown by it. Aren't you even going to consider trying?"

"I can't, Kira. I just . . . it's too complicated. I don't need more complications."

She heard her friend let out a soft sigh. "Well, that I understand. I can't tag you for running or hiding. Not when it looks like I've made it my own new life mission. It's just . . ."

Tessa turned and looked at her when the silence lingered and she didn't finish the thought. "Just what?"

"I didn't—don't—have any alternative paths. At the moment, anyway. No' unless I make my own."

"I want to make my own, too," Tessa said. "I think I have to."

"Maybe that's a huge part of why you're here in the first place. Because you think you can only make it on your own. Roan doesn't strike me as the possessive, controlling type. I canno' believe he'd want to dominate you, or your life. He's no' that man."

"Whose side are you taking here?" Tessa asked, but there was no bite in the question. She knew Kira was just saying what she thought was true. It was more than a little disconcerting how closely her thoughts and comments had mirrored Roan's.

Kira reached out and took Tessa's hand in her own, and squeezed. "The side that will end up with us both being healthy, happy, adult women who look at the world like a good, rich, rewarding place we want to be part of. That's the side I want us both on."

Tessa turned her hand over and squeezed Kira's in return. "I want that for us, too. I'm just not certain Roan is the solution. To any of it."

"Fair enough."

Tessa heard the pause as clearly as if her friend had said, "but." She caught Kira's gaze with a raised eyebrow of her own.

Kira sighed, then smiled. "Just . . . don't close any doors permanently quite yet. All right? Give yourself a chance to figure things out first."

"We're on an island. He's not going anywhere."

"Yes, but you can be—"

"Oh, he knows exactly what I can be."

Kira's smile grew then, and the twinkle came back. If it wasn't at her expense, Tessa would have been a lot happier about seeing such honest delight on her friend's face.

"And yet," Kira said, "he still wants to hang around you. Brave man."

"He's not afraid of me." That was as stunning as it was disconcerting.

"All the more reason to give him a chance." Kira gave Tessa's hand a final squeeze, then let go and walked back into the studio, sat down, and picked up her current work in progress. Without looking up, she added, "If nothing else, maybe you should stick around for the wild sex." Her glaze flickered to Tessa, then back to the bead she was threading on another long, waxed linen spoke. "I mean, come on. We're happening, hot single women. One of us should be getting lucky."

Tessa smiled back. It might have been a grin. Then they both snickered. "Okay, okay. I'll keep it under advisement. That part, anyway. I'm going to go play in my dark room. Happy weaving."

Kira pulled over her lamp magnifier and switched it on, merely nodding in response as she positioned the lens over her intricate beadwork, caught up once again in her own creative world.

When Tessa let herself into the pantry / dark room, she could hear Kira singing "It's Raining Men." "Not funny," she shouted out.

But it kind of was. And she was humming herself as she went to work.

Chapter 9

"Who started the tradition of strangling men with these things anyway?" Roan squinted into the mirror as he tried to do his bowtie correctly. "Had to be a woman. Like we're no' already willing to be at your every beck and call. Ye've got to make us feel tethered. Literally."

"Oh, *haud* yer *wheesht*. I've had enough of yer caterwauling. Ye'd think you were the one tying the knot." Eliza bustled over to Roan and pushed his hands out of the way.

"See? Tying a knot! That just proves my point. Marriage is bondage."

"Aye, that it is. The sweetest bonds ye'll ever want to be tied into, and dinnae you forget it."

"How can I? I've a noose about my neck, reminding me."

"Och, and you're only the best man. We'll be lucky to make it through the preparations when it's your turn."

Roan knew when to shut up. And that was quite probably a few comments back.

Eliza gave an extra smart snap to the freshly knotted bow, then stepped back, a calculating look in her lively blue eyes. "Cat got yer tongue now, eh?"

"I was merely trying not to imagine the horror. It's Graham's funeral—er, day, after all."

Eliza's expression turned more sincerely considering. "You've taken on quite the sour attitude now, haven't ye? I thought you approved of the union. Since when did yer views on holy matrimony grow so dark?"

Since he couldn't seem to get his mind off the only woman who would likely never willingly agree to enter into such an institution—with him or anyone else. But he could hardly tell Eliza that. Hell, he could hardly even admit it to himself. "Oh, I'm all for Graham doing it. Hey, maybe it's just wedding night envy. The rest of us poor blokes will go home alone tonight."

Eliza's expression said she didn't buy a single word of that.

"Perhaps you should go find out if Shay needs your estimable skills," he suggested.

"Shay does not," the man himself said, as he strolled into the small anteroom, off the main chapel of the abbey.

Though the vows would be spoken in the meadow, the procession was to begin from there. Complete with horse drawn carriage, transporting the lovely Katie, along with her man of honor. Roan's mouth twisted in a wry grin at the thought of that ironic little scenario. The man Katie had dumped at the altar was escorting her down the aisle as her witness. Who better to stand by her side than the only person in her life who'd stood by her all along?

Roan knew Katie had made an effort, more than once, to reconnect with her parents before the ceremony, but they had remained unwavering in their silence. Roan understood, perhaps better than anyone, what it was like be considered a choice by the very people who had brought you into the world, rather than a duty, much less a blessing. Whereas his mum and dad—teenagers both—had run off, leaving him on the doorstep of a pub in Castlebay on their way to parts unknown, never to be heard from again, Katie's had raised her as a family-owned corporate entity to be utilized to the best advantage by the very same family-owned corporation.

He supposed there was an argument to be made that Katie's parents had been raised in households with a similar mind-set and didn't know how to do otherwise. But, to him, the lack of basic humanity toward their own daughter was downright disgusting. At least his parents could be partially absolved for being too young to understand the full impact of the reckless choices they'd made. He'd come to think that leaving him to be raised by someone—anyone—else was perhaps the one true gift they'd given him.

But he couldn't say he'd stopped wondering whether they'd ever paused and considered what had become of their abandoned offspring.

Katie's parents were presently holding her trust fund and all of her worldly possessions hostage, thinking it was the leverage that would get their daughter—a.k.a. their corporate investment—to return herself to the asset column. He supposed it was sad, bordering on pathetic, they likely had no sense whatsoever that she could find complete and utter fulfillment without any of those things. She would never be going back to what they held dear.

Roan had seen her in her gown earlier, looking like a magical fairy goddess. She lit up so angelically when speaking of how excited she was to exchange her vows with her one and only, and he thought it was utterly tragic that her parents would never understand the true asset they'd lost and should have held dearest.

"I believe our carriage awaits," Shay announced, giving Roan a quick once over, then standing next to him as they looked into the full-length mirror perched in the corner. "We almost look respectable."

They were wearing their plaids and full clan regalia. McAuley colors for Roan, Callaghan colors for Shay. He was one of only a handful on the island of three hundred plus who wasn't McAuley or MacLeod.

"A shame we already know all the single women at the reception," Shay said, quite seriously.

"Aye. No' a chance we'll field the question," Roan said, adjusting his sporran.

"What question is that?"

They turned as Blaine waltzed into the room—which, was the only appropriate adjective, really. His gait was too regal to be a sashay.

The man was a bit godlike in appearance, in a magazine advert kind of way, Roan supposed. It was only when he moved . . . or talked . . . that one realized there was a goddess hidden beneath his mythical exterior. His arrival on the island hadn't initially been met with enthusiasm, given the villagers immediate affection toward Katie and fear he'd come to interfere with the impending nuptials. But once that fear had been put to rest, they'd quickly accepted the chatty and quick-witted Yank. Roan couldn't be certain his sexual orientation had been met so open-heartedly by some of the more devout and traditional clan elders, but life on a remote island wasn't for the faint of heart. Islanders were rugged individualists. In that regard, his very differences were seen as endearing quirks. And God knows, they all had them.

"What a true Scotsman wears beneath his kilt," Shay responded, still admiring his oh-so-serious self.

Blaine considered the response for a moment, appearing thoughtful, then tossed off a quick grin. "And here I was already a fan of any culture that endorses men wearing skirts. Hmm." He gave them both a cheeky once over.

Shay glanced at Roan, who glanced back. They shared a quick shake of the head. Then Shay looked back at Blaine. "Today, we shall let you live. But only because Katie would make our lives an eternal living hell if we were found responsible for anything happening to you."

"Not to worry," Blaine said, not remotely chastened. He tipped his top hat in their direction. "You're not my types anyway."

Again, Shay and Roan exchanged glances. "I believe we've just been insulted," Shay said, turning back to the mirror, serious as ever. "What's not to love?"

"Graham's reaction if the two of you scoundrels are late to

the meadow," Eliza said, hustling back into the chamber, only to stop short as she spied Blaine. "My, my, don't you look the vision."

Roan had no idea where Blaine had acquired his get up, though he wouldn't have been at all surprised if it was simply a part of the regular wardrobe the man traveled with. He had on pinstriped dress trousers, a dove gray, cutaway jacket with tails, and had completed the look with a deep rose pink cummerbund, cream silk ascot, dove gray top hat, and a slender black cane. The shame was that he actually carried it off with more elan than even the swishiest of Brits would have.

Blaine doffed his hat and bowed deeply in front of Eliza, then took her hand. "You are as delightful a vision as the first blush of spring." He kissed the back of her hand, surprising a delighted smile from her, and if Roan wasn't mistaken, a bit of a blush.

He hadn't thought that was actually possible. His estimation of Blaine rose a notch or two just for that feat alone.

"We were just heading out," Roan told Eliza.

"If I could have a short moment," Blaine said, sending a gracious smile toward Eliza, who didn't need further explanation that he'd wanted the short moment to be a private one.

"Dinnae be late!" she warned, then winked at Blaine, the blush still pinking up her ruddy cheeks. She bustled out, arrayed in quite the fancy mauve church dress, with a lace hat pinned to the back of her gray bun.

"We'll be along shortly," Shay assured her, then turned to Blaine. "What is it?"

Blaine waited for the office door to shut. Roan could have told him it wouldn't stop Eliza from hearing every last word if that was her intent. But it would be a waste of time.

"As you know," Blaine said, looking back at the two of them, "Katie has made overtures to her parents more than once since her arrival."

Roan frowned and felt a certain tension slide down his spine. "Are you saying they're going to somehow interfere in the proceedings today? I thought they'd maintained their silence throughout."

Blaine lifted a perfectly tailored shoulder. "They have. But I know the McAuleys—our branch, anyway—and though it doesn't surprise me that they've cut Katie off without so much as a single tear shed, I've had my doubts that they'd actually allow her to tie the McAuley name legally to anyone without some attempt at intervention. It's one thing to allow her to run off and have a tantrum, no matter how unseemly. Quite another to go off making decisions that could affect the corporate bottom line."

"What's going on?" Roan asked, the tension turning to dread.

"I've been keeping tabs."

"From here? How?"

"I might not have had the fortitude to do what Katie did, but one big difference in our manner of parting is that, as the tragic, betrayed victim, I still have my allies back at home."

Katie's family was bound to Blaine's through their joint industry of building expensive racing yachts as well as other high-end floaties. McAuley-Sheffield had been in the boating business together for several hundred years, in fact. The pairing of Katie with Blaine had happened almost at birth, their collective parents all but salivating over the legal union and what it could do for the family-owned business, especially when there was an ever bigger push to take the company public. Katie had ruined all that by walking out on their wedding day. Roan knew how the McAuleys had responded. He had no sense what Blaine's side had done after his defection.

"Are you in contact with your family, then?" Roan asked.

Blaine's jaw tightened a little, but otherwise he kept his tone upbeat and wry. "Let's just say that if you think the McAuleys are being chilly toward their daughter, my family is being downright glacial to me."

"They're not blaming you for the wedding being called off, are they? Katie said it was pretty clear that it was all her doing. I can see them transferring blame to Graham, but not—"

"No, it's not that. Not only that, anyway. Let's just say other information became public that day that was even more news-worthy to my family's assembled friends and business associates."

"Ah," Roan said.

"Indeed," Blaine said, not looking particularly upset about it, at least not outwardly.

Roan couldn't imagine such a pivotal moment being received so poorly as anything other than brutal, bordering on devastating. But Blaine seemed to have recouped well enough. Perhaps he hadn't expected anything different.

"The biggest difference between our circumstances now is that I had the foresight to do a bit of self-preservation planning. You know, just in case," Blaine went on. "I told Katie time and again she needed to squirrel away a little here and there. The Caymans are lovely for that sort of thing, as it happens." He waved a gloved hand—Roan had missed that detail—and said, "She didn't think it was necessary. Kind of ironic, given how things turned out, but she won't let me help her. Not in that regard. However, there are other ways friends can support friends. So . . . I've been keeping an ear to the ground."

"She doesn't know about that?" Shay asked.

"I tried to talk with her about it, but she was fairly adamant that I not stick my nose in. I had no intention of stopping, so I just stopped talking to her about it."

"What have you learned? There is still a ferry docking before the ceremony. Is there a surprise waiting us?"

Blaine smiled at him indulgently. "Oh, the McAuleys would never arrive by ferry. How . . . plebian."

Roan and Shay frowned. "The closest airstrip is on Barra," Shay said, referring to the nearest island to Kinloch. Even that was just a narrow strip on the sandy beach.

"You have docks, don't you?"

"For fishing boats, but we're hardly set up for anything elaborate."

"What I mean is, you have a harbor. That's why they make offshore anchors and skiffs for taxi transport."

"Of course they do." Roan sighed, feeling that the inevitable was upon them. Poor Katie. Nothing should dampen that day for her. "The wedding is less than an hour from now. Will they have time enough to say their vows?"

"Yes, but you know how they weren't planning on going anywhere for their honeymoon?"

"The flax harvest—Graham feels he needs to be here. They'll go after the harvest is done."

"But you could spare them for, say, the weekend, right?"

"That's what I tried to tell him, but—"

"A weekend in the Cotswolds would be lovely this time of year," Blaine added. "Lovely private cottage, a bit of hiking, taking in the beginning of the fall colors." He sighed somewhat rhapsodically, then went on with a sharp look in his eye. "In fact, I was thinking it would make a nice wedding present. Especially if they left immediately after the ceremony."

Roan was smiling as he glanced at Shay, who'd also cracked an uncustomary smile. "Great idea. Except the last ferry will be gone before—" Roan broke off as an odd sound vibrated through the air. "What is that?"

"I'm not much for boats," Blaine said, by way of explanation. "You understand."

They walked outside the abbey just as a small, sleek black helicopter landed on the smooth beach below, off to the west of the abbey, in the shadow of the ancient ruins.

"How did you manage—?"

Blaine smiled. "As I said, self-preservation planning. Comes in gloriously handy, doesn't it?"

Roan looked back at the chopper and grinned. "Aye. That it does."

"Now all we have to do is convince Graham to get on the damn thing." Shay looked at Blaine. "He's no' much for flying."

"I'm thinking once I explain that there's a yacht on the horizon with Katie's parents on board, along with their lawyer—"

"Lawyer?" Roan's eyes widened. "They're bringing legal representation to their daughter's wedding?"

"One never enters into commodity negotiations without legal being present."

"Bugger that," Shay said.

Roan had known her parents' attitude was bad, but Katie tended to play it down, make jokes at her own expense. Even so, he hadn't known it was quite like that. "Fine. I'll go have a talk with Graham." He took two steps toward the exit, then turned back and stuck his hand out to Blaine. "Thank you. You're a good friend."

Blaine shook his hand once, firmly. "You'd do the same for someone you cared about."

Roan's mind flashed immediately to Tessa. "Sometimes the path to giving aid isn't always so clear, or appreciated." He let that go, wishing he hadn't said anything. He was worried about Katie. "What if Katie doesn't want to go? What if she wants to confront her parents?"

"That's her choice," Blaine said. "But this is her wedding day. I don't think this will be the day she'll want to take them on. They had their chance to deal with this before now. I'm going to talk to her while you talk to Graham."

"She doesn't know? About any of it?"

Blaine shook his head. "I wasn't sure until this morning."

Roan nodded and turned to go again, but Shay asked Blaine, "What is it we're supposed to do with them? Katie's parents, I mean. Do you have a course of action?"

"It depends on whether they stay until she returns."

"They'd come all this way and not stay to see her?"

"They're coming all this way to prevent a wedding. Once that plan is thwarted, I doubt they'll see any real reason to stick around."

"That's pretty cold-blooded," Roan said.

Blaine smiled, but it wasn't like any smile Roan had seen on his typically amicable face thus far. In fact, it was downright chilling.

"Welcome to our world," he said.

"I'm beginning to see why you came here."

"If we can just get the two of them married and off to the Cotswolds, then I think the problem will resolve itself. For now, anyway."

Roan just shook his head. "Hell of a resolution."

Shay shook his head, too, but his tone was far more fatalistic. "I've seen worse."

"And people wonder why I have no desire to leave this place," Roan muttered as they exited the abbey, his thoughts on one person in particular.

Chapter 10

Less than twenty minutes later, Roan and Shay were standing proudly beside their best mate as he awaited his bride. Graham hadn't taken the news of the impending arrival of the senior McAuleys at all well, but Blaine had been right in guessing that when faced with disrupting Katie's wedding day—again—the option of a weekend in the English countryside had taken on a better shine.

The helicopter had made quite a stir with everyone. He and Shay had passed the word to Eliza that it was a honeymoon surprise. As expected, she had quickly set the gossip mill into action. The news had the women in the crowd swooning at the romance of it, and the men envious of the hot ride.

Despite being distracted by the latest turn of events, Roan automatically searched out Tessa to watch her work. She was lithe, graceful, and surprisingly unobtrusive. Aye, there were several hundred folks trampling the meadow grasses—the whole of the island had turned out for the happy occasion—but Tessa's focus was on the bride, groom, and their small wedding party.

"Katie'll miss the reception," Graham muttered to Roan. "Worked hard on it, she did. Wanted it just right for everyone."

Roan noted that Graham didn't seem too choked up by the same loss. "We'll throw another party when you return. I'm sure everyone will be quite happy to continue the celebration today as planned. Tessa can get it all on film."

"That is if it's no' still going on when you return," Shay murmured.

Roan smiled, then caught Tessa's gaze as she moved behind Father Maddy to capture the crowd. She paused, too, the camera she'd been about to aim hanging still for a moment.

She'd avoided him since their interlude the day of the rehearsal. Not that she'd been all that social prior to that, but she'd been all but nonexistent in public since. Her retreat didn't surprise him, but it hadn't, as yet, deterred him. He wasn't retreating from the field that easily. He knew from asking the most casual questions of Katie that Tessa had been in touch with her on last-minute ceremony discussions.

All that had done was alert Katie to the fact that there might have been another as yet untold part to his story that Kira had rejected him. It had been a half truth at best, but one he thought would put a stop to Katie's matchmaking efforts. But there had been a notably sharper look in Kira's eye and a slight edge to her tone when she'd stepped outside that afternoon to tell him they wouldn't be accompanying him. He'd thought perhaps Tessa had told her about their shared moment in the courtyard . . . but she hadn't alluded to it, and he certainly hadn't. He wondered what else Tessa might have told her.

Fortunately Katie had been a little distracted by other things and hadn't pushed the matter as she otherwise might have.

He'd intended to talk to Tessa at the reception later and at least put an end to their communication embargo, but that option appeared tentative at best. He assumed everyone would continue on with the festivities with or without the happy couple, but how much time Tessa would spend on it without the bride and groom, he couldn't be sure.

The unexpected moment they were sharing might be his only chance. And there was nothing he could do to capitalize on it. If he smiled, she'd scowl.

Instead, he simply held her gaze. Steadily, unwavering.

She didn't look away.

See, Tessa. I'm no' going anywhere.

Then a murmur rose in the crowd, followed by a round of clapping and cheers. The carriage carrying Blaine and Katie had arrived.

Roan glanced in that direction, and when he looked back again, Tessa was gone. Showtime for her.

As stunning and ethereal as Katie was with the dandified Blaine helping her down from her carriage, Roan found his attention fixed on the photographer capturing the moment—every bit as captivated by her as the crowd was with the bride.

"You've really got it bad, haven't ye?" Shay leaned over to murmur in his ear.

"Don't let Graham hear you say that," Roan said, going for the obvious joke. "He'll have my head. Though I doubt he'll start with that bit."

Shay straightened as the procession moved toward them. "I wasnae talking about the bride."

Roan shot him a quick look. "Then you're seeing things."

The tiniest bit of amusement laced Shay's deadpan expression. "Oh, aye. I see things."

Roan couldn't do much more than glance at him, because Katie was stepping up in front of Graham. To look at her, Roan would never have guessed her world had just been rocked by the news of her parents' impending arrival.

Roan glanced beyond Katie to Blaine, who had just handed her into Graham's care. Blaine gave him a brief nod. All was okay.

Good.

Roan turned to face Father Madaig as he began the ceremony. The crowd hushed. Roan had expected his thoughts would drift to Tessa, or the yacht heading toward their shores, or what to do about both of those situations. Instead he found himself truly listening to the sermon, to what Father Maddy was saying. When Graham and Katie turned to one another to recite the vows they'd written, he actually felt his heart constrict a little, and his throat went a wee bit dry.

Aye, he wanted that for himself, he did. He'd witnessed many, many weddings over the years. Granted, not as best man, and not when it was one of his best mates saying the vows. But never had he felt the way he did in that moment. As he handed the ring to Graham, he saw no fear or trepidation on his face, just the absolute joy of a man who knew he'd come into possession of the most precious gift he could receive. The smile on Katie's face, the brightest of sparks in her eyes, as Graham slid the ring onto her finger, left Roan feeling all but gutted.

He wanted what they had for his own, and had never more keenly felt the lack of it. As Katie spoke her vows in hushed but happy tones, Roan's gaze drifted of its own volition to Tessa. She was staring through the viewfinder of her camera, not paying the slightest attention to him.

Why you? he thought for the thousandth time. Why not someone like Kira? Why not any one of the dozens of other lasses that had crossed his path over the years? Why had he never, not once, felt the tug that he felt now . . . when it was directed toward a woman who wasn't simple or easy. No. Leave it to his heart to latch on to the most difficult, challenging, inconvenient woman he'd ever met.

Then briefly, she lowered the camera, and he could have sworn, even from the distance where she stood, that she looked directly at him.

But Father Maddy was announcing Graham and Katie to be man and wife, and Tessa whipped the camera back up while Roan turned to watch the two kiss as if it were the first and finest they'd ever shared. He felt a burning behind his eyes as Graham turned and embraced his best friend. Roan moved to kiss Katie's glowing cheek as Graham clapped Shay's back, then Roan and Shay stood side by side, cheering uproariously as bride and groom turned to face the likewise cheering assemblage for the first time as man and wife.

"You're a lucky, lucky bastard," Roan murmured, as he watched the two head into the crowd. Blaine got Roan's attention then and turned his finger in a circle, meaning they had to speed things up. Roan looked out past the crowd toward the shore. Sure enough, at some point during the ceremony, a very large, very sleek sailing vessel had come to anchor inside the small, calm sound just off the northern shore.

Roan moved into the crowd behind Graham and cupped his elbow. "Your company has arrived," he leaned in to say quietly. "Say your thank-yous, then let us get you to your whirly-bird."

"I've got it," Shay said to Roan. "Stay here and glad hand the crowd a bit. You're better at that. We'll leave Blaine to handle the parents."

"Aye, right then." Roan clapped Graham on the back and gave another quick hug to Katie. "Dinnae worry," he whispered in her ear. "We'll take care of everything."

She pulled back, and her gaze was nothing but pure joy. "Nothing can ruin this moment," she assured him. "Thank you for your help. We both really appreciate it."

Graham sent the crowd into a complete tizzy by scooping his bride up into his arms. "You'll excuse us," he said, a grin as wide as the brilliant blue sky splitting his rugged face, "but I believe we have a honeymoon to get on with." He turned and caught Katie's gaze, and his expression was completely swamped by his obvious adoration for his new wife.

Roan realized right then that things would be different. Yes, the two had been inseparable since Katie's arrival on the island. But the mates he'd grown up with, the bond they'd always had . . . was forever altered. He wasn't sad about it so much as bemused. What would come next?

He sought out Shay, thinking to share the philosophical moment—Shay being so overly serious he was generally stellar at those—but he was already herding the newlyweds toward a waiting car that would get them back to the abbey and the helicopter. The crowd was almost deafening, cheering and shouting, so Roan hung back and clapped and cheered along with them.

He felt a bump at his elbow, and turned to find Tessa standing next to him. "I'm torn," she said.

He was so caught off guard that he just said the first thing that came to mind. "About?"

"Whether to follow the happy couple and get their dramatic departure . . ."

"Or?"

Her gaze drifted out toward the harbor. "Or stay for what might be the better fireworks."

"You're not here as a journalist," he reminded her.

"Yeah." She smiled. "But which pictures would you rather see?"

He couldn't help it, he smiled back. "I'm still trying to understand what kind of family treats their only daughter this way." From the corner of his eye, he caught a bit of flinch on Tessa's face. It was barely more than a tic or tightening of her jaw, but he'd seen it nonetheless. He faced forward again, watching as Graham tucked Katie safely into the car, while Shay climbed in to drive them.

A movement off to his left caught his attention. It was Blaine, who'd taken one of the horses from its carriage tack and was presently and quite adeptly leveraging himself onto the beast's back. "What in the—"

Roan watched as Blaine nudged the animal and surged forward, looking quite comfortable astride. Roan supposed he'd played polo or something, given his upbringing—but what was more surprising was that he didn't appear as idiotic riding bareback in his formal wear as anyone else likely would have. "Where in the devil is he going?"

"My guess is there." Tessa directed his attention back to the sound, where a small inflatable speed boat was heading toward shore. "Rather surreal, isn't it?"

"Which part?" Roan asked.

"Which part isn't? Seriously. From what I gather, Graham

sailed off across the ocean to Annapolis and snatched a woman he'd never so much as laid eyes on from her wedding—to Blaine. Graham brought her back here for a business-only marital merger—didn't she just escape one of those?—because you all live and die by some four-hundred-year-old marriage pact law. By the time they got here, that had all changed and before you know it, they're marrying for real. You and she hook up like long lost litter mates, then Blaine shows up, but he's not trying to win back his bride. Oh no, he just wants to be her BFF and hang out." She glanced at Roan. "Unless you are all blind, you have to realize the man is as gay as the grass is green, so what was that wedding all about anyway? And now, supposedly, Mummy and Daddy dearest have arrived—too late—like some horrifyingly misguided dysfunctional cavalry, to snatch their only daughter back into the maw, but not because they're concerned about her welfare, oh no, but because her absence makes them look bad and they can't have a tarnished social reputation bring down the number of new yacht orders. Now the bride and groom are being forced to flee by helicopter to avoid that confrontation, and their gay almost-son-in-law has just taken off to confront them. On horseback."

"Well," Roan said at length, "when you put it like that . . ."

He heard a small, dramatic sigh. "So, you can see my dilemma."

"Aye." They stood for another moment as the crowd slowly dispersed after sending off the happy couple. People began to make their way toward the village, where the reception was still very much on the agenda. "Have you ever been married?"

"What?" She looked at him. "Where did that come from?"

Roan looked at her. "We're at a wedding. Not so big a leap."

"Oh. Right." Suddenly she didn't sound quite so dryly amused. "No. I haven't."

"Close calls?"

"No." She fiddled with her camera for a moment. "You?"

"No to both. No siblings?"

She looked at him as if he was being deliberately annoying.

And maybe he was. The last time he'd provoked her, they'd ended up kissing each other's brains out. So he didn't think it was entirely a bad idea to kick things off that way again.

"Why do you ask?" she replied, sounding anything other than interested in the line of questioning.

"Just . . . watching Graham get married was like watching a close member of my immediate family leave the roost, so to speak. In a good way, but a way that will forever change things. I wondered if that's how it feels when a brother or sister marries."

"I wouldn't know."

"I'd think it's close to the same. We're the closest to family we've got, all three of us."

"You're an only child?" she asked.

He smiled. "I wouldn't know."

She turned to him then, frowning in confusion. "What does that mean?"

"It means I don't know. I was abandoned as a baby. I have no idea if either of my parents ever procreated again."

Her mouth dropped open, then she shut it again. "I'm sorry."

"For what? I had a great childhood." He glanced at her. "They're right you know. It does take a village." His smile grew. "At least it did with me. But I believe I'm better for it."

"I doubted you."

"What? Why? About what?"

"Your comment about understanding being a misfit. I couldn't fathom it. You were born and raised here and are openly adored. I've never met anyone who so clearly fits his environment. So the whole misfit tag just didn't work for you. I shouldn't have judged, though. I know better."

"We all come to conclusions. That's normal. Like with me, I thought you were a bit of a snob. Maybe prima donna was a better term."

"Me? A snob?" She barked a laugh.

"It wasn't specific, more of an air, the way you carried yourself. I thought you presumed we were all backwoods bumpkins, living out here on our little scrap of earth. As if we were somehow beneath your notice."

"And I thought you were a pretty boy who got by on looks and charm and didn't have much motivation to do more than that."

Roan looked up as the helicopter flew over their heads. He waved. "Well, at least one of us was wrong."

She gave him a shot with her elbow, then lifted her camera and got a few departing shots of the whirlybird as it sailed into the sunset. "I guess that takes care of my shot selection dilemma."

"Where did you grow up?" he asked.

She lowered her camera and took aim toward the shore. The bright yellow inflatable skiff had landed. Blaine had dismounted and was waiting, legs braced, the horse standing next to him as if they'd ridden in battle together many times. It was quite the vision, what with the top hat and all.

"I sure hope he doesn't have to resort to using the cane as a weapon," Roan said conversationally.

Two people debarked from the skiff with the help of their skipper, and confronted Blaine on the small spit of sand, the waves lapping at their feet. Things appeared to get rather . . . animated.

"Even two to one, I'd put my money on him," she said, shutter whirring.

"Well, technically, he does have the horse as back up."

"True."

Roan listened as Tessa's shutter continued to whir. "So, small town? Big city?"

"I'm working."

"No, you're not. You're being nosy. I like it."

She glanced at him with a *you're impossible* look, then went back to shooting. "Big estate in a small town," she said after a few seconds.

That surprised him. Both that she'd answered, and the answer itself. "So, I wasn't far off then, after all. Woman of privilege. What does your family think of your globe-trotting job that takes you to the most dangerous places on earth?"

"I don't have a family. No, that's not entirely true. Kira is my family. I don't have any blood relatives."

"Not one?"

"Not a one. We're both little orphan Annies, it appears. Or little orphan Andrew in your case, I guess." She shot him a quick smirk.

He wasn't going to let her derail the conversation. He'd started it as idle conversation, to keep her talking to him, but he was truly intrigued. "What about the big estate part?"

"Well, my estate manager lived there with me, until I was sent off to boarding school. Overseas. The better to keep me out of the loop, don't you know. He continued to live there. At least until I was made aware that he'd filched my trust fund and invested it in some development scheme in Hong Kong. That was to cover up the fact that he'd already bilked the estate out of the rest of its assets."

"What did you do? How old were you when you found that out?"

"Seventeen. How I found out was when the school I was attending in London escorted me to the curb with all my worldly possessions. My tuition was long overdue and they'd finally determined there would never be any additional monies coming their way."

He gaped at her. "That's . . . an incredible story."

"It's a true story. I'm not sure, even in hindsight, if I'd have been equipped to handle things any differently. He was a very trusted employee and close friend of my father's at the time of my father's death. I thought he was loyal and cared about me, so I had no sense not to trust him. He was my sole legal guardian. It was a pretty easy ripoff for him, I must say. But I was too young to have any realization of that."

"How old were you when your father passed?"

"Six and a half. I was in boarding school by the time I was eight."

"What happened to him?"

"Well, when the cookie crumbled, he took off. To where, I had no idea. I had no legal representation or money to hire anyone to go after him. I lost the estate, everything. I wasn't a legal adult yet, so, fortunately, none of the debt followed me, but I was penniless and homeless. They tried to put me in a foster home, but that didn't take very well. I took off and managed to stay under their radar until I was eighteen. No one had any right to say what I did from that point on."

"He got away with it?"

She laughed. "You're so outraged."

"It's an outrageous thing to do! Leaving a young girl completely alone and destitute. The man should be strung up and have his knackers sliced off. In tiny pieces."

She pretended to flinch and it occurred to him she'd seen far worse than that.

"Remind me never to cross you," she said, still amused. "But I didn't say he got away with it, just that I couldn't go after him at the time."

"But you did. Eventually."

She nodded. "How do you think I became an investigative reporter?"

Roan grinned. "Really? Well. I rather like that story."

"So did the *London Examiner*. And the *Wall Street Journal*. And *Time magazine*. *60 Minutes* enjoyed it, too."

Roan grinned. "Well done."

She smiled, nodded in acceptance.

"So . . . you became the righter of wrongs then, is that it?"

"I became interested in exposing stories that outsiders might judge wrongly due to preconceptions."

"Like the poor little rich girl."

"Something like that."

"And the camera? When did that become the predominant thing?"

"Oh, I'd always lugged one around. I'm not even sure when that started. I was in school. And the camera was . . . like . . .

my friend. A way to see the world, judge it even, without having to be part of it, I guess. A way to grieve about my father passing, I suppose, be a little mad about it all. I was so unhappy on my own in school." She smiled briefly. "I met Kira there. It got better after that. When I started working, the pictures were the part that, for me, were telling the truer story. In a way the words—my words, anyway—were not. The words could only convey so much. The pictures were important, vital. They were what delivered the ultimate knock-out punch. That's what called to me."

He'd dug deeper into her career over the past few days as he'd struggled to come to terms with the strong feelings she provoked in him. But he hadn't dug into her childhood, or even her early career. There was so much to read about what she'd done since, he'd hadn't gotten to the point of digging that far back.

He had only about a million other questions on the tip of his tongue, but before he could choose which one to ask next, a small car came whizzing back up the single track road and stopped in a spray of rock and dirt right at the edge of the meadow.

"That's Eliza's car." Alarmed by the speed with which she'd come toward them, Roan started moving across the meadow, worried that something had happened. The chopper was long gone, so it wasn't anything to do with Graham or Katie. Probably a pub fight had broken out, or something of that sort. "What is it?" he called, as she scrambled to get her stocky girth out from behind the tight fit of the wheel. He'd never figured out why she drove the tiny thing in the first place. She'd always struck him as the type to drive a big, oversized utility vehicle. The better to intimidate folks with. "Is everything okay?"

Tessa was right behind him as they made it to the road before Eliza, still in her wedding finery, but with her bun slightly askew, had fully righted herself.

"Oh, good," she trilled, upon seeing Tessa with him. "You're both here." She waved a manila envelope at them. "We've gotten word!" She beamed at them both. "Came in on the ferry during the ceremony. It was at the office when I stopped by on my way in. We've won!" She looked as pleased and excited as a child on Christmas morning. "The calendar contest," she clarified when they both simply stared at her. "Ye've gone and done it, lad!" Her blue eyes twinkled like those of a woman half her age. "And you've snagged the best slot of them all." She smacked the envelope into Roan's chest. "*You* are Mr. December!"

Chapter 11

"It's not funny."

Kira smiled at Tessa. "Oh, I assure you, it's quite amusing."

"Well, amuse me by telling me where on earth—or on Kinloch, to be specific—we're going to get Christmas-themed photos. In September. The calendar people want at least three to choose from, preferably five. Why couldn't he have been Mr. October?"

"You don't have to have snow." Kira's smile widened. "You could always pose him in front of a roaring fire wearing nothing more than St. Nick's velvety red stocking cap."

It did not improve Tessa's mood in the slightest that her traitorous mind immediately latched onto that visual like she was a sex-starved fiend. Which she wasn't. Okay, so the sex-starved part might have been a tad close to the truth. But she took umbrage at the fiend part. Except, ever since the wedding, her imagination had taken on rather fiendish tendencies.

She'd spent the past two days printing wedding pictures . . . and the nights imagining a variety of calendar poses that would make even Kira blush. Most of those poses required . . . assistance. She envisioned him tugging her down in front of that fire, rolling her to her back on that fur rug, plunging his hands into her hair, his tongue into her mouth. She'd rise up to meet his thrust . . . Or she'd roll him over and ride him, the firelight sparking a halo around her red hair, his hips pistoning from the floor, showcasing the lean muscles in his thighs, the cut of muscle in his shoulders and biceps . . . She could frame him again, and again, and again, and there would never be a bad angle.

The only advantage of it all was that she hadn't suffered a nightmare in almost a week. Not since he'd kissed her out in the courtyard and distracted her every waking thought. She wasn't sleeping any more soundly, but if she had to choose, waking in an adrenaline rush caused by dreams of Roan playing his own Highland version of a sexy Santa beat the hell out of the reasons she normally woke up in a hot sweat.

"When's the deadline?" Kira asked as she bent her head back to the basket she was weaving.

Tessa blinked away images of naked Santa Roan and leaned against the framed entryway to the studio. She and Kira had both risen early. Tessa had been in the dark room since before sunrise, largely due to the very vivid naked Roan dreams she'd been having. When she'd heard Kira rustling about, she'd come out to get her friend's input on the latest inconvenience. "Two weeks. They're scheduled to go to press mid-October for an early November delivery. Apparently that's high season for calendar sales."

"Makes sense. Holiday shopping."

Tessa nodded. "The winners each get paid a fee for being included. Roan said all along he planned to funnel any income he derived back into the island economy. His bigger hopes are that the information about Kinloch he'll include in his bio will drive tourists here."

"That would be a very Roan thing to do," Kira said, sounding pleased.

It was on the tip of Tessa's tongue to ask her a few questions about Roan, just random curiosity stuff. What he'd been like as a kid, how it had really been for him being raised here with no immediate family.

"Being the last man in the calendar is good, I suppose," Kira said, "Keeps him in the public's eye longer that way. Unless they don't read his bit until it's his turn."

"Didn't you hear? Traditionally, Mr. December is always the cover guy."

Kira grinned and hooted. "Really! I bet that set his knickers into a knot."

Tessa didn't rightly know. She'd read the contents of the envelope while Roan was explaining his ideas for marketing, then she'd handed it all off to him and they'd agreed to discuss the photos they needed to take after Graham and Katie returned to allow her to finish their wedding photos. "I'll admit I've enjoyed a few amused smiles picturing his face when he got to that part."

"You weren't there? Pity. We might have gotten pictures of the moment."

Tessa's smile grew. "Now I wish I'd stuck around. He did tell me he wants to incorporate baskets into the shoot. You do some of the most innovative work on the island, so I told him you'd be happy to let me use your work in the shoot. I hope you don't mind."

Kira looked sincerely stunned. "Really? But my work is so . . . untraditional. Maybe you should stick with samples of what we've done for the past couple hundred years instead."

"I'll have a sampling. At least that's my plan. Roan knows all the weavers and I'm sure they'll be happy to contribute. But I definitely want yours in there. They have the most visual appeal."

Kira snorted. "Like anyone is going to be looking at the baskets."

"Again, you have a point," she said, grinning, "but, hopefully, when they flip the very last page to the bios, they'll read about Roan's lifelong work promoting the centuries-old Kinloch craft trade, and they'll go back to the picture and look at them. When they do, I'd like them to be looking at your work."

Kira sat back for a moment, but her surprised expression eventually turned to one of satisfied pleasure. "Okay."

"Okay? Just like that? You're not going to freak out on me later, or anything, are you?"

"I've decided I need to start thinking beyond my four walls here and the den of security I've made out of my weaving studio. It's become a place to hide now."

"What made you decide that?"

"I've thought a lot about our talk, what you said, about my no' socializing. And Roan's perception of me as someone who's not healthy and whole yet."

Tessa's regard sharpened at that.

"Dinnae worry, I've no' decided to set my sights on him. He's all yours."

Tessa merely gave her a quelling look. "Who says I want him? God knows, you're healthier and more together than I am. He's all yours for the taking."

"Right," Kira said dryly. "Now who's living in denial?" She went on before Tessa could reply. "But that whole conversation did get me to thinking, and . . . maybe it's time."

"For?"

"Making my move."

Tessa's eyes widened. "Really. Are you going to tell me who the lucky man is?"

Kira laughed. "Oh, I'm not ready to make those kind of moves. I'm just talking about stepping out into the world for more than milk and weaving supplies. And maybe thinking about my weaving as more than just therapy."

"Roan said you've been talking about pushing more innovative designs and incorporating other nontraditional materials."

"When did he tell you that?"

"When I was trying to convince him to make his move on you."

"Oh. Well . . . did he say anything about whether he thought my ideas were good?" She looked so uncertain, which was impossible for Tessa to fathom. Kira had always been the one with a natural direction, she always seemed to know where to step next, even when it was in a direction she hadn't planned. It was hard to see her so insecure. She'd always been naturally gifted.

"Roan seemed really intrigued by your ideas. Since when don't you have faith in your own skills?"

"Since I found out I sucked at being a wife," she said with surprising bluntness. "I thought I was a pretty damn good one. It's made me question everything." She held up a hand. "I'm not angling for a pity party, okay? Or a therapy session. I've dealt with it—I have—but even putting things in proper perspective, there's still fallout. As far as I've come in reconciling and laying blame where it belongs, there's still a process I have to go through. With everything, it seems. The more important and secure I should be about something, the more I worry. I don't want to be wrong again, or unable to see the obvious for what it is."

"Then I don't need to tell you that, without even hearing the gritty details of why you and Thomas are no longer man and wife, I can state unequivocally that it wasn't because you sucked. At anything, especially weaving. Or being a friend. Or anything else you set your mind to."

Kira looked at her for a long moment, then pushed back from the work table, crossed the small studio to where Tessa hung in the doorway, and hugged her. Tightly.

Tessa immediately hugged her back. It felt good. Grounding. Rejuvenating to her spirit—which made her aware all over again of how bereft of human contact she'd been. And still was. Despite the very human contact she'd had with Roan, it wasn't something that was part of her daily experience, nor had it been for a long time.

Her therapists had discussed it with her, told her she should get weekly massages, even a pedicure or having her hair washed in a local salon. That seemed ridiculous to Tessa, but they'd assured her it was part of her healing process. It was imperative Tessa get back in touch with herself. To do so, she had to let other people touch her. If she couldn't handle touching on a personal, intimate level, with friends, family, a lover, whatever, then she could start with impersonal touching. It took away the risk, the vulnerability, and the obligation to return the favor. But it was an important step.

Tessa had said she would. But she hadn't. She'd done everything else they'd told her to do, but touching hadn't seemed a particularly productive use of her time, and she'd never worked it into her schedule. The truth was that it had felt rather pathetic. The only way she could get a little human contact was to pay someone to wash her hair or rub her back?

Standing in the midst of a heartfelt, very personal human contact moment, she was crucially aware that it wasn't just the warm fuzzies of connecting with a friend that was making an impact on her, but the simplicity of the touch itself. It really didn't take much to make a difference. So . . . maybe she should have made time.

Hugging Kira made her feel very alone. Or, at the very least, she recognized the person she'd been when she'd arrived on the island was even more cut off and isolated than she'd realized. She'd tried to deny the truth of it, just as her instinct was to shrug off what she was feeling at the moment. Less risk that way. But she wanted the contact—hugging and being hugged. She wanted friends. She wanted more. She wanted a simple, heartfelt hug, from someone who mattered—and for it not to feel so monumentally abnormal.

Maybe she hadn't scheduled in the massages and the pedicures for that reason. She'd been afraid of wanting more. She'd been afraid that wanting and needing, but not knowing how to get it, might have pushed her over the edge—possibly right on the massage table. She hadn't been willing to risk another humbling mortification. She'd been feeling humbled enough, thank you, just going through counseling.

But she had to think about the possibility. Confront it. Deal with it. No longer was it some ambiguous want or need, but a specific one—hard to deny.

Kira stepped back and her cheeks were suspiciously wet. Immediately Tessa felt like a jerk. "I didn't mean to make you feel bad," she said. "I was trying to tell you that you're awesome."

"You didn't make me feel bad. You hugged me just now. Tightly. And . . . it was brilliant. It made me feel great." She sniffled a little, even as she choked on a bubble of sincere laughter. "It did for you, too, didn't it?"

Tessa's shoulders fell a little. Had they both really had it so bad that a hug was like a small miracle? She knew the answer to that, but it was mortifying to have her weaknesses exposed to someone she cared about. It made no sense since the someone she cared about was probably the one person who wouldn't judge, and could possibly even help. But, it just felt . . . hard. To feel like a failure in front of the one person she wanted to think well of her. "It did," she said, a bit horrified to hear the choke in her own throat. She wasn't going to cry. Not now, not ever if she could help it.

She'd come a very long way in her healing process, but she knew, without a doubt, if she ever let the tears come, she would shatter into a million pieces.

"I need more of that," she said, trying on the truth, then feeling the overwhelming need to escape. Baby steps, she told herself. She shouldn't be ashamed if she needed to take baby steps. It was better than no steps. "I'm going to let you get back to work. I need to keep on with the wedding photos. The happy couple is due back late tonight and I want to have a decent sampling to show them."

If Kira understood her retreat for the escape it really was, she didn't push it. And for that, Tessa was almost as profoundly grateful as she'd been for the hug.

"Pot roast for supper later. I'll want to put it on to stew in a bit." Kira said, smiling warmly. "You're on vegetable duty."

"Deal," Tessa said, already backing out of the doorway. "Just tap on the door when it's time for me to come out."

"I will."

But before she could make a full retreat, there came a tapping on the outside door. She and Kira traded surprised looks. She hadn't even heard a car or truck.

"I'll get it," Kira said. "Go ahead and—"

Hide, was the word that came immediately to Tessa's mind.

Another rap on the door. "Tessa," came a voice through the door. "It's me, Roan. Could you step out for a moment? Or can I come in?"

Kira glanced from Tessa to the front door, and back to Tessa. "Want me to ask him to come back another time?"

Tessa truly did feel ashamed. Clearly Kira thought she was some fragile flower. And maybe she was. But she'd been pretty good at not letting other people see her vulnerability.

"No," she said, when what she'd wanted to do was fall on the ground in abject gratitude for the save. It was for that very reason that she declined Kira's offer. "I'll go talk to him."

Kira looked sincerely surprised. "You're sure?"

Anyone else she'd have snapped at for getting too close to the truth. But not Kira. "No, I've never been less sure," she said, going with blunt honesty again. It was a bit less mortifying the second time. "We're not hiders anymore, right?"

Kira smiled. "No. We're no' hiders anymore. We're bold and we're out there and we're no' taking any prisoners."

"Badass non-hiders. That's what we are."

Kira snickered. "Exactly."

"Totally." They both tried to pull that off for another second, then laughed at themselves. "Sadly pathetic, that's what we really are," Tessa said, shaking her head.

"Yeah, but no one else has to know."

Tessa shot her a look over her shoulder. "Right." Except she knew she would be opening it to the one other person who somehow would know. Lovely.

"I can still tell him to go away."

"No," Tessa said, girding herself. "We have to build our asses up to the badness level at some point. But thank you." She shot her friend a smile. "I'm going to be expecting you to live up to the badass end of the non-hider bargain, so don't even think about backing down when it's your turn."

"Wouldn't dare."

"You would totally dare. So, fair warning."

Kira smiled. "Warning received." She made a shooing motion with her hand as Roan knocked again.

"Tessa—"

"Don't get your kilt in a knot, Mr. December," Tessa called out. "I'm coming."

"You tell him, badass," Kira said behind her as Tessa exited the studio.

Tessa smiled at that as she crossed the main room to the door. She paused with her hand on the doorknob and took a steadying breath. She couldn't seem to be around the guy without either pouring out her life story or throwing herself at him and shoving her tongue down his throat. She couldn't keep doing that. Either of those things. He had way too much of an edge over her already, and giving him more pieces of her puzzle was not the way to create a defined space between them. And that's what she wanted. That's what she needed.

A defined space between them that would allow her to figure out what she wanted to do next where he was concerned.

She opened the door. He grinned at the sight of her, the full dimple treatment. And her heart fluttered.

Yeah. That wasn't a good sign.

She put her hand on the frame, blocking entry. "Why are you here at the crack of dawn, banging on the door?"

Her attitude didn't so much as make him blink. If anything,

an amused twinkle lit his green eyes. "I'm on to you, you know," he said, as if he'd been reading her mind. She wasn't entirely sure he couldn't.

"Goodie. We're trying to work. In peace and quiet."

"I came in peace. And I can be quiet, if given proper motivation."

Then he did something that shocked her as much as it had the first time he'd done it. He leaned right in and kissed her. Had she guessed he'd even been thinking about it, surely she'd have blocked him. Surely.

Instead, he'd just moved in and kissed her. Just like that. Before she could gather her wits, he slid his hand under her hair and cupped her neck, pulling her mouth that much more intimately beneath his.

She blamed her lack of fight on being blindsided. Well, that and having spent the past two nights imagining him in various Mr. December poses. All of them requiring him to be naked. Any red-blooded woman would have responded. Right?

"Kiss me back, Tessa."

She shouldn't. What she should do was knee him. Make it perfectly clear in the most painful way possible that he didn't just get to lean in and kiss her. Not without her permission. Until further notice, she needed to make it clear she was off limits to him, to his charm, and most definitely his hands and mouth.

But was that what a badass non-hider would do?

Was she making space, setting ground rules? Or was it another form of her ducking and hiding? He said he was on to her. He knew she'd retreat if given half a chance. So maybe what a badass non-hider would do was give him what he wanted. But on her terms. He wanted her to kiss him back? Look out. She gripped his face and attempted to do just that and take control of the kiss.

But he was having none of that.

To her shock, he tugged her into his arms, pulled the door

shut behind her, then pinned her up against it. "I didn't say take over. Or make it about lust. Kiss *me*, Tessa."

"What gave you the impression I wanted you to come barging in here and shove your tongue in my mouth?"

He leaned in and kissed her chin. Then he kissed the tip of her nose, then her forehead. Each kiss was impossibly sweet. "I'm no' barging. And my tongue hasn't been at all involved. Yet. I'm merely kissing ye. It's fun. Try it with me."

"Don't patronize me," she said, but he kept up the gentle assault, and it was hard to maintain any sense of outrage. Especially when she wasn't shoving him off of her, and her body was wanting to go all pliant and warm.

"Kiss me back, Tessa," he urged her again. The plea was playful, but there was a tension in his body. His hard body. Pinning hers to the door.

He was confusing her. She didn't understand how to combat that kind of attack on her defenses. She didn't want to be any more vulnerable to him than she already was. But the other truth was . . . she did want to kiss him back. So much so that it simply couldn't be wise for her to give in to the desire.

He kissed her mouth, then the side of her jaw, then nudged her chin so he could reach the side of her neck. She sighed, and could feel him smile as he kissed her beneath her ear, then bit, gently, into the lobe. He made her knees weak, and her head swim. That couldn't be the smart choice. Smart was staying in control. Smart was calling the shots. Smart was being in charge of her emotions and not letting them be in charge of her.

He kept kissing her. Softly, so tenderly. Not only was it decimating any defenses she might have put up, it was also the most erotic seduction she'd ever been the focus of. How was that possible? He wasn't heated, or groping, or taunting her in any of the ways they'd taunted each other the last time. Sweet seduction was far more lethal. It was about more than simple— or even complex—lust. Sweet and gentle implied affection.

She wasn't sure she could handle being the object of anyone's affection. Had, in fact, spent most of the past two years—consciously or not—making sure no one would view her affectionately. It would undo the hard edge she'd worked so hard . . . so very, very hard, to build. It was survival mode. She couldn't be soft and pliant, needy or wanting . . . not if she had any hope of maintaining the solid, objective front necessary for her job.

A job you don't have any more.

Or rather, one she could no longer perform. And that wasn't Roan McAuley's doing.

But shouldn't she be more sorted out before letting herself go . . . and definitely before involving anyone else in the equation? Wasn't that why she'd stepped back after their last interlude? Clearly he hadn't gotten the message. Just because she'd talked to him at the wedding, didn't give him the right to—

"Stop," he told her, his lips still on the side of her neck.

"Stop what?" she said, surprised to hear how breathless she was. All she was doing was allowing him the most wicked access to the side of her neck and the curve of her shoulder. Maybe his hands had ridden up the sides of her waist a little. And maybe, just maybe, she was aching for him to cup them over her breasts.

"Trying to build up that wall. Brick by mental brick," he said.

"What?" She blinked her eyes open, which was when she realized she'd let them flutter shut at some point.

"I can hear the battle raging in there," he said, lifting one hand to trace a small circle on her temple. Then he drew it down along the side of her face, over her neck, and along her collar bone.

She wanted to sigh. She wanted to moan. "It's not that simple," she said, closing her eyes again.

"It's exactly that simple," he said, then tipped her chin down, so their faces were nose to nose. "Tessa."

She opened her eyes. "For you it's simple. Not for me. You'll have to take my word on that. I can't afford to get all tangled up."

"It's a simple kiss."

"Not with you. Last time I tried to make it just a kiss, you made it clear you were looking for more than a roll in the heather. And that's fine. But then it can't be with me. That's why I stepped back and put some distance between us."

"Until the wedding."

"It was a simple conversation."

"That you started."

She sighed. "Fine. But for me, it was just conversation. You can want what you want, but I don't have time or room in my life for more. I don't. I've tried to make that clear. By not encouraging more of . . . this."

He stroked his fingertips along her cheekbone, along her jaw, then slid them back into her hair. The tingling sensation his touch sent skittering over her skin was entrancing.

"Have ye given thought to the photos we're to take, then?"

She blinked again. "What?"

"The photos. For the calendar. Business, no' pleasure."

She tried to swat at his hand. "The calendar? Is that why you're here? What's all this then?" She shoved at him.

"We need to discuss the calendar, so if you're not willing to discuss . . . this, then we can talk business instead."

She scowled at him. "Right. Easy come, easy go. So much for sticking with it."

"Hardly easy." He let go and stepped back. "I'm not going anywhere. I'm still standing right here." He slid his hands in his trouser pockets and rocked back on his heels. His expression was still open, the knowing twinkle in his eye still on full display. "You're a tough woman, Tessa, but you know that. You're also a tender, soft, sweet, and incredibly delicious woman."

He said things that were so unexpected. He'd caught her off guard again and she said the first thing that came to her. "I don't know what on earth gave you that idea." But, rather than a dismissive comeback, it almost came out as a question.

He smiled and the dimple flashed. "Well, I have firsthand experience on the last part. If you were really as hard as you want people to believe, you wouldn't be so worried about my feelings. And you definitely wouldn't be at all concerned about your own."

"Who says I have feelings?"

"You just said you can't afford to get all tangled up. I dinnae think ye were talking about our legs." He slid his hands from his pockets. "What would be so tragic about havin' feelings anyway, is what I want to know?"

"I've got bigger things to worry about right now."

"Two heads are better than one. You don't have to solve everything by yourself."

"I'm not staying on Kinloch," she said, all but daring him to have a snappy comeback for that one.

"When are you leaving?"

She stumbled. "I-I'm not staying," she reiterated. That much was true.

"How long before you have to go back?"

"Why does that matter? All that matters is that, at some point in the not too distant future, I won't be here. And this is where you'll stay."

"Answer me one thing."

She wished she felt more confident about agreeing, but she honestly had no idea what he was going to ask. "What?" she said instead, remaining noncommittal.

"If the job wasn't an issue, and whatever these things you have that are distracting you from having a life—"

"I have a life."

"You have a career."

She faltered on that, and looked down to avoid him seeing anything she couldn't afford for him to see. She *had* a career. She didn't know what else she had.

"Tessa." Just her name, spoken so sincerely, so . . . quietly. "If you had a life, you wouldn't be here, trying to find one."

"I can't stay here."

He shifted his weight forward, but didn't crowd her. When he lifted his hand and lightly touched her jaw, she didn't move away. "Where do you have to go?"

"Wherever the next story takes me."

"You're going back to it then."

"What would make you think I wouldn't? It's what I do."

"So, the burnout you were talking about—a few weeks on a remote Scottish isle, and you're good as new? If it's nothing more than that, then why all the drama?"

She was suddenly tired, so very tired—of defending herself, of arguing, of trying to make him believe . . . something she already knew wasn't true. "I just want to be left alone to figure it out. Is that too much to ask?"

"No, no, it's not." He moved the smallest fraction of an inch, the way one might when dealing with a cornered tiger. No sudden moves. "But Tessa, you've been alone for a long time. You said as much yourself. You haven't figured it out so far. Maybe if you want a different result, you need to change the formula."

"Why are you doing this?" she asked quite seriously.

"Doing what, exactly?"

"Prodding me, provoking me, not leaving me the hell alone? It can't be a roundabout way to get me into bed, because you know you could have had that without any of the work. You want more, you say, though God knows why. I say I can't. And you . . . you just don't leave."

"Have you ever had someone want to be a friend to ye?"

She snorted. "We're hardly capable of friendship. Not by itself, anyway. We're . . . combustible."

"Okay," he said, with a shameless grin, "best friends, then. Best kind I know."

She shook her head and turned around, determined to go

back inside the croft. He could find someone else to take his stupid Santa pictures. No more talking in circles with him. No more talking, period. It was confusing her. He was confusing her. She didn't need confusion, she needed clarity.

He didn't stop her, but he did step up close behind her as she put her hand on the doorknob. He wasn't touching her, but she could feel the warmth of his breath right beside her ear. "You make it damn hard for anyone to get close enough to be anything to you. Everyone needs people."

"I have people. I have Kira."

She heard him sigh. A sigh of defeat? Why was it that her instantaneous reaction was disappointment? What the hell kind of perverse game was she playing with him? And worse, with herself? She prided herself on being direct, and she'd have sworn that was exactly what she was being with him.

But was she being direct with herself?

"Do you want to go back?" he asked. "To the job you left behind?"

"More than anything in the world," she answered, as fervently as she'd said anything. As she said it, she realized it was a different truth from before. She wanted to go back to her old life, meaning the life she had when she could handle the life she had. But did she *really* want to go back? To what that life truly was?

"Okay, then," he said. "I willnae bother you. No' like this anyway."

"Like this what?"

"This is selfish. Because I want you. I don't even know why, exactly, but I do, Tessa. You completely and utterly command my full attention. Without even trying. Clearly," he added with a harsh laugh, "you've done everything but shoot at me."

Her heart was pounding Why was he saying those things? Why couldn't he just go away? And stop confusing her? Making her feel things and think about things she didn't want to know, feel, or think about.

"So I'll stop beggin' ye. I'd like to think I have some pride," he said, the wry note tempered by true disappointment. "But that doesnae mean I canno' be your friend. I know, I know, ye have Kira, and shouldn't we all be so lucky as that? Ye could have no one better in your corner. No' even me. But, Tessa . . ."

She could have gone inside the house at any time. He wouldn't have stopped her. "What?"

"As ye go forward, back to your world, your job, your stories . . . ye'll burn out again unless you make changes."

She wanted to snort. If he only knew.

"You need friends. More than one. And no' just to lean on in the tough times. You need to be a friend. You need to expand beyond being an observer only. It'll ruin ye, ye have to know that, to sense that, ye ken?"

She turned to face him, and he was deep inside her personal space. Again. That time she wanted him there. Wanted to understand him, like she would try to understand the enemy . . . and the target. In all of her stories she worked to understand both sides, then conclude the most honest way to portray that view to the world.

"What makes you think you know anything? About me? About what I do, about how it affects me?"

"I've spent some time, looking at your work, reading your words. I know we're all built differently, but I don't know how anyone but the hardest of souls could subject themselves to recording what you do, with as much heart and sensitivity as you show—" He broke off, his expression changed.

She didn't know what she'd just revealed, but clearly something.

"You don't think you're sensitive? Tessa no one—*no one*— could see what you see when you look through your lens to the world, without caring. Without feeling. Like in Phuket, after the tsunami. The devastation was . . . beyond comprehension. There was that shot you took of the mother standing at the edge of what had been her home, her village, holding the hand of her child. All you saw was the back of them, their bare legs, bare feet, ragged clothes, no facial expression to move you, just the grip she had on that little boy's hand. His grip on the beaten up photo of his brothers and sisters. All of them gone. A sea of ruin in front of them . . . and all of it framed by the larger picture of what can only be described as paradise. You can't no' feel, no' have a knot in your belly, lookin' at that. The personal pain, the national tragedy, the stunning beauty."

He swallowed and she could see the emotions on his face waging war. "That was early on, when you'd just begun. You were so young, to have such a deep focus, such instincts. Those instincts remained clear and true as you grew. Your article on the human trafficking of Mongol women . . . the photos, how stark their lives were, why they were so susceptible to the head-hunters, and the unspeakable things that happened to them. The young son—seven years old—of the woman whose story was the framework of your piece . . . his was the purest face of innocence I've ever seen, then watching the change in him, in his eyes, as he's finally shown, unflinchingly, what had happened to his mother . . ." Roan closed his eyes for a moment, then opened them again. "How do you look into that face and not feel?"

He held her gaze then and there was something so stark there, she couldn't look away.

"So, no, I dinnae know you well, but I'm human. I know how just seeing those few shots affected me, photos of places I've never been to, never seen, of people I don't know and will never know. I'm no' the one there, seeing it unfold live, making the choices you're making, which means having a much deeper level of understanding of what's going on. And what will continue to go on long after you put that camera away."

She looked away, because he was taking her to places, mentally, that she'd been working hard to steer clear of.

Gently, very gently, he tipped her chin up. "I see you here, working to find your way back. To what, I don't know. I don't know that you do, either. But the bottom line is, I don't have to know. I can see, with my own eyes, where you are now. This isn't just a break, or a little burnout, is it, Tessa?"

"It's not your business, Roan," she said roughly.

"Then let me make it my business. Even if your time here is short, if you do find your way back let me help you with that. Let me be a friend. That can't be a bad thing, even for a short time."

"You don't get it all. I can't let myself feel. Anything. And friends demand feelings." She cupped his cheek when he would have spoken, for once surprising him into silence. "I've been a bitch to you. Because you scare me. You challenge me and I can't handle it. I can't. Or I won't. But I appreciate that you chose me to befriend, chose me to concern yourself with, though I'll likely never understand why. If it's not just about the sex, then—"

"I'm attracted to you. You're attracted to me. Look at us, we're all wrapped around each other because we're like two force fields or something. Maybe that makes it too combustible for you. I get that, but it doesn't stop me from wanting to help you anyway."

"Why?" she asked, honestly stymied.

"Because, when you smiled that first time, during the photo shoot for the calendar, it transformed you. You've smiled a bit more since. While you were shooting the wedding, you were more relaxed than I've seen you yet. And maybe the longer you're here, distracted from the world you left behind, you'll find it a more natural thing to do. That can't be a bad thing. For you. Specifically, for you.

"If you could see what's in your eyes, Tessa. You're angry, and you're defensive—understandable on both counts—but your eyes . . . they're . . . they're haunted. Then you smile like that and the shadows disappear and I'm captivated by that woman who's in there, behind the shadows, behind the fear."

She didn't know what to say to any of that. Much less how

to feel about it. "I'm the one with the trained eye. And yet you see things . . ." She trailed off. "I don't get you. I don't get this. People don't do this. Not without an agenda."

"Some people do. Not everyone has an agenda."

"They do in my world."

"Then maybe you should spend a little more time in mine."

Chapter 12

It wasn't like the last time they'd stood in that exact spot. Then he'd had no real sense of what—or who—he wanted. Well, he had, but he hadn't fully admitted it to himself, much less made a decision on what to do about it or how to handle it.

After significant time spent thinking about it, he knew exactly who he wanted and what he intended to do about it. He was going to find a way to lower Tessa's defenses. Shatter them if possible. Kissing her right off had seemed like the way to go. Or maybe it was just that, when she opened the door, kissing her was all he could think about.

He shouldn't be surprised that she was doing her damnedest to shove him away, but she was going to have to shove a bit harder. If she wasn't willing to accept his advances man to woman, so be it. For a while, anyway. He'd need a bit more convincing before he agreed that the spark between them wasn't worth pursuing. Limitations be damned. But that didn't mean he had to give up becoming her friend. From where he stood, she could use a few more of those.

"Let's go for a drive," he said. That had been part of his plan, too. Actually, that had *been* his plan. All of the rest . . . seemed to happen when they got within two feet of each other.

"Drive? The island isn't that big. We could almost jog it."

"I thought we could scout locations for the calendar photographs."

"Is there snow somewhere on Kinloch that I'm not aware of?"

He smiled. "We'll improvise. Come on, if nothing else, it gets us out and away from whatever is on our respective desks and—"

"I was hoping to get more of the wedding photos developed and put together to give to Katie and Graham when they get back tonight. I still have a ton to go through."

"I dinnae think that will be the first thing they'll be thinking about the moment they return. Surely the photos can wait one more day. You and I have a more critical deadline. We can get out, drive a bit, and brainstorm on how to meet the needs of the calendar people."

"You're awfully pushy for someone who's basically bumming a favor off me in the first place."

"That's why I'm good at my job."

"What, exactly, is your job, anyway?"

He backed slowly away from her and the door, snagging her hand at the last possible second, and tugged her forward. "Come with me and I'll explain while we drive."

"Better be a short conversation. We'll have lapped the island twenty minutes from now."

"See," he said, "then it won't take up much of your precious time."

"You're incorrigible." But she let him pull her with him to his lorry.

"Yet another good attribute to have in my line of work."

"I should go tell Kira I'm taking off."

"She's weaving, aye?"

Tessa nodded.

"She willnae even know you're gone, most likely."

The truth of that was clear on Tessa's face. He grinned, and added, "Stop trying so bloody hard to come up with a reason to no' spend time out of your cave, conversing with the little people."

"You're hardly the little people."

His grin spread even wider as he opened the passenger door. "Glad you noticed."

"I'm not keeping my own company because I think you or the other islanders are somehow beneath my notice and you know it."

"I do know it, which is why I'm working so hard here to get you to come out and play. To remind you of that, too."

"I like it in my cave."

"And you can go straight back to it when we're done. A friend would get you out of your darkroom isolation at least part of the time, show you what you're missing, remind you that being in the land of the living, with other living things, is no' so bad after all."

She climbed into the lorry, a bit of a scowl on her face. "Why couldn't you have decided to do this with Kira? Latch on to her. She could use a friend. One just like you, for that matter."

"She can come along next time."

She shot him a quelling look. "You're missing the point."

He grinned. "I know." He closed the door and he scooted around to the other side before she could get out and stalk back inside the croft. He even understood her consternation. If Graham, or Shay, or anyone else had tried such heavy-handed tactics with him when he wanted to be left alone, he'd be doing a lot more than scowling and grumbling. But the fact was, he had a Shay and a Graham in his life. And a Katie—even a Blaine. Not to mention a couple hundred other people, who reminded him, daily, why it was he lived there and loved being there, even on those days—especially, maybe, on those days—when he questioned everything.

In the end, he could grumble and scowl all he wanted. It wouldn't stop Graham, or Shay, or even Katie, from doing what they thought was best for him. That's what friends did. And he always got that—at some point.

He climbed in the driver's side and closed the door, glancing over at Tessa as he settled himself and turned the key in the ignition. Arms folded, gaze set straight ahead, she was quite obviously intent on merely putting up with his shenanigans only as long as it took to get right back again.

He put the truck into gear. "Oh, you'll want your camera." He shifted back to park, but she was already hopping out. "Wait, I can—"

"It's just in the back of Kira's car. I was out yesterday . . . using it." She reached in the driver's side and popped the boot on the small Fiat, grabbed a padded black canvas gear bag, then shut it and climbed back in the truck.

He wanted to ask her what she'd been shooting, anything to strike up a conversation, thinking maybe getting her talking about her passion would be a good idea. But she was already settled once again, gaze straight ahead, arms folded, her shield up. He supposed he should be happy when she'd gotten out to grab her camera that she hadn't raced back into the croft and locked the door. No, she'd come along. Grudgingly. But she'd come along.

He smiled to himself as he backed out of the courtyard and onto the track road. *Fine,* he thought, that was fine. For a start. He'd just do his damnedest to make sure by the time they got back, she'd have had a bit of a break, seen some lovely sights, and perhaps had a chance to chat a bit. Blow off steam, ask questions, or just get outside her own head for a few minutes. He was bold enough and arrogant enough to think it would do her good.

Guess they were going to find out.

He took the northern track, away from the village and into the higher elevations at the other end of the island, where the fortress was nestled between the biggest peaks, and the flax crops grew in the protected valley below.

"So," she said, a few minutes into the drive, "tell me about your job."

A quick glance proved she was still sitting, arms folded, staring out the front, certainly not looking at him. But she was instigating the conversation. He appreciated the effort.

Maybe it was the journalist in her, maybe she was truly curious about him, or maybe she was simply killing time. It didn't matter.

"The kind of weaving we do here is a traditional, but unique, form of basketry that uses a spun linen thread, made from the flaxseed plant, then waxed in order to give it a binding texture. The threads come in various ply widths and are dyed in a number of colors, all natural dyes from organic material here on the island. The various ply widths, the range of colors, along with other organic material like handmade beads, willow branches, pine needles, can all be woven into the intricate patterns.

"There are baskets, bowls, trays. Initially they were strictly for functional use, and were just one of many kinds of weaving done on Kinloch. Many people might still use waxed linen woven trays and baskets that way, but they are small, and retain a certain flexibility because they're made of thread rather than reed or willow. It is very much an artisan craft now, popular mainly as collectible works of folk art. Many are considered gallery quality, even museum quality. Our baskets now are far from the cruder weaving done by our forebears centuries ago. But one thing that hasn't changed is that if you buy a Kinloch basket, much like if you buy Harris tweed, you are guaranteed a product that is one hundred percent handmade, including the thread from which it's woven, created on this island, in the home of the weaver, using only organic material found and processed on Kinloch."

Tessa nodded. "Kira has told me a lot about the history. It's fascinating that the craft has sustained itself all these years. Amazing, really. How did you get involved in marketing the baskets? How was it done before you came along?"

"Historically, being so remote, we relied on word of mouth, mostly. With a reputation spanning hundreds of years, a large part of my job has long been done. Word has spread pretty far and wide. Our baskets are very well known all over the U.K. Word has trickled on throughout Europe, but not in any substantial, established, ongoing way. I was the one who thought to use new technology to establish ourselves as a global presence. Some of the work done here, most notably by your best mate, are true works of art. Kira, in particular, uses ancient Gaelic and Celtic patterns, along with meaningful clan symbolism, but with newer shapes, and she incorporates unusual and nontraditional organic material into the mix. It's really pushing the craft in a new direction, and she's already attracted a distinct, relatively new group of buyers."

Tessa nodded and appeared to think about that for a moment or two, then asked, "So . . . are you responsible for marketing, creating the catalog, getting the word out?"

"I do all those things, yes, but I also manage our accounts, finding the best shipping routes and rates, growing the client base directly. I don't do the packaging and actual movement of the baskets from the weavers to the ferry and onward, but I oversee it, as well as the traffic the work brings to Kinloch."

"You mean tourism?"

"Aye. Kinloch is a lovely enough island, but too isolated to be a direct vacation spot of any kind. But the weaving and the history behind it bring artists, crafters, and collectors from all over, who are interested in seeing the process from start to finish."

"So you're the tour guide as well."

"Something like that. I keep myself busy, at any rate." He glanced over at her and flashed a smile when she finally looked his way. "No' too bad for a man who lives off his charm and good looks."

She had the grace to look a wee bit abashed. "I've apologized for that, you know. Who had the job before you?"

"No one in particular. We've always operated as a co-op of sorts, and, surprisingly, it wasn't until recently that we've laid out a more regulated system and spelled out the terms of how it all works legally. Shay was largely responsible for that part, along with Graham. Prior to that, the weavers more or less worked on it together. It wasn't really a cohesively managed unit, and as a result, we suffered."

"What changed that? Was it Graham's direction? I understand he's only recently become the chief, with the wedding being the formal crowning, of sorts."

"Formally, yes, but, with Ualraig's declining health, he's been functionally leading us for a very long time. It was actually the blight that attacked the crops earlier on during Ualraig's reign as chief, and put us on the brink of complete ruin that eventually forced us to evolve entirely.

"Graham went off to university with the idea of learning new farming technologies in order to make our crop more resilient and consistent. I went off as well, to Edinburgh, with the idea that there had to be a better way to manage the business end. I'd always had a certain affinity and avid curiosity for computers and global connectivity. It seemed a good fit. And it was. Is."

"So you both left to get an education for the sole purpose of coming back and helping the island prosper."

"Is that so hard to comprehend?"

"Not at all. I had always thought my life would be something similar. Kira and I had markedly different paths mapped out from the ones we ended up taking. In fact, I suppose we're both at a crossroads of sorts again, with a future that's perhaps not what we might have had in mind."

A glance in her direction showed she was looking at him. The studied disinterest was gone, and she seemed truly caught up in the conversation.

Brilliant, he thought, quite happily. *Very good.*

"While you were away at school, were you tempted by the bigger world out there?" she asked, before he could follow up on some of the things she'd alluded to. "Did you consider not coming back?"

"No. I knew where my future was."

"Nothing tempted you about the big city?"

He grinned. "If you mean was I caught up in the allure of big city women, I certainly enjoyed my time there. But it was always with the knowledge that I'd come back. I'd have happily brought someone home with me, but that wasn't to be."

"Was there someone?"

"Oh, there was a string of someones. I had my heart broken rather regularly. Shay was generally disappointed in me pretty much all the time. He's the best mate a person could have, you know, loyal, honest, true. But he's also the most even tempered, unexcitable person I know. He has a very strong sense of humor, but it's so dry, I'm amazed anyone gets it but us. Yet the lassies crawl all over him. I've no' ever been able to sort that out."

"Shay went to school with you?"

"He was in Edinburgh at the same time, pursuing law, same as his father, with the same end goal as the rest of us."

"Where was Graham?"

"Studying in Glasgow."

"And all three of you came back?"

"Aye. Graham traveled quite a bit with his studies. Shay still commutes to Edinburgh to oversee his father's firm, which was handed to him upon Aiden Callaghan's passing."

"But you . . . you're just here."

"That I am. I can learn most of what I need as the world grows and expands from the very source I use to promote our baskets. My computer."

"Have you ever had the urge to go beyond here, beyond Edinburgh, to see the world? You grew up in such a remote place, I'd think the idea of getting out would have been captivating. Or was it overwhelming?"

"Not overwhelming, no. I enjoyed my time at university a great deal. But I was eager to return here and put my education to good use."

"So . . . you never leave. Ever?"

"I've gone on holiday, visited old school chums, though no' so much as the years continue on."

"And you're happy here, content."

"You say that like you simply can't fathom it being enough. But then, I dinnae have yer penchant for travel, or wanderlust. I'm curious, I suppose, to see some of the places we ship our baskets to, that would be quite a thrill, actually, but I dinnae want to live in a different place. I'd want to venture out, absorb, learn, see . . . but only so I could come back and put it to good use. So we'd all benefit. Of course, you must think me incredibly green. I guess, given that the world is your office space, it must seem almost suffocating to ye, being stuck in such a small place, surrounded by folks you know and who all know you. No place to hide, no anonymity. You can't simply be an observer here."

She didn't respond right away, though he'd noted her expression went through a series of rapid changes.

"It hasn't so far," she said at length, surprising him with her candor. "Been suffocating, I mean. In fact, it's been . . . comforting."

She'd willingly given him bits of insight into herself any number of times. But it always surprised him. He supposed that was at the core of why he'd continued to push, prod, and poke her into interacting with him.

"That's because you came looking for a cocoon," he said, as the quiet spun out, more comfortable this time. "While we're no' quite as backward or cut off as you might have thought, we do provide a very good nest for those looking to roost, or simply rest."

She maintained her silence, but her expression was thoughtful. She appeared to be thinking about what he was saying.

As they began climbing into the mountains, he said, "Does the idea of me choosing to stay in one place, especially one as remote as this, make you think I'm stunted in some way? Emotionally, socially . . . That I'm just no' willing to risk a life that's more demanding, that this choice is merely sticking with something safe."

She immediately looked at him. "Heavens, no. Why would you think that?"

He lifted a shoulder, kept his eyes on the road. "Just curious." He didn't just want to know more about her, he wanted her to think about him, too. She'd shown some curiosity . . .

but he didn't want to let her wall herself off again. He wanted to provoke her to consider him, to not be able to keep herself from asking for more. Whether it was as a journalist, or as a woman, he didn't much care. For starters.

"I think you—all three of you—coming back here, or, for that matter, heading off with the very intent of coming back here to improve not only your way of life, but the lives of everyone else here, is admirable," she said directly, and quite sincerely. "Furthermore, I don't think there's anything about struggling on such a remote, relatively inhospitable strip of land that is taking the easy way out. Your survival is a miracle and a testament to how sturdy and determined you are as a group—for generations. I have nothing but admiration for everyone here. In fact, that's why I was headed off that day to the shore to—" She immediately clipped that sentence off, and jerked her gaze to the window. "I have nothing but respect for what Kira is doing here, and, believe it or not, for what you're doing, too. Even the damn calendar idea has merit. You're not close-minded. At all. That's a good thing. I've learned many things from what I've seen, but first and foremost, I know when people are struggling, they have to be open to all things, new and old, in order to move forward, to survive."

She shut up then, seeming almost relieved to finally find a stopping point. He, of course, hadn't missed her slip of the tongue and she had to know he hadn't. She was likely praying to whatever God she believed in that he wouldn't push—while he sat right where he was, and wondered if he should.

She'd spoken so passionately about Kinloch, about the people, about their centuries old journey, and that stunned him a little. More than a little. He supposed, if he thought about what she'd done for a living up until her arrival, he shouldn't be surprised. Observing, understanding, figuring out the immediate hierarchy of the people whose story she'd chosen to tell, their past triumphs and losses, what the future might or might not hold . . . all of those things went into it. Could it be, from her slip of the tongue, that she'd decided to tell Kinloch's story?

Huh. That set him back. Given the rather brutal nature of the peoples and places she exposed and brought into the light, he wasn't sure what story she thought to tell. Aye, Kinloch had a very brutal history, as did most of their country, reaching back to the oldest recorded time. But the only thing brutal for the past hundred or so years was the blight. While that had been quite harsh, and potentially decimating to the clans, their suffering was nowhere near on the scale of those whose stories she typically told.

At the same time, the part of him that was good at his job latched on to the idea that getting Tessa to document their history would put the calendar project to shame in terms of exposure. All without a bit of skin bared to the world.

Should he just come out and ask? She'd give him a direct answer, or just as directly refuse, that much he knew. It was the part of her he didn't know, like exactly what demons chased her, that made him step forward with caution. "Ye've a good handle on us, aye," he said. "Not many do, but it's no' surprising that you get it. I appreciate that."

She nodded, but appeared lost in thought.

He battled the urge to blurt out the question, to know for himself and as further insight into her. In the face of her contemplative withdrawal, he opted to let it drop. For now. Pacing was everything.

They traveled on in silence for a few more minutes. The track became narrower and the curves tight as the incline grew ever steeper. Just before the peak, he turned off on an unpaved lane that was barely more than two grooved ruts, and littered with more jutting rocks than grass or dirt.

"Where are we going?"

"A potential calendar shot spot. Trust me."

She nodded, and appeared more alert and interested in the change in direction, but she still seemed distracted to him. His curiosity about her grew stronger. She was so strong, and at the same time, so vulnerable. She'd seen things that would level battle-tough soldiers. He believed she was just as tough, just as strong—even with her vulnerabilities clawing at her.

"Here," he said, as he slowed to take the last hairpin turn through some very narrow, deep ruts.

"These look like they were made over a long time," she remarked. "The ruts, I mean." She pointed. "They've even been worn into the rock in some places."

"Aye," he said, coming to a stop as the track abruptly came to an end. An outcropping of rock in front of them, taller than the lorry, blocked the view of what lay beyond. "Come on," he said, and climbed out.

He came around to her side as she was sliding out. "You don't have to get my door," she said, as he held it for her, then closed it after helping her down.

"I don't have to do anything," he said. "I'm fully aware you can do everything for yourself." He kept his hand under her elbow, holding her between him and the truck. "I admire that, I do. But you don't have to do everything all the time, Tessa. Let me enjoy pretending I can be a gentleman."

Her lips twisted the tiniest bit. "Why? You don't have to put on any act for me. You definitely don't need to try and impress me."

"It's no' an act. Nor about impressin' ye. I like getting your door. I like helping you up into your seat and out of it again. It's part of the dance. A good part."

"I don't dance. And I'm especially not good at that kind. Strikes me as more of a game."

"It's a courtship," he said.

Her gaze narrowed. "I thought you were content with trying to be a friend."

"Even friends can do courtly things," he said. "What is so wrong about enjoying a friendly gesture? Can you no' allow yourself that much? Think of it as a guilty pleasure, not an admission of weakness."

She started to say something then stopped. After a short sigh and what appeared to be a brief internal struggle, she met his gaze directly. "I'm sorry. You're right. I shouldn't be so touchy. Maybe it's because I'm not used to that part. The touchy part." She dipped her chin, but he gave her time, wanting to know what she was struggling so hard not to say, not to reveal . . . wanting, more than anything, for her to give him entrée to that part of her. The most private part. She was the only one who could do that. He couldn't force his way there.

He rubbed his fingers on her elbow, comforting her, but otherwise did nothing to alter their positions, or encourage her to do . . . anything.

Finally she looked at him again. "In the places where I spend most of my time, I try very hard to be invisible. It's better for an observer to not be observed. But to gain entrée into some of the places I most need to see, I need help to get there. I need to make my presence known to someone. In almost all cases, every single thing I do or say, every expression, every minute body motion, can be examined, analyzed for any possibility of deceit or impropriety. That I'm a woman makes it all so much more complicated."

She sighed just a little. "I'm hyper aware of where I am at all times, what I'm doing, how I look, what my expression is, what it should be, what I can't reveal on my face, and what could cost me my life if I do. I know—always—what those around me are doing. Every flinch, every blink, every sideways glance. And things like this"—she gently removed her elbow from his hand—"casual touching. It doesn't happen. It just doesn't. Nothing is casual in my world. If I touch, or am touched, it's with a purpose. Otherwise, I stay back, I stay hidden, I—" She broke off and shook her head.

He waited. He was humbled that she was sharing confidences with him, opening up in a way that couldn't be easy for her. That she wanted him to understand her made him very, very glad he'd gone to Kira's croft that morning.

He wished he felt better equipped. She was the most complicated person he'd ever met. And by far, the most compelling. The very last thing she'd ever say she needed was a protector or a partner. Yet she made him want to be both of those things.

He took her elbow again, very gently, but with purpose. She lifted her gaze to his . . . but didn't tug it away.

"I'm touching you because I like to feel connected. Aye, it's an ego thing, wanting to be the man to escort you, as it were. Any man would be honored—and very likely gobsmacked—to have you at his elbow. I know this man would. Beyond that, Tessa . . . it's about being connected.

"Touching in these little inconsequential ways is a form of courtship and connectivity that is its own reward. The little touches to the small of your back, the hand at your waist or elbow to help you into your seat, the pulling out of your chair. All of those things aren't because you need them, but because I do. It's supposed to make you feel good, smug even, that your man wants to have his hands on you at all times, and is finding socially acceptable ways to do that in public, because all he can think about is stripping that lovely suit or dress you're wearing from your impeccable body and delighting in touching you in all the ways he can't when the eyes of the world are on you."

Her eyebrows lifted . . . and her throat worked. She didn't pull away. Or step back.

"So it's courtship. And seduction. And ego. It's also just being there—so you know I have your back—I am always right there. It's a good feeling, to know that you're there, too . . . right within reach. I pay attention to those myriad little things . . . but for entirely different reasons. My attention comes from a place of comfort, of titillation, and of wanting to provide security. And no' just for you. It secures me, too. Grounds me. What you can always count on is that every single time I touch you, in whatever capacity, it will never be motivated by deceit, anger, or malevolence."

"Roan—"

"It's a lot, Tessa, I know. But you make me feel a lot. You make me think a lot. I would be a true and loyal friend to you.

But it would be a lie to stand here and tell you that I don't also want you in every way a man could ever want a woman. I'd honor those feelings, and be loyal to them, too. Because it's who I am. I know you dinnae have much experience with loyalty and honor in your world. But this is my world. And in my world, Tessa, you're safe. In my world, you can just be yourself . . . whoever that might be. Might be interesting, fun even, to find out. It doesnae matter what comes next and it can't matter why here, why now, or even why me. If you want to find out, if you want to figure it out, then just reach for it. You've done far scarier things, I'd imagine—"

"You'd imagine wrong, then." Her voice was a choked whisper.

He went completely still, because her throat was still working, and there was definite emotion in her voice, if not her eyes. Her gaze was probing, serious, and almost laser-like as she looked at him, into him.

"I reach because those whose stories I'm telling can't. I reach for the story. If there is anything personal or selfish, it's reaching for things that will enable me to keep reaching for more. I don't . . . I don't reach for me. Personally. I . . . I just don't."

"You can reach here," he said, continually humbled by her. He felt deeply inadequate at a time when he wanted most to be what she needed. "You can reach for me. I'm no' going anywhere. Not now. No' ever."

She looked down, her shoulders tensing, her jaw rigid.

He stopped thinking, stopped analyzing, and went with his gut. He lifted her chin, then cupped her face with a gentle hand. "I lied about one thing," he told her. "You do scare me. No' your anger, no' your pushiness, or your tougher than nails exterior. Your pain scares me. Your fear. Your past scares me. Mostly though, it's not knowing how to be your friend that scares me. Because you do need one. I want to find a way to earn that friendship. I think it could be the most rewarding thing I've ever had in my life."

"Why," she choked out. "Why me? I'm a lousy friend, I'm—"

"Beautiful, smart, sharp, caring, giving, with a heart bigger than the world, which you've given completely to the world. You're selfless, and you're brave."

"I'm smart-mouthed, and impatient, and bitchy, and—"

"Scared, and hurt, and human." He looked into those eyes that had seen so much, wondering what could she see in his. What had he been thinking, to fool himself into believing that he, of all people, was going to have the magic elixir to make someone like her sit up and pay attention. To him. Of all the arrogance and—

"You see me," she said, her tone one of awe.

His thoughts broke off right there, all but stuttering to a stop.

"Truly see me. Past all the bullshit, past all the"—she waved her hand—"and you just come out and say the most amazing things. The most blunt and direct things. You're not afraid of me. You're . . . I don't know what you are, Roan McAuley. Savior, saint, or the devil come to take me." She took a breath. "I do know you're the one man I can't get out of my mind."

His heart stuttered along with his thoughts. Then started up again—in double time. "Probably because I dinnae leave ye be."

"Precisely because you can't leave me be. No one else would keep at it, keep at me. But you do. I don't know if that makes you brave or a sadist."

"I wouldn't if I didn't think there was something there," he said. "I guess I was arrogant enough to think that my seeing past the hard front you put up was what set me apart. Was what you would notice. I couldn't stop noticing you. But I wondered what someone like you could really see in someone like me. I'm—"

"Caring, and beautiful, sharp and smart, with a heart as big as this island, a loyal heart, and a strong mind, with a caring soul that would work till its last moment on earth to make the world around him a better place for the ones he cares about. And who so clearly care for him. You're a very wealthy man,

Roan. Rich in ways I don't know if I'll ever be. You do scare me. Because I look at you, and I want what you have. So easily, so effortlessly. I feel . . . it makes me feel . . . broken. More than I already am. Like I can't ever hope to get that, to have that, because it's too sane and normal and nice. I've traveled too far, seen too much, to ever be able to have sane and normal and nice. People will look at me and know, somehow, that I'm none of those things, and so . . . I can't let myself want you. That would be admitting I want it all. And I can't have it. That's not going to work for me. I don't think I have it in me to reach and fail. I need to find a way to reach for the thing I know I won't fail at, that I know how to do. And I only know how to do one thing. This is not it. It's the opposite of this. Do you under-stand? Do you? I can't reach, Roan. I *can't.*"

She took his face in her hands and she kissed him. But it wasn't a conquering kiss, a dominant seduction, or a wrestling power play. It wasn't even a submission, or a reaching for what could be. It was . . . a cry for help.

A cry for him.

Chapter 13

If he would just kiss her back, she could lose herself in it, in the swamping waves of lust and want and need that he so effortlessly aroused in her with a mere wink of a dimple. If he would just kiss her back, she could shove away the terror of wanting and needing things she could never hope to achieve, never hope to own.

If he would just kiss her back.

Roan lifted his head, held her face to keep her from reaching for him again. "Tessa," he said quietly, calmly. "Look at me."

She opened her eyes. Expecting to see him all serious and kind, she was surprised to find him smiling, his eyes twinkling with something that looked a lot like affection. She knew that looked like, she'd taken pictures of a seemingly endless variety of it recently. At a wedding. She wondered what Roan would say if he knew she'd burned entire rolls of precious film on him and him alone. Painstakingly developed . . . then stared at for far longer than could be healthy. She'd captured a wide range of expressions on his face that day. But not one quite like the one she was looking at.

"Just kiss me," she said with a plaintive note in her voice that she would beat herself up over later.

"I want to. More than you can possibly know. But you're still just trying to drown yourself in it. Or maybe both of us. I could drown in you. I just . . . I want you to kiss me, Tessa. Me."

"Who the hell else do you think I'm kissing?" she said, not wanting any more of his armchair psychology at the moment. No matter that he'd been dead on—far too dead on—with each thing that he'd said. No one, not even Kira, understood her as that man seemingly did. How it was, she had no idea. But he did. And she was drawn to him like the proverbial moth to the flame.

The moth didn't usually fare too well in that particular confluence of events, did it?

"You're kissing me to not feel anything," he said. "I want you to feel everything."

"Oh, I'm feeling, trust me." She was tempted to slide his hand down to the front of her shirt, so he could touch for himself just how much she was feeling him. Her nipples were like hard pebbles, rubbing against the silk of her bra. Instead she shrugged out of his warm embrace and the shelter of his arms and stepped back. Immediately she felt far more bereft than she'd ever felt before. If that didn't scare her, nothing should. All the walls, all the defenses, all the shoving him away had been in vain. He'd slipped through to her most vulnerable places no matter what protective measures she employed. How did she defend against that?

"You just like to fix things, broken things," she said, trying to make sense of it as much for herself as to push him away. "You're compelled because you want to fix me."

"If that was true then why didn't I try to fix Kira?"

Tessa had turned away from him, her arms wrapped protectively about her waist. She whipped back around to look at him. "Don't you dare say anything against—"

"I'm not going to say anything against her, far from it. It's no secret that she was definitely not whole and happy when she came back, and yet I did with her what I am trying to find enough patience to do with you. I became her friend. Not to fix her, but because she could use one. I told myself that when the time was right, I'd let her know I was interested in maybe finding out if there could be more. It was just a normal attraction where the timing wasn't the greatest. I didn't befriend her to fix her, or to up my ante with her. I'm not calculating, Tessa."

"So why can't you just be a friend to me, then?"

"I thought I could, but I canno' separate one from the other, no' with you. It's so glaringly clear to me now, that whatever attraction I had for Kira wasn't . . . enough." He took a step closer and for the first time, she saw a bit of temper and impatience come into his eyes. "I sat back for a year, Tessa, more than a *year* . . . and did nothing."

"You befriended her. Hardly nothing."

"I was content with that, content with biding my time. I can't do that with you. I can't last a single day just being your friend. I want more, I want everything. I can't help it, I can't stop it, and I can't want our relationship to be anything less than everything it can be—whatever that is or might be. I'm compelled to do something about it, find out if I can make it happen, so I can get on with it, or get busy getting over it. But sitting around and doing nothing, sitting by and just holding your hand and being there for you? No. I can't do just that.

"I'd want to. For you. If I could, I'd be that, hell, I'd be anything, if it would be good enough for you. But the fact is, it's not near good enough for me. I've gotten a taste of you, not just in my mouth, on my tongue, but in my head, in my thoughts. You've infiltrated me. So no, I was wrong about what I said before. I can't just be your friend. I will be the best, most trusted, most loyal, and most dedicated friend you've ever had, along with your lover, your partner, your mate in every sense of the word. I'm no' saying we'd achieve it, we can't know that, but that is the goal, that is where I want to go. Anything less . . . I'd just be pretending I'm okay with that."

He walked up to her, and tugged her arms from her waist, then slid them around his. "So, when you kiss me . . . you need to be able to kiss *me*. You're too caught up in trying not to kiss me. Not for real. Not openly, honestly, with hope in your heart. Right now, I am still your friend. But I have every intention of getting us to a place where you can kiss me back."

"Roan, you make this so complicated when it doesn't have to be. If you'd just—"

"Am I really saying anything that's no' true?"

She glared at him, so frustrated she wanted to lash out at him, physically, verbally. "Why can't you just be like everyone else and take what you can get?"

"Because I won't settle for that. Kinloch would be doomed if I did that in my professional life. I find I won't settle for less in my personal life, either." He tugged her closer, wrapped her arms more tightly around him, and held her snugly in the circle of his own arms.

She fit him well. Perfectly, in fact. Legs, hips, shoulders. He was just that perfect bit taller than her, so she had to tip her face up to look into his eyes. It made her feel good, it made her feel . . . like the girl. She liked being the girl. Feminine, protected, maybe even a bit coddled. As he held her in the security of his arms, nestled up against him as she was, she couldn't help thinking if he would just lower his mouth, that same tiny bit, it would fit perfectly on hers. And there might be nothing more naturally right than that.

Her heart tripped, then sped up when his gaze drifted lazily to her mouth, then back up to her eyes as her lips parted. There was such emotion in his eyes. They crinkled at the corners, and were lit with joy. Just . . . joy. Such a simple, beautiful emotion. So pure, so honest. Why was it so hard for her to embrace it? Without fear, without worrying?

Roan did. Every day. Without even thinking about it. He reached for it, expected it to be there for him. Reveled in it, and did his charming level best to spread it to all who were around him. As if he was the damned pied piper or something.

But oh, she wanted to follow him and fall under that spell. To live joyfully as it if were as natural as taking her next breath. He was a man who was content with his life, successful in his endeavors, and very clear about his path for the future and his sense of where he fit into the fabric of it. He knew what he wanted and he didn't settle for less.

So, how was it that he was the man who wanted her?

He lowered his head, and softly brushed his lips over hers. She made a little noise in the back of her throat, but she didn't do anything to alter the kiss, letting him guide her into it. Her entire being softened as he kissed each corner of her mouth. He gathered her more closely to him, and her arms tightened around his waist. Naturally.

She didn't fight it. She didn't want to fight it.

He shifted his head, pressed a short, soft kiss to the fullest part of her mouth. Then again. And again. Short, sweet, gentle.

She moved against him, nestled more deeply. "I do like how you kiss me."

"How purely wonderful that is," he marveled, his deep voice a hushed whisper. "I won't grow tired of it, that I know."

"Good," she said, and allowed the smile that came so naturally. Along with it came a first taste of joy. Could it really be just that simple? Could she leave her defenses behind, the fear of what came next, the plotting and planning, and all the worrying about whether she could handle it all, and just allow . . . joy?

He was looking straight into her eyes and she let herself look back. Her heart tightened almost painfully as she felt a deep well of yearning unfurl inside of her. She wanted him. Really, truly, wanted. That very specific man. Not just to assuage needs, but to know him, to talk to him, laugh with him, be challenged by him, to have him, as part of her life and not just for a few hours, or a few days. It was a stunning revelation, and she felt it keenly, with stark, bald honesty.

With that confusion came an instinctive ball of dread, coiling inside her belly, choking the new tendrils of want. Fear licked at the edges of her inner calm. She'd be so open to him, so completely vulnerable. He would have significant power, because what he offered her was huge, as big as the wide world she'd traveled, and every bit as unpredictable. If she let herself want that big new world, where joy happened naturally, and love and need and want were a part of every single day, only to lose it—or, worse, discover she didn't have what it took inside her to return it . . .

Every muscle started to tighten, anxiety jacked up her pulse. No. *No!* She was going to relax and let go. She was going to trust. Him. And more important, herself. She could do it. She could have what she wanted and damn the consequences.

But Roan had already felt the shift. It was unnerving how easily he read her, felt the changes in her. It was also comforting. She latched on to that, to steady herself. He felt the fear in her, the tension, and yet nothing changed in him. Not even a flicker. She could be herself, even her broken, unable-to-relax-enough-to-just-enjoy-a-damn-kiss self . . . and he was still standing right there. She wanted to ask him again, why? She wanted to shake him, and ask him why he was taunting her with the impossible. Why did he think she, who was a veritable walking minefield, was worth the effort?

"I want to show you something," he told her. "Let's go for a walk. Bring the camera."

Just like that, the moment ended. No recriminations, no making her feel like a pathetic loser because, once again, she'd pulled back emotionally. She felt she'd made a huge stride forward, despite being left with a gnawing ache in her gut.

After she grabbed the camera case from the truck, she turned to find him smiling at her, dimple winking and eyes crinkling. Maybe he realized it had been a breakthrough for her. It wasn't a kiss. *The* kiss. But it was still a start.

He took her hand as if they walked hand in hand all the time, and started off toward a narrow trail through the wall of tumbled stones in front of them. When he wove his fingers through hers, she was the one to tighten their hand hold. He shot her a wink. And she was instantly infused with warmth.

So . . . they were flirting—attraction fluttering in your stomach like a firestorm of butterflies. It wasn't only rampant need and swamping lust. It was also . . . friendly. And playful. Joyful.

"It's just down the trail here, but step carefully."

He held her hand, helping her down the steeper parts, though she hardly needed the assistance. He had to know that, he'd watched her climb all over the rocks while taking shots of Graham and Katie's wedding. But . . . it felt good, so she accepted the help, liking the feel of his easy strength. She remembered what he'd said, about casual touches and keeping their hands on each other. He'd said he liked the feeling of being connected, that it was reassuring, comforting. Exactly what she felt at that moment.

An undercurrent of attraction continued to sizzle, making her quite aware of how strong his hands were, the hard width of his palm against hers, the scrape of calluses . . . and fingers she already knew could tug her tight or stroke her with such gentleness.

At that exact moment she made a pact with herself: she'd do her damnedest to stay in the moment and enjoy the outing for what it was. Keep the anxiety, the fear at bay, and use the time to get to know Roan, and maybe learn a little more about herself. To give herself permission to simply . . . feel. She needed to stop thinking in big picture terms and reduce everything to right now . . . one morning. One outing. No worrying about where it might lead and what might happen. It wasn't as if he didn't know she was grappling with mental crap. He knew . . . and he was still there. For that reason alone, she should be able to trust him. With that pledge in mind, she let him lead her, still hand in hand, down the steep, rocky trail.

"It gets narrow here. You'll have to turn to the side," he instructed. "Keep your back against the rocks. Do you want me to take the camera?"

"I've got it." She'd put the strap over her head so it went across her chest. The camera was such a natural extension of her, she hadn't thought about it. It was far less gear than she usually worked with. "Where are we—oh. Wow."

She'd inched around what was more a narrow ledge than a trail. Beyond that the tumble of boulders fell away to a steep drop-off . . . and a view that was breathtaking.

"That's incredible." The vista before her was framed on either side by two rugged rock peaks that soared higher than the one they were perched on, making her feel as if they were hugged between the two. Through the narrow gap in front of her, she could look below at the rock and boulder tumble that cascaded straight down for thousands of feet . . . all the way to the beach, and the cove beyond. If she looked forward, directly through the gap, the ocean played out as far as she could see, to the distant hazy horizon. "Such a primal juxtaposition between the jagged rocks and calm cove waters, heights and depths, distance and immediacy . . ." She was talking to herself as she unzipped her camera bag without even thinking about it.

Roan steadied her so she could use both hands. Her initial instinct had been to pull away, preferring to balance her own weight than rely on anyone to keep her centered, but she immediately quashed the instinct and let him brace her to the rock wall behind them. She reeled off a series of shots using the taller jagged peaks as a frame. What she wanted to do was lean out and take shots straight down, but she didn't have anything to tether herself with.

She looked around for a place to wedge her feet, or better, a place to lie flat on her belly, when Roan carefully turned so his chest faced the wall. He reached up with one hand and grabbed a stubby branch growing out of a deep crevasse in the wall. He tugged, it held; then he slid his free arm across her hips, his upper body strength easily pinning her. "There," he said, "go ahead."

She looked at him and wondered again if he could read her mind.

"Just lean slowly."

"Roan—"

He grinned. "I've got ye."

The corners of her mouth kicked up. "You wish."

"Aye, that I do. And often."

She shook her head, but she liked flirting. The smile that had been hovering came out in full. It was . . . fun. "It would be better if I lay flat."

"Many things are better that way, aye," he said with a cheeky grin. "But for this, the ledge is too narrow, your angles would be challenging. You can get a shot straight down from here, if you shift slowly."

"You sound quite sure of yourself."

"You're not the only one with a camera. The only difference is that when you risk your hide, at least it's for a good cause. I'm fortunate my remains aren't scattered down below."

"You were up here alone?"

"Aye. Hiking. I was doing some historical research."

"As part of the marketing for Kinloch?"

"It was personal curiosity, though the story is a good one for selling the island lore. There was a tale of an inland trail that led from the cove below up through a steep climb, then winding through the crevasses and passes, all the way back to the fortress, and I just couldn't see how that was possible. So I started hunting for it."

"Does it connect all the way to Flaithbheartach?"

"You've gotten pretty good with your Gaelic, ye know. I noticed it at the rehearsal. That 'tis no' a name that rolls easily off the tongue."

"I've managed worse. At least your language has vowels." Her smile widened. "Even if you do pronounce them all wrong."

He grinned. "I believe we were utilizing the language long before your lot even organized yourselves."

"True. Yet, you can actually understand us when we speak."

"Pretty mouthy for a woman presently being held from plunging to her death by the arm of the very man she's taunting. Living dangerously, lass."

"You've no idea," she said, but her smile remained. She trusted him. With a whole lot more than holding her to the wall, apparently. How was that possible? "Okay," she said, sliding the camera easily from it's padded pouch. Ready?" Was she, she wondered?

"Aye."

He firmed up his support as she set the f-stop and played with the other settings. She should have brought her regular gear, but she'd been working off her beloved old Nikon since her hike to the shore that fateful morning. The morning of her epiphany. The morning she'd almost gotten run down by Roan, and had begun to see him for who he really was. In her mind, the life-altering idea that had set her off on that hike, and her collision with Roan, physically and emotionally, had seemed tangibly connected in some way.

She looked through the viewfinder, then fiddled a little more with the aperture setting, and wondered what he would think if he knew why her camera bag had still been in the boot of Kira's Fiat. She'd taken off in the car the morning before, much as she had the epiphany morning, with the same goals in mind.

She'd spent most of the previous thirty-six hours developing prints and working digitally with the wedding shots. Not only had she found herself drawn, time and again, to the shots of Roan, but to her candid shots of the villagers and the wedding party. It pulled at her mind . . . and her heart. And her thoughts had wound back to her goal of depicting the history of that place, and how it had led to the islanders' current peace and quiet prosperity. She realized that the crux of the story was the people, more than the place itself.

She'd told herself the tug she felt was just the excitement of the story taking hold in her, as stories had in the past. That excitement was building. There was a story to tell. She not only felt it, she knew it.

It was entirely different from the way she normally approached her stories, as it was after the fact. She had the wonderful and rare luxury of time. Time to think, time to plot, time to plan. That was never the case in her previous work. It was gut instinct and go for it, pray she got what she needed as she developed her angle while the story unfolded before her very eyes, in all its glory . . . and all its brutality.

Excitement was there, and the drive to tell the story, every bit as strong, but completely different. The tug wasn't one of sorrow, or anger at injustice and inhumanity. The tug was one of . . . joy. Of hope. That, sometimes, things turned out for the better. Sometimes there were happy endings.

Huh. She hadn't put it together until just that moment. She was working from a joyous outcome, back to the beginning, to the roots of the story. She already knew how it ended. There was a certain kind of peace in that. And a glory, too.

She'd gone out looking for more of the story the morning before, driven by the photos she'd spent half the night developing, unsure of where the journey would take her, but trusting she'd know what she needed when she saw it. She knew it would involve people as much as places, which was why she'd noticed a bunch of kids playing soccer in a field behind the one and only small schoolhouse on the island. It was just east of the village, past the port road. She'd initially headed that way, intending to position herself to take shots of the ferry coming in, thinking about links to history and survival that single form of transportation provided to the islanders. Instead, she'd turned and aimed her long range lens on the field. The idea that those kids were playing soccer on the very field where bloody battles had taken place had captured her attention.

The surprise had come when she'd looked through the lens, zoomed in . . . only to discover their coach was the man presently pinning her to a rock wall.

"Vertigo got ye?" he asked.

She twitched, her thoughts jerking away from memory of the frames upon frames of film she'd shot of him with those kids . . . to the same man standing in front of her, a concerned look on his face despite the levity in his tone. "No, I'm fine," she said. She felt shaky, all right, but it wasn't a physical issue. "I was just . . ." She glanced at him, and she felt the same tug she'd felt looking through those shots of the wedding party and the guests—the tug of honest and real affection they had for one another, the tight bonds that had been forged through a lifetime of hard, unified work to keep their island colony thriving and alive.

She looked at him . . . and she felt the tug of wanting to be part of something significant. Not a wandering, anonymous member of the world at large, and not self-contained and safe within herself. But part of something—one thing—that was meaningful. And lasting. And unified. And very, very specifically not alone.

She lifted the camera and took a picture of his face, cheek pressed against the rock, green eyes laser sharp and focused on her. She got off three shots before he straightened slightly away from the wall. He kept his gaze on her, and his arm was still bracing her as he slid her closer to him. She didn't question him, or try to stop him as he edged her a few inches around the rocky outcropping, then eased her onto a curve in the rock . . . and pinned her there with the full weight of his body.

Wordlessly, she let the camera drop between them and slid her hands onto his shoulders, then around his neck. He was already lowering his mouth to hers. She kept her eyes on his until the last possible second. When his lips brushed hers, she let her eyes close so she could sink fully into the kiss. With no sense of the precarious ledge they were on, or of why he'd chosen that particular moment, she let him kiss her.

He didn't tease her like before. There was nothing playful or tentative or inviting about the kiss. Neither was it the lust-filled assault of the first kisses they'd shared.

It was . . . a plea. And a promise. He was kissing her like . . . like she meant something. Like the narrow edge beneath their feet could crumble at any moment, and it might be the only time he had to let her know how he felt. There was no desperation in it. It was ardent, but reverent.

He eased her mouth open, and she moaned a little as he took her fully. Her hands twined tightly around his neck and she was swamped with his scent, his taste, and everything he was becoming to mean to her. It was as if he was making love to her mouth, slowly, rhythmically, and she groaned at the way it pulled at every single part of her. She wanted him buried deep inside her, assuaging the stark, almost painful physical need she had for him. She wanted to stay, pinned in the protective shield of his body, connected only by their mouths in a way that was more intimate, more exposed, more vulnerable, than any mating she'd ever experienced. He was being open, honest, and raw with that kiss. It was fierce, emotional, and impossibly sweet.

She needed—wanted—to be a part of it, not simply a recipient. She needed him to know she was fully engaged. She slid her fingers into his hair, then touched his face, stroked his cheek. She didn't try to take control; she just wanted—needed—to touch him, so he'd know she was feeling all the things he was pouring into the kiss, into her.

Instinctively, she pressed her palms to the sides of his face, and gently disengaged him from the kiss. He looked at her, and there was such rampant need and hope . . . and fear in his eyes. She wanted to keep the first two and erase, forever, the last. But she knew she couldn't. Because she was scared to death herself.

Very deliberately, she ran her fingers along his face, his cheeks, his jaw, along the sides of his neck, around the rim of his ears, into his hair, along his scalp, then back along his temples. He kept his gaze on her the entire time, and she watched him right back. She hoped he understood what she was telling him.

She had no idea how to go about it, but she wanted him to know, when she pulled his mouth down to hers, that she was, for once, very specifically kissing *him*. With no other intent but that he sense what it was she felt when he kissed her.

She'd never thought of herself as a gentle person, so it surprised her that she found it easy to taste his mouth, take him in slowly, sip, tease, touch. She'd never thought herself particularly playful; her world was far too serious, too tense, for such a luxury. She'd always wondered how it was that people who were so oppressed could still retain their joy, their positive spirit, their hope. She marveled at it, even while she couldn't help feeling they were doomed to learn otherwise. That there was no hope, and there would be no end to the oppression. Yet, they soldiered on, in spite of the harsh fate life dealt them.

Oppression had hardened her . . . and she'd simply been an observer. How was it they'd kept themselves open to joy when she'd only watched and felt as if it had been bludgeoned out of her very psyche a long time ago?

But joy was the emotion infusing her, filling her with a warmth that came from somewhere deep inside her. She felt there was a bottomless well, as if it had always been there for the taking, but she hadn't known where to find it, or how to draw from it.

She moved his mouth onto hers so she could kiss him fully, deeply. Maybe he would feel her surprise and the banked excitement that was beginning to grow at the dawning of a new discovery.

Moving her hands to his neck, she wrapped her arms tightly around him, and, quite shockingly, joyously, kissed him with a happy exuberance that made her want to shout out loud, with laughter and a sense of freedom such as she'd never known.

He groaned as she poured all of herself into the kiss, smiling against his mouth, marveling at the laughter that was bubbling up inside her. How was it possible for any one person to feel this good? And all because of a connection being shared with someone who wanted everything she had to give.

Roan was grinning when he broke the kiss, though there was a stunned look in his eyes—which were glassy with emotion.

She was swamped with that same emotion, and feeling gloriously alive because of it.

"Wow," he said, shaking his head slightly.

"I know," she crowed, too pleased with herself to worry how that must sound. "I think I'm getting it."

"Oh, aye, I think ye can safely say that much." He laughed in the face of her obvious glee, even as he shook his head. "No' to look at a gift such as that with anything less than abject appreciation, which I can guarantee you I have . . . but where did that come from? From where we were . . . how did you get to that?

"I . . . got it from inside me," she marveled, feeling an almost overwhelming desire to wriggle with pleasure. There was a victory dance inside her just dying to get out.

"What was it you were thinking about, when you took that picture of me? I've never seen you like that, your expression so focused . . . and then almost beatific."

"I can't—I don't want to talk about it," she said. "Not yet. Not because I won't, I will. I just . . . this is so new. And so wild. I—for now, I just want to stay in the moment. I'll be analyzing it to death later for certain. There are things . . ." She paused, then grinned. "Wow. There are things I really want to tell you. I actually really do."

"Good," he said. "Bloody brilliant, in fact. But—"

"Can we go back and take some pictures?" she said, anxious to move on from the moment, and preserve it perfectly as it had been. "From where we were just standing? Oh, and can you explain to me how on earth this would work as a magazine spread location? And more about the trail to the fortress?"

"Aye, I can, and I will," he said, amused, but still looking like his world had been rocked.

Join the club, she wanted to tell him. He'd been making her feel that way on a regular basis since they'd first crossed paths. It would do him good to be on the receiving end for a change.

He started to shift away from her, back to ledge, but she held on for just another moment, until he looked back at her. "If it's okay with you, after that, I'd really like it if you'd hold my hand while we climb back out of here."

His grin was fast and perfect, even though surprise showed clearly on his face. "I will hold your hand always, luv."

She felt her cheeks warm a little. That was . . . new. And kind of nice, actually. "I just . . . I just want to feel. Okay? I don't want to think."

"As long as the eventual thinkin' doesnae turn things back to—"

"No," she said almost defiantly, more to herself than to him. "No. There is no going back. Not now." She looked at him, and wondered if he saw anything that looked like hope in her eyes. And joy. "I know where I'm going, Roan," she said, bursting to say it out loud. Hearing it, stating it, made it feel that much more real. "Finally. Thank God. I think I've figured it out."

She could see on his face the dozens, if not hundreds, of questions he was dying to ask, but didn't, because he was letting her feel. Letting her be in her moment. That settled something inside of her, that which always got jerky and nervous and anxious. He got it. He got her. She truly couldn't wait to tell him everything. It should feel odd, awkward, or, at the very least, portentous and nerve-wracking, to want to share something—anything—with someone else. It was all of those things, but the overriding emotion when she looked at him in that moment was excitement.

She reached to touch his face. "Trust me, okay? You need to trust me. You've asked me to take huge leaps of faith with you. This is the leap you have to take with me. I don't have all the answers yet. But I want to share the ones I do. I won't run. And I won't hide."

"As long as you'll talk to me. Tell me. Share the dreams, even if I'm no' included in them. Don't keep them inside. Good or bad. You dinnae have to analyze and ponder and figure it all out by yourself, ye ken, aye?"

"Aye," she said. "I ken that . . . and a lot more. No one is more surprised than me, but I'm actually looking forward to talking to you. I think you'll help me figure it out the rest of the way. I do. In fact, you're quite possibly the only one who could."

He smiled at that, then he grinned. "Now 'tis you who looks verily gobsmacked, just at the idea of it."

"I am. But it's a rather glorious gob, isn't it?"

"I believe ye might be right." He shifted his face so he could press a kiss in the palm of her hand.

And she was undone by him all over again. There was excitement, and anticipation, not dread, or fear. "Roan."

He'd begun to edge them around, but paused and looked back. "What, luv?"

She wondered how long it was going to take before the hot little thrill she got when he said that would cease to have that effect. She hoped it was a very long time. "Thank you."

He looked surprised again, and more than a little pleased. "For?"

"Being patient. Understanding. Not pushing."

The laugh barked out of him. "Right. I've tried to be understanding, but I've been utter crap at the patience part. I've done nothing but push ye."

"Then maybe I should say thank you for explaining yourself, and what you want from me. Then giving me some space to figure out what I want. And what to do about it."

He grinned. "I'd like to take credit for that, but we both know I'd have likely been pushin' again before I even returned ye to Kira's. It's only because you came around to it so quickly that I'm looking like the good guy here."

"You are a good guy, Roan McAuley."

His dimple flashed. "You're just sayin' that because you want my body."

Much like that day with the calendar shots and the kilt, she realized that he was maybe the tiniest bit uncomfortable being the direct recipient of praise and attention. When she'd first met him, she'd mistaken his good-natured charm as a kind of grandstanding for attention that was typical of men who looked the way he did. In her experience, anyway. But he just liked to put everyone around him at ease, make them smile, laugh a little. He wasn't comfortable in the spotlight himself. *Interesting*.

"I do want your body," she said, and had the pleasure of watching that constant sizzle of attraction between them make his green eyes go dark with want. "But I'm equally attracted to your mind." She smiled. "And your humor. Your generosity. Your strength. Your thoughtfulness. Your sensitivity."

He was all but squirming—which meant she had it exactly right, and was the most endearing part of all.

"That is what you wanted, right?" she asked, discovering the pleasure in being the one to say the things that made him think and feel. Maybe shake him up a little, force him to be the one to step outside his comfort zone. "You want me to be interested in all of you." She held his gaze intently. "And I am."

She swore she saw him swallow. Hard.

Her smile widened to a grin. It was turning out to be fun in ways she hadn't even begun to consider.

She winked at *him*. Imagine that! "Be careful what you wish for, Mr. December."

Chapter 14

He'd deeply underestimated her, which was about as stupid a thing as he'd ever done. The woman was nothing if not an overachiever. He'd been hopeful, of course, that she'd come around to giving him a chance. He'd thought it would take a lot of careful nudges and patience beyond anything he thought he might actually have, not to mention an inordinate amount of self-control. All of which he'd pretty much figured he'd be a spectacular failure at, given his track record with her thus far.

When he'd gone to the croft yesterday, he'd already wanted Tessa for what felt like an eternity, which made no sense considering he'd known her less than a month, but there it was. Like eons stretched out, end to end, that's how long it felt he'd waited, just to find her. Now that he had, he wanted it all so badly he could taste it. So badly, he stayed half hard pretty much at all times. When she got even close to his personal space—hell, when she so much as glanced at him—he went straight to the edge.

And that had been when she was actively trying to push him away.

He wasn't sure how he'd survive now that she had her sights set on him.

"She's coming to pick you up? In Kira's little death pod?"

"Aye. Any minute. We'll take the lorry, though. I don't fancy spending possibly my last moments inside a tin trap." Roan stared at the e-mail detailing the latest order from their newest client in Italy. A shoe designer, of all things. Seems they wanted to add the artisan basketry to their showroom floor. Said it went with the Tuscan influence and natural sunlight and . . . he didn't rightly understand the rest, but it didn't matter. They wanted several of the more expensive pieces still in inventory and were going to commission Kira, specifically, to do two more.

Shay sifted through the mail that had piled up while he'd been in Edinburgh. "Are the contracts in here from the Malaysian distributor you told me about?"

"What?" Roan looked up, not that he'd been all that absorbed in the e-mail. He already knew what it said. He was just trying to look busy and focused for Shay's sake. The last thing he needed was a lecture on his love life. He'd heard the one before about handing his heart away to someone who couldn't take proper care of it, and though it had been quite a long time since Shay had needed to deliver it, Roan wasn't in any mood for a repeat performance. Especially where Tessa was concerned. It was perfectly fine for him to be sitting there, quietly freaking out over the monumental step he was taking in his life, but if anyone else wanted to offer up a less than lovely opinion on the matter, or Tessa herself, then he couldn't promise he'd remain civil in her defense. Even with his closest mates.

He felt intensely protective of her, which should have made him smile, because she'd personally want to kick his sorry arse for thinking she needed protection of any kind in the first place. A more fiercely independent woman he'd never met. He rather liked that she could take care of herself. Though it didn't diminish his concern for her welfare, it was a comforting thing to know she could hold her own. But perversely, that only served to amp up his protective sensibilities further. That very ferocity of hers, coupled with her capableness, could lead her to jump into God only knew what kinds of situations. She thought she was superwoman, and in many dazzling ways she was. But in many other ways, she was just as vulnerable, insecure, and prone to self-doubt as anybody. Maybe more so. He thought of the glimpses she'd given him into what she was really grappling with on Kinloch.

"Hullo? Malaysia contracts?"

Roan blinked out of his latest Tessa reverie, which had been an almost constant state for him since he'd dropped her off at Kira's yesterday after those life-altering moments spent out on that ledge. In many ways, he was still out on a ledge.

"Not yet," he replied, clicking open a reply window to the Italian buyer's note. "There was an issue with the shipping time frame, but I was able to negotiate a compromise and I think we're all set. You'll need to give that part special attention, though. Nice guy, and enthusiastic, which we like, but I think that's partly a mechanism to get us to drop our guard. I wouldn't put it past him to try to slide in some proprietary language that'll give him an advantage when competing with our other retailers."

"I won't let that happen," Shay said, sounding somewhat distracted himself, as he continued sorting the mail into stacks. "So, what happened yesterday?"

Roan paused in typing his response. He looked up warily. "What about yesterday?"

Shay didn't even glance up. "Half the island is talking about it. And that's only because the other half is listening to the first half."

"About what?"

He looked at Roan with a steady gaze. "Seriously?"

Roan swore. While he'd been perfectly fine pushing Tessa to consider the possibilities between the two of them and completely impatient about starting things with her, he was in absolutely no hurry to share this new occurrence with anyone else. He supposed it wasn't going to remain a secret much longer. "We were scouting sites for the calendar photos we have to send in. That's all there was to it. Or all there was supposed to be. Things between us are—I don't know how to explain it—complicated. But good. Why is anyone discussing it in the first place? How the hell does anyone even know? We were on the high trail up from Smuggler's Cove back behind Flaithbheartach. Who would even know that?"

Shay lifted his gaze and gave him a steady look. "I have no idea what you're talking about. I meant the conversation between Katie and her parents. I've been in Castlebay since right after the wedding, working out a problem with Gunderson regarding our sharing communal waters for fishing. I know that Katie and Graham got home late yesterday from their honeymoon. I came back over this morning in time to see the senior McAuleys set sail. I was talking with Blaine earlier, and he got me partly up to speed. I understand they stayed moored offshore after the wedding and he said the reason they stayed was because they were threatening to find a way to get the marriage annulled and prove Graham is keeping her here against her will. They were demanding that Katie leave with them, and their lawyer was apparently using the fact that she refused to do so as proof of their claim. Have you talked to Katie yet?"

"*What*?" Roan sat back and raked his hand through his hair. "When did that happen? That's insane. How can they make that stick? I don't care how much money they have, anyone with eyes in his head can see she's head over heels. Can't they fathom she doesn't want to go back? Is there anything you can do to stop this farce before it starts?"

"I'm planning on calling her later today, but I wanted to get the full story from you. Are you honestly just hearing about this from me?" He rocked back on his heels, more than a hint of amusement in his eyes. "Must have been one hell of a hike yesterday."

"In more ways than I can describe," Roan said, too stunned by the news regarding Katie to be guarding his own comments. "But I want to hear more about this meeting."

"What meeting?" Tessa stuck her head in the door, then belatedly knocked on the edge. "It was open. Sorry, I don't mean to intrude."

"No, that's quite all right," Shay said, almost jovial as he motioned her to come in. He shot a quick look at Roan, quite clearly enjoying himself, then stuck his hand out to Tessa. "I know we've crossed paths several times now, but I wanted to personally thank you for taking on this calendar project for us. And it was good of you to take on the wedding photographer assignment, too. I know Graham appreciated it, and Katie talked about it nonstop the last we spoke."

She took his hand in a quick shake and smiled. "It was a lovely ceremony. I was flattered to be a part of it."

Roan watched them, thinking it all seemed quite . . . normal. So why he was sitting there, tense, he had no idea. It felt as if he was watching two worlds collide. Or something equally apocalyptic. His private fascination with Tessa was about to become anything but. He wasn't done processing what in the hell he was getting himself into. When he was with her, it all made complete sense, and he knew exactly where he wanted to be. But when they'd parted yesterday, and he was thinking about it all in what had to be a more rational state of mind, he'd started to question things.

Not his desire for her, or his intent to pursue a relationship with her . . . but whether or not they had any real hope of making that happen. He was thrilled . . . and terrified that she was finally willing to give it a go. But just because she'd said yes didn't make the process any less complicated.

He shoved his chair back and stood. "Are we ready to head off?" Not that he didn't want the two to make further acquaintance, but Shay was looking far too pleased with himself, and Tessa's change of heart was fresh enough that he didn't want to risk exposing her to too much of his world, too fast. He knew Shay and Graham would support him in anything he did, but while getting there they would be blunt and direct. Though he would appreciate their input . . . he wasn't quite up for the grilling session that would precede it just yet.

"We are," she said, and he noted that she looked . . . happier. And more rested, less haunted.

That made him feel good, eased his mind a little.

"I looked at the files you sent over last night," she added. "If you're as good as you say you are with digital photo editing, I think there are several locations that could work."

"Good." He rounded the desk and gave Shay a good-natured, perhaps a bit harder-than-necessary clap on the shoulder. "It's good to have you back," Roan said to him. "Will you be sticking closer to home for a wee bit now? Or will you have to go back to the mainland?"

"I'm hoping to be here for at least the immediate future, but I'm no' sure as yet. We reached a settlement on the case I've been working on all this time, which was a relief to us all as it was setting up to be a lengthy court fight. But there is another on the horizon that could prove challenging. Young ingénue French film starlet trying to get out of her marriage to an Oscar-winning British director twice her age. She's hoping for a rather substantial piece of his net worth."

"He had no prenup? Marrying a French actress? Who was his lawyer?"

"Oh, there's a prenup," Shay said. "We wrote it."

"Ah."

"Indeed. But that's still in the early stages. I'm no' going anywhere today," he said, with a meaningful look. "We'll have to catch up."

Roan narrowed his gaze, but Shay maintained a positively innocent demeanor. Roan knew better. "Don't wait for me, but if I get back in time, we'll do that. See what you can find out about . . . that other matter."

"Rest assured." Shay turned to Tessa, who was watching the byplay with open interest. "Good luck today with getting the right photos. We're all grateful for your superior expertise. I'm sure it was your keen talent that fooled the calendar folks into thinking my rather homely friend here was actual cover model material."

"Well, though the wedding gig was my pleasure," she said, "I don't know that I can say the same for the calendar shoot. The calendar subjects were a bit more challenging." She shot a dry smile Roan's way, then looked back at a far-too-satisfied Shay. "It's a shame you were gone, though." She gave him a quick, clinical onceover. "You'd have definitely given him a run for his money."

Shay's face turned ruddy, and Roan took a moment to appreciate his discomfort. "Aye," Roan said. "To think . . . this could be all about your coronation as the world's most eligible Highland hunk."

Shay frowned then, his expression growing more serious than embarrassed. "Ye know, speaking of which"—his gaze shifted to Tessa briefly, then back to Roan—"you should let me look over all the documentation we got from them regarding how the remainder of this promotion plays out. The calendar release schedule, any promotional plans, and payment structure, general requirements, that sort of thing. Simply to make certain we're complying with all the guidelines. We wouldn't want any last minute concerns because we didn't pay attention to the details."

Roan didn't immediately understand Shay's sudden concern, but shrugged and said, "It's all in the file there on my desk if you want to go over it while we're out. Looked pretty straightforward to me."

"Except the part where you're responsible for sending in the photos. That seemed a bit odd. Why is it you're taking them?"

"Actually, they have two shoots scheduled for all the winners, but they're all the way in Aberdeenshire. Seemed a bit of a bother, so I contacted them and explained who we had used for our winning photography and they agreed to let us send in our own shots—per their final approval. If we don't give them what they want, I'll have to travel over. Hence the tight deadline. We have to get them there before the final shoot."

Shay looked to Tessa. "Sounds like we really do owe you. If there is anything I can do in a legal capacity to make you feel more comfortable about lending your name professionally to this endeavor—"

"No, that's okay," Tessa said. "I'm fine with this. I trust that you will handle it properly."

"Us, aye, but if the calendar folks see an opportunity to sell more copies by exploiting your name . . ." He shrugged. "I'll look into that for you, if you dinnae mind."

"Not at all, and I appreciate the concern. But if it will help sell calendars and that forwards your cause here, I'm not opposed to my name being used. Though I wouldn't mind finding out what the parameters are and I'd prefer to give personal permission for anything beyond copyright notices being posted for my specific shots."

"I'll take care of it," he said. "If you get the shots today, or as soon as they're done, let me know, and we can finalize it at the same time."

"We're hoping to get them all today. We're setting them in the exact places where I've taken other shots during the winter months. That, along with a little creative Photoshop-ing, should do the trick to imbue them with Christmas-in-the-Hebrides appeal," Roan explained. "I'll let you know how it goes."

"Good. We'll talk later," Shay said, holding Roan's gaze a bit longer than necessary.

"We will, aye," Roan said, not sure if Shay wanted to talk to him about Tessa, or if there was something else that had triggered his ever-so-serious self.

Shay was already snagging the contract file from Roan's desk as the two of them said their good-byes and headed out.

Once outside, Tessa glanced at him, a wry smile curving her lips. "He seems a rather straightlaced sort," she commented.

"He's the mediator of the group, has been since we first became friends as children, and generally a rather overly serious sort—which makes him quite good at his chosen profession." He smiled. "I particularly enjoyed your having him on there for a moment."

"Oh, I wasn't having him on. I quite meant what I said." She barked out a short laugh. "You should have seen your face just then."

"If you believe I'm remotely jealous, have another thought. I'd have given much to be rid of this particular assignment and you know it."

She wagged a finger. "Faces don't lie."

"Yes, well, at least mine didn't go all dark and ruddy at first glance."

"True enough. Has he ever looked in a mirror, though? He must catch the wandering eye all the time. Does he not notice?"

"He's well aware, trust me. He's no' got much of an ego that one, no' about his looks at any rate."

"Oh, come on. I was hoping you were going to tell me that when you three are hanging out and he gets a few beers in him, he's like some wild, raucous party animal."

Roan chuckled, boggling at the very idea of it. "No' hardly. Though I'd admittedly pay large sums to see it. And would pay you even more handsomely to record it for all posterity."

Tessa was walking to Kira's little Fiat, but Roan pointed to his truck. "I thought we'd take the lorry. It will likely do better on some of the rougher tracks we're looking at today. Should we drop the Fiat back off for her so she'll have use of it for the day? We can start out in that direction if need be. I could follow you there."

Tessa shook her head. "She's already buried in the studio doing sketches for that Italian contract. I doubt she'll come up for air anytime in the next day or two at least."

Roan leaned past her and opened the passenger door. So far, it wasn't awkward between them at all. Quite the opposite, which surprised him, though he wasn't sure what he'd expected. She'd always behaved professionally. He had typically been the instigator, provoked, perhaps, by that very staunch professionalism.

More recently, he'd been aware of any opportunity to keep his hands on her, keep her aware of him, but, faced with even the casual touch required to help her up into the passenger seat, he found himself pausing.

She turned to climb in on her own, unaware of his dilemma, and he immediately reached to assist her, feeling rather idiotic for over-thinking even that small gesture. He didn't want the entire afternoon to go awry straight off, so he needed to get right with himself and quickly. "So, you've had a chance to talk with her then," he asked, trying not to sound tentative, or leading—though he was both.

"I have. She's very excited and a little intimidated by the specific request for one-of-a-kind pieces by her. But I think she's going to surprise herself at how she's going to rock this assignment. She's really . . . starting to blossom, I guess is the right way to put it. It's good to see. I'm pleased and excited for her."

At the last second, she turned back to him, which landed her almost directly in his arms, as he'd been reaching to help her up.

They both went still . . . and silent.

Finally, she said, "But that's not what you meant, is it? Talking to her about the Italian contract."

He shook his head.

"You wondered if I'd talked to Kira about . . . yesterday. The ledge."

"It's crossed my mind. But I'm glad to hear she's excited about the work challenge. It's a wonderful opportunity."

"It is. And to answer your other question, no, we haven't had the chance. She was weaving last night and focused and . . . it wasn't the right moment. Actually, that's not entirely true. She wouldn't have minded the intrusion, but I was still sorting everything out. I needed to think about what happened out there, put it in perspective, and make sure I was good with my choice. Then I got the photos you sent for us to work with today, and I looked through them. When I finally surfaced it was the wee hours, and she'd gone to bed. Then this morning, that Italian thing came, so . . ."

"Had you changed your mind about talking to her, or were you relieved to put it off?"

"Actually . . . I did want to talk to her about it." She tilted her head and focused more intently on him. "What about you? I know Graham just got back from their long honeymoon weekend, but did you and Shay talk?"

"Not yet. I told him we took a hike scouting locations, but—"

"I interrupted?"

"No' quite. We'd gotten side-tracked by other news at that point."

"Did you want to tell him?"

"I think it's a little like the situation with you. I want his input, his support, Graham's too, but I don't want to be made to defend my choices, or even deal with the good-natured ribbing I'll get. Now that one of our trio is newly wedded, I know it will be a more pointed discussion. I haven't exactly figured out what to say. Shay and Graham are essentially my brothers, my family, much like Kira is for you. Simply mentioning the hike alerted Shay enough that he's curious."

"So . . . you didn't want him to know."

"Word is going to get out if we spend much more time together. In that regard, I wanted to be the one to tell him. But I'd have likely waited until sometime after today."

"Why?"

"Because my thoughts have been a complete jumble since yesterday. I needed more time to sort things out before talking with them."

She pulled back slightly. "You're having second thoughts." She made it more statement—bordering on accusation—than question.

"I'm processing my thoughts. Big difference. Can you look me in the eye and tell me you've been nothing but one hundred percent positive about this since we parted ways yesterday?"

"Of course not, but I'm not the one who was all knowing and all seeing, like you were. You led me into this."

He could hear the tension—the fear—climb into her tone, could feel her body tense beneath the hands he'd placed on her upper arms to support her when she'd turned to him.

"I'm no' doubting the want or the desire for you," he said, sincerely. "Those are real, and they're no' going away. But I'm also not viewing this as some kind of fantasy or escape from reality. I want this—us—to exist in the real world, this world. You have every right to be worried about our chances, and I understand that, but that doesnae mean that I've no worries of my own. You would be more worried, and rightly so, if I was so blithe as to dismiss your very clearly stated concerns. I've listened to you, to everything you've said, and I hear your doubts, your fears. What you did yesterday, the leap you took . . . that humbled me. Deeply. And aye, I began to question if I was worth that leap for you. I dinnae doubt my sincerity or my willingness, but I canno' be so certain I will be what you need, what you want. I'm risking here, too. You're not the only one vulnerable in this."

She leaned away from him slightly at that. "Perhaps we should cut our losses now."

He pulled her closer. "We're not running, not hiding. Remember? I've no desire for that. I was only tellin' ye that I've been looking at this with a true eye, no' with my head in the clouds. I don't run, Tessa. I'm considering, and I'm thoughtful, because that's the smartest thing for both of us. When I'm with you, I feel certain."

"But when you're alone, you question everything."

"Have you no'? Have ye been more certain alone than you are when you're like this, in my arms, feeling me, seeing me?"

She searched his face in that disconcerting way she had, as though she was looking through a viewfinder while doing it, then finally shook her head. "No. You're right. I'm more certain here, with you. I did come to realize, while I was working last night, that talking with Kira, who knows you, might give me insight, or strengthen my conviction to reach for something for myself. Namely, you. Are you worried, because Graham and Shay don't know me, that they won't approve? That you'll have to defend your choice, as you just said?"

"I can anticipate the conversation I'll have with them. Their concern will be for my welfare, so they'll ask tough questions, partly because they want what's best for me, and partly because they dinnae know ye. I'm trying to find the answers to the questions before I give them that chance."

"When you're with me, you have such strong convictions. Can't you just tell them what you've told me? I'm thinking I'm the harder sell and I bought it."

He sighed. She was defensive. He couldn't blame her. How had he managed to botch it up already? "I speak from my heart with you, as I likely would with them, and aye, you're right. Perhaps I should trust that, trust my instincts, trust them."

"But you think they'll hear doubt because you're feeling doubt."

"It would be unrealistic if I didn't have a few. Of course I worry. You spent the bulk of the time we've been together tellin' me you can't do this. But you want to. I want it, too. When you capitulated, when you reached for me, I realized just how badly I wanted you. I'd be lying if I said that wasn't a wee bit terrifying. You have to be feeling that, too.

"Graham and Shay will give me support, because they want my happiness, but they'll also give their honest opinion. It's no' a bad thing, thinking things through as if they were already badgering me. It forces me to consider things I otherwise might no', and do so with more clarity." Before she could say anything else, he asked, "What about with you and Kira? Weren't you at least a little relieved when your chance to discuss our little adventure was postponed?"

"Yes," she confessed, and he felt her tension release, just a little.

He smiled at that. "Good. That's honest." He slid his hands up her arms and rested his palms on her shoulders. "I want that, before anything else, from you. I'll give the same. The trust we build is the foundation of everything that comes after. Dinnae mistake my doubts or concerns for lack of will, or desire for you. The best way to combat doubt or insecurity, is by figuring it out together, no' alone, in the privacy of our own thoughts.

"That means being honest with each other, bringing questions to one another, and no' feeling like the other will turn tail and run because either of us is simply being human. We'll need to be direct, even if it's no' what the other wants to hear. No' only to help each other, but because we both deserve to know the thoughts of the other. Especially if there are doubts. We've certainly had no trouble speaking our minds from the time we first met. I want to know that won't change between us."

"I don't know that I have it in me to be any other way. I've never been coy, and I don't play games. If anything, I'll be too blunt and you'll have to remind me to play nice."

His smile returned as he leaned, pulling her a bit closer. "Sometimes nice is overrated."

She smiled, too, but it was more a dry curve of the lips. "Yes, but not all of the time."

"You've demonstrated a lot of kindness," he reminded her.

"Just not to you. Not in the beginning anyway."

"Beginnings are just that." He cupped her cheek, toyed with her curls. "Everything after that counts, too."

She reached up, touched his hand. "You're impossible and amazing, you know that? You challenge me, annoy me, say the most direct things, but are so thoughtful, I can't find fault with your logic. When we're like this, I don't want to turn away from you, I don't want to be anywhere but right here. Then, when I'm apart from you, it scares me that I'm going to reach for you again and take such a big chance when I'm feeling anything but secure and strong in my own world. I don't want you to be a crutch, or a distraction from what I should be focusing on, and I worry about that. But when I'm with you like this, it feels . . . good. Normal. Healthy. And yet, who am I to judge that?" She laughed a little. "So, I'm humbled, too, and more than a little terrified that you want to tangle yourself up with me. How can I be sure I won't hurt you, or make you wish you'd never laid eyes on me?"

"It's the intent, no' the outcome. If your heart is in the right place, and you give your best, then what comes of it, even if it's a disappointment to either of us, is what comes of it."

She smiled and her aqua blue eyes fairly twinkled.

"What?" he asked. "What did I say to amuse you?"

"Nothing amusing, it was all truth. But do you listen to yourself? Take your own advice? Here you're telling me to leap and just be pure of heart, yet you say you're worried about failing me."

He had to grin at that, albeit sheepishly. "It's possible you have a point."

"I do, on occasion."

"Perhaps it's good we're drawn to each other. Spare the rest from having to sort us out and set us straight."

"Possibly you have a point," she echoed; then they both laughed.

"Ye've a good laugh, Tessa. I like hearing it."

"It's a bit rusty. But it definitely feels good."

"Well then, perhaps I'll start with that goal in mind. Make ye smile, make ye laugh. Things have to go well if we're doing that, right?"

"Sounds like an admirable plan. As little as a week ago, I'd have wished you good luck with that. Maybe it's something about Kinloch, and being on distant shores and away from . . ." She drifted off and he cupped her cheek more tenderly. She closed her eyes, and pressed her cheek against his palm, then took a breath and continued. "Away from bloodshed and brutality," she forged on, almost as if testing herself, "and tyranny and war . . ."

She opened her eyes, and what he saw in the depths moved him, and made him hurt for her. He wanted to move mountains or whatever it took to erase the memories that had put those shadows there.

"I worried that I was hiding," she said, her voice a bit thicker. "That I was using you as a shield, too. I pushed for sex with you because it's an easy thing to understand, obvious for what it is. And what it isn't. But what we're talking about isn't any of that. You're so much more than sex to me. And I've been discovering that Kinloch isn't so much a cave to hide in as a place to actually learn something, and grow. A place to look at things, at life, the world, and its history—both tragic and beautiful—in a new way."

"Will ye share that with me?" he asked, cupping her face with both hands now.

"I want to, which is stunning, in and of itself. Yes, I want to talk to Kira about us, about you, about making this leap. But I want to talk to you about me. About my world. About . . . everything. And that's more than stunning, it's . . ." She shook her head, smiling, but clearly a bit overwhelmed.

"It's okay," he told her. "I want to know it, I want to hear it all. And, aye, I want to talk with Graham, with Shay, have their support . . . but, Tessa, I also want to shout it to the world. I feel like I've waited for an eternity for you to arrive, and now that you're finally here I can get started on the important part of my life. Aye, that disconcerts me, but I canno' describe it any other way. I dinnae claim to know what we'll do, or how'll we'll manage, or if, after some time spent together, we'll still want to try. Only time can determine that. But I want this to be public, lived out in the open, in the real world. I'm no' hiding ye. Nor do I want to." He twined a curl around his finger, liking that she was smiling at what he'd said.

Her expression had softened—warmed—as he spoke. That alone eased some of his concerns.

"I don't want this to be some furtive, private thing . . . but I am at a disadvantage," she said. "You'll come under the close examination of every person you've ever known, but they do know you and love you, and they want to see you happy. I'm the outsider. It's not like it might have been with Kira, who was a known quantity and everyone would be cheering you both on from the start, happy for two of their favorite people."

"I told you, we're a hospitable lot. Our default position is to welcome and accept people new to our shores."

"For someone like Katie, yes. But, I'm—"

"She wasnae initially welcomed by all, ye know. There was concern that she wouldn't honor her commitment to Graham, that it was too odd a thing, too fickle, even by our forgiving standards, for her to have exited one wedding—to a person she'd known her entire life—only to leap, willy-nilly into another, with a complete stranger. And if ye think they've a shine for me here, it's hero worship where Graham MacLeod is concerned. Well earned, I should add, though I'll deny it if you tell him. Swell his head right up."

"Right," she said dryly, "I could tell that was a problem with him straight off. All ego." They shared a grin, but she went on to say, "I guess I shouldn't be surprised that everyone knew her entire story straight off, and I understand, completely, their concerns. But everyone clearly adores her now. I understand that, too. The wedding was like a fairy tale come to life. It's obvious Katie and Graham are committed to one another. You'd never know they'd met such a short time ago. Almost as if they were fated, or something."

"Aye, isn't it then," he said, and felt a bit of a shiver down his spine. He'd admired and even envied Graham and Katie's immediate deep bond, even if he hadn't entirely understood how it could happen so swiftly. He looked at Tessa and thought that now, perhaps, it didn't seem odd or hard to understand at all. "You're no' the first to say it. We did get past our initial skepticism of her quickly, because of their obvious dedication to each other, but don't discount your own credibility here."

"*My* credibility? What, because I'm Kira's friend? I doubt that has earned me more than the benefit of the doubt, which is admittedly more of a welcome than I usually get."

"I was speaking of rescuing us with the calendar contest, then going about sealing your goodwill by taking the wedding photos. Everyone is quite impressed with your credentials and deeply grateful that you helped so willingly. That you took it seriously, and worked hard to make the photography special for Graham and Katie made them feel special, too. That's no small thing in the islanders' eyes."

"I wish I could say it was all done out of the kindness of my heart, but you, of all people, know that's not true.

"That you took it on with honest dedication to do it well enough for us to win the contest, and well enough to work out all the angles and shots to make the wedding remembrances so special is testament enough."

"When I came here, I wanted to take a break from photography of any kind. I can say now, however, that I'm glad I did it."

He grinned. "It pushed us to cross paths, whereas we might not have otherwise. So, I'm thankful."

"I meant because it forced me to pick up my cameras, and think about my work and my ability in a way I hadn't before." She reached up and pushed his hair from his forehead. "But I'll agree on your take, too."

She started to take her hand away, but he covered it with his own, then wove his fingers through hers, keeping them linked as he lowered them. "I'll gladly accept whatever confluence of events it took for us to be standing here right now."

"I'll agree with that."

Their gazes held for a moment, then another. Roan had all but forgotten where they were standing, and didn't care who might have been watching. His thoughts were exclusively on her. "Ye said you wanted to tell me things. Yesterday, you seemed excited by the idea. I'm interested in listening."

"It's a new feeling, a new urge," she said, but smiled. "Scary, but, yes, it's exciting. I was hoping that today, while we're out, I could show you a few things, get your take on a few ideas I have."

"Is this about the calendar shots?"

She shook her head. "It's about a different project."

He remembered her passionate defense of the island, its people and history, and he wondered again if she had an idea to tell a story based on something she'd discovered there.

"If you have the time," she said. "I know we need to get the calendar stuff done first, so—"

He squeezed her hands. "We have time." He'd have made the time, even if he hadn't blocked out the rest of his day. It would make for a hectic schedule tomorrow, but taking a single day to get the photos done was better than going all the way to Aberdeenshire, which would have required his being gone for at least three days. And, he thought, standing there with Tessa in his arms . . . there were other benefits to staying on Kinloch as well.

She smiled then, and he could see the spark come back into her eyes, chasing away the shadows. He realized that was where he could begin. He couldn't erase her memories of the horrible things that had created those shadows but he could be part of giving her the space, time, and place to create new memories. Memories that were light to balance the dark of her past.

"I'm interested in whatever it is you want to show me," he told her. *And tell me*, he added silently. He hoped she'd come to trust him enough to share not only a new project idea but the dark parts of her life that had sent her to Kinloch in the first place.

"Good," she said, obviously pleased. "That's great."

She looked so pleasantly surprised by her own sincerity, he wanted to laugh and tease her a little, but he didn't want to dampen the moment in any way.

"I'd like to get your insight, too, if you're willing."

"I'm definitely willing."

She smiled then, and it was that purely joyous, transformational smile he'd been privy to only twice before. He added that to his list of goals. Things to make sure happened as often as possible.

She squeezed his hands. "Let's go for a drive," she said, echoing his request of the day before.

"That's a brilliant idea," he agreed. He'd go to the ends of the earth with her as long as she smiled at him like that. He twined one of her curls around his finger and gently tugged her face closer to his. "But first—"

"We're right in the middle of town," she reminded him as he dipped his head toward hers. "In case you wanted to tell your friends first."

He merely smiled. "I'm wantin' to kiss ye, Miss Vandergriff, right here in front of God and any witness who cares enough to watch. I'm making my pledge public. Do I have your permission?"

Her smile grew, but it was the anticipation he saw that both reassured him and fired him straight up.

"Aye, that you do, Mr. McAuley."

He felt her tremble . . . or maybe that was him. He chalked it up to the anticipation he, too, was feeling. It was rather an exquisite form of torture, the rush of want, the race of his pulse, the quickening of his heart. In that moment, there wasn't any trepidation.

As it was each and every time she stood before him, and he could smell her, touch her, feel her . . . everything came into startling clarity. He knew exactly what he wanted with absolute certainty. He was looking at it. All he had to do was trust his instinct at all times, trust what he'd been telling her. Trust himself.

"Then now we begin," he murmured, lowering his mouth to hers.

The kiss was different from any they'd shared. It was a promise. In her response, he felt a promise made in return. It was a challenge to keep from taking the kiss deeper, and giving in to the other raging needs he had for her. He ended the exchange by dropping one last light kiss at the corner of her mouth. "No' a bad way to start a day."

"I was thinking the same thing," she said, sounding a bit breathless.

He smiled against her hair, and allowed himself to anticipate the time when they'd both be breathless for entirely different reasons.

"Your chariot awaits, my fair lady."

She laughed, and let him help her into the lorry. "Fiery, maybe, but rarely fair."

"I can live with fiery." He levered himself up on the running board and took her mouth in a hot, fast kiss. "Fiery is good."

Leaving her with a bit of a stunned look on her face, and very clear desire for him in her eyes, he hummed to himself as he jumped down, shut the door and sauntered around to his side of the truck. *Aye,* he thought, *fiery is going to be damn good.*

Chapter 15

It should be harder than this.

That's what Tessa kept thinking as they drove to the westernmost end of the island, through the towering twin mountains, across the flax crop valley between them, and finally toward the far shore. It was the most inhospitable stretch of shoreline on Kinloch. The narrow track they'd taken from the loop road wound its rutted way through a rock-strewn field to an abrupt stop, right at the edge of a series of jutting cliffs.

The sheer drop ended in staggering piles of boulders and jagged rocks, all of them pummeled by the relentless crash of churning white caps. No beach, and certainly no calm cove, unlike the ledge they'd been on the day before that sported a stretch of beach beyond the tumble of rocks at the bottom, leading toward the calm of the cove.

Due to the surrounding currents, even the fisherman couldn't navigate the waters around this cape for fear of their vessels being sucked in and shattered against the rocks. Tessa had been drawn to it for its sheer natural ferocity. To her, it was kind of a metaphor for the people and the island itself—withstanding centuries of the myriad battering rams of wars, invasions, pestilence, and blight. It had been an incredible endurance cycle, requiring constant defense and enormous strength of will.

Roan rolled the lorry to a stop well before the cliff edge. "Here?"

She nodded. He had to know this wasn't about the calendar. Not only had he not sent her any pictures taken from that site, but there wasn't anything remotely playful or Christmassy about it. No amount of digital wizardry would change that. This location was about her. "Come on," she said, and climbed out. At the last second, she grabbed her camera. She had no intention of using it. She had a bulging file of photos taken from that exact spot already. She'd grabbed it as more of a comfort, and maybe a little bit of a shield, much like a child might grab her favorite teddy bear before facing a particularly intimidating challenge.

Roan met her at her door just as her feet slid to the ground. She was rapidly getting used to his charming brand of chivalry and thought. Perhaps she'd never tire of his simple, yet consistent demonstrations of care and consideration. She certainly hoped she didn't.

"I don't guess you have a blanket stashed in here anywhere, do you?" Had she planned better—or at all—she'd have thought to bring one. But when she left the croft she hadn't known she was going to go there. She'd known she wanted to talk to him, that it was important to tell him more of the truths she was dealing with, before they went a single step further, but beyond that, she hadn't really formalized a plan.

That kiss in the parking lot had rocked her more thoroughly than the one on their hike, and she'd immediately known where she wanted to have that particular talk.

Everything he'd said, everything he'd told her, had resonated in places so deep inside her, she hadn't known of their existence. Not truly. She'd have thought every one of those surprisingly sensitive and tender nooks and crannies had long since disappeared. Yet he so effortlessly tapped into more and more of them every time they were together.

That was unnerving and not a little terrifying, so she'd gravitated to the most powerful place she knew of, within reach, anyway. She'd need to draw on the primal ferocity of it.

"I've got a roll of furniture padding, for moving things. No' the most romantic, but clean enough, and comfortable."

She nodded, a little nervous at his use of the word romantic. If he was thinking tryst, she was afraid he might be disappointed. She doubted her revelations were going to inspire lust. She was hoping for compassion, and dreading the possibility of pity. "Let's see if we can find a smooth spot among the rocks." The ground was a jumble of rough surfaces, filled here and there with loose rock chips formed from centuries of relentless weather. There was no grass, but there were small pockets of smooth stone or hard-packed ground. "There, maybe?" she said, pointing to a spot a few yards away from the cliff edge.

"There?" Roan had scooped the thickly rolled padding from the rear of his lorry, and stood, shielding his forehead with his free hand to keep the wind from whipping his hair into his eyes. "A bit close, don't you think?"

She smiled lightly. "I was thinking that if you're preoccupied, worrying about being blown over the edge, then what I'm going to tell you will seem mild by comparison."

His smile faded, but all he said was, "Okay. Flirting with danger it is."

That he agreed to her request without question went a long way toward reassuring her.

"If I'd known, I'd have brought wine," he said as he rolled out the thick, quilted pad.

"This isn't a seduction," she said.

He glanced up at her, a reassuring smile on his face. "I know."

"Ah," she said, and smiled, thinking he might be right. A few sips might have loosened the tension that was quickly forming a crick in her neck. *Relax*, she schooled herself. *He'll listen, he'll understand.*

He might also run, her little voice added. But she squashed that. What happened, happened.

She sat cross-legged on the pad, dropping her camera bag in

the hollow formed by her legs. She was quite aware it was a posture that, while casual enough, didn't invite closeness.

Roan didn't look put out. He merely stretched out on his side, equally casual, making himself comfortable by propping his head on his hand. He remained silent, but seemed comfortably so, which put her more at ease. Who knew he could show such restraint?

"We've talked about my reasons for coming here not being as simple as taking a break, or even a mild case of burnout. I mean, you've drawn that conclusion, correct?"

"Aye. And, wherever this is leading, can I say one thing first?"

She felt the tightness creep across the backs of her shoulders. "Go ahead."

"You're twisting the strap on your camera case like you're strangling the poor thing. So I know you're nervous, and I'm sure with good reason. I just want you to know it's my nature to comfort, not to condemn. Whatever it is you're wantin' to share, it's safe with me, Tessa. As are you. Ye ken?"

She nodded. "I appreciate that. And I know it, or I don't think I'd ever consider sharing. I do trust you."

His expression warmed and his eyes glittered, as if he understood her words for the rare gift they were. "Good. Possibly the best news I've gotten all day," he said.

"I haven't talked with anyone about this. At least anyone I wasn't paying to listen to me."

His gaze focused then, and his expression grew serious and thoughtful. "All right."

"I just felt that if we're to take so much as another step in each other's company, then you need to know where I truly am. It's only fair."

"That may be, though I'm certain it doesnae make it any easier a thing to do."

"No," she said, dipping her chin, alarmed by the sudden sting at the backs of her eyes. "It definitely doesn't." *I will not cry! Not now, and most definitely not here.* It was hard enough, revealing to him her career-ending fragility, her decimating help-lessness to control her own mind. The very last thing she was going to do was finally cave in and have her cathartic break-down there. In front of him.

He shifted closer, still stretched out on his side, still giving her space, but within arm's reach. He stretched his free hand and simply laid it across her calf. A comforting presence that didn't require her to do anything other than accept it, and the warmth and reassurance it provided.

That simple gesture almost undid her completely.

How had she, in the short span of their acquaintance, be-come so needy, so grasping for any scrap of comfort?

"I'm sorry to put you through such a hard thing," he said. "But I do want to know. It'll be better for us both."

"I know." Instinctively, she reached out and covered his hand on her calf with her own. He'd told her more than once that she didn't have to go through things alone. She'd always thought that was what would make her the strongest, never re-lying on the comfort of anyone but her own self, her own mind. And look where that had gotten her. So . . . she reached.

When he turned his hand to the side, so they could weave their fingers together, there was an immediate rush of increased strength and fortitude, from nothing more than the steadying warmth of his palm against hers.

It didn't make her feel weak, or fragile. It made her feel . . . supported. Cared for. She, with an ease that was nothing short of shocking . . . drew strength from that. From him. Her reac-tion made her wonder what it was she'd been hiding from all those years.

"When I was little," she said, beginning her story in an en-tirely different place than she'd intended. Her thoughts had shifted to her childhood as very critical pieces of herself started to fit into place. She'd taken him to the rocky cove to illuminate him about her new plans . . . but was illuminating herself in-stead. She realized it was the more important thing she wanted him to know, needed him to understand. Not where she was going . . . but where she'd come from. "Really little," she went on, "I had a pony."

If he was surprised by the opening, he didn't let on. His expression was calm, relaxed, but his gaze was focused entirely on hers.

"I always wanted one of those," Roan said. "Was thankful later on, when I briefly had a crush on a girl who rode religiously every afternoon, that I'd given horses a pass."

Her lips curved briefly. "We had help for that sort of thing. I could just go brush him and love him and enjoy his company. I didn't have siblings, so I would tell him all of my darkest secrets and sorrows."

"You had dark secrets and sorrows as a little girl?"

It didn't surprise her that he'd picked up on that. She nodded. "My deepest, darkest secret at the tender age of five was that I longed for a mother. That I didn't have one was also my sorrow."

"Did you ever know your mother?"

She shook her head. "Not in any real sense. She died when I was a toddler. I had plenty of pictures, and stories from my father and the household help, but no real memories."

"Did your father want to remarry?"

She shook her head. "He was devastated, losing her. She had more than a few health problems, but she contracted pneumonia early in the spring the year I turned three, and she was too weak and . . ." She let her gaze drop to their joined fingers, and he began rubbing his thumb lightly along her index finger. "My father wasn't really the same after that, at least that was what the staff whispered about all the time. I had no real sense of him any other way. And he was happy enough around me, or certainly tried to be. I loved him very much and felt very much loved in return. I had everything I wanted and a very comfortable life, but I wanted a mommy. I think that hurt him . . . in a lot of ways."

"How old did you say you were when he passed away? Six?"

"Six and a half. Car accident. He swerved and ran off the road. When I was older, and understood more about pain and loss, I wondered, every once in a while, if he'd swerved intentionally."

"Would he have willingly left you behind like that?"

"I don't know that he thought of it that way. His despair was overwhelming, at least that's what I learned later, when I asked questions."

"He didn't get help? From people he could pay to listen?"

"Not that I'm aware of."

He continued stroking her fingers, letting her find her own way into the story. The real story.

"Then he passed, and I didn't have a mother or a father. I had George. Our estate and financial manager. My father trusted him above all others, and having chased away most of his closer friends with his grief, he'd appointed George as my guardian. I'm sure he thought George would do right by me. At least, I choose to think that. My father might have been lost in his own grief, and I suppose that was selfish of him, but I don't think he ever meant to harm me."

"So, before the age of seven, you'd lost both parents. And before you turned eighteen, you'd lost everything else. I can't imagine feeling so let down by every single important person in my life. I know people might not think it's fair, or right, but I can't believe you weren't just a little mad at both your mum and your dad for leaving you to fend for yourself."

"It's more understandable for someone in your position," she said, "you were willfully abandoned."

"Didn't some part of you, rational or not, feel the same way? Weren't you angry at your father, who you do have direct memories of, and most certainly George?"

She nodded. "I know I told you it was my anger at George, and what he'd done, that eventually introduced me into the world that would become my entire career."

"What led you from embezzlement and fraud to the kinds of stories you went on to tell?"

"Opportunity. I felt very much like a crusader when George was sentenced to a healthy stay in prison. Initially I went after corporate fraud, embezzlement on a much bigger scale, thinking if going after George helped me, one individual, tackling an entire company would help a whole bunch of people. I was fortunate because contacts came my way due to the glare of media, and I took full advantage. I was back in London following up a story when that terrorist bomb blew up a busload of people in Madrid. I'm not entirely sure why I dropped everything and went, but I did. That was when I truly thought I'd found my mission, my purpose. There couldn't be anything more important than taking on injustices being perpetrated on such a grossly horrifying scale. One story led to another, and I went to places I'd never dreamed I'd go. I was so taken with how oppressed people were so otherwise hopeful, and how their country was often such a place of beauty . . ." She trailed off, and finally lifted a shoulder. "It was an evolution, but I truly felt like I had a very specific calling. The more successful I was at it, the more determined I became, and the higher and deeper I reached."

"You've done some remarkable work, shed light on things that were important for people to know about."

She nodded, accepting his compliment. "I feel that I did. Or I wouldn't have kept going, especially when . . ." She trailed off again, finding it difficult to finish. "But I didn't tell you that part to toot my own horn. I'm telling you about my beginning, and my childhood, because there is a link from one to the other that isn't limited to my being betrayed as a kid, then growing up to crusade against other injustices. That's the obvious linear path. The less obvious one is that I also chose to remain quite singular and removed from everything and everyone around me. On the one hand, I was interacting with the entire world, a range of people that would boggle anyone's mind, so—contrary to popular belief," she added, with a surprising, but brief smile, "I did have people skills. But they were skills designed to elicit information without really giving any of my own, or any part of myself really. I told the stories of hundreds, if not thousands of people . . . but no one got to know my story."

"I'm more aware of that than you might know." He tightened, just slightly, his hold on her hand. "I told you I'd looked you up, read about you, read some of your articles, and I've looked through a large number of your photos. As I became more interested in you, I dug deeper, wanting to know more. And you're quite right, even in this information age, and despite the fact that you've won multiple awards, there is next to nothing to be found anywhere about you personally."

"Which is exactly my point. It wasn't that I was hiding myself, or choosing extreme privacy, though both of those things were often necessary in my line of work. There wasn't any 'me' to be exposed. I *was* my work. I didn't form relationships beyond the fleeting ones I needed to get the job done, and what contacts I did maintain were only for their potential use in future work. The only person who could claim to know me was Kira. Even then, I was a horrible friend to her. I didn't know how to be a friend. I mean, I tried, but whereas she was a natural at fostering that type of bond and keeping it strong, I sucked at it. It's only due to her perseverance that we have any relationship at all. And that all goes back to the pony."

His brows furrowed in confusion, and she realized that somewhere in the past five minutes, she'd let her guard down. She'd been talking to him, much the same way she encouraged people to talk to her. She didn't know if it was the strength of his hand in hers, or the comfort of his steady regard. But at some point, the dread had started to dissipate.

"Other than Kira, and maybe some of the house staff, the only meaningful relationship I developed was with a damn pony. And all he needed from me was the occasional carrot and apple that I sneaked out of the kitchen." She looked at Roan more directly, almost challenging him and his easy comfort and support. "So what I'm saying is that I don't know the first thing about fostering a relationship, about doing all the things people are supposed to do so that other people care about them, and continue to care. I ducked it. I told myself I couldn't get involved because of my job, but the truth of it is, a lot of the avoidance was based on fear."

"You'd lost everything you cared about. Except maybe the pony. So who can fault you?"

"I can. I mean, I chose my profession. I chose a path that would only challenge me in the ways I was willing to be challenged."

"Which happens to be ways that require the kind of mental strength and fortitude that very few, if any of us, have. You're remarkable for what you can do, and what you have done. Dinnae beat yourself up for the things you didn't excel in."

"Basic human relations? That's a pretty big thing."

"You just got done telling me you were amazing at human relations. So what if it wasn't the long-term kind? Even if you'd wanted to, how on earth would you have kept up?"

"Other journalists did. Hell, most of them had families, wives, friends."

"And none of them was you."

"You mean none of them were hiding. None of them were feeling sorry for themselves and their lot in life, and glossing self-pity over with a veneer of public works and a side of humility."

"You did what you did to get through your life, your path. And did a lot of good for others along the way. As I said, dinnae beat yourself up for that."

"It's just . . ." She sighed. *Here it is. The moment of reckoning.* "Maybe if I had, maybe if I'd worked on that part of me sooner, even acknowledged I needed to work on that part of me, I wouldn't be in the place I am now. Which is no longer being able to do the one thing I know how to do."

"And why is that, luv?" he asked, gently and with such sincere concern.

When she tried to tug her hand away, purely on protective

instinct, he tightened his hold. Then he slowly righted himself, never letting go, and scooted until he was facing her. He straddled her crossed legs with his own, then tugged her forward, until she was in the circle of his legs and body. He didn't otherwise hold her, other than their joined hands, but he did lower his mouth next to her ear when she dipped her head and pressed it against his collar bone.

"Ye were tender and gentle and kind all along, weren't ye?" he murmured. "You're exactly the kind of person who fosters relationships and nurtures friendships. You want that, just like we all do. Only you were taught, very young, that you can lose the things most precious to ye. So ye stopped reaching, stopped nurturing. No one will fault ye for that, Tessa. No one wants to be hurt like that again. And again."

"I was a child then," she said haltingly. "I grew up. I should have gotten over it. I did, briefly maybe, with Kira . . . but—"

"But then the rest of your world was ripped out from under ye. It's a testament to the tenderness and the heart in ye that you chose the path ye did. Helping others. The kind of others who are experiencing the worst sort of suffering there is. Who does that, Tessa, if no' someone with a big heart? Ye've let yerself love every single person you've written about, even if ye didn't know it. It's why you wrote about them with such passion, such honesty, and such truth that the rest of us, reading your words and seeing your pictures, couldn't help but be moved. Ye simply wouldn't—or couldn't—let them love ye back."

He cupped her cheek, but let her continue to press her forehead to his shoulder, keeping her face averted. She felt him kiss the top of her head, a sweet, tender kiss, pressed there once, then again. "But that doesnae mean you're not worth love. I know this. Because I've been falling in love with you from the first time I saw you smile. Maybe even before that, but that was the first moment when I knew the real power of you." He kissed her hair again, then nudged until he could press another to her temple. "So, if yer heart is all done feeling the pain of others," he said, so quietly it reached only her ears, "if it can't take any more, that's okay. It's done its job, and done it well. Now it's time for your story."

She felt something inside her crack then, and it fissured so rapidly she couldn't contain it, couldn't keep it from shattering into a million tiny pieces. The sob, when it came, almost choked the breath from her. She thought she might pass out from it if she didn't release it.

So, she did.

When the wracking sobs came, and came, in terrifying, gulping, breath-stealing waves, he held her, and rocked her . . . and did absolutely nothing to stop them.

And she let him. God help her, she let him.

Chapter 16

Roan felt like he was holding on for dear life. Her dear life. How she had become so dear to him, so quickly, he had no idea. But he'd been telling the truth when he said he was falling in love with her. She tugged at him so hard, in places no one had ever come close to reaching.

Maybe it was because her future was unclear, and his was not, that he felt such a sense of urgency with her. As if they had to figure things out between them quickly, or else life would interfere, and tear them apart before they knew enough to make the big decisions they were going to have to make.

But right then, the only thing that was important was holding on.

He didn't know much—hell, anything—about how to handle that kind of situation. But he did know her. Or he was beginning to. He didn't think she'd want sympathy, or coddling.

Her keening made his brain shut down and he closed his eyes, then squeezed them shut and gathered her closer. The sounds she was making were so raw, so . . . wrenching, it was like someone was tearing strips off her. It had to be cathartic, he told himself, praying like hell he was right. He doubted she had done that before, maybe ever. Certainly no one cried like that, grieved like that, fell to pieces like that, so profoundly . . . more than once.

So he held on, and would keep holding on, for however long

it took for her to work all the way through it, and get every bit of it out. He could only hope the tears would cleanse, heal, help . . . and not drag her to a place she couldn't crawl out of. No, no that wasn't her. She'd been fighting that fight for a very long time. And she was losing, but she'd tried to find a way— the right way—to stay in it. She wouldn't let grief get the best of her.

She'd told him yesterday that she'd finally figured out what she was going to do. He hoped with everything he had, even if it meant leaving Kinloch, leaving him and never looking back, that whatever she'd found to walk toward was going to take her away from her past. Away from anything that could cause her so much pain ever again.

He pressed a steady, gentle stream of kisses against her hair, as much to console himself as her. He stroked her back, and held her when she sobbed so hard she couldn't breathe. He wanted to cry with her. And he, the eternal pacifist, had a pri-mal, visceral urge to hunt down anything and everyone who had done this to her. Except he knew he was already holding the only person responsible.

Why? Why had she let it get so bad? Why hadn't she gotten out sooner? He still didn't have the full story, but it was fairly obvious to him that her work could easily take a toll on her as it would anyone fighting a war. She'd been in a war zone for years. It wouldn't surprise him at all if she'd been suffering some kind of traumatic stress. Who wouldn't?

It made sense that she couldn't keep doing the very thing that was torturing her. How it must have thrown her, hurt her, to be denied the only path she'd pursued, the one thing she'd allowed herself to want. Given all she'd been through, it seemed unfair. She needed to give herself a break, and most cer-tainly not feel like a failure. Her career would stand forever as proof of her success.

But he knew it wouldn't feel that way to her. He reminded himself over and over she'd told him she'd found a new path.

And he prayed, selfishly, that whatever she'd discovered, it wouldn't take her away from him. He'd only just found her.

As he held her he was making all kinds of bargains with himself, with God, with whoever would listen, that if she was willing to try to find a life that included him, he'd do whatever it took to make it work. He could compromise. She was making huge changes in her life already. He knew, even in that desperate moment, that Kinloch, in and of itself, simply didn't have enough to offer someone like her. She might not ever go back to war, but he couldn't imagine she'd find something lasting and fulfilling there. Not long term.

She'd gone there to heal. And it looked like maybe that was happening. But she didn't intend to stay.

Her sobs quieted, even if her body was still wracked with heaves and shivers. He rocked, he stroked, and he simply held on.

Finally, she pressed lightly against his chest, and he loosened his hold enough for her to straighten slightly away from him, though she remained in the cradle of his body. She didn't look up, and he wouldn't rob her of that basic privacy.

"I-I'm sorry," she choked out between gulps of air, as she tried to find her way back to some semblance of normalcy.

"Dinnae ye dare think to apologize for crying," he said, almost tersely. "Dinnae ye dare. Take your time, luv," he continued, more gently. "I'm no' going anywhere."

"I don't—do—that."

"I know. But you've needed to," he said. "You've needed to."

"It's"—she hiccupped air, and had to stop, still working to get her breath back to a steady rhythm—"mortifying."

He shifted his body around, so she was leaning her side against him, and he tucked her more fully against his chest, allowing her to keep her tear-streaked face averted from his. "No' with me. Never with me."

She was tense in his arms, and he thought she was going to

argue, or simply pull away, but then she sighed. A ragged, broken, hiccupping sigh . . . and finally gave up and leaned against him, pressing her cheek against his heart.

He held her like that until the wracking breaths finally subsided to an occasional shudder. "It's plaguing ye, isn't it?" he asked.

He felt her nod against his chest.

He stroked her hair, her back, and continued the slow rocking motion. "When you're asleep?"

There was a pause, and then she nodded.

"Ye canno' go back." He didn't make it a question.

"No," she rasped. "I can't."

"I'm sorry that hurts you," he said. "I'm sorry you'll lose something that means so much to you." He leaned back a little, and urged her swollen, tear-streaked face up to his. She was reluctant, but he gently persisted. It tore at his heart, the ravages he saw in her sad, sad eyes. "But I'm no' sorry you willnae be going back. Someone else can take up your cause. Ye've literally given it everything ye have. And that's something to be proud of, Tessa. Yer leaving the field of battle, but yer leaving it alive, and thriving. And I know you'll find another way to contribute, to do what you want to do, what drives you . . . but in a way that won't tear you apart." He kissed the swollen lids of her eyes, kissed the splotchy red of her cheeks, then gently, very gently kissed the corners of her mouth, and the softness of her full lips. "One that allows you to finally be you . . . and to be happy."

She sniffled all over again and slid her arms around his waist, holding on tightly as she buried her face against his neck. "I know it might not seem like it," she managed, her voice still so raw it was more whisper than words, "at the moment. But . . . I am, Roan. I'm not whole yet, but since coming here . . ." She made herself look up, and broke his heart all over again.

"I'm so sorry it did this to you," he said, stroking her cheeks. "But I am so proud of you for letting go, for trusting yourself to handle falling apart, and finally letting it all out."

"I'm not sure I could have done it on my own. Maybe . . . but . . . thank you." She held him more tightly. "Just . . . thank you."

If he'd felt humbled before, he felt triple that now. He pressed his cheek to her hair, and felt as if he'd run a marathon himself. He hated having to remind himself that it was far from over yet.

She took a deeper breath and sat up, facing him squarely, looking at him directly for the first time since she'd lost the battle for self-control. "I have been healing here. And you're playing a role in that." Her breath hitched, and she had to work to speak. "I'd figured it out, my path, that morning when you wrecked your bike—when I made you wreck your bike—I knew then. But you're the one who has helped me to accept it. To feel more confident in my choices. To push me to allow myself to want, to anticipate that happiness will be there, to believe in joy. My joy."

He studied her face and saw the truth of what she was saying. "I won't lie and say I have any idea what I'm doing," he said. "I don't. What you're dealing with scares me—but only because I want to help and I don't know how."

She hiccupped again, and gave him a watery smile that tugged at emotions he didn't know he had. "Your instincts seem pretty good to me."

His lips curved a little, and it was a welcome relief to feel like smiling.

"I wanted to tell you," she said, "about what I want to do. But you needed to know—need to know—just how broken I really am. Obviously, it's not over yet. And I don't know how long the process will take, or if I'll ever be free of the nightmares, the terrors, doubting my own mind and ability to control it. It scares the ever loving crap out of me, Roan. It might never be fully gone. So . . . so, I don't see how I can expect you to handle—"

He leaned in and kissed her. Short, and tender, but enough to stop her so he could speak. "I know what I expect of me. When

I have doubts, I'll tell you about them. But it won't keep me from trying. I just might need help from time to time, too, to make sure I'm giving you what you need."

"You're giving me more than anyone ever has. It's an embarrassment of riches, what you bring to me. What I'm worried about is that I won't have enough to give back."

"I'm here, aren't I? I wouldn't be if here wasn't something for me. When we don't have a clear path, then we'll help each other." He tipped her chin up and now that her breathing had smoothed out, kissed her a bit more lingeringly. "Trust that we can figure it out. You're already giving me more than I thought was possible."

Like the sun peeking out from a long storm, her lips curved, just slightly. "You have very low standards for yourself, then."

"On the contrary," he said, wanting to grin and shout to the world, he felt so triumphant. "I have the very highest of standards." He kissed her again. "At least I do now."

She kissed him back, and he felt himself stir. He fought against it; that was the last thing she needed at the moment. Even if it might be yet another cathartic release, he knew he wanted their first time to be joyful, not a bandage on a still healing wound.

As he gathered her and lay down on the padded blanket, he knew there would be a first time. If he was the luckiest man on earth, and he certainly thought he was in the running, there would be many more times to follow.

He rolled her to him and they lay with their legs entwined, her cheek on his chest, and allowed peace to seep back in.

"I want so much," she said, after a long time had passed. "I've expected a lot of me in the past, but I haven't really let myself want. But I do now. And I can't seem to stop."

"Why do ye have to stop?"

"I want to reach for it all. I want to explore this new path. I want to explore you, this, us. I want—"

"This new path of yours, will it take you away from here straight off?"

"No, but—"

"Then we have time to sort through it all. Find solutions." When she started to respond, he nudged her face up so their gazes met. "We're already working through this. Together. Trust that, and enjoy it. What just happened, brought us closer together. It's a turning point, a moment. I want more of those. We don't have to sort it all out today. Okay?"

She nodded, and the smile flirted again, reaching her eyes. "Are you always so wise?"

"Hardly ever. I'm more of a stumbler. But what I'm no' is a quitter."

"I never felt like I was."

"You're not one now. Retiring from the field of battle to live to fight another day is not quitting. Your battle strategy might be changing, but you're hardly running away. You're going with your strengths. And those have changed. It happens to all of us at various points in our lives. You're adapting. I don't know what else you could expect from yourself."

"A stumbler, huh?" She scooted up and gave him a rather startlingly passionate kiss on the mouth. "I wish I stumbled half as cleverly and wisely as you. But . . . point taken. I'll try. I will," she added when he gave her a doubtful look. "I'm nothing if not motivated."

He kissed her again, but when his body threatened to talk his mind out of his earlier decision, he gently disengaged himself, then helped them both to their feet.

She took a deep breath and a moment to smooth her clothes, run a still-shaky hand through her hair. "Now what? Calendar shots?"

"We've got time to deal with those. I'm thinking an early dinner. And maybe just some time to talk. About . . . anything or nothing. No pressure, just getting to know more about each other."

Her expression grew concerned. "I-I don't know that I'm really up for a public dinner. Not because I'm uncomfortable being seen with you," she hurried to add. "But . . . after that, I'm just not—"

"I didn't mean in public. I do know how to cook."

"You. You mean, you cook dinner? For me?"

"We do that here, on occasion. You should try it. Tonight, in fact." He bent down and quickly shook out the moving pad and rolled it back up. "Are you game?"

"Apparently. But you might have to explain the rules of this particular game to me."

They started back toward the lorry, and he was amazed and more than a little staggered by how easily they'd transitioned past such a monumental moment. Things still felt . . . good. Normal. Not awkward. "You sit. I cook. We eat. We talk."

"And?"

"And . . . you can help with the dishes—if you insist." He slid his hand in hers as they walked, and her eyes immediately took on a bit of that feminine sparkle again. *Good,* he thought, with a private smile. *So very good.*

"Okay," she said. Then she smiled. "That sounds good. Really good."

He smiled back . . . and enjoyed feeling a bit of that sparkle himself.

Chapter 17

Tessa had no idea what kind of place she'd imagined he lived in . . . but she knew she'd never imagined this.

He watched her as she took in his home and its surroundings. "It's—"

"A stable," she finished for him.

He flashed her a grin. "Aye. It *was* a stablehouse and hunting lodge back around the nineteenth century. Now it's a home. My home."

She walked up to the door. The house itself was all stacked stone, with a red gabled roof. It was surrounded by a low stone wall. What had been the stable doors, inset into the front stone wall, were sealed along the bottom half, with the upper halves having been turned into windows. The building was L shaped, with the short length disappearing around the far corner.

"But no horses?"

"I have a few sheep, but no." He smiled. "Never did change my mind about that." He stepped past her and opened the door. "You'll have to pardon my less than stellar housekeeping. I wasn't anticipating company."

"Please, that's the last thing you ever need to worry about with me. I haven't exactly spent my life in four star—oh . . . my." She stopped just a few feet inside the door, then turned slowly. She took in the story-and-a-half high gabled window and the wood beam ceiling. "This is beautiful. Truly."

"Thank you."

She walked across the hand-laid tile of the small foyer area, and onto the hardwood floor of the main room. "I think that is the biggest fireplace I've ever seen."

"Ye've got to be able to cook what ye kill."

She swung around to look at him.

"Hunting lodge," he quickly added. "No' me. But I didn't want to take it out. It's functional and it heats most of this place at night and all through the cold months."

To her left there was another tiled area that contained a narrow, galley-style kitchen, framed by a counter, which had what looked like hand carved stools lined up under it. The main room had functional, wood-framed furnishings, all on the large, masculine side. More from the hunting lodge, she presumed. "So, was this place already converted when you bought it?"

"No. I've spent most of the past eight years converting it. One stable at a time," he added with a laugh. "This was the lodge area, but the design was different originally and there was no electricity. All bathing facilities were outside. And the hunters' mounts lived right down the hall. But, when I took it on, it hadn't been used as anything for almost forty-five years, and that attempt had been to resurrect it for its originally intended use. It went up for auction when the last of the McAuley line who'd owned it left for the mainland, and so I took it."

"Were they related to you?"

"All of the McAuleys are related here in some manner, but this was a distant cousin at best. Much older, and fairly reclusive. He lived about a kilometer west of here and was a crofter. He'd let this place fall into complete disrepair when the hunting lodge didn't take off."

"With your handling tourism, did you ever think of trying to make it into a bed and breakfast or something?"

"I wasn't interested in being a business owner. But the concept called to me personally and I thought it would be a good project."

"Because you're not busy enough."

He grinned briefly at that. "Actually, I did briefly consider converting the section with the stables into a weaving school. Knock down some of the walls and turn them into studio classrooms."

She paused in her stroll around the room and looked back at him. "Really? That sounds . . . kind of wonderful, actually. What happened?"

He shrugged. "Like I said, I didn't want to run a business. I already had one or two or ten other things that I did. I talked up the idea, but no one wanted to step forward and take it on."

She thought that was kind of a shame, and couldn't help wondering if someone with Kira's vision and determination, and education, wouldn't have been perfect for such a thing. Of course, Kira hadn't lived here then, but still . . . She tucked that thought away in the back of her mind. "So, what did you do with the stalls? The building looks like it wraps around the back."

"It does." He pointed to a set of heavy double doors across the main room from the kitchen. "Those connect to the back hall, which is what used to be the center aisle of the stables. I had to completely gut most of it out to the exterior stone, and rework the interior entirely. The stone itself was easy to steam out and scrub clean, disinfect, but the rest, including the original stable doors, were replaced or removed."

"Right." She made a face. "Not the odor you really want to live with."

"No, no' really. It took three years to get it all right."

"Years? To fumigate?"

"And renovate. It was a process. But I can guarantee you'd never know that horses used to stand where I now spend each night."

"Your bedroom is back there? Where did you sleep for the three years it took to get that all done?"

He gestured to the couch—which was . . . functional, but didn't exactly leave him room to stretch out.

"I don't require four star lodgings, either," he said with a wink.

They shared a smile at that. She wandered over to the fireplace, which was almost as tall as she was and long enough to fit his entire couch into. "Who did the pen and ink drawings?" Over the mantel were several framed prints, all depicting scenes of island life. "They're all from here, aren't they?"

"Aye. I dinnae know the history of them. They're initialed, but no' signed. I found them stored in one of the stables that had been converted to a small office and storage space—a very rustic office. There were trunks in there, and crates full of mostly useless things. I really liked the viewpoint of whoever it was that drew them."

"I do, too. None of them are placid or even bucolic. I'm not sure how he made a simple pen and ink drawing look so . . . tempestuous." She turned to look at him. "Imagine what he could have done with pictures of the cliffs."

"Aye," he said, and smiled. "Imagine."

And, just like that, tension eased in and filled the room between them. Not the difficult or strained kind. The kind that made her thoughts drift back to the double doors . . . and the bedroom that was beyond them. She hadn't gotten the sense he'd taken her there with lovemaking in mind, nor, when they'd left the cliffs, had she been in any shape whatsoever to think about that.

But, standing in his space, where he lived, something he'd made into a home literally with his own two hands . . . her thoughts weren't entirely on the mortifying catharsis she'd had, also in his own two hands.

He hadn't made her feel badly about it, had, in fact, done quite the opposite—which was nothing short of a miracle in her book. He'd said many things that had given her much to think about, not the least of which were his feelings for her. She needed some time to regain control of herself, of her emotions, before thinking about what came next with the two of them.

But, she felt that he was way too far across the room. And the idea that the bed where he slept was just beyond those doors was admittedly tantalizing.

"I could give you a tour," he said, following her gaze.

She wondered what he might have seen in her face, but he didn't give any indication that he'd read in her expression anything other than continued curiosity for his home.

"Or," he offered, when she didn't immediately reply, "you could make yourself comfortable while I go see what I can put together for an early supper."

She turned her attention to a narrow stone patio she saw through the windows in the rear wall. The sun was further west than she'd realized. They must have lain on that blanket pad a lot longer than she'd thought. "Supper sounds good. But I can help. Just because I turned into a raving lunatic back there, doesn't mean I'm completely helpless. Really, I—"

"Tessa, I told ye. I willnae accept apologies." He said it firmly, but kindly.

It made her feel better, put her more at ease, post breakdown.

He smiled—which didn't hurt his cause. "But if helping would be a better thing for ye at the moment, how are your chopping skills? I have a vegetable plot out back, and half a roasted chicken. I could make potatoes."

"You garden?"

"Most of us do. How else would we have vegetables?"

"True," she said, and had to laugh at herself. She'd spent enough time in underdeveloped or besieged countries to know that many, many people didn't have a corner grocer to run to when they got low on green peppers and corn. She supposed she'd found more creature comforts on Kinloch than she'd been used to in some time, so she tended to forget the existence there, though comfortable, was still a bit rustic.

"I can chop," she said, and followed him into the kitchen.

He kept on moving through the narrow alley-shaped area to a door she hadn't noticed, situated in the back corner. He pushed open the door, having to use a bit of force. "Damp air from the ocean warps everything. I've re-sanded and reworked the floors in the main room I don't know how many times and they're still not entirely right."

"I thought they were beautiful."

"Thank you," he said, sounding quite pleased.

"You're welcome," she said, smiling. He was quite cute, too. She followed him through the doorway. "Where are we going?"

"Vegetables?"

"Oh!" she said. "We're picking them fresh."

He looked at her, and she laughed. It felt almost as cathartic as her tears. That she laughed far more easily still stunned her a little. That she had so much to laugh about stunned her even more. She wondered if he realized how much he'd enriched her life in so short a time. But that made her think about his other declaration, about falling for her, which she'd already firmly filed in the "think about it later" file. No way could she tackle that now.

"You'd think I still lived back in that manor house," she said.

He'd crouched down and pulled out what looked like some big orange beets from the tilled soil. "Where *do* you live?"

She'd crouched next to him so she could take them from him or pull some herself, but paused. "What?"

He glanced sideways at her. "Live. Do you have a home? A place you go to between assignments?"

"I'm never between assignments."

He rotated on the balls of his feet so he was facing her. "Are you saying you have no home? Where . . . do you keep your stuff?"

"What stuff?"

"Okay," he said, clearly trying to readjust his thinking. "So ye have no stuff, but ye have clothing, and, I'm guessing, a fair amount of photo equipment. Surely you dinnae travel with all of it."

She lifted a shoulder.

"Ye do? Really?"

"It's not that much. It all packs in these big, fiberglass trunks. I'm used to lugging or shipping them around. If I'm on a quick assignment, I just stash the trunks somewhere local, but if I know I'll be located somewhere for a period of time, I'll lease a place, set up a dark room, get Internet connection." She shrugged again. "It's easier than you think."

"For you, maybe." He continued to gaze at her, looking a little amazed. She found she didn't mind that. It didn't make her feel like a freak. It made her feel kind of . . . unique. Special, maybe. At least that's how he seemed to take it.

She smiled in the face of his complete disconcertment. It was a testament to how far they'd come that she was amused by his reaction rather than defensive. "For me, definitely. It's funny that you have no problem accepting that I'm completely screwed up over the things I've seen, but you can't wrap your head around the fact that I have a vagabond lifestyle. Where would I live, anyway? What would be the point of having a fixed location?"

"Where were you just before this? You said you'd been trying to get help to deal with how everything was starting to come down on you. Where did you stay?"

She rocked back on her heels, then pushed to a stand. She was surprised that she wanted to explain. He still wasn't entirely aware of whom he was involving himself with, despite his declaration of deep feelings. Nor, apparently, looking at her immediate surroundings, did she really know him.

"A hotel. I looked up the best doctors and that's where I went. Lodging wasn't all that hard."

"More than one," he said, not making it a question. "Doctor."

She nodded. "I wanted to be fixed, I wanted to get back to work. I tried . . . everything."

"What did they say? Did it help?"

She nodded. "Tremendously. In terms of dealing with the pain, understanding it. There were different doctors, different approaches, but they all agreed on one thing, which was that the only way I'd ever fully get past the horror of what I'd seen was to stop putting myself in the middle of it."

"For good?"

She lifted a shoulder, then nodded.

"And have you?"

Her lips curved a little. Maybe he did know her, because his tone was decidedly skeptical. "The breakdown sort of made the decision for me. I've been getting help for the better part of a year. But I'd start doing better, and I'd take an assignment. I wasn't completely stupid. I tried to take on things that weren't, perhaps, as horrifying or challenging. Didn't matter."

"The nightmares came back, the terrors?"

"Debilitatingly so. Eventually I knew I had to take a break, a sabbatical. I was doing more harm to my career and to myself than good."

"Did anybody else know?"

She shook her head. "I mean, clearly I was having burnout issues, everybody saw that. Nobody was particularly surprised. I never took a break. I had no reason to. There were always so many stories to tell."

"So . . . when you came here . . ."

"It was, as you said, a retreat from battle."

"Did you still think you could go back?"

She shook her head. "I mean, I wanted to believe otherwise, but I knew. Deep down, I knew. I wouldn't have come here, otherwise."

He stood, too, and brushed his hands off on his trousers. "And it's helped? I mean, I know you said you've come to some decisions, about work. But . . . how are you with the rest? Better?"

"I don't know, Roan. At first, yes. Then the nightmares came back, even here. But . . . for the past week or so"—her cheeks warmed and she smiled—"I've been a bit preoccupied. The dreams I've had have left me disturbed, but in an entirely different, far more interesting way."

He smiled then, too. And reached up to push a stray tendril from her cheek. "That sounds encouraging."

"It is," she said, and felt the real truth of her words. He invigorated her, and, for the first time, she truly felt . . . healthier. "It's not over yet, Roan. You need to know that."

"Are you violent? In your dreams? Is there anything I need to know? Special ways to help you if you're in one?"

Rather than be put out by his assumption they'd be sleeping together she was touched that his first instinct was to learn, to help, without even the slightest hint of pity. "I sleep alone, but the terrors just seem to victimize me. I didn't fight in battles, I merely recorded them. So . . . no, I don't think so. There are recommended ways to wake me out of them, but I've never had reason—had anyone—to try them to see what works. I usually just wake up terrified, heart pounding, drenched in sweat . . . and it takes a while to come down from that. But I do."

He stepped closer, and reached for her with his free hand. He took her hand, and tugged her gently, closer, until their bodies bumped. "Will you teach me? I dinnae want to hurt ye. I want to help."

Her heart, until then, had definitely been teased by the promise of what he might have to offer her. In that moment it swelled, and began to fall—right into his hands. It had been a big day. A landmark day. For her. She nodded, throat tight, and eyes still swollen and tender, stinging a bit with a fresh rush of emotion. She knew, looking at him, that if she was capable of love, true love, he would find a way to bring it out in her. And she wanted him to. She knew it would be swift and fast. Heady and thrilling. Good, and strong.

But there was nothing intimidating or potentially frightening about the sensation. Instead of feeling that she alone was responsible for holding up a wall against a tsunami-strength wave of terrifying emotion, she felt like the thing threatening her was simply the possibility of being swamped with . . . well . . . love. Whatever this welling sense was within her, the warmth and affection and powerful, powerful want . . . she welcomed it. She was all done ducking out. She was a badass non-hider now. For real.

"I can tell you what they told me," she said to him, "and explain it in a little more detail, then . . . if you want, we'll figure it out from there."

The look in his eyes changed from one of care and concern, to a darker, more crackling one of desire. She wanted to take the beets from his hands and toss them over her shoulder, then have her way with him right there. But she was smart enough, at least that's what she told herself, to know it was probably better for them to spend more time talking before . . . well, before.

"Dinner?" he said, lofting the orange tubers in his hand.

She could see him trying to bank his desire, stay focused on what he, too, thought was the better path for them to take. So, she nodded. But it took enormous willpower not to at least explore the idea of an alternate way to spend the next few hours. "What are those, anyway?" she asked.

"Sweet potatoes," he said.

"Oh. They look like orange beets."

He grinned. "You really aren't a farm girl at all."

"Despite having spent most of my adult life either in a sweltering hovel under a mosquito net, or in a bombed-out building under a mattress . . . apparently my childhood has also left lingering scars that I wasn't even aware I possessed."

"So . . . not a cook."

She shook her head. "Forager extraordinaire. You'd be amazed at what I can find at four in the morning, in the worst places imaginable."

"I'll take your word for it."

She shrugged, but she was smiling. "Have it your way, then."

"Oh," he said, the intensity leaping right back into his green eyes, all but electrifying them, "I intend to. At some point."

"You know," she said, throwing caution directly into the wind, and not caring, "we could talk about my ideas for the new kinds of stories I want to tell—starting right here on Kinloch, by the way. You might have a personal interest in that one. And we can map out the three or four best shots to take for this calendar project. Over dinner." She stepped right up against him and toyed with the button at the top of his shirt.

"Or?" he managed, and she was deeply gratified to hear the gravel in his voice, the thread of need. Glad to know she wasn't the only one feeling what she was feeling, wanting what she was wanting.

"Or, you could ignore my less than lovely appearance at the moment, and at least pretend I'm looking fabulous and dynamic and sexy . . . and give me the rest of that tour you offered earlier. Fair warning though, being as we promised honesty with each other at all times."

"Which is?" He tossed the sweet potatoes over his shoulder.

"At a certain point in said tour, I might try and have my way with you."

"Really," he said, then made her squeal by scooping her up in his arms.

"Roan, I am not a small—you can't just—"

"Does it look like I'm strugglin' under the unbearable weight of ye?" he said, as he carried her quite easily back into the house.

"No, but you don't need to—"

"Oh, that is where you're wrong," he said, his wide grin carving that dimple deeply into his cheek. "I have all kinds of needs. And carrying you in my arms? Just one of many."

She wrapped her arms around his neck and laughed. "Many, huh?"

He kicked the kitchen door shut behind him with force enough to wedge the warped wood back into its frame. "That I know of at this moment. I plan to add to the list as I get to know ye better." He slid her around in his arms and kissed her. "Find out what ye like . . . what makes your eyes go all—" He kissed her again, longer, lingeringly, pausing in front of the door to the back hallway, and pressing her back up against it, until he could turn her and wrap her legs around his waist. He pushed right up in between them, making them both gasp, never once lifting his head.

She locked her arms around his neck, her legs around his hips . . . and kissed him back, releasing the full tumble of emotions, needs, wants, confusion, and joy. The kiss was as wrenching, as cathartic, as her breakdown by the cliffs . . . but rather than deplete her, exhaust her, and leave her feeling hollow and empty . . . it started an energy, a focused, driving force, that grew the longer she simply allowed herself to fully experience it.

Finally, he lifted his mouth, and her lips felt all tender and puffy and . . . loved.

His eyes glittered as he looked into hers. "Like that," he finished. "I will happily make it my mission in life to find more ways to make you look at me, just like that." Then he was making her squeal, in surprise and delight, as he hiked her up on him, pulled her close, and shifted them so he could yank the door open at her back.

He carried her down a wide hallway, and she vaguely found herself thinking that he was right, it didn't smell at all like a barn, but that was about the extent of her awareness beyond the man presently carrying her. "You really do have a Rob Roy complex, don't you?"

"If you dinnae mind being the conquered maiden on occasion," he said, giving it right back to her, "then, aye, I can play savage heathen." He kicked the door open to his room and turned so they fell across what felt like a sea of down and linen.

He rolled her to her back and half pinned her to the bed, his hand on her wrist, the other cupping her face. "And, for the record?"

He leaned down and kissed her again. It was so sweet and ardent and perfect, she felt her heart tilt dangerously close to its final tumble.

"For the record, what?" she asked, when he finally lifted his head. Not that she much cared what the answer was. She was too busy looking into the face of the first and only man she was truly going to fall in love with. How terrifyingly wonderful was that?

She pushed fear away, and the thousands of questions that went along with it, and for once, just let herself feel and experience the joy.

"You're the most beautiful woman I've ever known. Never more so than right now."

"Roan—"

"Do ye want me, Tessa?"

She framed his face, and very deliberately looked right into his eyes. "Oh aye," she said. "I want only you."

"Ye have me," he murmured. "Ye have all of me."

Chapter 18

He thought he'd be more worried about taking proper care of her, being enough for her, allowing himself to care so much, so quickly, and being terrified he'd lose everything when she couldn't handle it and took off.

Instead, all he could think was, *thank you, God, for giving me this time, this moment . . . this woman.* He accepted the gift for what it was, knowing he was the richest man alive, no matter what came after.

He leaned down, and though she lifted her head to claim his mouth, he pushed her back down . . . and kissed her gently. Her cheeks were still ruddy from her tears, her eyes puffy and tender, and her lips soft and full and waiting for the taste of his. He took his time and kissed each part of her, soothing, tender, but also stirring . . . if the soft sounds she was making and the hips moving beneath his were any indication.

She finally slipped her wrist free from beneath his hand and gently cupped the side of his head, bringing his mouth to hers. "I want this," she murmured. "I want you. And I want to give back."

"You do," he said against her lips. "The way you respond to me makes me feel like I could slay dragons."

He felt her smile against his mouth. "Is this more of that warrior heathen thing?" she teased.

He nipped at her chin, then claimed her mouth with a kiss so heated and passionate, she was left panting—and so was he—when he finally lifted his head. "Maybe," he said, in answer to her. "Is that going to be a problem?"

She shook her head, and her eyes were gleaming. That lovely perfect smile hovered at the corners of her mouth, and he thought there was nothing they couldn't get through as long as she looked at him like that.

"If there were such things as dragons, I'd gladly slay however many it takes if it will keep ye looking at me the way you are right now."

"You say the loveliest things." Then she surprised him by rolling him to his back. "Just how is it that I look at you?"

He grinned. He'd thought to be gentle and tender and soothing given all she'd been through that day. But she was being playful. . . . playful, fun, teasing. Hot, passionate, physical. He could see that was exactly what they both needed. *Step out of the dark, indeed, and into the pure, rejuvenating, healing light.*

"In the way that tells me you want me," he said, grinning broadly as he gave himself completely over to her and whatever mood she wanted to set. "Want me bad," he added. "Not that I can blame ye, of course."

"Of course. Modest, even here. I like it."

"Oh, I plan to see that you more than like it." He made his move, rolling up and taking her with him, then flipping her down to her back, pinning her with the full length of his body.

"More than like it?" she taunted right back and the avid gleam in her eyes had him so erect he hurt. "How, exactly, do you plan to do that?"

"I have many, many ways."

Her eyes darkened as the pupils shot wide and her mouth parted, just slightly. He prayed he could keep his control long enough to take her on the promised journey of pleasure. Because one touch and he wasn't too certain he would be able to last. The first time, anyway.

"Big talk," she said.

"Aye, but small, delicately concentrated and concerted actions," he countered, then began unbuttoning her green cotton shirt. "In fact, there are two very concentrated areas I intend to spend a very focused and intent amount of time tending to right now."

"Do you?" she said, but her hips were bucking, and her eyelids slipped shut as she sighed when he flicked open the front closure of her sheer, mint-colored bra.

"Oh, aye, that I do. Green is a good color on ye," he said, promptly peeling the shirt off her. Using his teeth, the cups of her brassiere followed.

"Aye, indeed," was all she managed as he dragged the shimmery fabric slowly across her taut, dark nipples. She was tall, lanky, and her body was lean, with a light ripple of muscle. The body of someone who required it to hold up to a lot of steady work. She wasn't soft in too many places that he could see.

He leaned down and kissed the smooth spot between her bare breasts, then worked his way, with lips and tongue, around the soft swell of each of them, careful to leave the pebbled tips free from contact.

She was writhing beneath him with greater need, and her moans were coming in short gasps. Finally she lost patience and dug the fingers of her free hand through his hair, urging him to take what she so badly wanted to give him.

"Patience, dragonslayer," he murmured against her skin.

"I thought that was you," she panted.

"I would be. Will be," he said, shifting his weight a little lower, and pinning her wrists easily back to the bed, delighted when she let him. "But, at the moment, I feel like I'm the one breathing fire." He blew air directly across one nipple, then the other, making her buck hard off the bed under him. "You know what puts out fire?"

"What?" There was pleading in her tone, but it was the bald need that threatened to destroy what little control he had.

"This," he said, and flicked his tongue across the tip of one, then the other. She moaned and his own body grew rather insistent. He took one nipple in his mouth, laved it with his tongue, suckled it, until he thought he might drive himself over the edge as she bucked and arched beneath him, pressing directly against every straining inch of him. But he moved to the other, wanting to draw out the exquisite sensations, as long as he could.

"Roan," she pleaded. "Oh—!"

Her hips jumped off the bed as he nipped at the hardened tip, and at first he thought he'd hurt her, but then she kept bucking and moaning and he realized she was coming.

"I'm no' sure I'll be able to keep up with ye," he said, but he was happy at the prospect of trying. She'd been through so much, felt and seen so much tragedy and heartache, suffered so much of her own, it was stunning to him that she was so open, so responsive to him. Maybe it was because she didn't let anyone close and the deprivation had made her ultra sensitive . . . or maybe it was the heightened emotions from earlier sending her nerve endings into a frenzy.

At the moment, he didn't much care. Because he'd moved his nipping, suckling attentions to her other nipple . . . and swore she was climbing again.

"Roan," she said, first on a moan, and then sounding almost panicky. He looked up, alarmed that maybe, somehow, it was triggering something bad inside her head. But her expression was one of stunned pleasure, and he realized that she was as shocked by her response as he was. "Don't st— oh, exactly," she said through a long groan, as he went back to what he'd been doing. "Exactly that. Lots of that."

He grinned against her damp skin, liking how verbal she was, how frank, how . . . Tessa. Even in bed. It made him quite delightfully curious to find out what she'd be like if he . . . He scooted down further, sliding his hands down the sides of her waist, to her hips . . . and the waistband of her khaki trousers.

"Oh, that would be . . ." she began, but ended with a groan as he slowly tugged down the zipper to part the front panels of her trousers . . . only to find matching mint green silk. She had the body, mind, and spirit of a strong, independent, tough woman . . . yet she wore silk.

"What?" she breathed as he continued to look. She was writhing beneath the weight of him pinning her thighs. "A girl can't have nice things?"

She was pushing at him, goading him, but it only added to his pure delight . . . and ramped up his desire. "I was thinking utilitarian cotton," he said, "so you'll have to forgive me."

"I have plenty of those, too, if they're more your thing."

"Oh, these are purely my thing. Exactly my thing. Although if you move like this every time I'm on top of you, it likely will-nae much matter what you have covering your most delectable bits." He levered his weight up and jerked her pants down in one tug. "Because they're no' going to be coverin' much for very long."

She wriggled beneath him as he slid them off her legs completely, then returned his attentions to the scrap of shimmer she called panties.

A glance up showed she was grinning, even as her neck arched and she pushed her head back into the soft down of the mattress, her eyes tightly shut. "I can live with that," she managed tightly.

"Good to know," he said, then ripped the panties off her, too.

He teased her with his tongue, but there were other parts of him begging to be the thing doing the teasing, and he was straining to the fair lengths and breadths of his control.

Her body was so finely tuned to pleasure, he carried her over once again, and she was still shuddering and twitching as he yanked his shirt off, followed swiftly by his trousers. He reached for the nightstand, but she stopped him.

"It's okay. I mean, I'm okay. Protected. I—like to keep things on schedule," she said with a dry smile. "There are so few things I can do that with. And, clean bill of health, too. Well, for my body. I can't vouch for my mental state."

"Tessa." He rolled toward her, and moved up so they were even with each other, then pulled her close to him. The shock of her lovely, warm, bare skin sliding over his felt . . . tremendous, along the scale of rock his world, bloody fantastic. He lost his train of thought. "That feels—you feel so . . . brilliant," he said, like a complete dim nob.

"So do you," she said, sliding her hands along his back.

He thought his brain synapses might just blow their circuits all at once, the friction was so electric and delicious.

She looked into his eyes. "Roan, if you're more comfortable using something, I don't want you to feel—"

"I trust you. And you have nothing to worry about from me." He rolled her gently to her back and moved on top of her. "I'd rather not have a single thing come between us. If you dinnae mind."

She smiled up at him, and whatever part of his heart he might have still claimed as his own was well and truly lost then. It was all hers, for the keeping.

"I definitely dinnae mind," she teased. "And I definitely dinnae want to wait." She lifted up against him, sliding him between her thighs, pressing, pushing him right where he wanted to be. Her smile grew, even as she gasped when he pushed the tip along her slick, tender skin. "If ye dinnae mind."

Both groaned as he pushed slowly, steadily into her. She gripped him so tightly he thought he'd not last past the first thrust. She lifted her hips, took him in more deeply, then gasped and arched hard against him. They moaned in unison as he withdrew, then again as he thrust back inside her. From there they found their rhythm, naturally, easily. It was incredibly perfect.

He tilted her hips, urged her legs more tightly around his back, as he sunk more fully into her.

She climbed slowly. "Roan—oh, that's . . . so"—she bucked wildly against him as she went over the edge—"good," she ground out as she continued to move and shudder against him.

Hearing his name, and that urgent need, feeling her contract and pulse around him, shot him straight to the brink. He thrust harder, deeper, and she met him at each peak. He'd thought to savor the rush as it swept through him, draw it out, enjoy each slippery, jerking, shuddering thrust as he came, but instead he was yanked, almost violently over the edge, and literally growled as he came roaring inside her. There was no finesse, no tenderness, nothing about it that was anything other than raw, primal, and downright visceral.

As soon as he could pry his eyes open and see something other than stars twinkling in his peripheral vision, he had every intention of apologizing for being so rough. "Are ye okay?" he managed between pants.

"I'm glorious," she said, sounding happily, completely sated.

He managed to crack one eye and shift his heavy weight off her narrower frame. "Truly? I didnae hurt ye there at the end? I didn't mean to lose control like that, take ye like—"

"A fiery dragon?" Her grin was slow, wide, and very, very naughty. "Oh, aye, you can do that anytime. In fact, I might make it my new life's work to learn all the ways I can slay that dragon of yours."

She surprised a laugh out of him. "I'm going to regret that metaphor. I can see it already."

"Oh, I think I can make it something to look forward to," she said, rolling toward him, curling up along the length of his body—his fully and completely spent body.

So it was with stunned amazement that he felt himself twitch as she slid her hand over his chest and up along the side of his neck. He'd thought it would take days to see even a flicker of life resume, that's how entirely and thoroughly she'd taken him.

He gathered her closer, and urged her cheek down to his shoulder, letting his eyes drift shut as he pressed a kiss to her hair. "I look forward to . . . rising to meet the challenge."

She laughed, and that sound warmed him as much as her earlier moans and gasps had titillated him.

There were so many things left to say, left to know, left to figure out. But he refused to tarnish even a fraction of that moment. There would be a time for all of that later.

"Supper now?" he murmured against her hair, as he lazily stroked the smooth skin of her back.

"Supper later," she said, sounding sexily drowsy and replete.

He tugged the duvet up and over them and they snuggled amidst the stuffed feather coverlet. "Supper later it is, then," he said, and with her cheek pressed against his heart, he held her as they both drifted off.

Chapter 19

It was the screaming that woke her, had her clawing out from under very heavy mosquito netting, digging, digging, for her gun, her knife, anything to get the weight of the intruder off her. She realized, quite distantly, as she fought valiantly and ferociously, that the screamer was her.

There was shouting. It was her tormentor. She had to fight him off, had to save—wait, her name, someone was shouting her name. It was . . . Roan. Roan? What was he doing in Bogota?

"Tessa, it's okay. It's me. Tessa!"

He pinned her shoulders hard to the bed with his hands, then slung his weight over her, using his legs and feet to keep her from thrashing and hurting either one of them.

"Tessa! You're okay. I have you. You're okay."

Roan had her. It was Roan. He had her. She must be okay then. She stopped struggling, then immediately grabbed his arms. "We have to get out, we have to go! Now—they're coming!" She was frantic, realizing she needed to save them. He wouldn't know, wouldn't understand what it was like here. She had to save him. "No time, Roan. There's no time. Get up, come on!"

"Tessa," he said, and she felt him kissing her cheek. Had he lost his mind?

"Run!" she screamed. Didn't he get it?

"Tessa!"

Something about the sharp demand made her open her eyes. "Roan! We have to—" But then she stopped herself as awareness slowly started to sink in . . . followed swiftly by utter and complete mortification. "Oh . . . oh, God. No—" She looked at him, eyes wide. "I'm so sorry," she whispered, her throat knotted against a renewal of tears. Tears she would not shed. She'd done enough of that. "Oh, no."

He rolled off her, but pulled her with him, tried to tuck her against him. She instinctively shoved, needing space, air . . . time. To think, to get under control. Then get away. She couldn't be with him. She'd thought she could. But she couldn't. She cared. Too much. And no matter what he thought, she couldn't—wouldn't—put him through it.

"Come here," he said, gently at first, but then with a bit more urgency. When she tugged, he didn't let her go, wasn't the gentleman she'd known him to be to that point. "Just . . . come here. For a moment. Take stock, gather yourself."

"I'm trying to."

"Try it this way," he said. "And see how that works out."

She grudgingly let him pull her down to his side. "Don't you dare tell me this is okay. This is far, far from okay. I'm not okay, and I hate this. Hate acting crazy in front of you. And nothing you say is going to change that. I'm just telling you right now so you won't take it personally. But please, don't even try."

"Fine, no words of wisdom," he said. "So, just shut up then and let me hold you, okay? I want to hold you. Because it makes me feel better. Can you do that for me? After all, you tried to slug me half to death and you've got a pretty wicked left hook. I'm just tellin' ye."

She was so stunned by the words he was saying, she simply gaped at him.

And he had the nerve—the nerve—to smile. "Good. I thought that would get your attention." He pulled her again, more gently, so they were aligned, and held her with both arms wrapped around her. "I know you're feeling like an idiot at the moment, but the only idiotic thing you can do would be to shut yourself off. From this. From me. I'm no' some fragile flower, ye know."

She was silent for a long moment. "I thought you weren't going to armchair analyze me. Tough love, that's what you were dishing out just now and that feels just about right."

He tipped her head back, with just enough force so that their gazes met . . . and clashed. "I canno' be that tough with ye. But I can give ye the love part. Tessa . . . it is what it is. We'll survive it. Maybe I can help. When ye finally knew it was me, ye calmed right down." He smiled and stroked her face. "Ye tried to save me, in fact."

She glared at him. "How on earth can you think this is even remotely amusing?"

"I'm no' amused. But I am quite happy."

"Because I had a terrifying nightmare? They feel quite real to me when I'm having them, in case you were unaware."

He gentled his touch and his smile and she wanted to smack at both, even as she realized she was being awful because that would be the thing to push him away the fastest. And get her back to ground zero—which meant . . . alone.

That's not really what she wanted. Not at all.

"Maybe happy was the wrong word. I hate, with more passion than ye know, that you suffer. But you were in the midst of a terror, and rather than fight me, you tried to save me. Your instinct was to defend yourself, then protect me." He shook his head when she'd have spouted off again. "I'm merely pointing out that it made a difference. My being here. So, keep me here. And maybe, at some point, I'll be the one doing the protecting. In your dreams. And out."

She stared at him, as if he was an alien.

"We made it through," he said. "And we will again."

"Sometimes it's every night. I never know, Roan."

"We made it through," he repeated, "and we will again. And

again. I'm no' a quitter. Not on you, not on your terrors. Or havenae ye been listening to me?"

"Why would you willingly sign on for that?"

He took her face in his hands then, gently but firmly, and she saw anger in his eyes for only the second time ever. She'd been idiotic the last time, too, but apparently she hadn't learned anything.

"I'm a man who loves you. You, Tessa. All the parts that are hard, aye, but all the wonderful parts that are good, too."

Her heart tilted right on the edge, and she was terrified to let it fall. Wouldn't it simply shatter on impact? She couldn't be lucky enough to have this much goodness. Could she? "I don't feel all that good or wonderful. And I'm lashing out at the one good and wonderful thing I have."

"Answer me one thing."

She looked straight into his eyes, and promised herself she'd respond honestly, no matter what he asked. She owed him that much. Even if the answer wasn't what he wanted to hear. "Okay."

"Your heart"—he paused, and the earnestness, the openness, so plain on his face, shook the anger right out of her—"do I have even a part of it yet?"

Her defenses crumpled. Fully. Oh the things he said. "Oh . . . Roan." Her throat was tight and tears rushed to the corners of her eyes. Since she'd let them out, apparently they weren't going back into full seclusion ever again. Maybe that wasn't such a bad thing. It meant she was letting herself feel. That didn't have to be such a terrifying thing. "I wasn't really sure I had one, you know."

"You couldn't do what ye do without one. You know that now. It's why your work hurts so much, and tortures you so." He stroked her cheek, her hair, her forehead, all the while staring deeply into her eyes, searching. "I know your night terrors won't stop all at once. But that doesn't mean you can't start letting your heart feel for all the good reasons, the healthy, happy reasons. Even if it's no' me, you need to let—"

"It's you," she said. "It's yours. Whatever part is under my control, anyway. You're . . ." She couldn't finish. When she saw his eyes glass over, she thought she would never find words again. But they came, in a torrent. "I could hurt you, and I won't mean to. I don't react well to . . . any of this. My instincts are so strong to pull away and I . . . the very last thing I'd ever want to do is hurt you. You need to be with someone who can love you, the way you so deserve to be loved. I—you're everything any woman would want. You're everything I could want."

"Then take me," he said, his voice a choked whisper.

"Why me?" she pleaded, needing to understand. "You just up and decide it's me. Couldn't you just up and decide it's not? When I get to be too much, make it too hard."

"You fulfill me. You challenge me. You make me laugh. You engage me on every single level I have, and many more I didn't even know existed. Your heart, your dedication, your passion. Your need to shed light on the hard parts of the world, while doing your damnedest to ignore that they're killing you. Your very difference from everyone I've ever known is precisely what compels me. I didn't know that, couldn't have known that, until I met you. But I have now. And you're it for me. You're it. Your past, everything that has shaped you, intrigues and fascinates the hell out of me. The pain, the darkness scare me, and make me angry. I don't want that for you, but I can't make it just go away. I can't wave a wand and fix it. But you're a million other things besides the dark parts. I won't be perfect in handling all of it, but as long as we both understand that and are willing to work at it . . . don't we get to at least try?"

"And if we fail?"

"We know we reached. We know we let ourselves want. We took the risk."

"Maybe I can't take any more of those. Maybe I need safe. And secure."

"Do you want to be alone? Truly, Tessa? Because if you want anything, or anyone, in your life, then it's a risk you're going to have to take."

She dipped her chin, feeling suddenly weary. Down to her soul weary. She didn't want it to be so hard, not for him, and not for herself. She realized she was the large part, the only part, of why it was so challenging. "I'm trying to do the right thing, find the right path," she said, continuing the thought out loud. "I will take risks again. I don't know that I was ready to take them quite yet. I'm just starting to figure out who I am, what part of me I can get a grip on and take forward from here. I don't know that it's fair to me, but even more so, to you, to think I can handle a new career and a relationship, too. It feels inordinately selfish to take the risk, to jump right now. I need time. I wanted time."

"So . . . are you asking me to wait? Until you're ready?"

Her mouth dropped open, then snapped shut. What was she asking? "I-I'm making a mess of this. I can't think, I—this has been . . . a lot. Today. Has been a lot."

"Yes, it has. Back at the cliffs, I was so worried for you. But then I realized how strong you are. It's the core of you, your strength. You're bringing it to bear on your current situation and I have absolutely no doubt you'll persevere and win, because you won't rest until you do. That's why you tracked down every doctor and treatment there was. You didn't curl up and die. You fought back. You fought for your life. For yourself. That's who you are. You'd fight for this, too, for me. I have no doubts. You could make a mess of it, but I know you'll do your best not to. I wouldn't ask for anything more of you than that. But you ask a lot more of yourself than I do."

He leaned down and kissed her, and there was so much meaning in his touch, she wasn't sure what to do with it all. It scared her. Just as strongly, it made her want to leap. To say the hell with all her fears and worries.

Then he eased away from her. Fully—until he sat on the side of the bed. "My instinct, because I want you to be part of my life, is to give you whatever you want. Wait for you? Fine. Till the end of time? No problem. I've got nothing but time to give. I want you. So, waiting? I can do. Seems a small, easy price.

Hell, I've waited this long. But Tessa . . ." He stopped, looked away. He braced his hands on his knees, and she saw his shoulders tense, then slump a little. Broad shoulders, shoulders that were willing to take on all of her burdens, all of her pain.

Her heart, which she was just discovering the depths and breadths of . . . started breaking.

"Now is the time we've been given. We didn't get to pick, we didn't get to choose. But we can choose to take what's in front of us now, because now is when we have it . . . or we can toss it aside, walk away from it. Life is never neat and tidy, never perfect. If you want to work your way toward me, then I'll be here for you—whenever you get here. But if you're waiting for everything to be perfect . . . that's never going to happen."

"I want to be whole," she said, her voice a rasp. "I want to give myself to you, I do, but . . . as a whole person. Let me finish figuring that out."

He looked back over his shoulder. "Doing it on your own is what got you where you are now."

She flinched, but she knew he was speaking the truth.

"You don't have to go off alone to do this, to feel like you're only worth it if you have everything all polished and perfect. I'm not asking for polished and I sure as hell am not perfect. So I don't expect you to be. Tessa, I can't make you believe you're a worthwhile person. Just know that you are to me." He stood and pulled on his pants, then turned to face her. And he looked . . . hurt. "I want, and am ready to accept, the whole person you are right now. But I'd also like to know that you respect that I'm man enough to handle your problems. To handle you. Do you really think you're beyond my scope? Or that I'm just too stupid in love to realize what I'm asking for?"

She gaped. "I never meant—that's not at all what I was saying!"

"Then what are you saying, Tessa? Think about that, while you're working things out." He leaned down and picked up his shirt and shrugged it on. He walked to the door, then paused, sighed, and swore under his breath. His shoulders slumped.

"I'm . . . sorry. Very, very sorry. I'm not handling this at all like I want to. I'm not finding all the right words." He looked back. "I'm stumbling. I'm not trying to say hurtful things. I just . . . I'm angry and frustrated and I want what I want, too.

"So . . . for the sake of not making a bad situation worse, I'm going to take a hike. Literally. Clear my head and stop pounding on ye. I don't know what ye need, that's clear enough. So, I'll leave you to sort it out. Make yourself at home, or take the lorry back to Kira's. I'll get it later on. I'll be gone for at least several hours." He turned to look at her directly. "But dinnae mistake this for running. Or quitting.

"I want you. I want to fall all the rest of the way in love with you. I want to fall in love with you for the rest of our lives. I think that's how long it would take, and the journey would be nothing but a grand and glorious adventure, each step of the way. I know your life wouldn't be here, not fully. So don't think small. And I won't either.

"For now, you're demanding space. So . . . now ye have it. All that ye need. I'm no' going anywhere, Tessa, but I'll leave ye be. When ye've figured things out . . . let me know."

And with that, he was gone.

A moment later, she flinched—hard—as she heard the front door shut.

She sat there . . . dry eyed and hollow-hearted and wondered what in the hell she'd been thinking, pushing him away. No, shoving him away, and tossing his big heart and perfect, giving soul right after it.

He'd been gone less than a minute, but the void felt like a gaping chasm. Both around her . . . and inside her. She felt fully and completely alone. With nothing but more of the same, staring her in the face.

"Well . . . you got what you asked for, didn't you, then? You idiot."

But she did not leap right to believing that his abrupt departure was exactly the proof she needed that she'd been right all along about her inability to have, much less keep a relationship. That was what the old, righteously wounded Tessa would have done. The new Tessa, the Tessa who'd found herself falling in love, the Tessa who had a man in her life—a wonderful, loving, strong, supportive man—who was and would be the best damn thing that would or could ever happen to her . . . that Tessa rolled herself out of bed, yanked on her clothes, jerked the tight knot of her selfish, self-centered attitude straight out of her scared ass.

And went after him.

Chapter 20

The next time he decided to take a stand, then make a declarative exit, he might want to plan things out a wee bit better first. Like . . . hiking, for instance. It was generally smarter, not to mention easier to see the trail, when the sun wasn't hitting the horizon at the beginning of the trek. Also, it was generally considered to be a more productive pastime when it wasn't raining.

Although he did admit the foul weather suited his mood.

It was rare, exceedingly rare, for him to be provoked to the point that he lost his cool and spouted off without thinking through what he really wanted to say. He was just . . . well, he was scared.

There, he'd admitted it. Weren't they a pair?

He wanted things to go the way he wanted them to go, and, more often than not, they did. And everyone was happy. So, naturally, he'd been convinced that if Tessa just listened to him, she'd be happy. It was hard, not to mention humbling, to realize that he didn't know bloody bollocking crap about what she needed to be happy. He only knew what *he* needed. He needed her.

He wished he could start their conversation over again, that whole scene after she'd woken up from experiencing another terror. Of course it had freaked her out, of course she'd been mortified that she'd had one while with him. And not just any

time with him . . . her first time with him. And this after—
after—her major breakthrough and breakdown out by the cliffs.

Aye. So, the very next thing she needed was him lecturing
her on what she should do to make him happy. Because, after
all, the world did revolve around him. There in his little world,
anyway.

Of course she'd immediately wanted to extract herself from
the situation. She didn't know him well enough to turn to him,
and most definitely not instinctively. Yes, she had tried to protect him, even while in the throes of her nightmare. But did he
have to take that and shove it at her, then crow about how it
was proof that what he'd been telling her was true?

"You're such a bloody stupid arse," he muttered, stopping at
the end of the lengthy stacked stone wall that separated his
property—and his sheep—from the rest on the other side of the
boundary line. He really had no desire to climb up the muddy,
slippery trail just beyond the wall. Given how things were
going at the moment, he'd likely fall and break his idiot arse
and his idiot head.

He turned and looked back at the house. In the gathering
gloom and mists of pelting rain, he couldn't see his lorry, but
he'd have heard the engine—which meant she was still there. In
his home. In his bed.

And he was not. No, he was out there stomping about in the
rain.

"Because I'm the farklin' genius." He turned back toward
the house, hoping like hell that between where he was and his
front door, he came up with the right thing to say to make her
stay long enough for the two of them to hash it out.

He was so intent on his mission he rounded the near corner
of the stacked stone wall and all but plowed right into her. She
grabbed at his arms to keep from slipping and falling, and he
tugged her up against him to keep them both from going backward over the wall.

"Roan, I—"

"Tessa, I'm sorry. I'm a blithering idiot and you have every right to toss me. You've been through so much and I had no right—"

She shoved at him. "Don't you dare go making excuses for me. I have no excuses."

"I just wish you'd give us—what?"

"It's not like I haven't been handling this with professionals for almost a year now. I know what the hell is wrong with me, and I know better than to take it out on you. Or anyone. You're right. I am strong. I can get through this. I can and will move on. In fact, the stories I think I want to tell aren't just going to be good, they're going to be bloody brilliant."

"Damn right," he said, completely at a loss. Was she mad at him, or herself?

"Do you know what's really mortifying for me?" she demanded so heatedly he thought it best not to offer an answer. "Not the tears I shed earlier today. You were right. I should have shed them long ago. No . . . what is mortifying for me is the fact that I've been using this trauma like a crutch. I've been using it like a get-out-of-anything-Tessa-doesn't-want-to-deal-with-free card. *That's* what's mortifying. I'd like to think I'm better than that. Apparently I'm not even close."

"Tessa—"

"You're the wise one, you're the one with all the amazing insights. You should hang out a shingle, because you've made me understand and see parts of myself so much more clearly than I ever had or could. And as previously mentioned, not all of those parts are all that lovely. But . . . that's good to know. I need to know. So"—she paused, dipping her chin for just a brief moment, the length of time it took her to take in a deep breath, steady herself, before looking him straight in the eye— "if you're not thoroughly disgusted with me wigging out on a semi-regular basis—with the added caveat that I'm working on it, but I'm sure I will be a work in progress for some time—I was wondering if you'd ever consider playing dragon and dragon-slayer with me again."

"Of course, I wo— What?" He broke off as that last part filtered through. He hadn't expected . . . humor. He could see that she was shaking, and he didn't think it was the rain.

"Because I want to play. And it's more fun with another person. You taught me that. Okay, you taught me both of those things, the playing part and the two-are-better-than-one part. I want to flirt with you. I want to laugh with you. I want to be happy and take it totally for granted some of the time, because I've gotten that used to it. I want joy to be my default position. I want—" She took a breath, and smiled. Boldly. Bravely. "I want you. I want you, now."

She stood there for several seconds and he knew it felt like eternity. He already knew the answer, but he was momentarily in awe of her. She kept thinking he was the one with the strength and fortitude. But, frankly, he had a foundation of bedrock underneath him . . . she had one of shaky toothpicks. At best. And yet, there she was, finding the will, and the way, to go after what she wanted.

So he said, "If you're always willing to fight as hard for us as you are right now, then I'd be an idiot to say no, wouldn't I?"

"Yes, you would. Total idiot. Fool is the word that comes to mind. Short-sighted. And lacking in vision."

She was fidgeting. Giving him a good go, but fidgeting. Nervous and scared . . . but putting herself out there nonetheless. That was a woman he could love. That was the woman he did love. "Well, I'd like to think I'm no' an idiot. At least not in total. Occasionally I will be. You should know that. I've never been accused of lacking vision, though, so there is that. In fact, I even fancy myself a visionary."

"Well, then," she said, but trailed off as he kept her waiting.

"Well, then indeed." It wasn't the nicest thing he'd ever done, but one thing with Tessa was that he was going to have to keep her on her toes and not just capitulate on every point, even if he wanted to. He had to man up on occasion if he had a hope in hell of not becoming a completely besotted doormat—which might have its benefits. But he had some pride, didn't he? "Okay," he said, at length.

Hope sprang into her eyes, and joy leapt into his heart so hard he thought he heard it knock. All he knew was that it was a sight he planned on seeing many, many times.

"Okay." she repeated.

"On one condition."

"Only one?" she asked, a dry note edging into her voice, but there was such a glittering sparkle in her eyes, he was pretty sure the one being tortured by stringing it out, was him. It was a fine line he'd be walking with her. He rather relished figuring that part out. "One main one," he said.

"Besides fighting for us as hard as I'm doing right now one?"

He grinned. She was never, not ever, going to make it easy on him. Thank God. "Well, it's in tandem with that, really."

"Does it have to do with learning to cook?"

He frowned. "No."

"Gardening?"

"No' unless you want to."

"Sheering sheep? I love their little black faces, but I don't think I have the heart to strip them naked." She shrugged, folded her arms. "There, I've said it."

"Sheep face weakness," he said. "Taken under advisement."

"I can do laundry. And I'm not a slob."

"So noted."

Her expression smoothed, and she smiled. "Okay, then. Stipulate away."

"I want us to show each other our respective worlds, share them, as best we can."

She frowned, confused. "What do you mean? Teach you photography? And I'll . . . what, learn to weave a basket?"

He smiled, then shook his head. "No, though that might be worth the trade. I could enlist Kira's help in training us both. Then we could weave together each eve, as the sun goes down." He wiggled his eyebrows. "Then you could show me around the dark room. Or, you know, we could just play with blindfolds."

"Very funny, basket boy," she said, but he could see her fighting the desire to laugh.

"What I meant was that I presume you won't be content to live out your days on my admittedly lovely, but wee little island. I would never want you to feel trapped."

She frowned for real. "What are you saying?"

"You said you have a new path, new stories, or a new angle on old stories . . . but Kinloch is likely only one of them, so I assume you'll have others that need telling."

She nodded, opened her mouth, shut it, then started again. "A lot of places where I spent my time won't improve, not in my lifetime. In many cases, the opposite. But, being here, I've been moved by the way the islanders have worked and struggled and fought to survive, and not just the current generation, but for centuries. Yet, you all have not only survived, you've succeeded. I want to tell that story. And I know there are many others out there. So, what I want to do now is . . . find the happy endings, and tell the story of how they happened. I want to show that hope exists for a reason, and, sometimes, the good guys win."

He smiled, truly surprised. "Really?"

"Really," she said simply and with no defensiveness. "Do you think it's beyond me?" She was asking him sincerely.

"Of course not. It's perfect for you. In fact, it's a bloody brilliant idea. Your background and work should make it almost the perfect bookend to the first half of your career."

She let out a little sigh of relief and smiled. "I'm so glad you think that. Because I'm really excited about it. I have the time here, without anyone knowing my plans, to work on this first story and see if, in fact, I do have something that is meaningful." She pulled herself out of her reverie and banked her obvious anticipation. "Did you mean, earlier . . . that you'd want to go on assignment with me?"

"I said before there are solutions if you want to find them. I've been thinking that with the way things are going here, it wouldn't be a bad idea for me to get off the island and cultivate new markets, try a more hands-on approach. Katie can step in here and take on a good share of the work while I'm gone. And . . . who knows, perhaps we could collaborate and find stories and potential client bases in the same corners of the world. Or something along those lines."

She looked stunned. "Really? You'd do that?"

"Really. I'd love to do that. But the other side of it would be you staying here on a regular basis, too. No' being on the road all the time. There will always be stories, but you'll have a home now. And we'll want your shining face in it."

"We?"

"All of us. Your home won't just be my four walls, it would be all of the island, and everyone on it. I'd want—or hope—that you'd put down roots here, become part of the rhythm and life cycle here. Be part of something unified and centered and specific, while simultaneously tackling the world. My hope is you'll feel grounded by it, anchored, not trapped. That it will—we will—provide you the foundation and support for when you go off gallivanting, with or without me, then cheer you when you come home."

"I won't want to be without you." She smiled, even as the slightly amazed look stayed on her face. "I'm going to miss Kinloch, I already know that. Not just you, or Kira. But this place. I've come to terms with myself here, my life. This place has meaning to me. Beyond you, beyond Kira."

"So . . . you accept my condition then?"

In answer, she leapt up into his arms and wrapped hers tightly around his neck. "Yes. A thousand times, most definitively, and with absolutely no strings attached . . . *yes*."

He wrapped his arms around her and they spun around. "Good. Bloody fantastic, really!"

"And then some," she agreed.

"Good thing," he said, as she kissed the side of his face, noisily, happily, "we both know you'd be an unmitigated disaster without me."

"So, this would be strictly a pity case thing, then," she said, but was smiling and nibbling on his ear as she said it. "Well, I can take that. I have been rather pathetic, despite my best attempts not to be."

"The only thing pathetic about either of us is that we're standing outside in the rain, when there is a nice, rather cozy home straight back there."

"With a very big fireplace, I hear."

"And an even bigger bed—where I'd like a chance to start over, by the way."

"I thought we started off pretty well. We might need to work on the finishing part."

"Then that, too. I'd like to work on all of it with ye. Loads and loads of practice." He slid her down his body and she wrapped herself tightly into his arms as he pushed the wet hair from her forehead and framed her damp cheeks with his palms. He tilted her face up to his. "Fact is," he told her, "I'd be the unmitigated disaster without you. Stay here. Save me."

"Maybe we'll save each other then."

He kissed her and gloried in the way she kissed him in return. She held nothing back, and he reveled in the utter abandonment and total commitment of it.

"Aye," he said, "I think we just might."

Epilogue

"You're going to have to drop the kilt."

"I thought we'd agreed that it was more the illusion of nudity."

Tessa rested her hands on top of her camera, keeping the tripod steady. "Honestly, Roan, you'd think I hadn't already seen it all before."

"That's no' the point now, really, is it?" Roan adjusted his stance and tried to keep the damn red cap from sliding down onto his face. The white ermine trim was shedding. "It's about pride now, luv. I do have some, ye ken. Despite what this ridiculous cap would suggest."

"You've got the claymore," Shay noted. "It's no' like anything will show anyway."

"Why are you even here?" Roan wanted to know.

"Creative consultant."

He looked back to Tessa. "Really?"

She lifted a shoulder in mild apology, but he could see her fighting a smile.

That sort of back and forth had quickly become the norm for them, but they'd found it increasingly harder to keep a straight face for any real length of time. Usually their standoffs ended with neither of them standing at all.

Shay flipped open the folder. Again. "Their notes say that it was the whole mighty sword part they found the most interesting and asked that you work it into at least one of the selections you send in. You've already got the other two, and . . . no sword. So, she's right. Straighten the sword, man up, and ditch the plaid."

"Don't you have a border dispute or salacious French divorce case that needs your immediate attention? And Katie's parents, has that been figured out?"

"Resolved the renegade sheep issue this morning. Katie's parents don't have a hope in hell of getting their daughter out of her marriage. And . . . uh . . . I have someone working on the preliminary research on the other thing."

Shay's uncustomary stutter caught Roan's attention. Anything to prolong the disrobing. "Someone? Since when do you have a research assistant?"

Shay flipped open the folder again. "You're losing daylight. We should wrap this up." He looked up, his expression once again composed. "You're already skirting the rules with"—he waved his finger between Roan and Tessa. "We don't need to give them any reason to discredit your entry."

"You said the contract only stated I needed to be an eligible bachelor when I first entered. They can't own my life ad infinitum after that."

"You have several launch events you'll need to attend. You two can't be . . . obvious."

"We'll be fine," Tessa assured him. She crouched down behind the camera. "Okay, a little to the left. Move the sword just a . . . got it. Okay." She fiddled with the settings. "Drop it."

Roan swore under his breath . . . and let go of the plaid.

"I heard Blaine took off on the ferry yesterday," Tessa said conversationally to Shay, as she ripped off a fast series of shots. "Okay, Mr. December." She straightened and grinned, then shot Roan a rather saucy wink. "Your days of exposing yourself in public are officially over." She glanced at Shay. "He wouldn't be heading to Edinburgh, would he? Blaine, I mean."

Suddenly Shay was looking at his watch. "I've got a conference call coming in. I should go. Glad we've wrapped this up."

He glanced at Roan, who was making quick work of rewrapping his kilt. "Literally."

"Everyone's a comedian." Roan tucked in the plaid, then pulled on his T-shirt and shrugged the old wool sweater back over his head. It was October and there was a distinct bite in the air. Thank God he didn't have to prance around naked any longer. Outside, at any rate.

His thoughts strayed to the launch events. He wasn't excited about them. One was in Glasgow, the other in Edinburgh. Tessa was coming with him, which helped. Tessa and room service. And indoor naked prancing. He wasn't complaining about that part. It was what was coming afterward that made the launch events tolerable. They were planning a short trip from there so they could both do some preliminary research. In Malaysia.

His gaze shifted to her and he watched as she expertly packed her gear. And thought about the dinner they had planned later that evening. In bed.

They were rushing to get the photos done and digitally transposed onto the winter shots because he'd called in sick the past three days and ... so ... they were a wee bit behind on the deadline.

"I couldn't speak for Blaine or his itinerary," Shay said, shuffling the folders and making his escape toward his car.

"Well, since he seems to think he's going to be in Edinburgh off and on for at least the next four to six weeks, we're hoping it works out to meet up with him for dinner after the launch party. You want to join us? I mean ... if you're going to be heading there around the same time. For that divorce case." Tessa brightened. "Hey, I know," she called out to Shay's rapidly retreating back. "You could bring your new research assistant."

Roan walked over to her and hefted her tripod bag over his shoulder. "You really shouldn't poke at him like that. It seems harmless, but it's like prodding a sleeping bear. Fair warning."

She looked at him and smiled. "We all know he's using Blaine

Donna Kauffman

to hunt up dirt on that French film actress—which is brilliant, by the way. I'm just trying to get him to own up to it. It's so . . . dirty. And he could use a little dirtying up. That's all I'm saying."

"Speaking of dirtying up . . ." He waggled his eyebrows.

"If that's your way of trying to get me to help you weed the garden, I think we learned our lesson two days ago when you told me what to cut and what to pull, and you lost your entire carrot crop."

"I still dinnae see how you could possibly mistake a carrot top for a weed."

"They're both green, right?"

He nodded. "But—"

She shrugged. "There you have it. I can't be expected to distinguish with my untrained eye."

"That's fine, because, actually, I was thinking that I'm feelin' a bit faint again." He made a face and patted his tummy.

"Aw. That poor, poor tender stomach of yours." She tried not to grin, but there was no hiding the desire that brightened her blue eyes.

He tried not to grin. In anticipation. "Aye," he said wanly, milking his performance. "It's a miracle we were able to get the photos done at all, really."

"You're a downright superman, given your declining health, for spending yesterday converting that back stall—"

"Guest room."

"Same thing—"

"Ye canno' call them stalls." He hoisted the claymore and they set off toward his lorry. "It's a slight to all the hard work I put into making them guest rooms."

"I'll just call it my new darkroom," she said with a cheeky grin and lifted up to buss him on his cheek.

They'd spent the entire last three days inside and around his house. He'd intended to just take one day to work on the photos they'd neglected the day before. But one day had become two, then suddenly he was telling Eliza he had the stomach flu.

Everyone knew, of course, that Tessa was staying on to help "nurse him back to health." He didn't care. Neither did anyone else. In fact, everyone they'd seen today had seemed quite delighted.

He didn't regret a single minute, either. He and Tessa had taken that time to talk, learn more about each other, and, essentially, commit themselves to each other.

He stowed her gear in the back of the lorry. She leaned in next to him, shoved her gear in, then dropped a kiss on the side of his neck, as if it was the most natural thing in the world, before heading around to climb in the passenger side.

He straightened and closed the rear doors, quite well aware of the foolish grin on his face. She never ceased to amaze him. And he hoped that never changed. He found he didn't so much mind her being a focused overachiever when he was the primary target.

He climbed in the cab and started up the engine. "How long do ye think it will take to doctor up this last shot?"

"It's the most basic background of the three of them. An hour or two."

"I was thinking I'd put together something for supper, and we could pack it and take it out to the cliffs."

She slid a glance his way, and a sexy smile to go with it. "Will there be wine this time?"

"And a real, honest to goodness blanket."

"Hmm. Sounds like a plan." She folded her arms across her middle. "Of course, it is getting a little chilly, being later in the day."

"True."

"What if we spread the blanket in front of the fireplace in the main room? I mean, we wouldn't want you to catch cold, what with your already weakened system and all."

"No," he agreed solemnly, "we wouldn't want that." He pulled into the lane that led back to his home, which wasn't a kilometer past the photo site they'd just left.

They slid out of their seats as soon as he parked and met at the back of the truck. They silently pulled out the gear as if they'd been doing this in tandem for years rather than days. She slung three straps over her shoulders and neck and hefted out one of the two aluminum cases. He grabbed the other one, and pulled out the tripod bags. They turned at the same time, and caught each other's gaze . . . and smiled.

"Do ye like Christmas, Tessa?" He hadn't meant to ask. Not yet. But he'd already gone and done it.

If the question caught her off guard, she didn't show it. But their conversations had been so far ranging the past seventy-two hours, he doubted any subject would surprise either of them. Except, perhaps the one he had on his mind.

"Haven't celebrated it in a long time, but I've nothing against it. Why?"

"We'll be getting back from Malaysia right before the holidays. Everyone here loves that time of year. It's cold and pretty inhospitable weather, and the days are short, so we really make the most of the merry occasion. Decorate, have different celebrations honoring any number of saints we can find a good reason to throw a *caleigh* for."

"Sounds nice." She walked with him to the front door. "Did you want me to work it into the story? Is there historical significance?"

They stepped inside and he stopped her from heading straight back to the room he'd begun making into her photo studio.

She turned back, a questioning look on her face. He slid the straps from her shoulders and eased the other one over her head, setting all the equipment on the floor.

"What is it? You can just ask," she said. "I won't mind."

"I'm hopin' ye still feel that way in a moment."

"Roan . . ."

"It's my favorite time of year. I think it's the most hopeful, because it's during a time when things appear bleakest. We have to work to stay cheerful, and we do. Willfully. Happily. I want to willfully make you happy."

"As do I." She stepped closer to him and reached up to cup his cheek. "What is it, Roan? Whatever it is—"

"I want ye to think about a wedding."

"You mean, being the photographer? Is someone else getting married? I don't think that would be a problem, but I should probably talk to them before we leave for the Malay—"

"No, ye willnae be taking the pictures of this wedding."

"Oh. Okay. If it's just making sure we get back in time to attend—"

"Tessa"—he cupped her elbows and pulled her closer—"I want ye to think about *our* wedding."

Her eyebrows climbed. "We've been under the same roof for three days and already you—"

"I want you under the same roof for all of my days. I'm a traditional sort, Tessa. I'm no' saying we have to marry this Christmas . . . I'm saying I want you to be thinking about it. During the holidays. And if it's a yes, we'll plan the wedding for whenever you want it. But . . . you should know, I'm going to push. A wee bit."

"You? No."

He smiled at that.

"I just have one question," she asked.

"Only one?"

She tipped up on her toes and slid her arms around his neck, so their noses almost touched. "Do I have to wait until Christmas to give you my answer?"

"Aye," he said.

Her brows furrowed in surprise. "Really?"

"I want you to be certain. For now, I just wanted you to know it's what I want for us. So you have time to work it all through. I just . . . I wanted you to know. That's all." He smiled. "Fair warning, and all that."

"Then I promise to give it close consideration."

He breathed a sigh of relief. He knew it was ridiculously early to say anything about something as huge as marriage, but the past three days . . . he just knew. And he knew how he'd be the longer they went on. So, better getting it out in the open.

"Good. That's all I ask."

"Well . . . I plan to ask for a lot more," she said.

His brows lifted. "Do ye now?"

"I'll want to know exactly what I'm getting myself into."

"All right."

"And," she said, twining her fingers into his hair, and teasing his mouth closer to hers. "I like to do really, really in depth research."

"Ah." His body was on board with that idea instantly.

"I like to know my subject, inside and out." She started to unbutton his shirt. "In fact, I like to start at the basics. Strip things down to their bare essentials. Get to"—she loosened his kilt—"the meat of it."

He swallowed hard. Overachiever, indeed. Was he ever to learn that lesson about her?

"Would you like to start the formal interview here?" She jerked the kilt so it fell on the floor, then yanked her shirt over her head. "Or back in my office."

"Actually," he said, kicking the plaid away, "I was thinking that, in order for me to be, ye ken, the most relaxed and . . . open . . . to all of your probing questions . . . ." He bent and put his shoulder down, then stood and straightened, with her draped over it.

"Roan!"

"We should start where I'm most comfortable."

"I don't think you're showing your interviewer the proper respect."

He kicked their bedroom door shut behind him, then slid her over his shoulder and down on the bed, following straight down on top of her. "Oh, I plan to show you the utmost respect. In fact . . . let me count the ways."

"Roan—"

"One." He shifted his weight and worked his way to . . . "Two . . ."

She squirmed, then giggled. He thought that was the most delightful sound he'd ever heard.

"What, I'm dying to know, is three?"

He showed her.

"Oh. *Oh!*"

They were married before Thanksgiving.

Here's a sneak peek at Maggie Robinson's
MISTRESS BY MIDNIGHT,
in stores now . . .

London, 1820

Laurette knew precisely what she must do. Again. Had known even before her baby brother had fallen so firmly into the Marquess of Conover's clutches.

To be fair, perhaps Charlie had not so much fallen as thrown himself headfirst into Con's way. Charlie had been as heedless as she herself had been more than a decade ago. She was not immune even now to Con's inconvenient presence. She had shown him her back on more than one occasion, but could feel the heat of his piercing black gaze straight through to her tattered stays.

But tonight she would allow him to look his fill. She had gone so far as having visited Madame Demarche this afternoon to purchase some of her naughtiest underpinnings. Laurette would have one less thing for which to feel shame.

Bought with credit, of course. One more bill to join the mountain of debt. Insurmountable as a Himalayan peak and just as chilling. Nearly as cold as Conover's heart.

She raised the lion's head knocker and let it fall, once, composing herself to face Con's servant.

Desmond Ryland, Marquess of Conover, opened the door himself.

"You!"

"Did you think I would allow you to be seen here at such an

hour?" he asked, his face betraying no emotion. "You must indeed think me a veritable devil. I've sent Aram to bed. Come into my study."

He *was* a devil, suggesting this absurd time. Midnight, as though they were two foreign spies about to exchange vital information in utmost secrecy. Laurette followed him down the shadowy hall, the black-and-white tile a chessboard beneath her feet. She felt much like a pawn, but would soon need to become the White Queen. Con must not know just how desperate she was.

Though surely he must suspect.

He opened a door and stepped aside as she crossed the threshold. The room, she knew, was his sanctuary, filled with objects he'd collected in the years he'd been absent from Town and her life. Absent from his own life, as well. The marquessate had been shockingly abandoned for too long.

She had been summoned here once before, in daylight, a year ago. She was better prepared tonight. She let her filmy shawl slip from one shoulder but refused Con's offer of a chair.

"Suit yourself," he shrugged, sitting behind his desk. He placed a hand on a decanter of brandy. "Will you join me? We can toast to old times."

Laurette shook her head. She'd need every shred of her wits to get through what was ahead. "No thank you, my lord."

She could feel the thread of attraction between them, frayed yet stubborn. She should be too old and wise now to view anything that was to come as more than a business arrangement. As soon as she had seen the bold strokes of his note, she had accepted its implication. She was nearly thirty, almost half her life away from when Conover first beguiled her. Or perhaps when she had beguiled him. He had left her long ago, if not quite soon enough.

A pop from the fire startled her, and she turned to watch sparks fly onto the marble tiles. The room was uncomfortably warm for this time of year, but it was said that the Marquess of

Conover had learned to love the heat of the exotic East on his travels.

"I appeal to your goodness," Laurette said, nearly choking on the improbable phrase.

"I find good men dead boring, my dear. Good women, too." Con abandoned his desk and strode across the floor, where she was rooted by feet that suddenly felt too heavy to lift. He smiled, looking almost boyish, and fingered the single loose golden curl teasing the ivory slope of her shoulder. She recalled that her hair had always dazzled him and had imagined just this touch when she tugged the strand down.

She had hoped to appear winsome despite the passage of time, but her plan was working far too well for current comfort. She pushed him away with more force than she felt. "What would you know about good men, my lord?" She scraped the offending hair back with trembling fingers and secured it under the prison of its hairpin. It wouldn't do to tempt him further. Or herself. What had she been thinking to come here?

"I've known my share. But I am uncertain if your brother fits the category. A good, earnest young fellow, on occasion. A divinity student, is he not? But then—I fear his present vices make him ill-suited for his chosen profession. Among other things, he is so dishonorable he sends his sister in his stead. Your letter was quite affecting. You've gone to a great deal of trouble on his account, but I hardly see why I should forgive his debt." He folded his arms and leaned forward. "Convince me."

Damn him. He intended her to beg. They both knew how it would end.

"He does not know I'm here. He knows nothing," Laurette said quickly, and stepped back.

He was upon her again, his warm brandied breath sending shivers down her spine. She fell backward onto a leather chair. A small mercy. At least she wouldn't fall foolishly at his feet. She closed her eyes, remembering herself in such a pose, Con's head thrown back, his fingers entwined in the tangle of her hair. A lifetime ago.

She looked up. His cheek was creased in amusement at her clumsiness. "He will not thank you for your interference."

"I'm not interfering! My brother is much too young to fall prey to your evil machinations."

Con raised a black winged brow. "Such melodramatic vocabulary. He's not that young, you know. Much older than you were when you were so very sure of yourself. And by calling me evil you defeat your purpose, Laurette. Why, I might take offense and not cooperate. Perhaps I *am* a very good man to discourage him from gambling he can ill afford. But I *will* be repaid. " He leaned over, placing his hands on the arms of Laurette's chair. His eyes were dark, obsidian, but his intentions clear.

Laurette felt her blush rise and leaned back against her seat. She willed herself to stay calm. He would not crowd her and make her cower beneath him. She raised her chin a fraction. "He cannot—that is to say, our funds are tied up at present. Our guardian. . . ." She trailed off, never much able to lie well. But she was expert at keeping secrets.

Con left her abruptly to return to his desk. She watched as he poured himself another brandy into the crystal tumbler, but let it sit untouched. "What do you propose, Laurette?" he asked, his voice a velvet burr. "That I tear up your brother's vowels and give him the cut direct next time we meet?"

"Yes," Laurette said boldly. "The sum he owes must be a mere trifle to you. And his company a bore. If you hurt his feelings now, it will only be to his ultimate benefit. One day he will see that." She glanced around the room, appointed with elegance and treasure. Brass fittings gleamed in the candlelight. A thick Persian carpet lay under her scuffed kid slippers. Lord Conover's study was the lair of a man of exquisite taste, and a far cry from Charlie's disreputable lodging. She twisted her fingers, awaiting his next words.

There was the faintest trace of a smile. "You give me far too much credit. I am neither a good man, nor, despite what you see here, so rich man a man I can ignore a debt this size. We all need blunt to keep up appearances. And settle obligations."

Laurette knew exactly what his obligation to her cost him and held her tongue.

Con leaned back in his chair, the picture of confidence. "If I cannot have coin, some substitution must be made. I think you know what will please me."

Laurette nodded. It would please her too, God forgive her. Her voice didn't waver. "When, Con?"

He picked up his glass and drained it. "Tonight. I confess I cannot wait to have you in my bed again."

Laurette searched her memory. There had been very few beds involved in their brief affair. Making love to Con in one would be a luxurious novelty. She was not prepared, however; the vial of sponges was still secreted away in her small trunk at her brother's rooms. She had not allowed herself to think the evening would end in quite this way. But she had just finished her courses. Surely she was safe.

"Very well." She rose from the haven of her chair.

His face showed the surprise he surely felt. Good. It was time she unsettled *him*.

"You seem to be taking your fate rather calmly, Laurette."

"Did you arrange it? That it would come to this?" she asked softly.

"Did I engage your brother in a high stakes game he had no hope of winning? I declare, that avenue had not occurred to me," Con said smoothly. "How you must despise me to even ask." He motioned her to him. After a few awkward moments, Laurette walked toward him and allowed him to pull her down into his lap. He was undeniably hard, fully aroused. She let herself feel a brief surge of triumph.

Con placed a broad hand across her abdomen and settled her even closer. "How is the child?"

Was this an unconscious gesture? Con had never felt her daughter where his hand now lay, had never seen her, held her.

She fought the urge to slap his hand away and willed herself to melt into the contours of his hard body. It would go quicker if she just gave in and let him think he'd won. "Very well, my lord. How is yours?"

"Fast asleep in his dormitory, I hope, surrounded by other scruffy little villains. I should like you to meet him one day."

She did not tell him that his son was already known to her, as his wife had once been, improbably, her friend. "I don't believe that would be wise, my lord."

"Why not? If you recall, I offered you the position as his step-mama a year ago. It is past time you become acquainted with my son, and I with your daughter." His busy fingers had begun removing hairpins.

Laurette said nothing, lulling in his arms as his lips skimmed her throat, his hands stroking every exposed inch. In dressing tonight, she'd bared as much of her flesh as she dared in order to tempt him. She wondered how she could so deceive herself. Nothing had changed. Nothing would ever change. And that was the problem.

Laurette pressed a gloved finger to his lips. "We do not need to discuss the past, my lord. We have tonight."

"If you think," he growled, "that I will be satisfied with only one night with you, you're as deluded as ever."

An insult. Lucky that, for she suddenly retrieved her primness and relative virtue. She straightened up. "That is all I am willing to offer."

He stood in anger, dumping her unceremoniously into his chair. "My dear Miss Vincent, if you wish me to forgive your brother's debts—all of them—I require a bit more effort on your part."

"A-all? What do you mean?"

"I see the young fool didn't tell you." Con pulled open a drawer, fisting a raft of crumpled paper. "Here. Read them and then tell me one paltry night with you is worth ten thousand pounds. Even you cannot have such a high opinion of yourself."

Laurette felt her tongue thicken and her lips go numb. "It cannot be," she whispered.

"I've spent the past month buying up his notes all over town." Con's smile, feral and harsh, withered her even further. He now followed in his father-in-law's footsteps.

"You did this."

"You may think what you wish. I hold the mortgage to Vincent Lodge as well. You've denied me long enough, Laurie."

Her home, ramshackle as it was. Beatrix's home, if only on brief holidays away from her foster family. Laurette had forgotten just how stubborn and high-handed Conover could be. She looked at him, hoping to appear as haughty as the queen she most certainly was not.

"What kind of man are you?"

Treat yourself to a preview of MY FAIR HIGHLANDER, the next from Mary Wine,

coming in August 2011.

Armed Englishmen riding across Scottish land only meant one thing, and it had nothing to do with friendship.

As she had just learned, they would use violence to gain what they wished without any remorse. She looked at the dirty plums crowning the English knight's helmet and decided that they fit him well.

"If ye've any sense, ye'd start for the border before Ryppon discovers what ye were about with his sister." Laird Barras leaned down over the neck of his horse. "And if I see ye again on my land, I'll not leave ye drawing breath to test my goodwill again."

His voice was hard as stone, leaving no doubt that he was a man who would not hesitate to kill. He looked every inch the warrior, but Jemma discovered herself grateful for his harshness, even drawing comfort from it. The man was saving her life and sparing her a painful death too. The English didn't wait but began walking toward England. It was humbling to set armored men on their way without their horses, but to return the animals would see the men becoming a force to be reckoned with once more. Laird Barras proved to be merciful by sparing their lives, but he was not a fool.

He turned to look at her. The night sky was beginning to fill with tiny points of light and that starshine lit him. It cast him in white light, making him appear unearthly, like a god from legends of the past. A Norseman Viking that swept across the land, unstoppable because of his sheer brawn.

A ripple of sensation moved over her skin, awakening every inch of her flesh. It should have been impossible to be so aware of any single person's stare, but she was of his. His stallion snorted and pawed at the ground a moment before he pressed his knees into the sides of the beast. Lament surged through her, thick and choking as she anticipated his leaving.

But he pulled the stallion up alongside her, a grin of approval curling his lips up when she remained in place without a single sound making it past her lips. Jemma found herself too fascinated to speak. Too absorbed in the moment to ruin it by allowing sounds to intrude.

"Up with ye, lass. This is not the sort of company ye should be keeping."

He leaned down, his thighs gripping the sides of his horse to keep him steady. Her gaze strayed to his thighs and she stared at the bare skin that was cut with ridges of muscles, testifying to how much strength was in him.

"Take my hand, lass. I'd prefer not to have to pull ye off the ground again."

But he would. She heard that clearly in his voice. That tone of command that spoke of a man who expected his word to be heeded no matter what her opinion might be.

Of course, staying was not something she craved. She lifted her hand and placed it in his outstretched one, only to pull it away when his warm flesh met her own. That touch had jolted her, braking through the disbelief that had held her in its grasp. Her body began to shake while her face throbbed incessantly from the blow that had been laid across it. She suddenly felt every bruise and scrap, her knees feeling weak as the horror of what she had faced sunk in deep to torment her mind with grisly details of what the English had been intent on doing to her. The idea of touching any man was suddenly repulsive and she clasped her hands tightly together.

"I thank you for your . . . assistance . . . but I will return to . . . Amber Hill."

Jemma looked around for her mare, but in the night it was difficult to determine which horse was hers in the darkness. The younger boys had several horses each and she couldn't decide which one belonged to her. She suddenly noticed how cold it had become and the darkness seemed to be increasing too, clouds moving over the sky to block out even the star shine.

"Give me yer hand, lass. 'Tis time to make our way from this place."

His voice was low now and hypnotic. Lifting her face, she found his attention on her, his eyes reflecting the starlight back down on her. Jemma lifted her hand but stopped when she felt her arm shaking. The motion annoyed her but there seemed to be nothing she might do to banish it.

"Do it now, lass. This is nae a safe place to linger."

"But is going with you a safe thing to do?" She truly wondered because he looked so at ease surrounded by the night. All of his men sat in their saddles without any outward sign of misgivings or dread for the deepening darkness. Her words didn't please him. His expression tightened and something flashed in his eyes that looked like pride. A soft grumbling rippled through his waiting men.

"I will nae strike ye."

Which was better than she might expect from the horseless Englishmen standing nearby. For all that they were her countrymen, she discovered more trust inside her for the Scots. There was no real choice, she hungered for life and the Scot's offer was her only way to hold onto that that precious thing.

Lifting her hand, she placed it firmly against the one offered. Barras closed his hand around her wrist and she jumped to help gain the saddle. He lifted her up and off the ground to sit behind him.

"Hold on to me, lass."

There was no other choice. She had to cling to him, press her body up against his in order to share the saddle with him. Her thighs rested against his and the motion of the horse made her move her hips in unison with his. The thick scabbard strapped to his back was the only barrier between them. She actually welcomed the hard edges of the leather scabbard because it kept her from being completely immersed in his body. There were several things she should have been dwelling on—the English left behind in the night, or the way her brother was most likely going to have her flogged for riding so late in the day. There was also Synclair to consider. The knight was going to be far more than unhappy with her for slipping out the moment his attention was taken away from her. He was not a man that made the same mistake twice.

Instead she was completely focused on the man she clung to. Her arms reached around his slim waist. It was amazing how much warmth his body generated. Holding so tightly against him kept the chill of the autumn night from tormenting her. The wind chilled her hands on top where the skin was exposed, but her palms were warmed by the man she held onto.

Her head was tucked along one of his shoulders, one cheek pressing against the wool of his doublet. His sword was strapped at an angle across his back, the length of his plaid pulled up over his right shoulder helping to cushion the weapon. Suddenly, the Celtic fashion of dressing was not so odd. Instead it was quite logical and useful. That bit of thinking made him seem less of a barbarian and more of a very efficient warrior.

Her heart accelerated and that increased the tempo of her breathing. She drew in his scent and shivered. It was dark and musky, touching off a strange reaction deep inside her belly, a quivering that became a throbbing at the top of her sex. Each motion of the horse sent her clitoris sliding against the leather of the saddle, and the scent of his skin intensified the sensation somehow. It was unnerving, and she licked her lower lip because it felt as dry as a barley stalk. Every hot glance he had ever aimed at her rose from her memory to needle her with a longing she hadn't truly admitted she had for the man. Now that she was pressed against him, she chastised herself for not jumping at him. No matter how often she had listened to other women talk of their sweethearts, it had never been something she longed for. Now, her body refused to be ignored any longer, it enjoyed being against him.

If Barras noticed, he made no comment, which she felt herself being grateful for. Sensation was rushing through her, filling every limb and flooding her mind with intoxicating feelings that seemed impossible to control. Her fingers opened up, just because she failed to squash the urge to see what his body felt like. Tight ridges of hard muscles met her fingers; they covered his midsection and even his clothing did not disguise them.

His men closed around them, the sound of horses' hooves drumming out everything else. But a slight turn of her head and her ear was pressed against his shoulder, allowing her to hear his heartbeat. Another shiver raced through her, rushing down to her belly where a strange sort of excitement was brewing. Her mouth was dry and her arms tightened around him because she feared she might lose her hold on him due to the quivering that seemed to be growing stronger along her limbs. It was a strange weakness, like too much wine gave to a person. Even her thoughts felt muddled.

A rough hand landed on top of hers. Jemma flinched, her entire body reacting to the touch. His fingers curled around hers, completely covering her small hand in his. But it was his thumb that she noticed the most because it slid around her wrist to the delicate skin on the underside. That tender spot felt the rougher skin of his thumb stroking across it before pressing against the place where her pulse throbbed. It was a strangely intimate touch, and she yanked her hand away from beneath his and curled her fingers around the wide leather belt that kept his kilt in place. She felt his chest vibrate and knew that he was chuckling, even if the wind carried the sound away before she heard it.

Jemma snorted, enjoying the fact that she could make whatever sounds she wanted. But his head turned to cast a sidelong glance at her and she realized that he'd felt the sound just as she had felt his. Jemma was startled to discover that she was communicating with him on some deeper level.

A much more turbulent one, her thoughts returned to the way he'd looked at her in the past.

They rounded a hill and a fortress came into view. It was almost black against the night sky, with thick towers that rose up against the hills behind it. A wicked-looking gate began to rise, the grinding of metal chain cutting through the pounding of the horse's hooves. Her breath froze as fear tapped its icy fingertips against her.

This was not Amber Hill.

It was not even England.

She shuddered, unable to contain the dread creeping through her. It stole away the excitement that had been making her so warm, leaving her to the mercy of the night chill. Indeed life might become very frigid if she awoke in a Scottish fortress without there being any marriage agreement. The gossips would declare it her own fault for riding out without an escort.

Laird Barras rode straight under the gate and into the courtyard without hesitation, his stallion knowing the way well. But he had to rein the horse toward the front steps instead of the stable. The animal had not even fully stopped when he turned and locked stares with her.

"Welcome to Barras castle, lass."

Keep an eye out for Sylvia Day's
PRIDE AND PLEASURE,

coming next month from Brava!

"And what is it you hope to produce by procuring a suitor?"

"I am not in want of stud service, sir. Only a depraved mind would leap to that conclusion."

"Stud service . . ."

"Is that not what you are thinking?"

A wicked smile came to his lips. Eliza was certain her heart skipped a beat at the sight of it. "It wasn't, no."

Wanting to conclude this meeting as swiftly as possible, she rushed forward. "Do you have someone who can assist me or not?"

Bond snorted softly, but the derisive sound seemed to be directed inward and not at her. "From the top, if you would please, Miss Martin. Why do you need protection?"

"I have recently found myself to be a repeated victim of various unfortunate—and suspicious—events."

Eliza expected him to laugh or perhaps give her a doubtful look. He did neither. Instead, she watched a transformation sweep over him. As fiercely focused as he'd been since his arrival, he became more so when presented with the problem. She found herself appreciating him for more than his good looks.

He leaned slightly forward. "What manner of events?"

"I was pushed into the Serpentine. My saddle was tampered with. A snake was loosed in my bedroom—"

"I understand it was a Runner who referred you to Mr. Lynd, who in turn referred you to me."

"Yes. I hired a Runner for a month, but Mr. Bell discovered nothing. No attacks occurred while he was engaged."

"Who would want to injure you, and why?"

She offered him a slight smile, a small show of gratitude for the gravity he was displaying. Anthony Bell had come highly recommended, but he'd never taken her seriously. In fact, he had been amused by her tales and she'd never felt he was dedicated to the task of discovery. "Truthfully, I am not certain whether they truly intend bodily harm, or if they simply want to goad me into marriage as a way to establish some permanent security. I see no reason to any of it."

"Are you wealthy, Miss Martin? Or certain to be?"

"Yes. Which is why I doubt they sincerely aim to cause me grievous injury—I am worth more alive. But there are some who believe it isn't safe for me in my uncle's household. They claim he is an insufficient guardian, that he is touched, and ready for Bedlam. As if any individual capable of compassion would put a stray dog in such a place, let alone a beloved relative."

"Poppycock," the earl scoffed. "I am fit as a fiddle, in mind and body."

"You are, my lord," Eliza agreed, smiling fondly at him. "I have made it clear to all and sundry that Lord Melville will likely live to be one hundred years of age."

"And you hope that adding me to your stable of suitors will accomplish what, precisely?" Bond asked. "Deter the culprit?"

"I hope that by adding *one of your associates,*" she corrected, "I can avoid further incidents over the next six weeks of the Season. In addition, if my new suitor is perceived to be a threat, perhaps the scoundrel will turn his malicious attentions toward him. Then, perhaps, we can catch the fiend. Truly, I should like to know by what methods of deduction he formulated this plan and what he hoped to gain by it."

Bond settled back into his seat and appeared deep in thought.

"I would never suggest such a hazardous role for someone untrained," she said quickly. "But a thief-taker, a man accustomed to associating with criminals and other unfortunates . . . I should think those who engage in your profession would be more than a match for a nefarious fortune hunter."

"I see."

Beside her, her uncle murmured to himself, working out puzzles and equations in his mind. Like herself, he was most comfortable with events and reactions that could be quantified or predicted with some surety. Dealing with issues defying reason was too taxing.

"What type of individual would you consider ideal to play this role of suitor, protector, and investigator?" Bond asked finally.

"He should be quiet, even-tempered, and a proficient dancer."

Scowling, he queried, "How do dullness and the ability to dance signify in catching a possible murderer?"

"I did not say 'dull,' Mr. Bond. Kindly do not attribute words to me that I have not spoken. In order to be acknowledged as a true rival for my attentions, he should be someone whom everyone will believe I would be attracted to."

"You are not attracted to handsome men?"

"Mr. Bond, I dislike being rude. However, you leave me no recourse. The fact is, you clearly are not the sort of man whose temperament is compatible with matrimony."

"I am quite relieved to hear a female recognize that," he drawled.

"How could anyone doubt it?" She made a sweeping gesture with her hand. "I can more easily picture you in a swordfight or fisticuffs than I can see you enjoying an afternoon of croquet, after-dinner chess, or a quiet evening at home with family and friends. I am an intellectual, sir. And while I don't mean to imply a lack of mental acuity, you are obviously built for more physically strenuous pursuits."

"I see."

"Why, one had only to look at you to ascertain you aren't like the others at all! It would be evident straightaway that I would never consider a man such as you with even remote seriousness. It is quite obvious you and I do not suit in the most fundamental of ways, and everyone knows I am too observant to fail to see that. Quite frankly, sir, you are not my type of male."

The look he gave her was wry but without the smugness that would have made it irritating. He conveyed solid self-confidence free of conceit. She was dismayed to find herself strongly attracted to the quality.

He would be troublesome. Eliza did not like trouble overmuch.

He glanced at the earl. "Please forgive me, my lord, but I must speak bluntly in regard to this subject. Most especially because this is a matter concerning Miss Martin's physical well-being."

"Quite right," Melville agreed. "Straight to the point, I always say. Time is too precious to waste on inanities."

"Agreed." Bond's gaze returned to Eliza and he smiled. "Miss Martin, forgive me, but I must point out that your inexperience is limiting your understanding of the situation."

"Inexperience with what?"

"Men. More precisely, fortune-hunting men."

"I would have you know," she retorted, "that over the course of six Seasons I have had more than enough experience with gentlemen in want of funds."

"Then why," he drawled, "are you unaware that they are successful for reasons far removed from social suitability?"

Eliza blinked. "I beg your pardon?"

"Women do not marry fortune hunters because they can dance and sit quietly. They marry them for their appearance and physical prowess—two attributes you have already established I have."

"I do not see—"

"Evidently, you do not, so I shall explain." His smile continued to grow. "Fortune hunters who flourish do not strive to satisfy a woman's intellectual needs. Those can be met through friends and acquaintances. They do not seek to provide the type of companionship one enjoys in social settings or with a game table between them. Again, there are others who can do so."

"Mr. Bond—"

"No, they strive to satisfy in the only position that is theirs alone, a position some men make no effort to excel in. So rare is this particular skill, that many a woman will disregard other considerations in favor of it."

"Please, say no—"

"Fornication," his lordship muttered, before returning to his conversation with himself.

Eliza shot to her feet. "My lord!"

As courtesy dictated, both her uncle and Mr. Bond rose along with her.

"I prefer to call it 'seduction,' " Bond said, his eyes laughing.

"I call it ridiculous," she rejoined, hands on her hips. "In the grand scheme of life, do you collect how little time a person spends abed when compared to other activities?"

His gaze dropped to her hips. The smile became a full-blown grin. "That truly depends on who else is occupying said bed."

"Dear heavens." Eliza shivered at the look Jasper Bond was giving her. It was . . . expectant. By some unknown, godforsaken means she had managed to prod the man's damnable masculine pride into action.

"Give me a sennight," he suggested. "One week to prove both my point and my competency. If, at the end, you are not swayed by one or the other, I will accept no payment for services rendered."

"Excellent proposition," his lordship said. "No possibility of loss."

"Not true," Eliza contended. "How will I explain Mr. Bond's speedy departure?"

"Let us make it a fortnight, then," Bond amended.

"You fail to understand the problem. I am not an actor, sir. It will be evident to one and all that I am far from 'seduced.' "

The tone of his grin changed, aided by a hot flicker in his dark eyes. "Leave that aspect of the plan to me. After all, that's what I am being paid for."

"And if you fail? Once you resign, not only will I be forced to make excuses for you, I will have to bring in another thief-taker to act in your stead. The whole affair will be entirely too suspicious."

"Have you had the same pool of suitors for six years, Miss Martin?"

"That isn't—"

"Did you not just state the many reasons why you feel I am not an appropriate suitor for you? Can you not simply reiterate those points in response to any inquiries regarding my departure?"

"You are overly persistent, Mr. Bond."

"Quite," he nodded, "which is why I will discover who is responsible for the unfortunate events besetting you and what they'd hoped to gain."

She crossed her arms. "I am not convinced."

"Trust me. It is fortuitous, indeed, that Mr. Lynd brought us together. If I do not apprehend the culprit, I daresay he cannot be caught." His hand fisted around the top of his cane. "Client satisfaction is a point of pride, Miss Martin. By the time I am done, I guarantee you will be eminently gratified by my performance."